Hope and Ashes

LEGENDS OF CORALIA

Hope and Ashes

KATE JENKINS & MORGAN MOREAU

4 Horsemen Publications, Inc.

Dedication

As always, for David who's upset at me because I will let him read *Corrupted Tides*, but not *All Is Quiet in the Cosmos* or *Through the Embers*. He's also not allowed to read my books, but he says that's fine.
For my parents, especially my mom, who's very upset with the amount of cursing in our book. Wait till she reads this one.
For Kala, who's going to be bugging us for book 4 for a while.
For Emerson and Adriana. The encouragement and love has been greatly appreciated.
For Morgan, my coauthor, who puts up with my crap and throws around my full name like it's candy, especially when I'm acting up.

~~ Kate

For Gavin and Avery who will always have Aunt Yippee's heart. You are both loved and valued beyond measure, and you can always come to me for anything.
For David and Finley, who always come to me for coins. I don't even care about the half-eaten gumball I found in my purse.
For Alane, even when she asks if I know what song is playing.
For Grey, who consistently demonstrates strength, courage, honesty, and love.
For Katie, my coauthor and coconspirator, despite her TikTok videos about me.
And Tom Welling for being a good sport about my book 1 dedication.

~~ Morgan

Table of Contents

Cast of Characters

Agnes Aballe: Human. Queen's Maid.

Alba: Elf. Palace Servant.

Aphros: Nereid. King of the Nereid people

Rhoslyn Almeida: Human. Sister of the Earl Veitel.

Wrenn Almeida: Human. Earl Veitel.

Borin: Human. Guard. (Deceased)

Cadan: Riken's Army Commander

Carac: Human. Guard. (Deceased)

Ceto: A Nereid advisor to Aphros.

Garibald Crobán: Lord (Deceased)

Tolan Dethenal: Half-human, Half Elf. Palace cook and for-pay arena fighter.

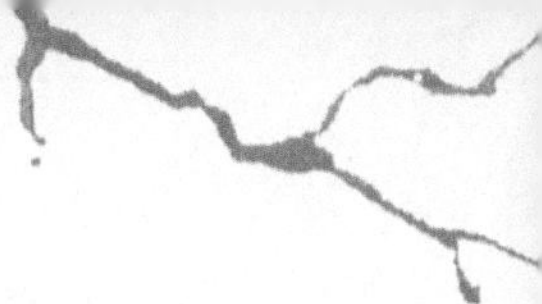

Jayden Drake: Nereid. Duke and Ambassador.

Alaoin Bialaor Eiero: Human. High King of Fythias

Xavier Eisenhart: Human. Head of Riken's Guard.

Lady Cecelia Elrick: Human. Wife of Lord Elrick

Lord Elrick: Human. New Captain of the Guard, Minor Lord (Deceased)

Farner: Young soldier in Riken's army.

Thomas Fletcher: Human with magic. Arrow maker and political activist.

Collette Venora Josselyn Gaillane: Human with magic. Queen of Coralia

Gaillard: Human. Works for Ian.

Gisela: Elf. Palace Servant.

Gwane: Human. Child worker in Wildrun

Cremisius "Crem" Hawke: Human. Commander of the Queen's Guard.

Diana Hawke: Human. Palace cook.

Mallan Hialti: Regent of the Azmarin Empire

Ian: Human. Tavern owner in Galel.

Indir: Elf. Survivor of the Urhadell massacre.

Howle: A Veteran of the King's Guard

Barris Ilthane: Human. Barron of Pontus Bay.

Jarin: Human. Guard. (Deceased)

Kenrick: A young guard.

Alexander "Pops" Leassitor: Shifter. Retired Mercenary

Larent Leassitor: Shifter. Mercenary.

Morrley: Human. Works for Ian.

Nieven: Elf. Survivor of the Urhadell massacre.

Nora Leassitor: Shifter. Retired Mercenary

Lynessea: Merperson. Wife of Lord Barris

Nawalya: Elf. Mercenary.

Rowan: Human. Guard. (Deceased)

Rulf: Human. Guard. (Deceased)

Sadon: Human. Guard. (Deceased)

Sara Whyldon: Human with magic.

Sargarus: Human. Former King of Coralia.

Riken Saullet: Human. Baron of Wildrun.

Arian Tal'Dela: Elf. Mercenary.

Brath Thancred: King of Azmarin (Deceased)

Rion Thorax: Human. Furrier.

Zephraim Villot: Human. Earl of Norbrick. Brother to the Queen.

John Whyldon: Human. Captain of the Queen's Guard.

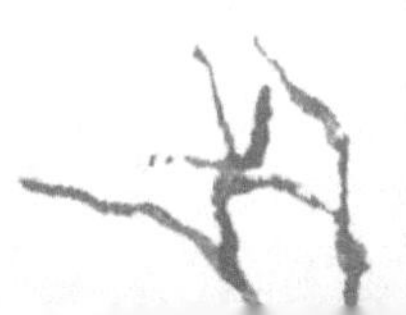

Azmarin Empire
Quenall
Barcomb Mi
Myrefall
Coralia

Other Locations
Catillatio: The Capitol of the Azmarin Empire
Gulf of Galel: Gulf bordering Galel and the Azmarin Empire
Sherrose Caverns: A cave system in Quenall
L'orilan
Fyithas
Pontus Bay
Galel
Nereid Kingdom
Veitel
A'lierdeen
Wildrun
Farner
Branlin

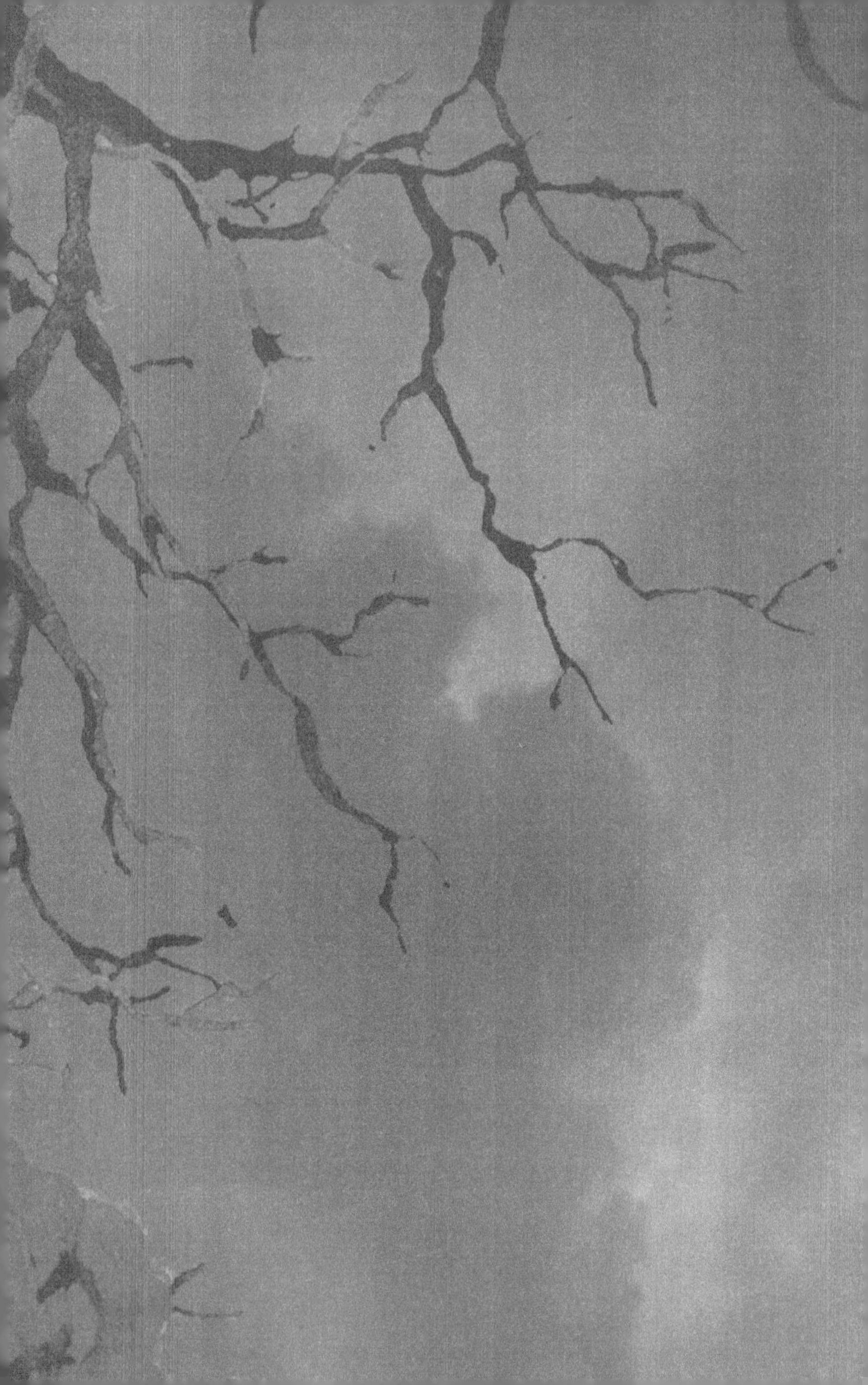

Chapter One

A hunting party gathered at a table in the crowded inn. Large beer tankards sat in front of drinkers and were drained regularly enough for the barmaid to happily return to the table every few minutes with refills. A boisterous laugh echoed from the largest of the group, his bushy ginger beard giving him a jolly appearance, but his sheer size spoke of the potential for real harm if he so desired.

Ginger Beard's laughter filled the room, and he gave the occasional pat on the back to another man sitting near him. The companion looked a little older, though his tanned skin and crow's feet around his vivid blue eyes potentially spoke of a much harsher life. His brown hair was also neater and smoother than the coarse red mane belonging to Ginger Beard. The second man seemed to enjoy himself as the ginger man carried on. There was enough alcohol all around to show why such moods were dominating the table.

"Oh, sit down, you big oaf," a woman commanded Ginger Beard. Her carob hair, pulled back and plaited, rested on her shoulder, and the rosiness of her freckled cheeks showed she too had been indulging in drinks throughout of the evening.

"You know very well half the deer Crem missed were because of your heavy steps!"

"I haven't heavy steps!" Ginger Beard declared. "I may not be as graceful as you," he motioned towards the woman who surveyed him in an amused way. "But I walk like a normal, proper man."

"How dare you call me graceful!" the woman retorted with faux outrage, slamming the palm of her hand down on the table. She turned to the man Ginger Beard had been patting on the back. "Did you hear him?"

The man nodded, his blue eyes twinkling with contained laughter. "I did indeed." His tone took on a playful quality, and he leaned back in his seat to survey the woman. "What I cannot figure out is why you are allowing it."

"What is she to do about it?" Ginger Beard asked with another boisterous laugh.

"I imagine she could do a great number of things you might just experience if you keep pushing her," the man supplied. He took a moment to pick up his tankard and take a deep sip.

Ginger Beard, however, turned his attention back to the woman. "What could a little thing like you do to the likes of me?" he asked her. He stood and walked around the table so he stood beside her, a tactic meant to emphasize his lack of fear.

The woman surveyed him, looking unimpressed by his actions. "Do you remember what I did to you last time, Rion?" she asked the man, her tone casual even with the threat-laced words.

Rion or Ginger Beard's expression fell. "Ah, Joss, you don't have to be so cruel. I was just having a laugh."

"So was I," Joss replied simply. "It's hardly my fault you're so sensitive. Have a seat, have a drink, and lighten up, or we won't bring you along next time."

Chapter One

Rion scowled before he took a seat and resumed his drinking from a large tankard. He pointed a large finger in her direction. "You're a devious wench who gets away with it because you look so innocent."

"You've known her far too long to be surprised," the third man said.

"She's a tricky thing! Nothing a husband taking her over his knee wouldn't cure. Mark my words," Rion declared, causing the third man and Joss to laugh hysterically.

"I'm trying to picture such a thing," the third man declared between each fit of laughter. "All I can see is a lot of blood."

"I'd not be married to a man who thought they could get away with such things," Joss replied as her laughter cooled down. "And I'd castrate the man even thinking it."

Rion gazed forlornly at his empty tankard. He held it aloft to catch the barmaid's attention. "A swift beating from a husband would knock the obstinance right out of you. You might be sweet underneath all of your hostility."

"I am quite sweet to those who deserve it," Joss replied. Her playfully curt expression suggested otherwise.

"Who told you such lies!" Rion asked, throwing an arm in the air to show he was done arguing the point. He was distracted by a newly filled tankard of ale.

Joss settled back in her seat, picking up her tankard once more, and glanced at her other companion. "I think Rion is losing his touch, Whyldon," she said, naming the man with blue eyes.

"Perhaps," Whyldon agreed. "You could also be growing meaner. I'm not sure which option I side with."

"And I'm mean?" she asked with a laugh. Other groups around the room were gathered in various areas, talking, and laughing as they celebrated the victories of the day. Some belonged to other hunting parties as the impacted mud on their

boots and long cuts from low-hanging branches suggested. Others were traveling and had settled in for an evening of rest before picking up tomorrow and resuming the activity.

"When you want to be, you are," Whyldon replied, bringing her attention back to him. "You allow Rion and his ilk to rile you up, but you handle yourself quite well. To suggest you do not easily deliver crushing blows to his ego would be disingenuous, and I would never accuse you of such a thing."

She responded by giving Whyldon a knowing smile and resumed looking around.

"It's a hard life to lead, trying to balance mercy and kindness with strength," she quipped back at Whyldon. "And anytime Rion opens his mouth, I forget about the mercy and kindness." She shrugged, as though to say there was nothing she could do.

Standing from her position at the table, she grabbed her now empty tankard and took it back to the bar, pushing it towards the woman so she might get a refill.

Once her drink was refilled, she turned to head back to the table but found her path blocked by Tolan, though she didn't seem to mind as the empty mug in his hand indicated they'd shared the same idea. He gave her an apologetic expression, looking down at her but not moving. "Didn't mean to block you," he said.

"How can I be so sure?" she asked him, amused by the encounter. He nearly chuckled as she gave him a once over, knowing the slight lift of the corners of her lips indicated she liked his well-muscled tan and dark hair.

"I suppose you could take my word for it, but you seem like you'd say anything to be contrary to whatever defense I could muster."

She nodded. "I've been accused of similar on more than one occasion."

"*I think your friends have suggested as much about you.*" He motioned his head in Rion's direction, though the woman in his lap prevented the man from noticing he had gained their focus. After having watched the group all evening, Tolan was happy enough for the woman's companions to have other distractions.

"*He likes to complain. I fear if he faced any true discourse, he would be quite unprepared.*" She shrugged. "*Should I let you get to your drink?*"

"*I seem to have been distracted,*" he admitted, though he issued no complaint. "*Perhaps you could join me?*" She grinned and nodded her consent.

He motioned her forward, leading her to a table not too far from where Rion and the others sat. Now close, he could easily see the freckles dotting her nose and cheeks, and the intelligent dark brown eyes he swore tempted him. "*Did you have a good outing?*"

"*It was quite successful,*" she replied.

"*I'm glad to hear it. Seems like some of the others didn't have such luck.*" He thumbed back to a group of younger men in another corner who were grumbling about lack of game. Tolan didn't pay them much mind. Not when he was seated across from Joss.

"*And what brings you here?*" she asked. The way she focused on him with her large, dark eyes left him feeling a little giddy.

"*I was looking for work,*" he explained with a shrug. "*It seems things have changed since last I was here, and I'm considering other options.*"

She nodded. "*I've heard a lot about the changes since I've been on my hunting trip, but I've not made much inquiry.*" She took another drink. "*What sort of work were you doing before coming here?*"

"*I have a lot of different skills, but I find gladiator fights pay the best. I'd been hoping to spend time fighting here, but the queen has ended the sport.*"

She nodded and offered an amused smile. "*I hear she's ended many former practices.*"

"*Good. It's not the best for me, but if she ended even a quarter of the old king's practices, it would better the kingdom.*"

"*Again, there have been a lot of changes,*" Joss agreed before taking a sip from her drink. "*And a lot of complaints. I'm interested to see how it all plays out.*"

"*Hopefully, it will work out for the best. I'll have to see what's here for me or move on.*" He gave her a slight smile, though Tolan knew he wasn't really worried. Things would work out, and for now, he was happy to be in the company of someone he found so incredibly enchanting.

"*What do you think you might do since arena fighting is no longer allowed?*" she asked. She leaned forward, resting an elbow on the table. He found himself longing to reach out to her.

"*I don't know. I hadn't planned anything other than coming here to fight. But if I am lucky, a merchant will need a guard or a cook.*" He gave a slight shrug and took a moment to study Joss. "*You are very beautiful.*"

"*Am I?*" she asked, though the playful smile she shared with him indicated she knew as much. "*Tell me... What do you like especially?*"

"*Well, your smile, for one. The way your hair catches the candlelight. And the flush on your skin from both joy and drink.*" He felt as though he could go on and on about her and never quite find the end of his interest.

"*Those are very nice reasons,*" she teased, dark eyes dancing wickedly. "*Though they are compliments I could pay you, as well.*"

Tolan looked down at himself. "I don't know if beautiful would apply to me, not like it does to you."

"Why would beautiful not apply to you?" she asked. "You are quite a man to behold."

Tolan gave a small smile. "Well, it is not a word often applied to me, but from you, I can accept it."

"You should hear it more often," she replied. She reached out and placed a hand on his forearm. "You are rather exemplary."

Tolan's smile grew. "If you don't have any other plans for the night, we could have a more in-depth conversation about beauty."

"Perhaps more privacy is needed for such a discussion?"

"As luck would have it, I have a room upstairs."

"You should show me."

Standing, Tolan held out a hand. "It would be my pleasure." She took his hand and rose from her seat, following him upstairs.

Tolan sat in the back of the tavern, ignoring the din of the drunks around him as he attempted to devour watered-down rabbit stew with wilted, weathered greens and spoiled potatoes. Not for the first time, he pondered if he would have just been better off staying on the road, fending for himself as he figured out his next steps, instead of trying to eat.

As he picked at his dinner, Tolan's thoughts were drawn to his usual subject: Collette. In the time since he'd left her in Azmarin, he'd accomplished far more than he thought he ever could. All it had cost him was a title and a kingdom, sacrifices he'd make again and again for her.

There was a part of him forever mourning the family he'd been denied by his father. The family and the peace of living

in Fythias were among all the things he was so keenly aware he lacked. Another, louder part of himself, the one currently winning and dictating his actions, did not regret a moment of the life he lived. Without it, he would never have met Collette, and he would give up anything for his queen.

Taking a bite of the stew, he grimaced. His heart reminded him he did actually have several regrets. Letting the man who should have been his father treat him and his mother the way he did was one. Not siding with Nawalya for the conflict in Lanthia was another. Not fixing things with Larent, and leaving him without notice was a huge regret, one he knew he would grapple with for as long as he drew breath.

Leaving Collette the way he had… Tolan knew he would never forgive himself. After sneaking out in the middle of the night, he'd made it five days before he felt the weight of the monumental harm he'd caused. His decision to leave had been hastily made, a combination of the high of having a plan, his anger with Larent, and his shame of having nothing to offer Collette while she struggled to regain her rightful place on the throne.

He waited for his regret to wane as he traveled, regret for not sharing his plan, or bringing Collette and the others along, for planting a seed of doubt in her mind about how much he loved her. It had been too late to turn back, and as he'd made his way to Fythias, he prayed she would understand and forgive him. Forgiveness would prove difficult, of course. Larent would make it so. Tolan had no doubt his scorned ex-lover would happily remind Collette of his abandonment.

Taking another bite, Tolan decided to wash away the lingering taste of stew with a gulp of ale, only to almost spit out the foul-tasting liquid. No, he was done. A meal off the road had been a bad idea. Standing, he threw some coins on the table and was about to turn to the door when movement from the front of the tavern caught his attention.

A scrawny man sat at a table, surrounded by people, food, and drink. They laughed and talked, and roared on occasion, none of which would have caught Tolan's attention had the scrawny man not held a simple, gold bracelet between two long, pale fingers.

The sight of the bracelet reminded Tolan of the night he'd fled. He'd placed the golden trinket near Collette so she could find it, having carried it with him since the tournament months ago. His blood ran cold as he contemplated the possible ways her bracelet was now in a random, roadside inn.

"Took it off of her before I left," the man bragged to his fellow drinkers. He laughed heartily and twirled the golden trinket around a couple of thick fingers a couple of times before it clattered on the table. He laughed again at the sound and swiped it up before others could grab it and pass the thing around.

"And we're supposed to believe you took out the queen?" A man bellowed with disbelieving guffaws.

The scrawny man chuckled again. "In truth, I did have some help from a big wolf." He threw back a large gulp of his drink. "But she is gone."

Without thinking, Tolan moved towards the table, grabbed the spindly little man by his shirt, and slammed his back into the bar top. "Say that again," he growled.

The man dropped the bracelet again, unable to retrieve it. He looked up at Tolan, visibly frightened by Tolan's height and physique. "W-what do you mean?" he stammered.

Tolan pulled the man off the bar before slamming him against it again. "You just bragged about murdering Queen Collette with the help of a wolf. I want the whole story now, and I will know if you lie."

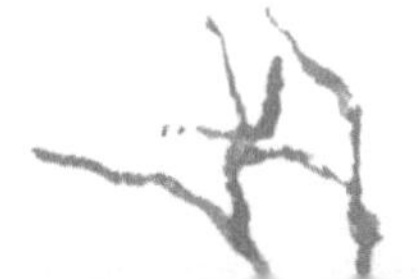

"The—uh—the wolf did most of it," the man replied, his eyes wide with fear and his complexion growing paler with each passing second. "His claws are what got her."

"I'm running out of patience," Tolan warned. Somehow, he was managing to keep his fear from surfacing, perhaps because he wasn't convinced the stranger before him, or Larent, could have possibly taken her out.

"I don't know what else to say," the man pleaded. "It was late in the day, and the wolf was huge. Bigger than any wolf I've ever seen."

"Was he there when you got there?"

"Yes," the man replied, his voice quavering. "But he wasn't a wolf at first."

Closing his eyes, Tolan forced himself to calm down. He *knew* Larent wouldn't hurt Collette, or he thought he did. Something must have gone wrong. He took another deep breath, fighting away his panic with everything he had. He opened his eyes again and focused on the assassing menace lacing his voice. "How did you hurt her?"

"I had a sword," he confessed, clearly believing Tolan's threat.

"And what did you do with said sword? I assume you know which end goes in a person or you wouldn't have one. Now," he said, slamming the man against the bar to punctuate each word. "Did. You. Harm. Her?"

The man groaned in pain with each impact. "I tried," he admitted. "The wolf is the one who killed her."

"So you didn't stab her, slice her, scratch, or knick her?" The man shook his head in response. Tolan doubted his sincerity. "I guess you get to live as long as you can answer my next question."

"What question?" the man asked, his voice raspy with pain and fear.

"Where did the attack happen?"

Chapter One

"A few days travel from Galel. In the woods. There is a town a few hours walk from there."

"Looks like today is your lucky day," Tolan said before throwing the man to the ground. He spotted the bracelet and crouched to pick it up, pocketing it before striding out of the tavern.

Once he was out in the cold night air, his panic started to set in. Was the man right? Tolan felt like he'd been terrified enough, to be honest, but honesty only spoke of his perception. He took another deep breath through his nose, trying to calm himself enough to form a plan.

He needed to find them. He needed to confirm the truth, and spirits help Larent if Collette was dead. Another breath and Tolan forced himself to think through the problem. They'd been close to Galel. Whyldon was from Galel, and they'd been gone long enough it would be safe to visit the area.

Galel wasn't much of a plan, but it was a start, and despite the late hour, Tolan started down the path in the direction of the farmlands of Coralia.

Chapter Two

Agnes and Diana made their way down the cave passage, their steps careful and silent. Every few minutes, they paused, looking around and listening for evidence of being followed. The Sherrose Caverns made for an excellent hide-away. Well-hidden on the perimeter of the city, the existence of the place wasn't widely known. Even those walking by would easily miss the constricted opening because of the wild over-growth of trees, bushes, and grass.

Noting they were alone, and presumably safe, Diana motioned for Agnes to continue forward, the path narrowing the further they traveled from the entrance. Diana tried to ignore the unopened letter she carried. Passed to her by one of the spies of the followers of the true queen, she'd urgently aban-doned her post at the palace to get it into the hands of her hus-band, Cremisius Hawke. Agnes had insisted she not go alone.

As they walked, Diana made sure to offer the older woman a reassuring smile. She could see Agnes's anxiety increase as they came upon the first of the sentries. Pausing long enough to provide the most recent hand signal the members of their resistance group had agreed on, the young soldier stepped aside so they could pass. Finally, they entered the main cavern.

Commander Hawke stood at a makeshift table, surrounded by Howle, Lord Barris, and three individuals who often accompanied Barris. As usual, Crem and Howle were engaged in a heated discussion while Lord Barris watched, a small smile on his lips.

Diana still didn't know the names of Barris's companions, a deliberate choice for security, though she'd learned most of their faces by now. One was tall, with olive skin covered in faint indigo and blue markings running down her neck and arms. Her strangely narrowed pupils glittered a pale gold color in the flickering lantern lights, contrasting vividly with purple-blue hair. At times, Diana was certain she witnessed a violet shimmer on the elegant woman's skin.

Her companion was stouter and broad in the shoulders and chest. His skin was much darker, and his vivid eyes were bronze, though a blue glimmer brightened his stern features. Agnes often remarked neither could possibly be human.

The third companion tended to Barris more closely than the others. A shock of orange hair and dark freckles made him look younger than he was, and perhaps perceived youth explained why he was the one to fetch drinks or extra parchment. He, too, had the same gold eyes.

Agnes paused in her steps, remaining close to Diana. They were a rare sight in the caves. Despite Cremisius Hawke being wanted for treason and the death of Lord Elrick, the false king and queen had not seen fit to punish the cook for her husband's crimes. It had been decided she would remain in the palace as long as she was safe.

Diana confidently walked over and joined the group, entering the scant space between her husband and Lord Barris. Diana had no strong dislike of Barris, but she was content to

keep him at a distance until his devotion could be tested. She ignored him and held the letter out to Crem. "We received intel from the morning watch," she explained.

The voices of the others quieted down. Although she was neither a leader nor a decision-maker for the group, Crem had made it clear he expected his wife to be treated with respect by all members.

Crem took the letter, his brows raising in concern once he took in the quality of the paper and the intricate red wax seal. He broke the seal, and unfolded the paper, eyes immediately scanning the words scrawled across the page.

When he finished and read the letter a second time, Diana's alarm. The narrowing of his brow spoke a subtle cue of stress and fear, enticing Diana to put a hand on his forearm as she stepped closer. "What is it?"

Taking a deep breath, Crem folded the letter and set it on the table before placing a hand on top of his wife's. "There are rumors Queen Collette is dead," he reported to the group at large. He paused and let the news wash over everyone before continuing. "The report is incomplete, and there isn't much to it. I doubt its validity."

The blood drained from Diana's face as Crem spoke, her mind demanding an answer as to why they had worked so hard to restore the rightful ruler to the throne. Barris snatched the letter from the table. All parties ignored Howle's cursing, which was getting more creative as the seconds passed.

"Do you think the story was planted or based in truth?" Diana asked.

"If it were true, I think we could safely assume we'd have more than hastily jotted down rumors. Zephraim would surely know, and official announcements would be made. We'd have word from Whyldon or other members of her travel party."

Crem frowned before continuing. "If I had to wager, I'd bet she was attacked, maybe even injured. But she's not dead."

A murmur went through the room at the mention of Whyldon. His skill as a soldier had been unmatched, as had his protection of their queen.

"What if the news is true?" Barris asked. "What would we do?"

"We have tasked ourselves with removing Zephraim from the seat of power," Crem pointed out. "A replacement would have to be found if the news were true, but her possible death doesn't eliminate the need for Zephraim and his ilk to be ousted."

Howle snorted and thumbed at Barris. "If he stays true, we could always put him on the throne."

Crem gave a snort as he surveyed Barris for a moment. "Diana is spying at the palace, and we have others listening throughout the kingdom. Someone out there will have information. They will find out if she is alive or not. I think we can avoid appointing a backup ruler for now."

Barris nodded, his gaze briefly settling on the Mer companions. Concern flickered across his face as he took them in. Quenall was quickly becoming more and more unsafe for them. "Let me know what you discover and how I can assist from there," he requested of Crem, who nodded in affirmation. He looked to Diana. "Does Mistress Hawke need an escort back to the castle?"

Diana shook her head. "No, thank you. I would like to visit with my husband a little longer. Agnes might appreciate the assistance."

Barris looked at the older woman, a blinding smile growing on his face. "I would be happy to escort you back." Barris offered an arm to the older woman which she took with some caution. He and his companions left without further discussion.

Howle did not leave the cave, though he retreated to the far side of the cavern to provide Crem and Diana a semblance of privacy.

The former commander took the opportunity to gather Diana in his arms, pulling her flush against his body. "I don't want you to go," he said softly.

"I don't want to leave," Diana assured her husband. "But someone has to be there," she reminded him. "And it can't be you. We both know what they would do if the royal guard got their hands on you."

Leaning forward, Crem rested his forehead on hers. "You worry over me far more than you should," he gently lectured, his voice full of infinite fondness. "They will turn on you eventually, you know. The moment you consider they might come for you... Promise me you will run."

"I swear." Diana put her arms around his waist, keeping her husband close for a few moments. "I would never do anything to hurt you, including getting myself hurt."

"You better not," he mumbled, kissing her with a gentleness no one could guess he possessed. When the kiss ended, he said, "Tell me you carry your dagger on you at all times."

"I haven't given it away like I did the last one," she teased, trying to get him to smile. "Not even to a queen."

"I still can't believe you gave Collette those boots," he said with a small laugh.

"Yes, you can," she said, drawing him in for another kiss. "You know I could have done nothing less."

"I can still pretend to be bothered by it, though."

"You can," Diana agreed. She did not want to leave him. She missed her husband, though his known connections and loyalties had removed his ability to remain at the palace. Somehow, despite the connection, Diana had not yet been deemed suspicious. "I will need to leave soon."

"I know." He kissed her again before tearing himself away from her. "You'd better go before I decide to keep you."

"One day, I might just let you," Diana replied. She was sorry to leave him, and she longed for the days he would casually enter the kitchens of the palace and accuse her of having a sassy mouth. Those were gone, at least for now. Unable to help herself, she approached Cremisius again and kissed him deeply, her hands cupping his face. Even after it broke apart, she lingered for a moment. They were both aware every meeting could be their last. "I will see you soon," she promised before forcing herself to leave. "Stay safe."

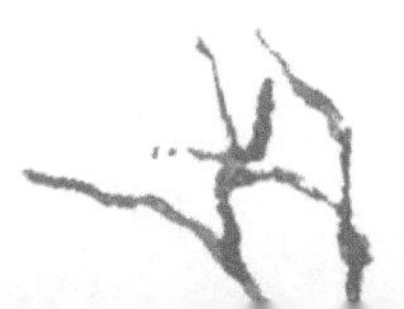

Chapter Three

The drone of voices in the council room seemed more positive than usual, though Zephraim paid little attention. His fingertips drummed against the table, and occasionally he heard words like "crops," "winter," and "Azmarin."

They'd received official word King Brath was dead, and there was concern over who would replace him. Some of the council saw an opportunity to lend support and make it known Coralia was a big player once again. Perhaps they were right, but Zephraim didn't care. As he sat in the relatively safety of the council room, he could see the red-tinted vision of his sister, feel the tear of her skin as claws sank into her flesh. He could hear her screams and smell the hot, pulsing spill of blood.

Why had he done it?

He looked up as someone mentioned the need to promote a new commander and captain for the guard. With Cremisius Hawke wanted for murder and treason and Elrick dead, he needed to make a decision.

"Elrick's widow needs time to mourn before we officially appoint someone," he reminded someone dully. "And I believe it was insisted upon by many of you to submit suggestions after Elrick's memorial."

Murmurs of affirmation were noted as Zephraim's thoughts went back to Collette. Killing her had been the kindest thing to do. Had she been apprehended, either by the Azmarin or one of his own soldiers, she'd have faced a prolonged, painful death. Perhaps she'd have suffered other horrors before then. People did exceedingly cruel things.

"Have you considered names?" a young baron asked. He was of little consequence as his holdings were minuscule.

"I've considered all submissions, as I promised I would," Zephraim assured them. "Though I understand some of you seem very comfortable voicing your concerns."

"Are you learning towards anyone in particular?" another lord, an older man by the name of Anson, asked.

"I'm sure I am," Zephraim replied. He looked at Riken, who was strangely quiet. He was always not-so-subtly offering his opinions through even less subtle jabs at his king's ability to rule. Zephraim could not help but wonder if Rhoslyn inspired this silence. "Is there anything else?" he asked the group at large.

When nothing of consequence was brought up, Zephraim rose from his seat and left the chambers, not sure where he was heading.

Vaguely, he was aware Riken rose and followed, though Zephraim didn't acknowledge his presence. Riken's sudden deference over the past weeks was something he needed to be wary of, even if he didn't speak of it to anyone. He wanted to trust Riken, and more importantly, his wife. Had he not been preoccupied with his sister, and what he had done, he might very well have figured out a means of investigating their loyalty to him, both as a king and as a husband and friend.

A young girl, one he thought might be named Gisella, came running down the corridor and skidded to a halt in front of

him. Breathless and red-faced, she held out a piece of parchment. "My apologies, your Majesty," she huffed out. "There is urgent news."

Zephraim accepted the letter, thanked the girl, and dismissed her. He slid his finger under the red waxy seal and opened the letter.

His Royal Majesty, King Zephraim of Coralia,

We have received word of the death of your sister, the false queen. An assassin traveling near the border of our two countries has been overheard bragging about ending her life in several taverns.

After we apprehended the man and interrogated him, we were able to confirm the location. The evidence there suggested she was slaughtered. We've heard no additional rumors or received reports of sightings. We will diligently report further with any news.

Yours,
Mallan Hialti, Regent of The Azmarin Empire

"They know she's dead…" Zephraim said out loud.

Riken heard Zephraim's words and paused ascending the steps, keeping a few paces away. "Zephraim?" he said in honest concern.

Zephraim looked to Riken, noting the genuine expression, something he hadn't experienced from his friend for some time. "The new regent of Azmarin has written," he said, knowing his voice sounded hollow. He handed the letter over. Riken took it and began reading. The king watched the changing expressions on Riken's face, noting something strangely triumphant blooming on his face before turning sympathetic.

"I am sorry," Riken said, once again sounding more genuine than he had in months.

"So am I," Zephraim admitted. He knew he could not explain what he had done or how he had contributed to the news. No matter what else they had indulged in, blood magic was never a welcome subject. "Despite everything, I wish things could be different. It should not have been so destructive for her to admit she was a failure as queen."

Riken looked back at the letter in his hands, scanning it once again before holding it out to Zephraim. "Traitor she might have been, but she was still your sister. We should go get a drink or two in remembrance as the Mother would want."

Zephraim thought of turning down the offer. He wasn't sure getting drunk was the solution, but he offered Riken a tired smile and nodded. "Sure."

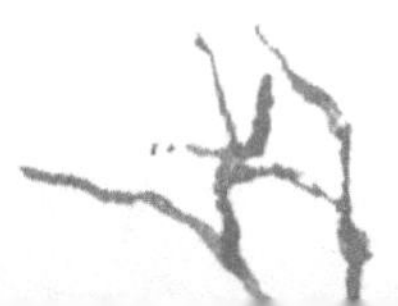

Chapter Four

As colder weather settled in, the sun provided sufficient warmth as Jayden dried off. The sun glittered on his skin, highlighting the subtle red and gold markings on his neck, chest, and arms. No matter how often he observed himself in the sunlight, he never grew used to the brilliant differences. He'd spent the day underwater, seeing to his duties. He'd have still been there, had he not been summoned to the king with some urgency. Once he was dry, he dressed in a clean linen shirt and some trousers, making use of his safely store clothing.

Jayden began the short journey to the royal residence, not quite a castle, but a grand estate all the same. He admired the coral-colored roof and rough, white sandy surface of the frame. As he got closer, he spotted Ceto waiting in the distance. Her bright red hair, even pulled back neatly on her head, still competed in brilliance with her dark red scales.

"Did something bad happen?" he asked when he was within hearing distance.

"Potentially," Ceto replied. She was dressed similarly to him, though the sleeves of her shirt had been rolled back. The faintest green shimmer on her forearms showed every time they stepped out of a shadow. "Aphros received intel. There are rumors Queen Collette was murdered."

Jayden stopped walking and turned to gape at her in a rather unattractive way. "She can't be dead. Aphros knows better than to trust rumors." He shook his head and motioned for them to continue walking. "Unless the news is from Quenall itself?"

"From what I understand, it's not officially from Quenall," Ceto replied. "And the news doesn't explicitly say she is dead. There were just reports." They greeted a guard who stood by the entrance to the estate before walking inside. "If she is dead, it will be terrible for all of us."

"If she is dead, we should go below and never resurface," Jayden said. He wondered if it was possible to move their location altogether, but it was not quite time for retreat just yet.

"You want us to live like the Merrows?" Ceto asked him with a playful grin. "Good luck convincing Aphros. He thinks they are strange."

"He's not wrong, but you have to admit, they are safer than we are."

Jayden directed them up to the second floor of the estate, seeking Aphros in his office. "I can't help but think if she was dead, an official announcement would have been made already. Strategically, it would be the smartest move."

"Someone was probably bragging in an effort for free drinks or attention," Ceto said in agreement. She pursed her lips. "Still, Aphros is going to worry. He had many hopes when it came to Queen Collette."

"And the news came not long after the worm on the throne sent veiled threats our way. The soldiers will be next." He sighed as they reached the king's office. "It will be fine. It has to be."

Ceto nodded. "We just have to figure out how to ensure Nereid victory should the worst happen." She looked at the door and took a breath before knocking.

"Enter," Aphros called from inside.

Jayden opened the door and motioned Ceto forward before following her inside. He found Aphros standing by an open window, peering out at the scene. "I hear you received some troubling news?"

Aphros did not move from his spot, though he looked back at the two. His expression was troubled, perhaps not to the degree indicated by Ceto. "Potentially," the Mer king confirmed. "If the news is true, it's certainly troubling."

"I will go to Coralia and verify the information myself, if it pleases," Jayden offered. He knew it was dangerous. He also knew his cousin might object, but he wasn't just a diplomat. He could protect himself.

Aphros turned from the window and went to his desk, taking a seat. "You were planning on going to Coralia to hunt for her, were you not?"

"Yes, but your intel makes the trip more dangerous. I'm willing to bet King Zephraim will send searchers." Jayden already knew Zephraim hadn't bothered to look for his sister thanks to their spy.

"Take someone with you to increase protection, if you'd like," Aphros suggested. "Going back into Coralia without Collette on the throne is going to be dangerous no matter what."

Jayden bowed his head in acknowledgement before looking at Ceto. "I may have an idea of who I would like to accompany me."

Aphros raised a brow but nodded. "Work it out between you and get started. "If she's out there and hurt, she'll need backup."

"Of course," Ceto confirmed. "We will be gone by the day's end. I'm going to pack and gather supplies." Without waiting for recognition from the others, she took her leave.

When it was just the two of them, Jayden looked at his cousin. "What are you planning to do?"

"I'm going to get my spy to increase his network within Coralia," Aphros stated, looking at his cousin. "I think some discussions with Fythias are also in order. In person."

Jayden nodded. Both actions made sense to him. "Should we start sending our people below?"

"Relocation would buy time, but not necessarily a lot," Aphros said, letting out a long breath. "There are others who can go beneath the water who are not pro-Mer."

"There are also the depth charges to consider," Jayden mentioned, remembering stories from when the trade of Mer scales had been widely implemented. "They can use those to wait us out or worse."

"Exactly." Aphros sighed again and stood from the desk. "As much as I would hate it, if it came to it, I'd evacuate rather than issue an undersea retreat."

Jayden took a breath. "Let us hope we can avoid evacuation."

"I agree," Aphros said. "Just be safe while you're there. I haven't been so apprehensive about anything in a long time."

"I will do my best cousin." Coming around the desk, Jayden pulled the other man into a tight hug. "Be safe as well."

"You know me," Aphros assured Jayden, hugging him back. "I will allow Ceto to burn Coralia to the ground if the throne cannot be returned to the rightful ruler."

"If the Queen is dead, I'll help her."

Chapter Five

Barcomb Mill was much more comfortable than what Arian had expected. The house owned by Whyldon was spacious and more than accommodating. There were enough rooms for everyone in the travel party, and Arian was thankful for the possibility of privacy and rest. After coming upon the scene where Collette and Larent had nearly died, Arian found he craved the space.

He was alone in the bathing chamber now, leaning back against the back of a steel bathtub and staring at the ceiling. He knew he was wallowing in self-loathing and recrimination. As he allowed the conversation with Thomas to replace in his head, he saw visions of the bloody clearing dance before him.

"Because people don't die when Larent and Nawya make mistakes." "You put far too heavy a burden on yourself." "We are each other's destiny."

He had allowed himself to be distracted. The worst had happened to Collette and Larent because he'd lost his focus. How could he forgive himself?

Submerging his head in the tub, he allowed his memories to take him.

"Arian! You pointy-eared fucker, I need you!" Larent screamed out.

Arian knew the worst had happened. He abandoned thoughts of plunging a dagger into the back of the man who'd sprinted past and took off towards the camp, vaguely registering Thomas followed close behind.

They arrived in the clearing only a couple of minutes later. The once white snow covering the area was dotted with footprints, mud, and the vivid red of fresh blood loss. Arian cursed in every language he knew and hurried over to Larent's side. The man was screaming and shaking as he clung onto an apparently lifeless Collette. She was the priority.

Arian fell to his knees and began rummaging through his medical pack, pulling every possible potion, salve, and medicine he might need. He lined these up for easy access, looking up as Whyldon and Nawalya joined. "Get Larent away from her!" he barked out. "I cannot treat her with him hovering."

They obeyed without objection or question, and Arian ignored the guilt he felt as Larent desperately struggled. He pushed the anxiety aside as his fingers went to Collette's neck and wrist. He found a pulse at both points, though it was weak. There was a chance.

"Thomas!" he shouted again. "I need the cloudy blue potion, the orange with the 'D' on the stopper, and the glowing red one." He pointed in the direction of the vials waiting for use before starting his examination of Collette. "Toss me a rag as well."

He lifted her shirt, intent on seeing the bloody wound, only to lean back on his heels upon spotting what looked like a stab wound, and strangely, claw marks freshly healed into shiny scars. He pushed back the memories and discussions of Nawalya's visions. Now was not the time to question the validity.

"What the fuck is this?" Arian demanded, angered by the information the three had kept to themselves. He looked to Whyldon as he indicated the healed scars. He noticed Larent had passed out, and Nawalya was on the ground holding him.

"She's got healing magic," Whyldon said. "She probably did it to stop the bleeding."

"And no one thought to share her ability to use healing magic?" Arian demanded as he reconsidered his strategy.

"Sargarus hated magic," Thomas said as he handed the requested vials to Arian. "Even in his own daughter."

Not knowing how her magic worked, or how much healing she'd managed, Arian knew he needed to be careful. He picked up the glowing red potion and pulled out the stopper. It would help with the blood loss. He tilted Collette's head and poured the liquid into her mouth, then massaged it down her throat. He waited a few seconds before testing her pulse again. It was stronger. Thank the spirits.

He continued working, circulating through the remedies he felt safe providing while having Thomas hand him different things from the medical pack. Every so often, Arian glanced towards Larent. He was breathing, and his body was still, but Arian couldn't help but worry. "Any idea what is wrong with him?" he asked Nawalya.

She shook her head. "He's feverish, sweating, and exhausted, but I don't see any signs of injury."

"Check his pulse, eyes, and breathing," Arian instructed. He used the rag and a salve to clean away the blood from Collette's skin, noting no change to the fresh scars. He felt secure enough to avoid further treatment, though she'd need more potion later, and probably for several more days.

He began picking up and recorking the empty vials when a gasp from Nawalya made him whip around.

"Larent's eyes," Nawalya remarked. "They're red."

"*And you're sure there are no injuries on him?*" Arian asked again.

"*Nothing,*" she confirmed. "*He's perfectly fine otherwise.*"

"*Red eyes indicate a struggle, doesn't it?*" Thomas asked, still hovering close by to hand over whatever Arian demanded.

"*It could,*" Arian confirmed, before pausing once more to examine Collette's wounds now she was stable. "*These are claw marks,*" he said, his finger tracing the healed wound. He got up to observe Larent's symptoms. Kneeling, he pulled back the shifter's lids and frowned. "*Possession?*" he asked, looking at Nawalya. It had to be. Larent would never willingly hurt Collette.

"*Or blood magic,*" she replied, dread in her voice.

Arian nodded, his face flushed with the guilt he did not speak. He went to the medical pack, taking it from Thomas. He quickly found a bottle of thick black liquid marked with a W. With Nawalya's help, he poured most of the contents down Larent's throat. It helped with his pale complexion, but Larent remained unconscious.

"*If they are stable, we need to leave,*" Thomas said, gathering the empty vials Arian had abandoned. "*The man responsible ran past us. He might be gathering aid.*"

"*You two saw him?*" Whyldon asked. He was walking the clearing, presumably looking for any additional clues as to what happened.

Thomas nodded. "*We did. He was a scrawny thing and sliced up. Nothing serious, though.*"

"*Where would you have us go?*" Nawalya asked. "*The next town is miles away and safely getting the two of them there would be impossible.*"

"*Barcomb Mill is closest,*" Whyldon said. "*My family home is there, and it's cared for by my sister. It's not ideal, because Zephraim knows I travel with Collette.*"

"We don't have much choice," Thomas argued. "These two are in bad shape. Besides, we haven't seen any soldiers."

"They've likely retreated by now," Arian said as he finished repacking. "And it's like you said. We don't have a lot of choice. Traveling will be hard on them, and I need to restock my kit. It's easier to do if we have someone safe and stable to hide."

He would have a breakdown later. Right now, they needed to get moving. Walking over to Nawalya, he placed a hand on her shoulder. "It's not your fault," he said. To the whole group, he said, "Let's pack up camp and move out."

No, the scene in the clearing was not Nawalya's fault. It was his. From the moment he knew about the vision, he should have told Whyldon and Collette. He never should have allowed Larent and Collette to be alone together. He should not have allowed himself to get lost in one perfect moment with Thomas.

He was vaguely aware of the burn igniting his lungs, informing him he would need air soon. As he contemplated rising to the surface again, he felt two hands grasp his upper arms and force him up. He sputtered and blinked. Slowly, Thomas came into focus.

"We already have enough sick and injured people around here. The last thing we need is your accidental drowning," Thomas said.

Arian gulped in breath, giving Thomas a thin glare through the hair plastered to his face. "I was not trying to drown myself. I know my limits."

"Really?" Thomas said, eyebrows raised. "I came to tell you Larent was awake, and I waited for a very long time before I pulled you out."

Arian hesitated, considering how his actions looked from Thomas's point of view. His eyes slid away from Thomas. "I just needed a moment." To decompress, to lose himself in his grief, to wallow in his guilt.

"I can tell you need a lot of moments, lately," Thomas said. "Dealing with two potential deaths… It's a lot."

Arian felt more guilt churn in his stomach at Thomas's words. He had not been treating Thomas well since they'd met in Azmarin. He opened his mouth to apologize, but instead, the wrong words tumbled out. "It is my fault. I was not there to protect them." Heat rose in his cheeks as his eyes prickled. Now was not the time for a breakdown.

"You can't be everywhere and prevent everything," Thomas reminded him.

Taking a breath, Arian forced himself to rein in his emotions. He wasn't ready to delve into how guilty he felt, and it wouldn't be fair to drag Thomas into his shit. "I should not have left them alone." He took another deep breath and pulled himself from the tub, grabbing a towel to cover himself as much as to dry off. "You said Larent is awake?"

Thomas nodded. "He's confused, and he's in pain. But he's awake."

Arian allowed his shoulders to sag. "Good." He pressed his lips together. "It also means he may do something very stupid." Larent's impulsiveness was enough motivation for Arian to dress.

Consciousness slowly came to Larent, though it arrived with a fuzzy sort of blankness he associated with being drugged. It wasn't often Arian felt a need to keep him unconscious, but when he did, he always had a good reason. As he couldn't really feel his body, he contemplated the possible sources of

whatever wound he was fighting off. He wasn't sure how long he remained in thoughtful bliss as he drifted in and out of sleep.

The clearing. The assassin. The total lack of control. And the blood. Copious, bright, metallic blood. It suddenly came back to him.

Collette!

He'd hurt her. No... he'd done worse. He might have killed her.

He tried to sit up, but his body wouldn't cooperate. Hands pushed him back against the mattress. "Stay here. I'll get Arian," he heard Thomas say. Before he could respond, the other man was gone.

Alone again, the struggle to regain control of his body remained difficult. He also suspected waiting around in bed would result in Arian putting him under again. Gritting his teeth, he forced himself into a sitting position, groaning as pain radiated from every muscle in his body. He suspected it felt even worse without the forced consumption of potions.

He made his way from the bed, using whatever was in reach to support his weight. He had to see her. She had to be alive. He would accept no other answer.

The door opened before he reached it, and in walked the person he least wanted to see.

"She's alive," Arian said, and Larent almost slumped onto the floor in relief. "Now, get back into bed."

Arian's commanding growl suggested anger, but their years together allowed Larent to look past it to find true worry.

"No," Larent replied, straightening a bit.

"What do you mean no?" Arian asked, his voice tinged with outrage. It almost made Larent want to laugh at the idea he would listen to a word Arian said right now.

"I mean no. I am going to Collette." He waited for Arian to move, and when he didn't, Larent gave his own orders. "Get out of my way, Chuckles."

Arian's expression changed to one of frustrated pity. "You don't even know where she is."

"I will if you tell me," Larent countered.

Arian ran a hand threw his hair. "Tell me what happened first."

"No." Larent shook his head. "I have to see her, Arian. I have to. I hurt her. She was dying in my arms." His voice broke with the last sentence, and he had to pause to pull himself together. "You will take me to her. We can talk after."

Thankfully, Arian caved. "Fine," he said, crossing his arms. "She isn't awake yet, and I will put you back to sleep by force if you wake her up." Arian reached out, offering an arm of support. Larent took the assistance without complaint.

"How much nasty shit have you forced me to drink?" he asked as they stepped out of the room.

"How long have you been under a blood magic spell?" Arian shot back.

"Good point."

Chapter Six

Noises brought consciousness to Collette. Her heavy eyelids protested, fighting to lure her back into a deep slumber. Every part of her longed to drift back down into the warm embrace of unconsciousness.

She groaned, opened her eyes, and glanced blearily around the room without moving any other part of her body. If she did so much as breathe too deeply, she was positive she would scream from the pain radiating from her torso and into her limbs. *Where am I?*

Everything ached. Her head throbbed. Her throat was dry and scratchy. Even her arms and legs pulsed with the discomfort from resting too long in one position. Had searing pain not licked at her side, she might have attempted to find ways to alleviate the rest of her ailments. Collette groaned as she extended an arm in a small stretch, the minuscule movement radiating across the abdomen and down one leg. "Fuuuck," she breathed through gritted teeth.

She remembered. Larent had attacked her, and she'd almost died. She'd tried to help Larent block his possession. It seemed to have worked, but where was he?

Chapter Six

Pressing her hands against the mattress, she forced herself into a sitting position, letting out a slow, long hiss with the movement. Her stomach twisted and sweat formed on her forehead. She was pretty sure she would either vomit or pass out from the sheer agony of her injury. Pain was still better than death, she thought, but paused in her efforts as muted discussions sounded outside her room. Before she could decide how to proceed, the door quietly opened, and a very pale, ill-looking Larent supported by Arian appeared.

"You should not be awake," Arian spoke first. He released Larent at the other man's silent insistence. "And you definitely shouldn't be sitting up."

"And you shouldn't be lecturing your queen, but here we all are," Collette replied. She found herself agreeing with him, but when she was still, the pain wasn't so bad.

Arian raised an unimpressed eyebrow, though his well-concealed amusement at her response showed in his eyes. "I think I've told you before I do not consider myself your subject."

"He considers you a friend," Larent said as he reached the bed. He was careful to not just collapse, though the effort was strained. Once settled, he didn't say anything. He just looked at her.

"Hi," she replied, reaching out for his hand. "You don't seem to be doing much better than I am."

"I'm fine," Larent said, waving off her concern with a forced laugh. "I just have random aches. You're the one with the stab wounds and claw marks."

"Poke him in the side, and you'll see how fine he is," Arian muttered.

"You're not fine," she said, agreeing with Arian.

Larent snorted. "It's just a deep ache." He closed his eyes and took a deep breath. "I clawed you, and the bandit stabbed you. So, I got off easy."

"I could always ask Arian for a more accurate report, you know," Collette said. She looked over at Arian as he went through his bag of medicine and potions. "You'd tell me, wouldn't you?"

Arian glowered over his shoulder at the two of them and ground leaves into a bowl. "You are both lying about being fine in order to make the other feel better." He nodded at Collette. "You almost died from blood loss and other complications." He motioned towards Larent. "I don't even know where to begin explaining the adverse effects blood magic had on your physical and emotional state. You being alive and not under its influence is almost unheard of. I don't know our next steps."

Larent rolled his eyes. "He's being dramatic. If we both say we're fine, we're fine."

"We know for sure it was blood magic?" Collette's brows knitted together in thought. "I thought so, but I'd never experienced it before."

"It could be possession, but..." Arian said, glancing over to Larent who picked up the thread.

"Possession is very different from blood magic. If it was possession, I wouldn't have really been me anymore. I'd have not been there at all. I saw the attacks in the clearing. My wolf had just been holding the magic back until I shifted." Larent shook his head. "The moment I transformed, I heard Zephraim telling me to kill you, and I could do nothing to stop it."

Whatever bottle Arian was holding suddenly crashed on the floor. "Now we know what caused the headaches," he muttered as he grabbed a towel to clean up his mess.

"I saw Zephraim," Collette confirmed after she reflected on what had happened. "When I touched your head, he was there. Angry and distorted. Maybe he decided he was done with you once he thought I was dead."

Chapter Six

Larent sighed. "Most likely not. Which means the only way to avoid killing you or anyone else is to not transform." His voice was dejected, but his expression was resolved. He looked to Arian. "Unless you know of any suppressant potions?"

Arian shook his head. "No. Blood magic is outside my area of expertise. I'm not really sure I understand how Collette managed to help get you back into human form. I've never heard of healing magic countering blood magic spells." The shattered glass cleaned up, Arian resumed his preparations. "You could always ask your grandparents. They might have some ideas."

Larent groaned. "I could. Shit, I need to write to them anyway before Nawalya sends a letter about what happened." He looked at Collette, giving her a tired grin. "I'll let you add a postscript to the bottom of the letter if you like."

"If people think I'm dead, it's safer to keep a low profile," Collette pointed out.

"It is," Arian confirmed.

Larent pursed his lips in a fake pout but nodded. "Fine," he said. "Really though, how are you feeling?"

"Like shit," Collette confirmed. "Turns out, puncture wounds hurt like a bitch."

"Who knew," Arian snarked.

Larent tried to laugh but stopped as pain flashed across his face. "I know I had no control of what happened. Saying I should have been stronger means shit against blood magic. But I'm sorry," Larent said, squeezing her hand.

"I know." She hated the sorrow she read in his eyes. "And I'm never going to blame you. I know you'd never choose to hurt me."

"Never," he breathed, moving closer. "I would choose death over hurting you. I don't know if you were conscious enough to hear me, but I meant what I said." As he spoke the words,

Larent ignored Arian who stood at the dresser continuing to make his potions, pretending to make himself smaller.

"I heard you," Collette replied. She'd absorbed the words before he'd started screaming, sounds she'd memorized as she'd faded into blackness. She'd never forget. "And you have to know I feel the same."

"I hoped, but…" He raised a hand to rest above her right breast, over her heart. "After everything you went through when Tolan left, I refuse to push."

"I know," she said, nodding at the memory of Tolan's abandonment even as she contemplated the feel of his hand so intimately pressed against her heart. Two very conflicting emotions swirled through her, but she would find a way to reconcile them. "Part of me will always love him. Maybe even miss him. But… I still look at you, and I know I'm home. I think you, of all people, understand the feeling."

Larent nodded, a relieved smile blooming on his face. "I do, and we can go at whatever pace you need," he promised her.

Collette couldn't help but give him a gentle smile. She didn't care about how much she hurt, or the fact she was in hiding from the world, or even how broken-hearted so many people had rendered her lately. She was going to trust Larent.

Noting Arian looked on the brink of jumping out a window, she decided to provide him with a little levity. "And on the days where physical affection is beyond me, I know Arian will appreciate the hugs."

"Arian will not appreciate the hugs," Arian said with a hint of relief in his voice. He turned to them, a bowl in his hands filled to the brim with purple liquid. Walking to the bed, he held it out to Collette. "Drink this. It will help with the pain."

"And taste terrible," Larent added, causing Arian to glare.

"It smells terrible," Collette said, giving the potion a dubious look.

Arian's gaze transferred to her. "Would you prefer to stay in pain?" he asked.

"We've got to talk about how overly affectionate you are, Arian," she replied with a sigh. She took the bowl and drank it, though it took a couple of tries to get it all down. It was horrendous and reminded her of something spoiled.

Arian rolled his eyes and walked over to the dresser. Picking up a pink vial, he came back and held it out to Collette.

"Wait," Larent said with a pained cackle. "Remember, you really *do* like Collette."

Arian rolled his eyes again. "It will help with the taste."

"I doubt it could be worse." Collette drank from the pink vial as well, finding the new potion a much more pleasant experience. The flavor was lighter, fresher, and vaguely reminiscent of mint. It eliminated the grotesque remnants of the pain potion.

Larent gave Collette an expectant look. "Well? What was it like? He never gives me a taste."

"If you don't tell him, I'll make sure to give you one every time you have to take a pain potion," Arian countered.

She gave Larent a sympathetic look. "I must do what Arian wants. I can't take pain potion alone again."

Larent groaned dramatically. "I get it. It hurts, but I understand."

Arian cleaned up the dresser, and as the last of his supplies were tucked away, he spoke. "As much as I dislike breaking up your emotional declarations, I need to see the others, but I am reluctant to leave you two alone together."

"Really?" Collette asked, though if she were being fair to Arian, she understood the concern.

Arian braced his hands on the dresser, cutting off anything Larent wanted to say. "Just for now. The suppression appears to be holding, but I want to be sure."

Collette nodded. As much as she hated it, Arian was right. They needed to be careful a little longer. "Okay. Since we have no one to play chaperone."

Larent muttered and groaned but held out a hand for Arian to help him, which the elf did with little complaint. "I'll be back soon. They can't keep us apart for long," Larent announced, and Arian rolled his eyes.

"Sleep," he told Collette. "If you need help, I can make you something. And don't try to heal yourself any further. You're already weak, and it would set you back."

"But I just woke up," she joked, primarily because Arian looked almost as bad as she and Larent. He clearly needed something less dire and two near-death experiences to focus on.

"I will drug you," Arian reminded her as he helped Larent from the room.

"Hey, Arian," Collette said as she watched the scene.

Arian stopped pulling Larent from the room. "Yes?"

"Love you, too."

Arian sighed, shook his head, and left with Larent, leaving Collette to go back to sleep.

Chapter Seven

Whyldon looked up as Arian and Larent came down the stairs, Larent being assisted by the elf. Larent's pale skin and purple-shadowed eyes confirmed he'd been put to ill use by an unknown party.

Whyldon's sister, Sara, stood at the counter, dividing vegetables into bowls. Her dark brown hair, now streaked with gray, was pulled up into a messy bun, telling him she planned on manual labor. The number of bowls set up on the counter suggested she intended to recruit help.

Thankfully, no one commented on her resemblance to Collette, and it went far beyond the hair. Their complexions, the way they laughed, the oval face shape and strong jaws, even the freckles made it evident Collette's paternal parentage had long been assigned to the wrong man. Only Sara's blue eyes greatly differed.

"Good morning," Sara greeted Arian and Larent.

Arian nodded his head in greeting. He made to keep going to the large wooden table which sat only a couple of steps from the kitchen workspace to deposit Larent, but he found the other man refusing to move, eyes locked on Sara. Larent blinked several times before turning his head to stare at Arian and Nawalya.

"You know we can't have them standing in the same room in front of anyone else, right?" he asked as Arian got him to the table.

"The resemblance is obvious to those of us who weren't in the know," Thomas said cheerfully from where he sat at the table, finishing up his breakfast. "Which, until you woke up, was just me."

"John likes to keep secrets," Sara said. She walked over to Larent with a bowl of thick oatmeal and placed it in front of him. "Eat," she instructed.

"I feel stupid for not realizing sooner," Larent said wryly. "I'm Larent, by the way. Thank you for the food."

"We've met," Sara said warmly. "You were unconscious, but it happened." She looked over to Arian. "You sit and eat as well."

Arian pressed his lips together. Whyldon half thought he would argue, but after rubbing his ear, which Sara had gotten ahold of the day before, the elf begrudgingly took a seat and dug in. "Do you need assistance today?"

Sara pointed in the direction of the vegetables she'd been separating. "Those need peeling, shelling, and prepping. I find myself with more mouths to feed than usual."

"It's the least we can do to help make the work less of a burden for you," Thomas said. Already, he was on his feet, gathering bowls and utensils to wash from those who were finished eating.

"Where is the nearest village?" Larent spoke up, and a quick glance in his direction told Whyldon he hadn't been focused on eating.

"About a half-hour walk from here," Whyldon replied, looking at him with curiosity. "Why? It's the middle of winter.

You can barely walk, and a new face would draw unwanted attention as we're supposed to be hiding."

Larent gave him a pained grin. "I'm not stupid. I'm gonna write to my Nana and see if she has any information on blood magic."

"Writing, while potentially helpful, may also be unwise," Whyldon pointed out. "There were soldiers here for a lot longer than we suspected. I fear they could be back."

"Be nice, John. He's been out." Sara finished with the bowls, and she began handing them out to members of the table. She also placed one where Thomas had previously been sitting. Clearly, washing dishes did not earn a reprieve from cleaning vegetables.

"I would feel better knowing more about what happened sooner rather than later," Larent said, shrugging. "We could have her send a response elsewhere."

"We can figure something out," Nawalya said, rising from her seat to put a comforting hand on Larent's shoulder.

"Is it necessary?" Whyldon asked.

"It could be. Nana Leassiter has a lot of useful knowledge and a rather large library. Collette and Larent confirmed blood magic was used on Larent, but I do not know how she managed to suppress it." Arian wiped his mouth with a napkin. "Nana Leassitor might have answers."

"Larent could still be a danger?" Nawalya asked.

Arian shrugged.

"Does your nana know anything about stopping or combatting blood magic?" Sara asked. "I'm well-versed in healing and protective magic from many species and practices. I haven't heard of anything working against blood magic."

Larent sat back in his chair, looking more exhausted.

"I do not believe so, but I am unsure how Collette suppressed the blood magic." Arian let out a breath. "Larent's eyes are no longer red. So, I am hopeful, but I do not know."

"She shouldn't have been able to stop him," Sara said. "She gets her abilities from our family. Suppressing a blood magic spell... It's not healing magic." Sara said. She looked to Whyldon. "Any ideas?"

Whyldon shook his head. "None. Adorra never spoke of any abilities."

"Larent only succumbed to the blood magic when he was a wolf," Thomas pointed out. "He theoretically held off for days, maybe weeks, as long as he stayed human."

"True…" Arian said, turning a pointed gaze to Larent. "No shifting."

"No shifting. I promised Freckles," Larent said with an unhappy but resolved sigh.

"Good. We have time to gather more information. If you think Nana has information, I could go see her. It wouldn't take more than a few hours," Nawalya offered.

Arian nodded. "We know Zephraim is behind the possession, and I doubt he's going to back down."

Larent sat up. "Wait. Where are we, exactly?"

"Barcomb Mill, in Galel," Whyldon said. "My estate." He looked at Arian. "How do you know Zephraim is involved?"

"Larent confirmed hearing the commands to attack Collette in Zephraim's voice, and Collette saw him in Larent's mind."

"Healing magic shouldn't allow you to see and hear a possessor," Nawalya said with concern.

"She's awake?" Whyldon asked.

"She was," Arian confirmed. "Hopefully she went back to sleep."

"And what did she have to say in addition to confirming Zephraim's involvement?" Whyldon prompted.

"Here's a better question," Thomas interjected. "How does Zephraim know how to use blood magic? A lot of people don't know about it, let alone how to use it."

Whyldon sighed. "King Sargarus dabbled with things he clearly did not understand. When Collette ascended to the throne, she came across his collection of dangerous magical items and spells. She got rid of some of it. Locked up the rest. My guess is Zephraim discovered them and made stupid choices."

"He did spend time with Larent," Arian said slowly.

"Larent's mission was to get close to Zephraim by any means," Arian said. Whyldon gave him a questioning look. "You need a piece of the person you use the magic on," Arian explained. "It is possible Larent left something of himself in Zephraim's chambers, hair possibly, or something else."

Nawalya opened her mouth to argue, but closed it again, brows furrowing. "How was the fool lucky enough to use blood magic when Larent is at his most dangerous?"

"If we accept Zephraim used blood magic, I'd wager he wasn't skilled enough for it to work while Larent was in human form," Whyldon provided, meeting Nawalya's gaze. "He'd been trying before he shifted."

"He'd also be aware Collette has been traveling with Larent," Arian said. "And it would explain the headaches."

"Collette and Larent claimed they were married while you were at the Azmarin court so Brath wouldn't demand a union with Collette," Thomas said. "One letter from anyone there would have been enough to get back to Zephraim. And it's not as though Brath wasn't scorned by Collette's rejection. Or her physical assault."

"You know what doesn't make sense? Why did Zephraim need to use Larent at all?" Nawalya asked, her brows knitted in

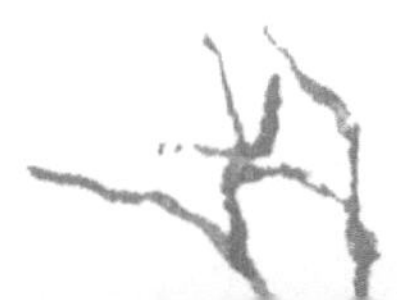

frustrated confusion. "Why not use the blood magic on Collette and be done with it?"

Thomas scratched his chin, eyes pointed at the ceiling. "He might have tried Collette first but something went wrong."

Arian made a thoughtful face at Thomas. "It's possible Rhoslyn had all of Collette's personal items removed as soon as she was arrested. It's also possible he was so angry about Larent being with Collette, he did not consider using something of hers." Arian gave a small shrug. "I truly don't know."

"He's petty enough to consider going for her since the two of us were so intimately involved. He likes to take stupid shit personally," Larent added. "I can guarantee if a letter got back to him about us, he went for me on purpose."

"I would wager Zephraim intentionally avoided trying the spell on Collette," Whyldon said as he considered the information. "I don't care how angry he is or what he truly believes her to be guilty of, their sibling connection has meaning."

Nawalya nodded in agreement.

"I wish those bonds had stayed his hand. He had to know she would not have killed Wrenn." Arian shook his head. "Any other questions before I drag him back to bed?" He thumbed towards Larent who stuck his tongue out.

Whyldon shook his head. He knew they would spend a lot of time in the coming days going over what had happened and questioning how Collette had been able to push back against the blood magic, but for now, they played the waiting game.

Arian stood and offered his hand to Larent who took it gratefully. Once on his feet, Larent leaned on Arian, and the two headed for the door. Before they could exit, Larent called back to Whyldon. "Oh hey, Collette and I decided to give the whole being a couple thing a try." He wiggled his fingers in goodbye as Arian forced him through the door.

Whyldon fought to not roll his eyes. Of course, they did.

Chapter Eight

Collette didn't know how long she'd slept, but when she woke, she knew it had been long enough for Arian's potion to start wearing off. A little more observation told her it was much later in the day as the position of the sunlight streaming into the room.

Her side and abdomen ached, drawing attention away from the time she'd spent sleeping. She found if she was mostly still, she could handle the pain, but soon, she'd have to call for Arian.

Peering blearily around the room again, her gaze landed on Larent who was beside her, awake but looking like he wished otherwise. Somehow, she'd ignored the feel of his weight on the mattress. As no one else was present, she felt like he'd seen himself to her room and bed without clearance from the others.

She said, "When Arian lectures us, I'm claiming innocence."

Larent blinked sleepily and gave her an equally sleepy smile. "I'll say the same." He removed the pillow placed between them and moved closer to her. "How are you feeling?"

"About the same as earlier," she said. "What about you?"

"Slightly better, I think, but I haven't tried to get up yet."

"Did Arian drug you again?" Collette asked. She shifted slightly so they could better talk, and the pain from the movement only made her press her lips together for a couple of moments before it subsided. Still, she gingerly pressed a hand over the scars on her abdomen, feeling the raised bumps beneath the fabric of her shirt. "You know whatever potion he gave you had more to do with your walking situation than the magic."

"Arian tried, I fought. He was worried about hurting me, so he left the potion on my bedside table. The moment he was gone, I left it there and came here. Stupid, I know, but…" He gave a careless shrug, leaving no doubt of his desire to be close to her.

"Should I assume he's monitoring us by the door, or have you gotten away with your scheme?"

"I have no idea, but as he hasn't checked on us, I think I've gotten away with it for now." Larent offered her a wide smile and sat up, taking her hand with his. The new position made it easier for to speak.

Collette returned the smile, thankful she could look at him head-on. It made it easier to relax and prevent further strain on her injuries. She was already feeling exhausted thanks to the combination of medicinal potions Arian had given her. "Slightly different question. Should you have taken the potion Arian gave you?"

Larent gave an enthusiastic nod. "Oh yeah. I'm going to suffer for it later, but I couldn't not be with you. Even though I know I shouldn't be here."

"I want you here. You belong here."

"I could hurt you. I have hurt you." Larent directed his gaze away from her and but could not hide the deep regret in his voice.

Chapter Eight

"Zephraim hurt me," Collette argued. "You had no control over what happened, and we know how to prevent it from happening again."

"It may have been him in control, but my claws were responsible." Larent made a face and sighed. "I need to tell you something. Something I should have told you the minute I found out."

She raised her eyebrows, watching him even if he wasn't looking at her. "What is it?"

Larent sighed again. "Nawalya had a vision of me attacking you. She's been seeing it since before the overthrow." When Collette didn't respond right away, he quickly added, "She and I convinced Arian not to tell anyone."

Collette stared at him for a minute, wondering how and why the three of them had not thought to say anything. "Why didn't you tell the rest of us?"

Larent shifted so he was on his back and looked up at the ceiling. "Because I was afraid," he said simply.

"Afraid of what?"

"Tolan or Whyldon might have convinced you to leave, for one. But really I couldn't stand the thought of you being afraid of me," he confessed. "So, I decided to focus on how often her visions don't come true. Nawalya kept quiet out of fear of losing Whyldon."

"Larent," Collett interrupted. She wasn't sure what she wanted to say at first, and her brows knitted together as she considered her next words. "I've never been afraid of you. Even now, on the other end of what happened. But you should have told me."

Larent nodded again, relief in his expression. "I should have, even it if meant you leaving. I'm sorry."

She let out a huff of air, although it was partially motivated by the reminder of the pain she was in. "We survived," she said. "No more hiding things. Okay?"

"Not a problem. Do you want to hear about all of her visions from now on? Cause some of them make no sense."

"It's probably best you three avoid keeping me, Whyldon, and Thomas in the dark, even with the uncertainty. We are together or we aren't. I know what I prefer despite the three of you still struggling to let us in."

"If it makes you feel better, it took forever for them to let me in when I first joined them, but I'll talk to them."

"Thank you," Collette replied. She yawned, knowing she was soon going to be losing the battle of consciousness. "Frankly, I think Arian is about three seconds from stabbing all of us and walking away, so the frankness will help."

"Stab us, yes. Stab you, no. He is fond of you. Which is why you're telling him we were fucking around with your attacker."

She groaned at the thought. "Do we have to tell him?"

"It's Arian. He'll find out anyway." He ran a hand down his face.

"As your queen, I've made an important decision," Collette replied simply.

"What decision?"

"I'm not saying a damn thing to Arian about what we did." She pointed at him with emphasis. "And neither are you."

Larent laughed. "You got it, your Majesty."

Chapter Nine

Ceto looked around the sparse beach, not at all surprised to see the humans fled the rocky shores of the Gulf of Galel during colder months. It was a real shame because there was great beauty in the steely blue water, the rolling waves, and the white foam ebbing and flowing across the dark rocks dotting the beach.

As she stepped away from the retreating water, she couldn't help but shake her head. Did the humans not appreciate the natural allure of their lands, or were they unequipped to deal with the discomfort of frigid winds? Either way, the lack of human presence made things easier for her and Jayden, especially since they were noticeably Mer even when in their land form.

Determining they were alone, she finger-combed her damp hair before piling it into a messy bun and securing it with a cord. "What do you think? Do you prefer the stones here or the white sand of our lands?" she asked Jayden in jest.

Jayden shook his hair out, but there was nothing to do about the water clinging to their hair and skin. "I will always prefer our lands and waters. I find most things in Coralia to be dull and lacking in spirit and life."

"Is it your anti-Coralian bias determining your conclusion?" All Mers, regardless of location, had good reason to be hard on Coralia. Ceto was also keenly aware stepping foot on Coralian soil was tantamount to asking for trouble. Still, she was determined to keep as sunny a disposition as possible.

"Both actually, though I am not completely anti-Coralian. Other than the elves, most who live here seek to control, tame, or conquer nature. It has taken away something vital from their towns and cities. From the land itself in some places." Jayden vaguely gestured around them, and it caused Ceto to chuckle.

"One could argue our own cities are not made in the promotion of nature, Jayden," Ceto said with a grin. She removed her travel pack from her shoulder and knelt down to begin looking through it. She finally came across the map she sought, and she pulled it from her bag, unrolling it. "Besides, it's winter. You can't seriously expect everything to be bright and colorful."

Despite having traveled by water, the map was dry and in good repair, so all of the elements of Azmarin, Coralia, and the seas to the east were in perfect condition. "Okay, so where do we think they crossed?"

Jayden knelt beside her so he could see the map. "Where did the rumors place Collette prior to news of the attack?"

"Honestly, there's nothing definitive in any of the rumors I've heard, including the message Aphros received," Ceto said. She traced her fingers along the border. "I think, perhaps, we can narrow down the area…" she said. "We know she left Catillatio heading back towards Coralia."

"I doubt she would stay on the main roads, but I think they might be our best and safest route." Jayden tapped the map. "We might miss her, but we might get lucky."

Ceto nodded and returned to studying the map. A handful of options remained. "Okay," she said, looking up to Jayden with a grin. "If we stick to the main roads, we can choose from three options. She could have gone to the west towards the mountains and Quenall, which would be a foolish choice."

Jayden shook his head. "She's not foolish, but I hoped she would be on her way to us by now. Or somewhere she could get help."

"I'd wager she'd want to do the smart thing. So, we assume she'd take the path far east and travel along the coast down to Pontus Bay." She traced the path on the map with a finger. "But if she's injured, I doubt she'd choose Pontus Bay."

Jayden let out a frustrated breath, shaking his head again. "I wish we knew who she was traveling with so we could narrow down possibilities."

He grew silent as he thought, and Ceto watched the subtle changes in his expression.

"Let's take the south road, the one cutting through the middle of Galel." A decision made, Jayden rose to his feet. "It's the most logical choice, and the small villages branching off either side present opportunities to hide. If luck and the gods are on our side, we might discover them."

"We've a plan." Ceto traced the chosen path before rolling up the map and putting it away. "We might always hear more on the road to give us a better idea."

Jayden nodded. "If not on the road, there are always the taverns."

"Weren't you the one who said I wasn't allowed in taverns anymore?" Ceto asked and adjusted her pack so the strap crossed her torso, making it easier to carry.

Jayden made a thoughtful face. "Yes, but I can rescind the order if you promise not to get us arrested again."

"I believe you had as much to do with getting kicked out as I did," Ceto pointed out. They started walking towards a distant road, the rocks lightly crunching beneath their feet. Ceto had no problem coming up with things to talk about and memories to

revisit. Based on the map, it would be hours before they found a village to settle in for the evening.

"Are you accusing me, your ambassador, of breaking someone's face and starting a bar fight because someone called you a finned bitch?" he asked her.

"I would never accuse you of anything," Ceto said with a laugh. "But I would happily recall the great historical moments of our dear ambassador."

Jayden laughed. "I would love to hear your version of events while we travel."

"I'm sure you will hear more than your fill," Ceto returned. Slowly, they put distance between themselves and the waters, and Ceto couldn't help but look back when they made it to the road.

"It gets easier, being away from the water. The need never really goes away, but it gets easier," Jayden said sympathetically.

"Yet, every step we take brings us further away from safety."

"I find it best to focus on other things."

"A most pragmatic way of handling our journey." She took a breath. "Well, let's get started."

Chapter Ten

Diana yawned as she used a forearm to push hair back from her face. The fire in the hearth roared with renewed life, filling the kitchen with a warmth not found in the hallways and corridors in winter months. Even so, the cold licked at her exposed forearms, neck, and face as she kneaded dough for the various pastries and breads to be added to the day's meals.

It was early morning, and the sun wouldn't make an appearance for another half hour or so, and Diana was one of the few members of the palace residence who rose in the early morning. She supposed the rest were warm in their beds, but she did not envy them. She relished the time to think, to observe the world around her without putting on a show or guarding herself.

More than a week had passed since she'd last seen or spoken to Crem. It was a normal existence since Elrick's death, and it wasn't one she was particularly happy about. She missed Crem. She missed their lighthearted bickering and his frequent visits to the kitchens whenever he had a spare moment. Sometimes, she wished her husband didn't feel the need to fight for seemingly hopeless causes. Even as such thoughts filled her mind, she knew she could not have fallen for him if he were different. People needed help, and Crem was in a position to provide it.

And it wasn't like she had the liberty to suggest she missed him. He was seen as a murderer and a traitor, and outward expressions of affection would mark her just the same. She sighed, dumped the kneaded ball of dough into a bowl, and covered it with a cloth. She'd let it be for a time so it could rise.

The ceramic thudded against the worktable as she sat it aside. She knew Zephraim had an affinity for eggs, so she decided to prepare the dish. As she gathered enough from the wicker basket serving as storage, she was surprised to find herself joined by the king. What was he doing here? Never in her life had she recalled Zephraim coming to the kitchens for any reason beyond grabbing a bottle and going on his way.

Giving a slightly awkward bow, she placed the eggs on the counter. "Your Majesty," she said, keeping her eyes downcast to avoid his gray eyes. "Is there something I can help you with?"

Zephraim didn't answer at first, instead choosing to walk around the small area nearest the fireplace. He ran a hand along the wall before continuing to the mantle above the fire. "Nothing, really," Zephraim replied. "Please, go back to your work."

Diana hesitated for a few moments but carefully began sorting the eggs into piles. Some to boil. Some to scramble. Some to use in other dishes. Her shoulders remained straight, her posture near rigid, as she focused intently on the king.

"How are you getting on, Mistress Hawke?" Zephraim asked after several moments of uncomfortable silence.

"What do you mean, Your Majesty?" she asked, looking over her shoulder. She almost felt sorry for him. His pale features looked all the more exaggerated by the sleepless shadows beneath his eyes, and his red-gold curls somehow seemed to hang limply on his head. As he stood near the fire, arms crossed and gaze distant, she pondered the wisdom in questioning him.

"Your husband is exiled, and you are alone," he replied, turning to look at her fully. "Even if you are loyal to me, I know your marital love has not vanished."

"Oh," Diana said, hands slow and careful in her work. "I suppose you are right, Your Majesty. I do still love my husband, even though he has made choices which prevent me from sharing my life with him."

Zephraim was silent again. "And you are struggling?"

Diana hesitated in her response, but she judged honesty to be wise. "I am," she replied. "Cremisius is a great many things, and not all of them bad. He involved himself in a cause I disagree with, but his treasonous actions don't make it easy to forget the fondness I have, and will always have, for him."

Zephraim let out a short, bitter bark. "I know how the loss and disappointment feels," he muttered quietly.

Diana pressed her lips together, wondering the wisdom of what she was about to do. "Are you referring to your sister, Your Majesty? Or someone else entirely?"

Zephraim sighed and opened his mouth to answer before shaking his head. "It doesn't matter."

"It does, though," Diana argued. She turned to face the king, wiping her hands on her apron. "You are our king. You of all people should be surrounded by those you care about, and those who care for you and will support you."

"Do you really think any of them support me?" Zephraim asked after another pregnant pause. He gestured vaguely towards the door, but Diana understood him to mean the nobility. "The ones who offer praise wish for reward. The ones who criticize pressure me to capitulate with commands. Those who claim my friendship also claim things they have no right to."

Diana swore she saw sorrow in his eyes, and the short walk to the chair usually occupied by Crem and the collapse into it showed Diana just how troubled the king was.

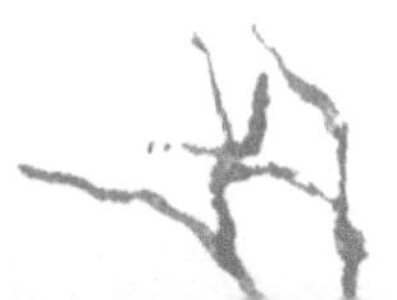

"I trust none of them," he confessed.

"A wise choice, perhaps," Diana said. She gave her own sigh, knowing Crem would disapprove of her honesty, or of how she intended to go forward. "I am not suggesting our former queen is innocent of the accusations levied against her, but the quickness in which certain members of court so readily jumped to prosecute and convict her leaves me worried for you."

Zephraim looked up from the seat, meeting her eyes with his own. He'd definitely had no sleep. "Do you think they'd do the same to me?"

"Perhaps. Some of them at least." Diana gave him a tight smile. "The staff hear things others might not. Some of those behind your sister's arrest cared very little about her involvement with the Mers or what happened with Lord Veitel. In truth, they sought to remove her because her decrees impacted their purses. We're all aware of their motivations."

Zephraim gave no response, but Diana detected no trace of anger in his expression. If anything, he looked all the more defeated. "How can I best offer you my support, Your Majesty?" she tried.

"I wish I knew," he said. He looked around the kitchen again and gave a great sigh. "I should let you tend to your responsibilities," he stated. "I know talking to me has been a distraction." He rose from the seat, his shoulders rounded even at full height.

Diana shook her head. "Not at all, Your Majesty," she insisted. "I'm more than happy to listen should you ever need it."

Zephraim gave her a weak smile and nodded. Without another word, he dismissed himself, leaving Diana to wonder what had driven him to the kitchen. When Gisela entered moments later, concerned despite her obvious sleepiness, she gave Diana a quizzical look. "What was he doing in here?" she asked in a whisper.

Diana shrugged and went back to work, considering how she might get the details of the encounter back to Crem.

Chapter Eleven

Riken made his way down the corridor to the queen's sitting room, his steps determined, but light. Zephraim's unhappiness had permeated so much of court life since the contentious last council meeting, the king's displeasure had taken the form of forced distance between himself and Rhoslyn. Zephraim watched them, interrupted them, and did everything but officially order the two to be separated anytime they were in the same room.

It had only been a few weeks, but those weeks left his hands and arms longing to reach out for her, to caress her smooth, fair skin, to be surrounded by the light, floral scent Riken attributed to only Rhoslyn.

Separation was untenable in the long term. He loved Rhoslyn and craved her presence down in his bones. Which was why, upon being informed by Xavier Eisenhart, one of his trusted men, the king had sequestered himself in his office and would be there for some time. Riken sought out his love. Arriving at the door, he glanced around to ensure there was no one around to report him and rapped on the door three times. If they were lucky, he might secure more than a few minutes with her.

His words seemed to catch in his throat when the door opened, finding her just as lovely as always. He stepped inside and gathered her into his arms. "Thank the Mother you are alone," he breathed before kissing her deeply. He groaned as she returned the fervent kiss and pressed herself flush against him. It was easy to get lost in her as his lips devoured hers, and his fingers trailed through her soft, cinnamon hair. "I know we must be careful," he breathed out when the initial kisses ended. "But I might kill them if anyone comes to interrupt us."

Rhoslyn let out her own breathy laugh. "You and the other lords completely overstepped in the last council meeting. He's angry, and I'm left to suffer without your warmth."

Riken sighed and nodded before pressing his forehead against hers. "I know, and I am sorry for it. Still, it is so tempting to throw caution to the wind and do as we please." He smiled as her arms tightened around him, letting him know she felt the same.

"And when do you think such a time will arrive?" she asked.

"I believe you insisted it was once he failed the kingdom, and we had lost hope in him. Unfortunately, I don't think we're there yet. You might let me know if you've changed your mind on being a widowed queen."

"You like him, and you would hesitate," Rhoslyn replied after a moment. "Either way, we'd need someone to pin the blame on."

She knew him well. Despite everything, including Riken's belief of Zephraim not being sturdy enough to be king, he did like the man. "There is always the cook," he said, his voice filling with spite at the thought of Diana Hawke. Were it up to him, she'd be disposed of.

"You have never liked Diana," Rhoslyn noted. "She poses a threat, of course. And her husband is suspect. But what has she done to you personally?"

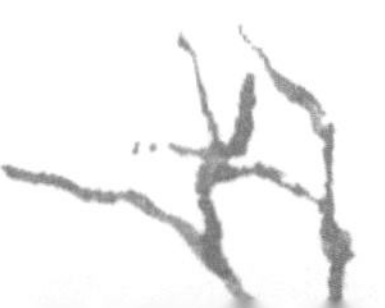

Riken felt his lips curl in a sneer, and he released Rhoslyn so they could talk. Once she seated herself in one of her chairs, he took the seat closest to her. "I don't like how she looks at us, as though she's better than us and knows it. It's the way she looks at you, with contempt, when you aren't looking. The way she watches Zephraim with pity, as if he deserves it." He shrugged. "I'm also willing to bet she agrees with her husband and reports to him whenever she gets the chance."

Rhoslyn rolled her eyes. "Of course, she agrees with her husband. She always has, and she was well-liked by Collette. Unfortunately, having an opinion she does not voice or act upon, as far as we know, cannot be punished as treason."

Riken knew she was right, and as much as he yearned to act decisively, he knew he could not without undermining their current positions in the political charade. "Which is why we frame her for poisoning Zephraim… and Lady Elrick."

Rhoslyn let out a chuckle, pressing a hand against her chest. "Lady Elrick does seem rather attached to you as of late. Should I be jealous, Riken?" she teased.

"I belong to you, heart, body, mind, and soul. I would kill myself before betraying you," he said seriously. Rhoslyn's duties regarding Zephraim were a matter beyond his feelings, one he would eventually deal with. "Lady Elrick's interest is concerning, though. She's approached Zephraim regarding a possible alliance with me through marriage. Our king has asked me to consider it."

"You're not marrying her," Rhoslyn agreed, her eyes narrowing in thought. "Do we have any easy paths of resistance? Any way to prove Cecelia Elrick as an ill-suited choice for you?"

"Other than the mountains of proof of her indiscretions during her marriage to Lord Elrick? No. Cecelia is very good at hiding her wrongdoings, and unfortunately, very good at pointing out how compatible we actually are. I am starting to think she was the brains behind Elrick."

"Can we connect any of her lovers to Collette? Any of her supporters, or suspected travel companions?"

"I don't know, but it is something I can look into. I'll have limited time since she's also pointed out to Zephraim I have increasing control over the soldiers."

"If you find nothing definitive, make something up. A planted seed will delay Zephraim." She tilted her head and took in Riken. "And for the Mother's sake, do not allow another council session to go down like the last one. You pushed the line far more than you should have."

Riken hung his head at her admonishment. He knew she was right, even if prodding the king had felt so good at the time. "I know. I let my frustrations with his inaction push me further than I should have. And the news he received after the meeting didn't help." He took a deep breath and looked at Rhoslyn. "Has he mentioned anything more about Collette?"

Rhoslyn shook her head. "He's been very quiet since he got the news. Melancholy, even."

"He did care for her, despite everything," Riken said with a sigh. "Another complication, I'm sure you know."

"I know," Rhoslyn replied. "Still, he turned on her first and with very little prompting. Everyone followed his lead. He bears the weight of his betrayal to Collette."

"He does. Mother, I hope he's not having major regrets." Riken knew regrets would require new plans and tactics. "We will need to discuss our plans further. For now, I have a proposal," he said as he rose from his chair. He offered a hand to Rhoslyn.

She took his hand. "Tell me."

"How about we find a quiet place and enjoy ourselves?" he asked, pulling her close again. "There are several abandoned rooms on the fourth floor where he wouldn't come looking."

"You could possibly convince me," Rhoslyn said. She placed a hand on the back of his neck, pulling him down for a kiss.

Chapter Twelve

The cool evening air seemed to make the problems of the past few months seem distant, but Whyldon knew they lingered on the periphery. They'd been lucky so far. He also knew Collette's survival was a miracle. The injury was more severe than the queen liked to admit, but she didn't deny how close to death she'd been.

Whyldon sighed, crossing his arms as he took in the setting sun. He thought of Tolan, something he rarely did with any fondness. He could not conceive of a decent reason for the man to have abandoned Collette. Despite any weaknesses he'd detected in Tolan's character, Whyldon believed Tolan loved Collette. Then there was Larent. He didn't know what he thought about the romantic angle and the blood magic situation.

Whyldon tried not to dwell on these things as he stood surveying the land around him. Distantly he noted a farmer maneuvering a plow across the small patch of earth next to his little hovel. He would soon retire when the sun went down, but the man continued to work as though he did not notice the change. As a boy, Whyldon had done the same thing more times than he could count. His parents had been loving, but they had instilled their children with an understanding and appreciation of work.

Being back home after so many years serving the royal family brought to light how little so many of those who had cast Collette from her role in Coralia had never experienced an honest day's work. The thought angered him all the more, but he was not afforded the opportunity to dwell on it as a smaller figure approached to stand beside him.

"Your companions are settled for the evening." Sara brushed her hands against her skirts as though the action confirmed her words as true.

"Good to know," Whyldon replied, his attention pulled away from surveying the land and landed on his sister. "You have no idea how much we appreciate staying here."

"You are sufficiently rattled. I can infer the appreciation." She offered Whyldon a wry smile. "At least you missed the soldiers who visited some months ago."

"We'd have not been foolish enough to be here months ago," Whyldon provided in defense.

"You're only here now because you had nowhere else to go." A genuine smile spread across Sara's face, and she placed a hand on Whyldon's arm. "You should relax. You are safe for now, and Collette will live. She just has a long recovery ahead."

Whyldon nodded in acknowledgement, though nothing in his posture indicated he was in any way relieved.

Sara continued, "It strikes me she'd have found a way to keep going if you had not been so close by. She is quite stubborn, though I venture you agree our little family has its fair share of stubbornness."

Whyldon nodded. "I believe our mother cast it as a defining trait." Even now he could remember her proclaiming over her luck at having such willful children.

Sara laughed again. "She did. Of course, she'd be put out with you, were she here."

"Oh?" Whyldon asked.

"Well, it's not every day the true Queen of Coralia strolls in, looking so much like every other woman in the family," Sara replied evenly. "I know it's not a secret. Everyone staying under our roof knows by looking at me. You might consider chatting about it with her, though."

Whyldon gave no reply, and he continued looking out in the distance. Sara changed topics. "You should go in and have a bite to eat. You are just as exhausted as the rest." Placing her hand on his shoulder, she pushed him towards the warmth of food and shelter.

It was probably a good idea. The aroma of delicious stew circulated through the cottage, and the simmering fire provided a protective warmth. The others were already at the worn table, eating and drinking, and Whyldon joined them without ceremony.

As he filled his bowl, he silently observed Nawalya moving from person to person. She rested a hand on Thomas's shoulder for just a moment before moving forward to brush her long fingers across Arian's neck. A small peck of a kiss on the top of Larent's head followed. By now, he knew her well enough to know she needed these small connections to ground her and comfort her through difficult times.

"We thought you were going to skip the meal," Nawalya said to Whyldon. She ran a hand through Larent's hair. He was starting to look better, though his exhaustion still clung to him. "You should get to bed soon."

Larent rolled his eyes. "At some point, you have to quit sending me back to bed."

"It is late," Thomas pointed out. "Sleeping does happen come nighttime." He was not eating. Instead, he was leaning

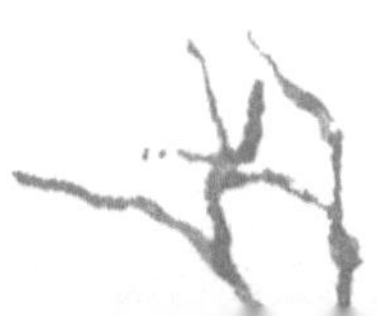

over a long roll of parchment, quill in hand. Whyldon could see the inks stains on his fingertips, and he wondered what the fletcher might be writing.

Whyldon backed Thomas's point. "I'm surprised any of you are still up," he commented. "Delicious food aside," he added, shooting his sister a playful look.

"I'm not tired," Nawalya explained, finally taking a seat at the table. "And even if I were, I'd not sleep well on an empty stomach."

"Did Collette eat?" Whyldon asked.

"She did," Sara confirmed. She made herself a bowl and joined the table as well. "She's getting out of bed and walking around, much to the chagrin of Arian."

Arian growled. "She needs more rest. Maybe one of you can talk sense into her."

"Do you really think she's going to listen to you?" Thomas asked, offering Arian a smile. He looked back at his work as he spoke. "You're lucky you got her to sleep as much as she did the first few days we were here."

Arian shrugged, meeting Thomas's gaze. "I see three paths forward. I can send Whyldon to talk to her, or I could have Larent talk to her, but I fear it would lead to more problems." He paused to smack the back of Larent's head when the shifter perked up. "Or I could drug her," he added. "I think it best to start with Whyldon."

"Do you really think she's going to listen to me?" Whyldon asked with a snort.

"Or submit to being drugged?" Thomas added.

"One can hope," Arian muttered and eyed the cup in front of him as though he were seriously considering drugging her.

"Collette is stubborn, but she's not unreasonable," Nawalya spoke up softly. "Sit down with her and explain your worries and recommendations. Do not drug her without her consent."

"I wasn't going to," he shot back.

"You were thinking about it," Larent popped off, looking just as unhappy with the thought.

"I think we're all in agreement doing anything to break her trust would be the end of the existing relationship," Thomas pointed out without looking up. "And by extension, our little travel party."

Arian's face reddened. "I would only do if left with no choice. If she opened her wounds or worse happened."

"I think we all know her wounds reopening won't happen," Whyldon spoke up. "Her wounds are scarred over, and there is no sign of internal problems. As much as I think she should be resting, you might be grasping for justifications." He knew anything done secretly or forced upon her would be seen as betrayal, and they didn't need to break her trust.

Arian scowled and looked down. "Things can happen," he muttered, though his new posture made it clear the elf knew he couldn't win.

"Any ideas about the healing situation?" Sara asked, leaving Whyldon thankful for the topic change. "What she's described is beyond the healing abilities I know."

Nawalya shook her head. "She's not the first person we've met who can heal, but what she was able to do for Larent is far beyond anything we've experienced." She looked at Arian who shook his head.

"Maybe she's not fully human," Larent joked.

"It would be on her mother's side, if so," Sara said.

Whyldon snorted. Sargarus wouldn't have accepted Adora as a wife had she any bloodline other than human. "I think we can safely assume Sargarus marrying a non-human is unlikely."

"Agreed," Arian said before sighing and throwing a thumb in Larent's direction. "Is there anything else we need to discuss before I force Larent to retire?"

"I would suggest his willingness to retire should be taken into account," Sara said, but she went back to eating. After a moment, she said to Thomas, "You have spent a lot of time writing tonight."

"I have," he agreed with a cheeky smile.

"And what are you working on?" Nawalya asked Thomas.

"Potential plans for how we intend to proceed come spring," Thomas replied.

"Should we not wait for Collette to join us before we make any real plans?" Nawalya asked, her brow creased in concern.

"We should," Thomas agreed, offering Nawalya a smile. "But it seems to me there is a distinct lack of planning about where to go and what to do. I'm laying out options as I see them."

"The Nereids would be the best option," Nawalya said. "Once the weather grows milder, we can go to Pontus Bay, get a ship, and sail."

"Assuming they are willing to help," Whyldon agreed.

Nawalya's brow furrowed again. "They may not have a choice but to help."

Arian silently reached out and squeezed her hand. "Did you have another thought?" he asked Whyldon.

"She can have the support of the Nereid and every other Mer in the world and still not have the support of her people. Regaining her throne isn't exactly a process of grabbing an army and taking things back." Whyldon imagined a direct challenge from the Quenall population would make news. "We don't know if Zephraim has been challenged."

"Do you know what the general consensus was before you left?" Arian asked Thomas. "While we were there, I would have said the majority approved of Collette."

"I suppose it depends on whom you ask," Thomas replied with a shrug. "I think most in the city support her, but there is something to be said about everyday people being more supportive of consistency in their lives. Of course, there are outspoken dissenters as well."

Arian sighed. "Some supporters are better than none, but it would be better if we knew exactly what was happening. I believe if it came down to it, unless Zephraim is an outstanding leader, the people will back Collette."

"With what I know of him, he won't be a great leader. Bet the people who put him on the throne will try and remove him sooner rather than later," Larent said as he tried to stand.

"We should be thinking bigger than just Quenall," Thomas pointed out. "I know a lot of the conversations have focused on the city since it's home for the Gaillaine family, but Coralia is much bigger."

Arian reached out and grabbed Larent, pulling him back into his seat. "Stay for a moment longer, and I will help you up, you ass."

"Love you too, Chuckles."

Arian rolled his eyes. "We could approach the elves. They might be willing to help. I do not know which members of the nobility would join us. So many seemed against her or neutral."

"There are some minor lords, but the ones like Elrick, Crobán, Riken, and Barris would not join us," Nawalya added.

"Again, you're acting as though the people and the events in Quenall speak to the larger stance of the relevant players throughout Coralia," Thomas pointed out.

"There are many tradesmen and merchants, and even gentry in Galel who would likely support Collette," Sara added in support of Thomas's point.

Nawalya nodded and stood, gently touching Thomas's and Arian's shoulders as she passed. She leaned down to kiss Whyldon before arriving at Larent. "I'm going to help him to his room," she informed the group.

"Thank the Lady. I'm not built for these conversations." He stood on his own but allowed Nawalya to put an arm around him.

As they made their way from the room, Arian turned back to the others. "Politics are not our area of expertise. Normally, there is already an army or the possibility of one. Something so monumental and complex escapes me."

"It's not exactly my area, either," Thomas said. "But thinking bigger than Quenall is needed, and we have the time to plan."

"How do we envision starting?" Arian asked, leaning forward and resting his arms on the table. He was clearly just as weary as the others. "Do we put her up in front of the people and let her inspire them? Do we continue to pretend she has passed and use her memory to turn the crowds to our side?"

"Depends," Whyldon said with a shrug. "There is a level of safety maintaining the death story. It's not as though she could defend herself if attacked right now, but maintaining the story might kill any momentum we have."

"I worry the people will be disheartened by her death. I am also concerned if we continue with the ruse, when they find out the truth they will feel betrayed," Arian said thoughtfully.

"And if we reveal her fate now, people will gather where she is based on where the news originated," Sara pointed out evenly. "There isn't a right answer. No matter how you proceed, there will be drawbacks."

Arian nodded before sighing and moving to stand. "I think we should shelve the discussion until Collette herself is able to join us."

"Agreed," Whyldon said. "In the meantime, perhaps we think about small groups of two or so going to Galel to see what we can find out about the political tide?"

"I could try to contact some of the villages and groups we've helped," Arian offered as he rose from his seat. "It's possible they will stand with the queen."

Chapter Twelve

"As long as you are careful in your communication," Whyldon said. "We don't need easily interpreted letters ending up in the wrong hands." The very notion, especially when Collette was recovering, was a horrific prospect.

Arian nodded, understanding dawning on his face. "I'll consider my options," he replied before heading for the exit to the house rather than going upstairs.

Thomas looked over to Whyldon, concern marring his generally cheerful expression. "I think a few of us going out into the local villages is a good idea since Arian didn't voice an opinion."

"I think so as well. Obviously, we would avoid Veitel and Wildrun if nothing else."

"Why don't all of you chat come morning?" Sara suggested. She had finished her dinner and was walking around the table, collecting the discarded bowls and cutlery. "I'll clean up."

Thomas took Sara's suggestion as his cue to finish his work, and he rolled up the parchment he'd been using. "Thank you, Sara. I'll be sure to help with breakfast come morning."

She offered him a warm smile. "I will hold you to it." Thomas packed his items and retreated upstairs. Sara put a hand on her hip and surveyed her brother. "You as well," she said.

Whyldon offered her a smile. He would not argue with his sister, no matter his reluctance to retire. "I know, I know."

Sara approached him and put a hand on his shoulder. "She is well, and you're all safe for now. Standing around and worrying over what hasn't happened is good for no one."

Whyldon let out a breath and nodded. "You're right. But I'll worry all the same."

"Now go to bed. I'll make sure Arian comes back inside."

"Good luck," Whyldon said, and with another sigh, he headed upstairs.

Chapter Thirteen

He erupted in laughter, rich and deep and infinitely warming, and she reached out to touch him, to be enveloped in the comfort of his embrace.

"I've missed you…" she whispered, relaxing in his arms. It felt like the first time she had truly been able to breathe since he'd left.

He gave her a puzzled look, like he didn't understand. "I was only in the kitchen, love. I promise not to linger so long next time. I would not want to keep my queen waiting when she misses me."

"Good," she replied, holding him closer. "I do not want to be separated from you again."

"As much as I wish I could stay by your side, you, my beautiful Queen, have a council meeting, and I have work today."

"We could ignore those responsibilities," she insisted.

He sighed deeply and shook his head. "As much as I would enjoy spending the day entirely in your company, I must leave."

She argued the point, trying to think of any way to convince him, but nothing swayed her lover's mind. Even as he casually strolled away, she was devastated by the loss, by the callous way he ignored her pleas.

Why did he not look back? Why did he ignore her? Why had he left?

Tolan…

Collette's eyes opened, though the darkness prevented her from seeing much of the room. A sense of dread and guilt pooled in her stomach. The dread came, knowing it was unlikely she'd ever lay eyes on Tolan again. The guilt came because of the man sleeping next to her.

She turned her head to look at Larent. He'd completely ignored Arian's insistence they maintain distance when not monitored, and she wondered if the elf had given up. She knew she loved him, without a doubt, as she studied Larent's handsome, sleeping face in the darkness. She could not imagine a moment without him.

Her love for Larent did not change her love for Tolan, nor did it provide closure for the abrupt end of their relationship.

Why she should be lying awake in the middle of the night contemplating her love life when she had other things, huge things really, to contend with, she could not say. Regaining the throne from Zephraim was critical. If her brother changed no laws and resumed no prior behaviors associated with the reign of Sargarus, he would still be too weak to keep the demanding vultures at bay.

She shifted into a more comfortable position, deciding she would try to force herself to sleep. She almost sighed as she saw Larent's eyes slowly blink open, knowing her restless movements woke him. He gave her a sleepy smile.

"Hey there, beautiful," he whispered in the dark. "What woke you?"

She offered him a smile, knowing he would see it despite the darkness. Everything about Larent, his warmth, his genuine

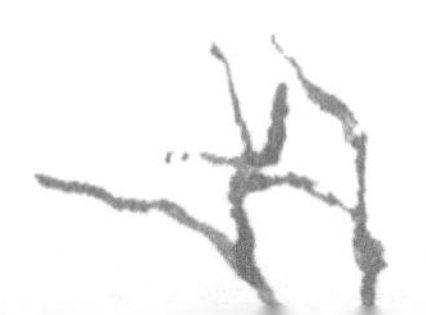

adoration of her, and his willingness to engage in conversation despite the late hour, all helped to soothe her. "Ongoing insomnia," she answered truthfully.

Larent nodded and, reaching out, pushed a strand of hair behind her ear. "You've never slept well, have you?"

"Not in a few years." She carefully shifted closer to him, thankful her movements weren't as painful as they had been when they'd first arrived at Barcomb Mill.

He wrapped his arms loosely around her once she settled, allowing her to control the space between them. "So, since you took the throne, yeah?"

"Very good guess," she agreed quietly. As big as the house was, she didn't want her voice waking the others. "It's gotten worse lately."

"Of course it has. You've been under so much stress, and there is so much uncertainty as to what tomorrow could hold. Fuck, I'm surprised you sleep at all, Freckles." He gave her a wolfish grin. "I would offer to wear you out, but I think Arian would come in, knives out and stab happy."

She moved even closer so she could put an arm around him. "I think Arian is about two seconds from losing it on all of us, anyway. We should avoid vexing him."

"Well, if he would get more than five hours of sleep every fortnight, he'd likely be in a better mood." Larent sighed. Arian looked for reasons to avoid sleep and had for as long as he'd known him.

"If he's not careful, I think he might find himself subjected to a sleeping draught."

"Let's drug his tea," Larent joked, laughing. It was infectious, and it served to distract her from earlier dreams. As he settled, he spoke again. "You would be very proud of the group, by the way."

"Why would I be proud?" she asked curiously.

"Even though everyone was debating possible next steps, they decided it would be best to wait for you to make any plans. You've made progress with them."

"Interesting," she said, pleased to hear changes were coming. "What ideas were presented?"

Larent shrugged as much as he could while lying on his side in bed. "Rallying the people. Seeing if we can find nobles who side with you." He grinned and wiggled his eyebrows. "Thinking about the rebellion outside Quenall."

"Imagine," Collette replied.

"Thomas has already started writing out potential options for you. Once you feel like challenging Arian and going downstairs, I'm sure it will be shared with you."

"Good. Now I have more reason to defy Arian," Collette said. "Getting my people to support me is a big place to start."

He leaned forward and brushed a kiss against her lips. "You're brilliant, Freckles."

"Practical and well-versed in running a country." She initiated another soft kiss.

"Brilliant," he whispered in return, kissing her again. When it ended, he brushed his nose against hers. "Did you want to talk to me about the thoughts keeping you up, or would you like to try to sleep? I know a lot has happened, and much more will continue to happen. I want to do whatever makes you happiest."

Collette knew she could have divulged the dream and her lingering thoughts of Tolan, and Larent would have listened without judgment or selfishness. She wanted to focus on the present, to let them enjoy one another without worrying about things they could not change. "We should probably try to sleep, especially since I'm not the only one recovering."

"Careful," Larent teased. "You're starting to sound like Chuckles."

"I ought to send you back to your own bed," she said, lightly shoving his shoulder.

"But you won't," Larent argued. He kissed her again. "Night, Freckles."

"Night, Larent."

Chapter Fourteen

Candlelight flickered in the dark room, and Thomas hovered low over the desk so he could read the words on the pages of his notes. He didn't know which of the basic options Collette might choose, or if he had considered all possibilities, but he knew they needed to be actively coming up with viable plans while they hunkered down for winter. Collette and Larent were healing, which meant the worry over keeping them alive had subsided.

He yawned and stretched, deciding he needed to get some sleep. He knew most of the others had already found their way to their rooms. Nawalya and Whyldon had settled in quite early, and Larent had not so subtly taken himself to the queen's room. Arian alone had not yet ventured into the house, and though Thomas first thought to let him be, he eventually decided Arian went without sleep far too often.

Thomas stood and washed his hands in the wash basin situated on the dresser. Once his hands were dried, Thomas let himself downstairs and out the door where he looked around for Arian. Snow covered the ground, and the decline of storms meant the layers of snow were thinner and tightly packed from melting under the daylight.

Arian stood by an old oak some distance from the house, every line of his body screaming of tightly coiled tension and bone-deep wariness. Thomas had no choice but to approach. "What are you doing out here?" he asked as he came to stand beside the elf.

Arian wasn't surprised to hear him speak. At least, the very deliberate response he gave suggested as much. "Keeping watch."

"No, you're not," Thomas said. "Try again."

Arian hung his head. "How do you read me so well?"

Thomas considered how he wanted to answer the question. Arian wasn't difficult to read with a little time and effort. It wasn't the full answer, anyway. So, he gave the answer he thought was more genuine. "Because I love you, I suspect."

Arian further stiffened, though Thomas wondered how such a thing was possible. He wondered if he'd said the right thing, but there was no taking it back.

"You barely know me, Thomas," the elf whispered.

"I know you well enough to know what I think and feel," Thomas easily countered. "I've known it almost as long as I have known you."

Arian didn't respond and chose to look up at the star-strewn sky. A long period of silence followed, but Thomas was not deterred. They were a matter of when, not if, and he was willing to give Arian space.

Which was why, as Arian extended a hand to him, Thomas raised his brows in surprise. He did not hesitate, and he found himself being led back to the house as soon as their fingers were laced together.

They moved quietly back into the house and up the stairs, and Arian led them to his bedroom. As he closed the door, Thomas looked around, quickly noting all his possessions, including his travel and medical packs, were sitting on a desk, seemingly ready to go at a moment's notice.

The bed was untouched, but Arian pushed Thomas so he was seated. The elf turned to his pack, removing items until it looked empty. He removed a stack of folded letters which he silently passed to Thomas before stepping away and turning to look out the window.

Without asking, Thomas opened the first, and he smiled to himself as he took in the precise writing belonging to Arian. It suited him. Thomas slowly worked his way through the letters, knowing with each passing one he and Arian had been feeling much the same way, even if Arian had never said the words. Some of the letters were simply accounts of experiences Arian had in the months since fleeing Quenall. Others spoke of missing Thomas, of wishing more could exist between them. Much time was dedicated to hoping Thomas was safe.

When he made it to the end of the fifteenth letter, Thomas folded each of the pieces of parchment and nearly stacked them. "You have a way with words."

Arian shook his head and continued facing away from Thomas. "When written instead of spoken, possibly," he conceded.

"We can agree on written."

Arian sighed and walked back to Thomas, taking a seat on the bed without touching him. Clasping his hands together, Arian stared down at his knees. "I feel deeply for you, Thomas. Maybe even love, but I believe you deserve better than me. I am broken. I have done horrible things, and I will likely do more. I don't have anything to offer you."

Thomas smiled to himself. "I believe we've had a very similar conversation in the past, Arian."

"I know," Arian said. "And yet, I still feel like you are losing out by picking me." He turned to face Thomas. "But I am also selfish."

"How are you selfish?"

"Because I should tell you not to… not to love me. To find someone safer, less broken. Yet I wish to keep you for myself."

Thomas turned, gently palming Arian's cheek so they were nearly nose to nose. "Then keep me," he replied. "And I shall keep you."

Arian briefly smiled. Thomas vowed to do more to help his smile appear more frequently and last much longer. "Would you stay? I do not sleep because I do not wish to be alone."

"You won't be alone," Thomas promised him. As Arian leaned in, Thomas closed his eyes and kissed him. He cupped Arian's jaw, letting the pad of his thumb brush along the other man's cheekbone in slow, gentle strokes. He wanted Arian to know he was cared for and adored.

Arian shuddered at the touch, breaking the kiss to rest his forehead against Thomas's. "I cannot promise there will not be days when I pull away," he said in a whispered confession.

"I know," Thomas replied. "I am patient, and I love you. I won't run from you."

"I may run. I know myself well enough to admit as much. But I won't run far, and I swear to come back to you."

"And not just because you are helping with our very long, uncertain mission, right?" Thomas teased.

"No. It's because you are here," Arian responded seriously.

"Good," Thomas whispered, and he kissed Arian once more. "Now, you need rest."

Arian rose from the bed, pulling his shirt off and revealing his pale skin, dotted here and there with scars. Thomas would ask about them one day. For now, he followed Arian's lead, removing his own shirt and folding it. When they were ready, he prompted Arian to get into bed.

Arian nodded and climbed into the side facing the door. He started to lie down but sat back up. "There is a knife under your pillow," he explained as he reached under the pillow on Thomas's side and pulled out a long, sharp dagger. "I apologize," he said as he tucked it under his side of the mattress.

"I'd be more surprised if it wasn't there," Thomas promised him. Once Arian was as relaxed as he could get, Thomas joined him, scooting close and spooning against the elf. "This okay?" he whispered.

Arian shuddered at first but soon relaxed. "Yes."

"Good," Thomas replied. He kissed the back of Arian's neck. "Get some sleep.

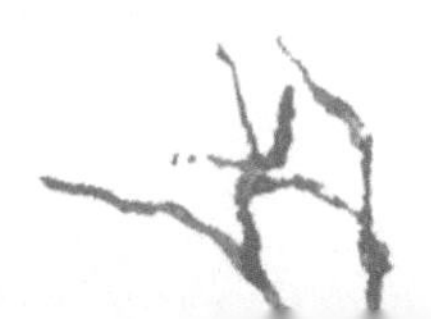

Chapter Fifteen

"*Now remember,*" *Diana said as she straightened Tolan's tunic, giving the rest of him a once over to make sure he was presentable. "Be respectful, bow, and only speak when you are addressed."*

She snapped her fingers, and Gisela appeared carrying a gleaming platter to Tolan, and practically shoving the thing in his arms.

Tolan couldn't help but laugh. "I don't know why it's so important for me to serve the first course myself, but I stopped arguing the point over an hour ago. Stop pushing me around, and let me get the food out there before it gets cold." He gave Diana a smile and headed through the large doors into the dining hall, only to pause and turn back around as he realized he'd be serving the royal family.

"You could have warned me!" he said, only to get a laugh from Diana in return. With a pained sigh, he headed back out the door. "There will be payback, I promise."

With as much grace as he could muster, Tolan walked to the table and placed the trays down. "Your Majesty. Captain," he said, his head and eyes lowered. "I hope you enjoy your meal." He bowed and stepped aside, waiting to be dismissed as per orders.

Captain Whyldon was the first to speak. "Her Majesty and I thank you," he said, taking the time to glance in Tolan's direction. So many of the nobles did not.

To his surprise, even the queen addressed him. "Yes, thank you."

Tolan glanced towards the kitchen again, spotting Diana who stood just out of sight of those currently dining. She gave him a reassuring smile before abandoning him to go back to the kitchens.

Different courses came and went, Diana passing trays off to Tolan when food was ready and whispering instructions when it was time to refill glasses and clear empty trays and dishes. On one occasion, Tolan made the mistake of locking eyes with the queen. Rather than wrath at his insubordination, he saw amusement and mischief, but he did not know what to make of it. Soon, the meal was finished, leaving the queen and her captain with wine and sweet fruits as they chatted.

"Have you heard from Rion?" she asked Whyldon, the name ringing familiar in his mind much like the sound of her voice.

"Not in weeks," Whyldon said. "He did say he'd write when he got home. Knowing him, he got distracted along the way." The captain took a bite of fruit, chewed, and swallowed. "He's never been one to write letters."

"His decision to retire irks me all the same," she declared. "Do you think I could order him to return?"

"I think I'd be figuring out what you wanted to do when he inevitably committed treason against you."

Tolan hid a laugh behind his hand, disguising it as a cough, catching a look from the captain. He found amusement in how easily annoyed the captain was, and intrigue as the queen's dark eyes glanced over at him again. They were such beautiful eyes...

She refocused on the captain, leaning forward as though they were alone in the room. "Treason? He'd have to get in line, don't you think?"

Tolan once again had to hide a laugh, though he made sure to keep his eyes downcast so as not to catch the captain's eyes. The bit of biting sarcasm rang through Tolan's mind, and he suddenly knew why her voice was so familiar. How had he not made the connection before now? As the queen and captain spoke, Tolan took the opportunity to study her, and he realized his own stupidity could be the only explanation. Though she did not wear the braid or hunting garments from when they first met, her long, dark hair was the same hair he'd run his fingers through. The playful eyes had captured his attention weeks before in a tavern miles away. Her smile, and those lips, were the same ones he'd sworn himself addicted to after their shared night. All the silk and finery she wore shouldn't have hidden those features from him.

He saw the wine glasses drained again, approached the table to offer more, but the captain shook his head.

"I've had enough," the captain explained to the queen. "I have an early morning. Crem wants to break in the new recruits."

"I might come to watch," she replied. She, too, declined more to drink, and rose from her seat.

Tolan held still, not sure if he should bow or leave the room. He decided bowing was always proper, and he made sure to bow lower and more formally than any he'd given while serving the queen. He also happened to watch her from lowered eyes.

Once she'd exited the room, followed by the captain, Tolan straightened. Grinning over at Diana who had joined him, he asked, "How did I do?"

"So far there have been no complaints," Diana said. "But I'll hear them regardless. Captain Whyldon is friends with my husband."

Chapter Fifteen

Tolan laughed. "Poor thing. What's my next job?" he asked as he pondered how quickly he could make his escape to check on someone very important.

"You know what your responsibilities are," Diana said with a laugh. "Now get to them. I have things to do before I turn in for the evening."

"I could have forgotten," he joked but headed to the kitchen to clean up, hoping to finish as quickly as possible.

Tolan hurried through putting away food and cleaning the dishes, his body vibrating with excited anxiousness. When Diana finally waved him off, he did not head for his room in the servant's quarters. Instead, he headed outside.

His connections to old acquaintances had ensured he knew the castle well. Whereas their knowledge was used in pursuit of assassinating the old king, he had much different motives. These motives saw him scaling a wall and thanking the Mother for his half-elvin blood.

Even as he climbed, he found himself wondering about the security risk of the unbarred windows leading to the queen's chambers. King Zephraim the Wise, Collette's grandfather, had removed the bars in a show of good faith, which had paid off. From what he understood, King Sargarus had insisted on replacing them a generation later, but expensive wars prevented follow through. He wasn't sure why Collette hadn't restored them, but he was sure he could ask her.

Reaching the balcony, he pulled himself up and over, feet quietly landing on the stone. Looking around at the rich furniture, he knew he had the correct rooms, and luckily his target had been held up. Tolan decided to have some fun, and he took a seat in a chair with the best view of the room and waited, hoping she would come alone.

He grinned as his wish was granted, though it took a moment for the queen to register him. She'd been smiling to

herself as she read over a letter. By the mother, she had the most radiant smile.

He waited for her to look up, and when she did, he was surprised and delighted to see she was neither angry nor afraid.

"Hello, again," she greeted, tossing the letter on her desk.

Standing, he strode over to her. "You told me your name was Joss." He wrapped an arm around her waist and pulled her snugly against his body. A small part of him prayed she didn't decide to gut him, while another larger part egged him on.

She smiled in delight, and an arm draped loosely around his neck in encouragement. "Joss is only one of my names."

"Clearly," said with a small laugh, lowering his head to capture her lips.

Keeping himself together proved more difficult than any other task Tolan had ever faced. Every step, every attempt to move forward, to keep from giving into anger, pain, and soul-deep sorrow tested him. So, he focused his energy on finding the group. Based on the information he'd obtained from the would-be assassin and his knowledge of the members of his former travel party, Tolan had narrowed possible locations of the fight to a half dozen. After determining the most likely, he'd gotten back on the road, intent to find out whatever he could.

He tried to keep up with his sleep while traveling, making sure to eat as often as his rations and his route allowed. However, he found his dreams plagued with nightmares of her death, and his food tasted like ash. His mind and body were so focused on his goal he couldn't even contemplate what he might do if his tracking confirmed the worst.

Weeks after the fateful encounter at the tavern, Tolan was convinced he was on a fool's errand. None of the sites he'd investigated yielded answers. Arian would make sure to conceal their presence, but Tolan knew blood and panic would make the meticulous elf less careful.

As he came across the clearing at the third site he visited, he was tempted to continue without much investigation. Only when he happened to step on a discarded potion vial hidden in the old, sludgy snow did he realize he might have gotten lucky. He carefully began surveying the area, looking for any signs of disturbance. Brushing aside the newer area of snow, he knew he was at the right place. Signs of old, dried blood had been preserved by snowfall, and the larger than normal wolf tracks had his heart pounding in his chest.

A part of Tolan didn't want to search. Accepting the results meant she was likely dead. The more he dug, the more blood he found. With no real conscious thought, his knees hit the ground and he let out a primal scream of rage and sorrow, unable to stop, uncaring, or maybe unseeing, the other figure emerging from the woods.

He didn't look up as the footsteps grew near, but his sobs and screams faded. If Collette was dead, Tolan had no desire to move forward.

"What are you carrying on about?" a deep voice asked him.

Tolan had his dagger in hand, throwing it wildly in Rion's direction. The days without sufficient rest made him sloppy, and it landed with a thud somewhere to the right of the intended target. Rising to his feet, Tolan took a fighting stance.

"Here to make sure she's dead? To gather proof for her fool brother?" Tolan spit out, his rage and anger finally taking over, not allowing him to see the man in front of him as anything other than a threat.

As defensive as Tolan knew he was, the man across from him seemed the opposite. He was tall, broad-shouldered, and imposing, but his casual stance and slightly tilted head told

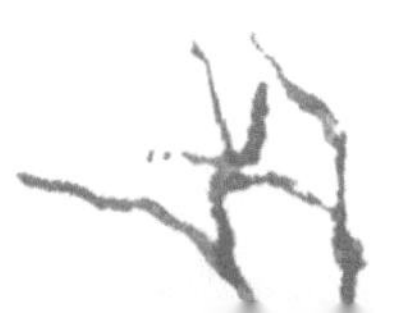

Tolan he wasn't planning to fight. The vivid, ginger hair and beard did somewhat detract from his looming stance, admittedly. "Why would I support anything Joss's idiot brother stood for, exactly?"

The nickname cleared some of the fog from Tolan's head. Very few people knew Collette's nickname. Straightening, he took the man in, really took him in. "Rion?" he asked as he put away his blade.

"Who else?" Rion asked. He stepped away from Tolan and looked around, his expression contorting into something resembling anger and worry as he spotted the copious amounts of dried blood. "You think the blood is hers?"

Exhaustion hit Tolan all at once. He didn't know Rion, but he felt better having someone who knew Collette nearby. "I know it is. The wolf tracks confirm it." He held up his hand, the golden bracelet belonging to Collette hanging from his wrist. "The man who claims responsibility had her bracelet."

Rion nodded as he continued searching the area. "There's a lot of blood," he commented after a moment. "And poor concealment. Interesting."

"Her attempted assassin took minimal credit, but he claimed a wolf finished her off." Tolan took a deep, shuddering breath. "Other than the wolf, she had three additional companions. If she was bleeding out or…" He paused, unable to get the words out. "They would have taken her and gone." His breath hitched harder. "And I wasn't there to help."

"The poor concealment suggests they were in a hurry," Rion said more to himself, not acknowledging Tolan's words. "She could be alive."

Tolan felt a small spark of hope bloom in his chest, one he desperately wished to cling to. "Arian has worked miracles in the past, but I don't know. I don't know where they would have taken her."

In his right mind, Tolan knew Larent wouldn't hurt her, but he wasn't in his right mind. Right now, looking at all the blood, all he could think of was tearing Larent apart with his bare hands.

"Was Whyldon with them?" Rion asked, his attention fully on Tolan.

"He never left her side."

"We should try Galel. It's close, and Whyldon has a home there."

Tolan nodded. "Were you out here looking for her?"

Rion snorted. "She's got herself in a bit of trouble. Of course, I'm going to help."

Tolan didn't know what sort of companion Rion might make, but he saw no reason for them to continue their journey separately when they had the same aim. "Would you mind if I travel with you?"

"You might as well," Rion decided, fingers scratching at his chin through the thick red beard. "Just… try to be a little less dramatic, yeah?"

Tolan gave a slight, shallow nod but said softly, "I just should have been there."

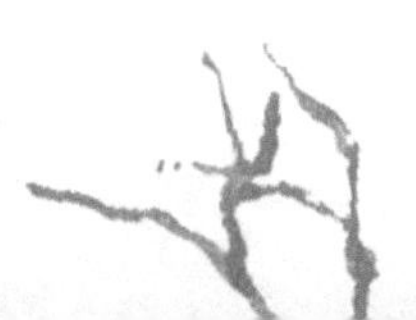

Chapter Sixteen

Riken was very, very unhappy, mostly with himself, for the unfortunate situation he found himself in. The last time he was in such a predicament, he'd been young and naive to the lengths others were willing to go to secure his hand, an alliance, or both. He'd since honed skills to keep others at bay. Yet, here he was, his back pressed against the balcony railing, hands held up for everyone to see, palms open. He would give the harpy no cause to claim he had touched her, nor cause to claim marriage was warranted. He would not be trapped by Cecelia Elrick.

Of course, he knew he should never have excited the ballroom for a breath of fresh air, not when Lady Cecelia Elrick had done her best to catch him alone. He'd needed the reprieve after watching Zephraim and Rhoslyn move about the room, talking with banquet attendees as Rhoslyn did her absolute best to portray a loving and utterly devoted wife. He wasn't even sure what the purpose of the grand feast was other than an opportunity for Zephraim to do something other than mope while he publicly paraded around the room with his hands on Rhoslyn.

He wanted to end Zephraim.

Riken shuddered in disgust as Cecelia ran her index finger down the front of his jacket. "An alliance between the two of us, and our estates, would be so beneficial," she purred in a silken voice, looking up at him from lowered lashes thinking it made her look coy instead of just stupid.

It wasn't as though Riken could say Cecilia was unattractive. Her pale gold hair and light gray eyes held an appeal. Riken knew exactly why the deceased Lord Elrick had chosen his bride. Despite her mourning dress, she made quite a lovely picture. Still, even with her beautiful face, Riken would not be tempted.

"I have made it clear I am not interested in marriage. I am a confirmed bachelor and happy to stay such."

The pout she gave was exaggerated, meant to draw attention to her lips and make men want to kiss them. The said attempt at flirtation did not work on him. He liked lips a little less plump, more bow-shaped. Lips belonging to the woman who held his heart.

"You say you are a confirmed bachelor, and yet you spend all your time with the queen, a married woman and our ruler," Cecelia cooed, though the sweetness of the words did nothing to hide the conveyed threat.

Riken forced his body to remain as relaxed as it could in its present situation. He knew she wanted a reaction, and he refused to give it to her. Glancing past Cecelia, he saw several people, Zephraim included, watching them with mild interest from just inside the ballroom, illuminated by candle and torchlight. Unfortunately, none of them looked bothered enough to come to his aid. Cecelia was fortunate they had witnesses, or he'd throw her from the balcony in much the same way Lord Crobán had found himself tossed.

He gave Cecelia a look of annoyed impatience. "You insult my honor and the honor of her Majesty, and I will not stand

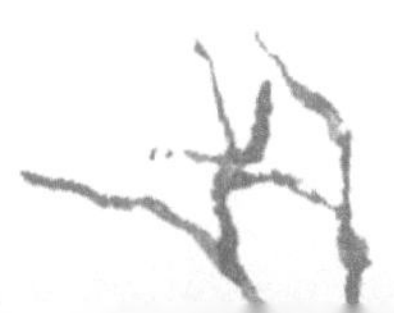

here and listen. I reject you and your suit. As I always have." He moved to step around her, only for Cecelia to grasp his arm, her nails digging in deep. Whatever venom she was about to spew cut off as a delicate throat cleared, catching their attention.

Cecelia whipped her head around, her pale hair swaying with the movement, though the sight of Queen Rhoslyn, dressed in a beautiful pale lilac, forced the other woman to immediately let go of Riken's arm. She gave a quick curtsey and a hasty murmur, "Your Majesty."

"What is this?" Rhoslyn asked, playing confused as though she were unaware of what she'd encountered. "Why are you assaulting Lord Riken, Lady Elrick?"

"Oh, Thank the Mother," Riken said, knowing from the venomous look Lady Elrick had heard his words. He stepped behind the queen, keeping a respectful distance between the two. Yes, he was hiding behind his lady's skirts, but he didn't give a shit.

"My queen, I was just trying to discuss with Lord Riken the benefits of strengthening our alliance. With my husband passed…" She dabbed her eyes as if anyone believed she mourned him. "My lands are in need of protection. I am in need of protection. Lord Riken is the perfect candidate. My soldiers respect him, and our lands are close together." She gave Rhoslyn a shy, weak smile.

"You did not answer my question, Lady Elrick," Rhoslyn returned, only a hint of sympathy in her voice. She looked down, smoothing an imaginary wrinkle from her silk skirt. "I'm not hearing an explanation as to why you assaulted Lord Riken."

"Oh but I wasn't, Your Majesty. I was just trying to get him to stay a little longer. He always seems in such a hurry to run off. You know how men are."

Cecilia giggled a little as though she and Rhoslyn were sharing a joke at Riken's expense. He sneered, about to say something when he felt another presence behind him. Glancing back, he turned and bowed deeply. "My King."

Cecelia curtsied again, and Rhoslyn inclined her head. Riken noted she took on the near saccharine expression of the ever-doting wife once more, and his jealousy flared behind a carefully concealed mask of delight at being joined by their king.

"What's the commotion?" Zephraim demanded of the group. "Just because you are on the balcony doesn't mean you are not heard."

Cecelia started to simper and smile again, moving closer to the king. "Oh, nothing to bother His Majesty about. I was just trying to have a private discussion with Riken, and I fear Her Majesty misread the situation."

Riken raised his eyebrows at the woman's audacity. Not only was she lying to a king, pathetic though he was, she was placing blame on Rhoslyn. He would not stand for it. "We were not. I was trying to leave, and Lady Elrick tried to stop me. Our queen saw and intervened on my behalf."

"It is true," Rhoslyn confirmed, her eyes narrowed briefly in Cecelia's direction. "I witnessed Lady Elrick forcibly grab Lord Riken. I cannot abide by disrespectful behavior directed towards our friends and our court."

"Perhaps you should have notified someone," Zephraim suggested to his wife, and Riken raised his brows in genuine surprise. Zephraim never publicly chastised Rhosyn.

Zephraim sighed, his hands going to his hips as he turned his face up at the darkening sky in apparent frustration. "Lady Elrick, I must insist, despite your recent losses, you will not vex Her Majesty."

Keeping her head down, Cecelia managed to give Rhoslyn a dirty look, one almost expertly covered by her hair. "I apologize, Your Majesty. I will try not to monopolize your favorite next time."

Snide comment made, Lady Elrick flounced away before anyone could say anything.

"Are you sure I should marry such a creature, Zephraim?" Riken said in a wry, mostly joking tone.

"I think she wouldn't be a bad choice for you," Zephraim replied with a shrug. "Even if she is overly assertive. As her husband, you could tame her. And all the benefits she mentioned do exist."

"Overly assertive?" He gave Zephraim a warm grin, knowing he needed to get back on Zephraim's good side regardless of anything else. "I couldn't marry her. She wouldn't take her vows seriously, and I won't be in such a marriage."

"You would make it work," Zephraim said noncommittally. "But I will take your concerns under advisement."

"My king," Riken said, low so his voice didn't carry. "I am not going to marry her. We would both be unhappy, good political match or not. I will marry for love and nothing else."

Zephraim's expression darkened. "You will do as you are instructed by your king, regardless of how much you disagree," he said. "I do apologize, however, if my orders put a damper on your ability to flirt with my wife."

Riken's lips pressed together, but he inclined his head. Zephraim's days were becoming numbered. Lady Elrick wouldn't last the week.

"Zephraim," Rhoslyn said, coaxing her husband into a better mood. "Let's not be hasty with our words."

"I'm not," Zephraim replied flatly, but no other accusations were made. He looked to Riken. "Perhaps, rather than worry about a potential marriage you do not welcome, you would be up for another task."

"I am at your command," Riken replied, eager to show any willingness for non-marital commands.

"We've word the Nereid grow anxious since my sister was reported dead. I need someone in the area for oversight while the Mertrade goes back into production."

Riken's eyes widened in surprise. "I am more than happy to help, my King."

"I thought you would be interested," Zephraim said. "We can discuss specifics tomorrow. For tonight, my wife and I have banquet attendees to see to." He extended his hand to Rhoslyn, and she took it without hesitation.

"Enjoy the festivities, my King. Your Majesty." Riken bowed deeply and waited until they were mingling again to make a discrete exit. He had a death to plan, and he needed to speak with Xavier.

It was late, and Zephraim was blackout drunk. Those were the only reasons Rhoslyn dared to seek out Riken. The accusation on the balcony had been enough to inform Rhoslyn, at the very least, there was suspicion of Riken, and she wouldn't doubt it extended to her.

She would have to think of ways to assure Zephraim she was utterly loyal to him. The truth did not matter, not when he had no actual proof. Still, as she silently crept along corridors and down the stairs, she made sure she was not watched.

Finding Riken's rooms was of no consequence. She'd been there before, though the frequency had dropped considerably in the past weeks. She'd hoped to rectify the prolonged distance, but with Riken easily agreeing to be sent away, her wish would not be granted.

Letting herself in without knocking, Rhoslyn closed the door behind her, glaring at her lover as he came into view. She gave no mind to her hair which hung loose about her shoulders

or the dressing gown she'd changed into after the banquet. "What were you thinking?" she demanded as she approached.

Riken took a step back, eyes going to her hands as though checking for a dagger. It was a smart move on his part. Rhoslyn was not above making her displeasure known.

"Which part?" he asked her in a soft, placating voice. "Because if I had been thinking any less, I'd be in jail for murder, or worse, treason."

She narrowed her eyes. "Let's start with being stupid enough to get yourself cornered by *her*. Then, we can move on to openly defying Zephraim."

Riken sighed and sat on his bed. "I saw her talking with one of the other men she's interested in. I made a mistake in thinking she would not follow me out." He ran a hand down his face. "I assumed Zephraim would understand, what with all his drunk talking when we were younger of marrying only for love." He took a deep breath. "He cannot force me to marry her. She won't live past the end of the week if he insists."

"Even so," Rhoslyn said, her anger marginally subsiding. "You cannot tell him what you are and are not going to do. Now, when something unfortunate happens to Lady Elrick, where do you think they will look?"

"I am aware. Which is why I am going to take the opportunity offered to me and leave for a little while." He held out a hand to her. "As much as I am loath to do so."

"You seem giddy over the opportunity," Rhoslyn accused, though she consented to take his hand.

Riken shook his head. "I find myself pleased at the prospect of being able to go out and further our goals. Being away from the castle will allow me to claim innocence when Lady Elrick dies in a robbery gone wrong."

"Let's not be hasty in whatever death she succumbs to," Rhoslyn replied. "We don't want you in more trouble. At some point, I'd like you to be welcomed on your return."

He looked up, meeting her eyes with his own, and Rhoslyn felt herself soften to him. "Leaving your side makes me feel like my heart is being ripped from my chest, but after Zephraim's display towards you tonight, I need to leave or murder him. I will not have anyone treat you disrespectfully."

"Perhaps it is time for my husband to find himself victim of some great accident," Rhoslyn said and allowed herself to be seated beside her lover.

"You would be a beautiful, widowed queen, and I would lay my weapons and my might at your feet to command as you will. I would kill him right now if you so wished. We could blame the cook's husband."

Riken's devotion was something Rhoslyn was certain of, something she could rely on without fail. But he could, and had, acted rashly that evening and on other occasions. Dealing with Zephraim had to be intentional and well-planned. "We have to be careful," Rhoslyn said regretfully. "Another big change in leadership may press the people's tolerance. We couldn't move too quickly."

He nodded in agreement. "Which is another reason I need to go. Maybe, if I am gone, you can find out what he thinks he knows and why he has suddenly turned on us. It has to be more than one meeting." He took Rhoslyn's hands. "Maybe, you can take control, so when something does happen, no one cares."

"I will use the time to our advantage," Rhoslyn assured him. "And if something terrible befalls him while you are gone, you would have to hurry home."

"I would be here within moments of receiving your summons," he swore. "I'm going to leave my best man, Xavier, here to assist you. He arrived recently to provide updates from

Wildrun. He's cunning and deadly, loyal beyond measure. He will do anything you ask as if he were me."

She smirked. "Oh, I am certain there are things he cannot quite live up to where you are concerned."

Riken threw back his head laughing. "Oh, my Goddess. I do so love you and your wicked humor." He ran a hand down her cheek, and she watched as his expression grew serious. "I am going to kill Elrick's widowed bitch for how she treated you tonight. Would you like it to be quick or very slow and painful?"

"I'd rather it be slow and painful," Rhoslyn replied without having to consider it. "She should know better than to openly implicate me."

Riken nodded. "I will make sure it takes hours for her to die."

"Good," Rhoslyn replied. "You do know what appeals, my love."

Riken chuckled. "I would do the same to the bastard you call 'husband' if it were in my power. Instead, I will go out and make the world perfect for you."

"We are slowly accomplishing all of our plans, my love," Rhoslyn replied.

"Yes, we are." He gave a sigh. "I really thought Zephraim would be more on our side with everything. Where did he and Collette go wrong, you think?"

"Collette was high-minded and idealistic, but she wasn't stupid nor weak enough to be swayed," Rhoslyn said, her head slightly tilted as she spoke. Thinking through the answer, as obvious as it was, needed the appropriate attention. "Zephraim is weak, but angry and arrogant."

"I wonder what it would take to break him," Riken mused, but he sighed again and turned to embrace her. "I do not want to leave you here with him."

"I will be safe with you gone," Rhoslyn consoled him. "I have taken care of myself most of my life."

"You weren't queen for most of your life. You were safer before." Pulling away from her, he reached over to his nightstand, a dark heavy thing, and pulled out the items he had been gathering since he left the ball. "I retrieved these for you."

The first item he held out was a petite stiletto dagger. "My mother used this dagger to keep herself safe. The night she died was the only night she wasn't carrying it."

The other item, a small box with a hidden latch, didn't need explaining. It would contain poisons, several different types. "Keep them in my chambers if you wish to avoid suspicion. I will not have you without protection, even if I believe your own skills are more than sufficient."

"You underestimate the experiences of a ranking woman," Rhoslyn replied, though she made sure to tuck away the dagger. Riken needed reassurance as they would be separated.

"Seeing as I am not a woman…" he replied. "How much time do we have?"

"He was passed out drunk when I left him," Rhoslyn said.

"We should make the most of what could be our last night together for a while."

Rhoslyn stood and moved to Riken. She pulled up the skirt of her night clothes and straddled his lap, initiating a heated kiss.

Riken crushed her to him, returning the kiss, and soon, Rhoslyn was removing both of their clothes.

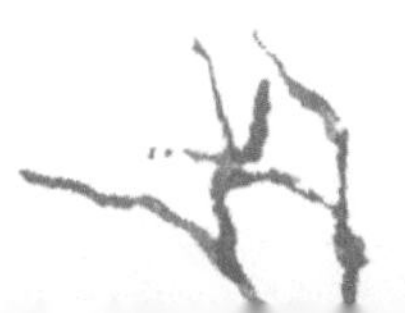

Chapter Seventeen

Crem walked slowly through the dark, slightly damp underground tunnel. He clutched a crudely drawn map in one hand and a small lantern in the other. The flame illuminated the rough stone walls of the tunnel, but it offered little warmth. Knowledge of the tunnels had been given by Howle, and their small but determined group used them for transporting those at risk out of the city.

Not all of the tunnels indicated on the maps remained open or in decent enough repair for use. Avoiding collapsing, dangerous escape paths seemed the least they could do, so when they had some downtime, one of them grabbed a map and walked the tunnels, marking them if they were still a valid option.

Today was his turn. Exploration was often boring work, allowing his mind to ponder melancholia and loneliness. He missed Diana; her warmth, her laugh, her smile, the way her hand felt in his. The past several weeks marked the longest they had been apart since before their wedding, and he hated it with increasing frustration. He would play the hand dealt to him by the Mother and his own choices, and pray no harm came to her because of it.

Crem marked one of the side passageways as unstable after noting weak support beams and debris scattered along the ground. They could still use the tunnel, assuming they could avoid creating more potential for a cave-in. He'd talk it over with Howle.

With a sigh, he debated returning to the resistance base, but paused as he overheard a low murmuring ahead of him. Not knowing who would be in the tunnels or why, Crem unsheathed his sword, extinguished his lantern, and slowly crept forward with imperceptible steps.

As he turned a corner, he spotted the low light of another lantern. Two people stood together, their bodies pressed close. Crem thought he recognized the male of the pair, but he couldn't make out the other person.

"You're injured," said a strong, velvety female voice.

"It's a flesh wound," replied the male, confirming Crem had stumbled upon Barris, the Golden Lord. Now a little close, he could see the lord's tan skin and rich black hair shining in the lantern light. Barris's piercings twinkled, as did similar piercings worn by the woman.

"It's not a flesh wound if I have to stitch it up," the woman said, her hand ghosting across what Crem could see was a long, jagged slice across Barris's upper forearm. She pushed the lord away and moved to a pack sitting next to them. No longer hidden by Barris's large form, Crem recognized the woman, whose olive skin shimmered indigo and sea green, her long rich black hair highlighted in the same colors. Crem recognized her as one of Barris's Mers, Lynessea.

"You're only upset because you wanted to add a new tattoo there, and thanks to a lucky strike, you can't," Barris joked.

"Oh, I could. It would just be less than pleasant for you," was Lynessea's playful response. She stood, a needle and medical thread in her hands. Without a word Barris turned so he was

leaning against the wall, his injured arm close to the light so the woman could sew up his arm. "Would you like something for the pain?' she asked, her voice a little more sympathetic.

Barris shook his head but looked away as she began.

Crem watched the two, wondering if he should show himself or stay. It felt wrong to be spying on those who were supposed to be allies. However, Crem knew he would stay, because he didn't trust Barris, not yet. He and Barris had spoken at length the night the man saved him from Lord Elrick's failed ambush.

Admittedly, Barris had ample evidence to prove his trustworthiness. Years worth of correspondence between himself and King Aphros of the Nereid had been presented. Barris had also allowed Crem to inspect his Merscale jewelry. The adornments which were meant to look as though they'd been taken from the Mer had actually been shed scales provided by those Nereid he was closest to. Still, Crem did not understand why Barris had originally joined the Nereids, or even when, and none of his questions had provided real answers.

"I'm fine," Barris reiterated, cutting into the silence. "It truly was just a lucky strike, and the tattoo can wait. I still don't think I deserve one for killing Elrick." The lord's uninjured arm came up to stroke Lynessea's hair.

"By slaying him, you protected yourself, and therefore, you protected us. It was an act in service of the Gods. Aphros, and our priestess, agree. You will get another tattoo to honor them," Lynessea replied.

"We give thanks to the Goddess of the sea," Barris murmured in prayer. "I will accept the tattoo since you wrote to the priestess. I still think killing Elrick was the right thing to do, but it does not deserve a reward."

"All the more reason you deserve it. The gods reward the humble," Lynessea started.

"And punish the vain," Barris finished. "We have been very lucky. First, because almost no one in Quenall bothered to learn the Nereid religion, and second, we were able to avoid Jayden while he was here. He would have taken one look at the tattoos and known who I was."

"You give my cousin less credit than he's due. He would have said nothing, but as Jayden has not met you, his interest in you would not have been good. Myself and the others worked hard to keep you out of his sight." Lynessea leaned down and bit the end of the string as she finished the stitches. "But don't lie and tell me you weren't interested in meeting him."

"I was very interested. I've heard much about him, but you, my charming and beautiful wife, are skilled at keeping me out of trouble."

"The Goddess knew someone had to monitor you, or you'd have given the game away by now," Lynessea teased as she leaned forward to kiss Barris but pulled away almost as quickly. "Now, Cremisius Hawke must be getting cold standing in the shadows like he is. Let us greet him like a friend so he may learn to trust us," Lynessea said, startling both Crem and Barris.

Without hesitation, Crem stepped into the light and was surprised to be greeted with warm smiles. "I would apologize but—".

"You don't trust us yet," Barris interrupted. "We understand, but it's good you're here. I needed to talk to you. Riken is being sent away. We need to plan for his departure, and maybe it's past due for us to spend time together. Trust is earned, after all."

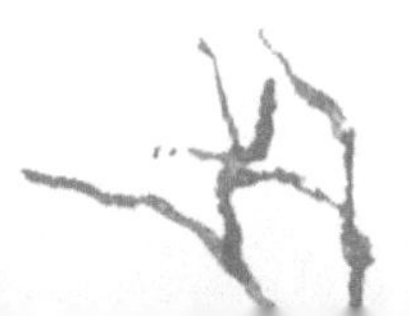

Chapter Eighteen

The Black Lantern stood as an ancient reminder of the wonders of Galel. No one quite remembered when the old inn was first erected, or how many times it had undergone repair over the years, but it was a place long spoken of by the grandparents and great-grandparents of the current locals.

Jayden found himself sitting at the bar, taking on the warm ambiance created by the cozy accommodations and roaring fire as he chatted with the innkeeper. All the while, he steadfastly ignored the commotion from behind him. Ceto could hold her own.

"I wish I could help, but we never saw the true queen," the owner, a tall, lean man named Ian said. His warm, flirtatious smile showed delicate lips and straight, white teeth, features Jayden could well appreciate. So much so, Jayden blatantly raked his eyes up and down the human. He was attractive, perhaps in his late forties, though slimmer in build than Jayden normally liked. The long copper hair did something for Jayden's insides, and he decided he would like to take the man up on the silent offer of sex rumbling between them all evening.

As long as Ceto was in no hurry to move along, of course.

"It's alright, my friend. I knew it would be a long shot," Jayden smoothly replied. He winced as he heard a table break. "I will pay for any damages," he said, leaning forward so only Ian could hear. With a sigh, he looked over his shoulder to see if Ceto needed his help with her bar fight.

He found her standing over her victim, rolling her shoulders. She offered him a cheerful smile. "All good," she promised as the large man with greasy hair groaned. She mouthed, "Go flirt."

He watched as Ceto slammed her foot down on the man's hand and decided Ian was far more interesting. His happiness over traveling with a fellow Nereid could not be expressed, especially with a companion like Ceto. Her strength and intelligence made for excellent travel conditions, and he could not understand why humans valued their women less.

But Ian was gorgeous, and Jayden yearned to create a scenario where he saw more of the innkeeper before they departed. "So, what can you tell me about the area?" Jayden asked with a charming smile, reaching out to caress the owner's hand. Ian didn't pull away, a good sign.

Another crash from behind had Jayden wincing again. Reluctantly, he turned his body to check on Ceto. She was brushing her hands together while her plaything was on the ground, a couple of feet from where Jayden last saw him, and unconscious. Jayden couldn't help but smile at his proud companion.

"I'm glad you're having so much fun," he said as she joined him at the bar. He moved his right hand down to his coin pouch, only to have Ian wave him off.

"I'll take it from them. Assholes like him know better than to mess with my customers." The decree seemed fair to Jayden since Ceto had only attacked after tolerating a half hour of verbal abuse about both her gender and her species. Ian left the bar and walked over to the downed man. He thoroughly searched and stripped the offender, and when he was done, Ian took the man by the legs and dragged him outside in the snow.

Jayden took the moment of privacy to lean towards Ceto and in a low voice said, "He says Collette hasn't been here or at least they never saw her."

"Do you believe him?"

Jayden thought about it. "Yes, I do."

Ian soon rejoined Jayden and Ceto at the bar, looking no less happy than he had prior. "I think this calls for a drink," he determined. Without waiting for Jayden's reply, he took out three glasses and filled them with a dark whiskey. He downed his with ease and put the now empty glass into a basin with other soiled cups and dishes. "Are you two going to need a room for the night?"

Ceto had her whiskey glass in hand, though she hadn't yet tried the liquor. "We'll need two rooms if you have them," she said, her eyes darting towards Jayden before returning to Ian. Jayden might have hugged her and gave a subtle, thankful nod.

"It just so happens I do have two rooms," Ian replied. He excused himself long enough to walk back to what Jayden assumed was an office, and soon the innkeeper returned with two keys.

"I guess we're staying the night," Jayden said as his and Ian's fingers touched.

"Wonderful," Ian said. "I will let you two settle in, and I'll be sure to check in later to make sure neither of you needs anything."

"I look forward to it," Jayden promised the man, holding in his smile.

Ian went off to clean the mess Ceto had made and see to the other guests. When Jayden looked at Ceto and saw her grinning excitedly, he had to work very hard not to laugh. "He's attractive," Jayden said in his defense. "And it's been a while."

"I'm not judging you for liking the squishy human," Ceto said before finally taking a drink. "You should have fun when the opportunity presents itself. You won't always have opportunities, especially if we do manage to find Collette."

Jayden rolled his eyes, but he was beaming. He nursed his whiskey for a few moments. "And no one has caught your attention while we've been on the road?" he asked. He realized he didn't really know much about many of the personal aspects of her life. He would have to learn more about her since their days together seemed limitless.

"Not yet." She shrugged. "But if I disappear a few days before the trip is over, you'll know why."

Jayden laughed. The evening's events had sufficiently demonstrated Ceto's ability to take care of herself. "Unless I see signs of a struggle, I promise to avoid knocking down doors and interrupting you."

"See? You're already basically prepared," Ceto said cheekily. "Just enjoy your evening and remember we can't take pets with us. Aphros wouldn't like it."

"You're terrible," Jayden declared. He downed his whiskey, finding it a bit sweeter than he was used to. With his drink drained, he went up to the room number indicated on the key, giving Ian a wink as he passed.

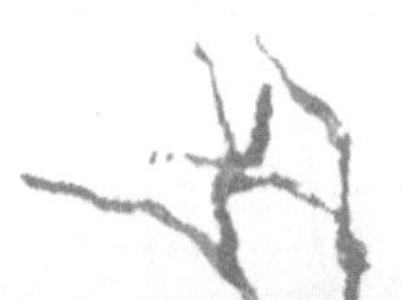

Chapter Nineteen

After weeks spent mostly in bed, Collette was starting to feel better. Occasional glances in the mirror confirmed she didn't look better. The dark circles under her eyes and her overly pale skin showed just how badly her fight had affected her. Everyone in the Barcomb Mill house agreed blood magic was behind Larent's possession. What wasn't known was how her magic had fought it. She shouldn't have been able to help Larent at all, and the working theory was whatever she tapped into hadn't been well-liked by Zephraim's spell.

Still, it didn't hurt to stand and walk. At least, it didn't hurt much. She had to monitor herself for exhaustion, something Arian insisted on once he understood he would never have the ability to make her stay put. She supposed she could finish healing the remnants of her claw and stab injuries, but trying to finish the healing process with magic was asking for a setback.

Venturing downstairs, she found the house mostly empty. Sara was an early riser, and her hard work around the property continued despite the guests. She had likely recruited most of the others to help with chores, something Collette wished she could participate in if only because it would help pass time.

Finding the sitting room, she spotted Arian, though she did not ask how he'd managed to escape helping. Instead, Collette thankfully sank into one of the old, but incredibly soft chairs. She found the chair more homey than anything back at the palace. Truthfully, the room was too small for the two chairs, table, and sofa squeezed around the stone fireplace, but she adored it.

"What are you doing inside?" she asked Arian as her fingers slid along the fuzzy green fabric covering the chair arms.

Arian looked up from a small, equally worn book. The cover suggested it covered home-healing remedies, and Collette knew it would be a natural thing for Sara to keep.

"Someone told Sara I have not slept the last handful of nights. She demanded I sleep, and when I refused, she threw a book at me." He lifted the book up emphasis.

"Was it Thomas?" Collette asked. Even having spent so much time unconscious, news had been regularly provided thanks to Larent and Whyldon.

"He is the most likely culprit. However, Nawalya has been eyeing me with concern for a few days. She and Thomas are both suspects," Arian said in a tone very near joking.

"You should make sure they both see you wearing your grumpiest expression," Collette suggested.

"Oh, I made sure they were subjected to it on my way into the house," Arian said with a smirk.

Collette snickered. "Good for you. Your wrath is the least they deserved."

"They deserve more, but I understand their concern," Arian admitted.

Collette nodded and sank further down into her seat, determined to stay there for a while. "There is much to worry about these days."

"They should worry about you, or something more important than if I am getting enough sleep," Arian stubbornly argued. "My lack of sleep is not a new development, and I have found myself resting more than normal as of late."

"I imagine it gets weary, having to worry about me so much," Collette said. "And from what I've seen, you've been struggling."

"It does not," he replied simply to Collette's first statement. "Though, I am curious as to what you think you've observed?"

Collette looked down as she thought about how to phrase her response. Admittedly, the signs she observed were subtle, and Arian kept his expressions neutral at best. "You've been more melancholy since the attack," she replied. "You hide it well enough, but I can see it."

Arian didn't reply or fidget, but he did look down in what Collette assumed was silent guilt.

"I thought so," she said gently. "So, what's wrong?"

Arian held in a breath for three counts before audibly releasing it. "Thomas and I have been talking about what happened," he started. "However, I fully believe if I had not walked off from the clearing, you would not have been injured."

Collette had been prepared for self-blame to eventually come up. The others had been off while she and Larent were left to their own devices. The assassin, in her view, was only a catalyst for what would have been a larger issue with Larent's blood magic possession. "I have some things to say, but I need you to promise me you will listen and not give in to anger."

Arian straightened in his chair, crossed his arms, and surveyed her with a raised eyebrow. "Why do I believe making such a promise is not in my best interest?"

"Getting angered could be detrimental to my ongoing recovery?" Collette suggested.

"Then let us compromise. I will only be displeased with you, if necessary, and I will withhold judgment when Larent is concerned. Fair?" Arian asked.

"It is," Collette agreed. She took a deep breath and almost wished she hadn't as her stomach reminded her of her healing injuries. "The stabbing and claw marks aren't your fault. Eventually, Larent was going to shift." Pointing out the truth was absolutely vital. Arian didn't need to suffer from guilt because of something he could not control. "Additionally, it's also possible Larent and I were fucking around with the guy who tried to kill me."

Arian pressed his lips together, his face going blank as he tilted his head to the side. "You were fucking around with a man who had intentions of killing you?" he asked calmly. "Am I hearing you correctly?"

"You said you wouldn't get mad at me," she reminded him. "Again, there is every possibility we'd have ended up in the same situation had we disposed of the man. There was nothing you could have done."

"We compromised on displeasure towards you," Arian reminded her, his expression turning frustrated rather than neutral. "And I am. I'm also angry with Larent. He knows better."

"He lets me sway him," Collette said in Larent's defense. "And again, he would have shifted at some point regardless of what did or didn't happen with the assassin."

"If I didn't know you were a superior combat fighter compared to Larent, I would concede to your argument," Arian shot back, raising a hand to massage the bridge of his nose. "Larent shouldn't have needed to turn into the wolf because you could have dealt with an opponent yourself. He should have encouraged you to finish the job. Instead, you toyed with the assassin and nearly bled out. I despise your injuries, and there are not enough words to explain just how much." He took a

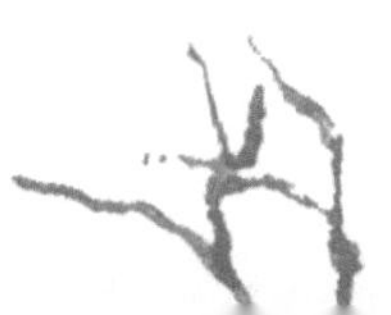

deep breath, his expression and body language considerably calming from the effort. "But you are right in the inevitability of his shifting. Had Nawalya and I been there, we would have put him down, hard."

Collette continued somberly, "We both know in other circumstances dealing with Larent under the control of blood magic would have resulted in death." She let out a long breath. "I'm not happy I was hurt. I'm less happy about what happened to Larent, but all things considered, the outcome isn't as bad as it could have been."

"It wasn't," Arian agreed, looking down again. "Still, Larent and I will be having words about the appropriate response to assassins attacking any member of our party. Once you're both better, we will double down on training, especially since I fear we are here until spring." He gave her a vicious grin. "I hope you like snow."

"He needs training," Collette agreed. "He'd win against most people, but someone with refined skills could really do damage." The idea was horrible to her, and she had no arguments when it came to ensuring Larent was well-prepared for whatever they faced. "And if he's training, obviously I'm helping. I'm sort of invested in him. You too, while we're on the subject."

Arian gave her a small smile, a rare expression on his angular face. "I have an idea for training Larent, but I will need to go into town. There is a weapon that could help him be more lethal than any sword or dagger we could place in his hands."

"I trust your judgment. His sword skills could improve with work, but honestly, he's so used to relying on shifting, I'm not sure we could do enough to close the current deficit."

"I'll send a letter to one of the capable blacksmiths in the area," Arian said thoughtfully, and he took on an air of satisfaction with the new plan in place. Her remained quiet for a moment, and even though his head was tilted downwards, Collette could see Arian was studying her closely.

"Yes?" she asked.

"If you did choose not to be queen, to take Larent and go, not a single one of us would blame you," he said softly. "Nawalya and I would put together a plan to remove Zephraim and the others."

Arian didn't look at Collette while he spoke, as if he knew she would take this badly. She might have, had she not known he was trying to offer her an out. "I'm not going anywhere," she said simply. "We've got too much to do."

"It is important for you to know you have options."

"I know I do," Collette assured him. "But thank you."

Arian nodded and looked back to Collette. He picked up a different line of thought when he next spoke. "Earlier, you said you can easily sway Larent. He and Nawalya can easily sway me. He told me you knew about Nawalya's vision." He grimaced as she nodded. "I am sorry for not telling you. I should have."

Collette had not expected the apology. She should have given she'd come to understand the depth of emotions carefully concealed by neutral expressions and biting remarks. "I can't say I don't care about not knowing," she replied. "I needed and deserved to know, even if you thought it was just a possibility. I'm angry and hurt the three of you chose to conceal the information."

Arian leaned forward, resting his chin on his hand. "I wanted to tell you, but I also understand the nature of Nawalya's visions enough to know most do not become reality. Both of them seemed sure Whyldon and Tolan would convince you to leave, and I allowed the possibility to sway me. I swear to you, had Nawalya had the vision again, I already planned on informing you."

"I'm not easily swayed," Collette reminded him. "Not when it comes to stuff I wouldn't want to do. I'd like to say I'd be more interested in learning about what would lead up to such a vision coming true." She turned as she heard someone enter the room, spotting Whyldon, bright blue eyes narrowed into dangerous slits.

Collette had seen her guard captain angry a number of times throughout her life, almost always justified and never overly harsh. Never had she witnessed him so ready to turn on those who should have been counted as friends.

When he spoke, his words were quiet and deliberate. "Am I to understand Nawalya, you, and Larent were aware of a possibility of her—" Whyldon motioned towards Collette "—being attacked by Larent, and not one of the three of you did a damn thing about it?"

Arian cursed under his breath and stood. "Nawalya had a vision, yes."

Arian's confirmation resulted in the firmer set of Whyldon's jaw and balled fists at his side. Without speaking, Whyldon turned to leave the room.

Collette carefully rose from her chair. "This is going to be bad."

"Very, very bad," Arian agreed.

The two followed Whyldon, and by the time they were out of the house, the distinctive chaos of raised voices issued from the west side of the house. They were not the only ones to approach the scene. Thomas was already standing close by Sara, both holding baskets of eggs, and both looking on in uncertain surprise. Larent was standing about a foot from Nawalya's right, taking in the scene.

"You three didn't think it was important to convey my fucking daughter might be killed by him?" Whyldon demanded, pointing at Larent, who took a step back.

Nawalya stood still, her face blank, but her eyes were moving from Larent to Whyldon, Thomas, Sara, Arian and Collette. It could be considered calculating, but somehow, Collette knew she was both threat-assessing and looking for a way out. The elf stepped forward, putting herself between Larent and Whyldon before the scene could further escalate. "I take full responsibility. I am the one who had the vision. It was my choice to keep it secret," she said in an uncharacteristically firm voice.

"You take responsibility now," Whyldon replied, letting out a sarcastic bark of a laugh. "How is this okay? How can you justify it? How can you stay here, around her, knowing what happened?"

"Whyldon," Collette intervened, stepping forward. "You need to calm down. We are not going to have explosive arguments about the vision."

Whyldon turned to face her, his eyes and mouth showing just how livid he was. Collette met his gaze, refusing to back down even if it felt as though she should. "How would you like to address it, Collette?" he asked her, his tone icy. "Or were you planning on it? You seemed to be aware of what happened already."

Collette's calm expression dropped for a second, showing how deeply her guard captain and newly confessed father's words ate at her. Nothing in the information he shared was news to her, even if the confession was a step Whyldon had not taken. Still, she was beyond surprised by his willingness to be so sharp with her. "Larent told me."

Both Arian and Larent moved forward to intervene, but they stopped when Nawalya raised her hands. "You said the consequences would be on my head," she said, looking at Arian. "I'm accepting my chosen fate." She glared at Whyldon. "You may take your anger out on me as I am the one who lied by omission.

However, you will find yourself regretting your words if you speak to Collette with disrespect again."

Nawalya's tone was sharper than Collette had ever heard. She opened her mouth to speak again, but Sara interrupted her.

"John, you need to go find something to do so you can cool down," she commanded, hands resting on her hips. "No matter what's happened, you don't need to take such a tone with anyone here."

Whyldon glared, but he did not contradict his sister. He took a deep breath, looking at Nawalya. "There is no justification for concealing your visions, especially when they almost came true. I'm done with the three of you." He didn't give them time to respond, instead turning around and marching off towards the house.

Nawalya sagged like a doll with her strings cut, her breathing coming out in small pants like she was about to cry. She forced herself to calm and straighten. Arian and Larent went to her, but she motioned for them to stand back. Collette finally understood why Nawalya led their missions.

"I'm fine," Nawalya assured them. "Thomas, would you mind retrieving my things from the captain's room? I think I will need different accommodations from now on."

"Of course," Thomas said. After handing his basket to Sara, he put a comforting hand on her arm before retreating to carry out her request.

Nawalya looked at Collette, her eyes softening. "He did not mean what he said. I am sure he will apologize to you soon enough."

"He fucking better," Larent muttered. He closed the distance between himself and Collette and wrapped his arms around her in a comforting hug.

"You shouldn't worry about me," Collette said. "Some harsh words are hardly the worst thing I've experienced lately. You're the one he went off on," she reminded Nawalaya.

"I'm fine, and everything is going to be fine." Her smile grew as she spotted Thomas returning with her neatly packed items. "Sara, you mentioned needing meat, and I suddenly desire to hunt."

"I would appreciate it," Sara said. "But you should take someone with you. You'll have plenty of light, but you never know what you'll encounter."

"Thank you," Nawalya said to Sara. She retrieved her pack from Thomas. "I am going to put this in the barn, then I will be on my way."

"The barn?" Arian asked, true concern marring his face.

"Just in case," Nawalya replied as she started walking towards the large structure on the far side of the property.

Arian closed his eyes and rubbed his temples. "Sleep is for the weak," he said, his tone full of forced humor.

Chapter Twenty

Larent wasn't terribly worried about the group, and that was saying something. So far, all their efforts had been met with pushback or outright failure. Tolan had fled like a little bitch in the middle of the night. Zephraim used blood magic and nearly killed Collette in the process. The fractured relationship between Whyldon and Nawalya threatened the group's possible future. Even moments of peace had been tainted.

But Larent was more focused on the way the confrontation had affected Collette. Out of everyone, she was the least deserving of Whyldon's wrath, and Larent couldn't deny how the flash of raw pain on her beautiful face had enraged him. He wanted to go after Whyldon and demand the man grovel for his offense. No, he wanted to fight the guard captain even when he knew he'd likely lose. He just knew he couldn't. It would hurt Collette, and Larent would do anything to avoid causing her pain.

So he would do whatever he could to cheer her up.

Collette had suggested a walk to clear her head, and Larent was happy to oblige while Thomas, Sara, and Arian resumed chores. They wandered aimlessly around the grounds but stayed close enough for safety reasons. Collette was in hiding and injured, after all, and if something unexpected happened, he wasn't in much better shape.

He put an arm around her, drawing her close as they walked. She had no coat, and the winter air couldn't be ignored. She leaned against him, and Larent found himself calming.

"You look angrier than I've ever seen," she observed.

He nodded. "I understand Whyldon's anger, but he had no right to take it out on you." He added a shrug in emphasis, as though he hadn't seriously contemplated tearing into Whyldon.

"True," she agreed in a quiet tone she rarely ever used, causing him to frown. "But honestly, he was rather tame compared to the way many have spoken to me this year."

Larent silently paused their steps, and he turned so they were facing each other. "Whyldon is your father. Your real father. I also know, despite how little you are willing to talk about it, Sargarus treated you like shit. Coupling those facts together makes me want to rip Whyldon's face off." He half-expected her to be angry with him, or for her to argue the point. Instead, she stepped close, letting her arms circle him as she rested her head against his shoulder. He wrapped his own arms around her, both in an attempt to enjoy the closeness and to make sure she stayed warm.

"Yeah," she agreed. "When spelled out, Whyldon's behavior was not okay."

"What Nawalya, Arian, and I withheld from you was more than shitty, and Whyldon should be mad at us. You weren't part of our bad decision."

Larent looked back at the white, timber-framed house, noting the black circular designs contrasting so vividly against the snow. He could barely spot Arian helping Sara carry something. Thomas walked back to join them. "I'm going to have

words with him if Whyldon doesn't apologize. Arian might stab him, though."

"I would appreciate everyone leaving Whyldon alone," she objected. "He's not a bad person. I understand his anger even if the way he expressed it was unpleasant."

Larent let out a frustrated breath, wishing she would draw a firmer boundary regarding what she tolerated from people she loved. "I'll tell you what. We will attempt to keep things civil with him. If he does anything remotely similar to how he treated you today, I'll punch him in the face. Repeatedly."

She was amused, if the way the corners of her mouth twitched up were to be trusted. Good. He preferred her in better spirits.

"I doubt he will," Collette replied.

"I hope so," Larent replied. "But I'm being practical here. This mission isn't getting any easier, and Nawalya, Arian, and I aren't going anywhere. There's bound to be more conflict."

She loosened her hold on him, and they soon resumed walking. A few minutes passed before Collette spoke again. "I take it Nawalya is going to respond poorly?"

"The answer is complicated," he replied, unsure of how to explain himself. "Nawalya will probably put on a brave face, as if we were on a mission. She won't want Whyldon to know how much she's hurting. All the same, Nawalya has been hearing Whyldon's voice since she was very, very young. The emotional stress might trigger more visions. We're in for a good time." Their movements slowed as they came across a particularly icy patch of land near the tree line, and Larent maneuvered them back to more reliable footing. "Do you think he'll try to make you leave?"

Collette shook her head. "He's smart enough to know better. It's safer, having more allies to surround me." Now she shrugged. "And I love the three of you, so I intend to stick with you. If he wants something different for himself after today, he will have to make a choice."

Larent smiled. "And I plan on sticking with you. For Nawalya and Whyldon, though, I get the feeling it's over, permanently."

"As bad as I feel for Nawalya, I understand his anger. Given what happened, could you expect him to not be so upset?"

"Nope," he said, gazing at Collette. "Why aren't you more upset?"

"I am upset," she replied.

They approached a fairly dry tree stump. He removed his heavy overcoat, placed it on top, and motioned for Collette to sit. She looked tired, and thankfully, obeyed his silent request. Although he believed he could read her well, Larent knew she was good at keeping thoughts and feelings concealed. She'd had to learn the skill for the sake of survival. "From what I've seen, and what you've told me, Whyldon has done everything in his power to keep you safe. From my perspective, both of you have every right to be angry." He paused then, wondering if his next words were wise and knelt in front of her. "And if you want to be more blatant in how upset you are, with me or the others, you are allowed. We're not going anywhere. I'm not going anywhere."

Again, she smiled, a sight so intoxicating and perfect, he nearly forgot to breathe.

"I know," she said.

"Good," he replied, returning her warm smile with his own. He moved to take a seat beside her, and again, he draped an arm across her shoulders. They sat in happy silence for some time, Collette leaning against him, breathing steady as she rested. He needed to talk to Arian about doing something to speed up her recovery.

"Arian knows, by the way," she said.

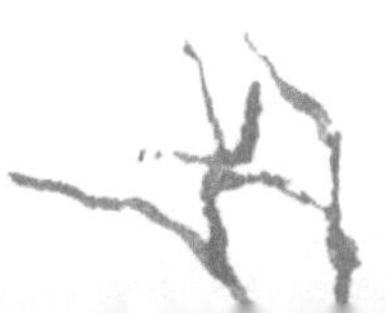

Larent had no idea what she was talking about, and his expression changed several times as he considered and dismissed several possibilities. What would Arian object too the most? He and Collette taunting the thug that tried to kill her.

"Oh shit," he breathed out. "Was he mad? How dead am I?"

"He's displeased with me, and he's angry with you because you know better than to play around with people waving swords in your direction."

"Great," Larent complained. "Arian is such a bitch when upset."

"He actually mentioned training, which I think is needed no matter how unpleasant he makes it."

Larent groaned dramatically, seriously dreading whatever bullshit Arian devised. "By the Lady, if either he or Nawalya let Nana and Pops know I neglected my human training this badly, they would come here and kick my ass." He looked to the left, half expecting his grandparents to appear at any moment. "Considering they are only four hours away by foot…" He let out a sharp breath. "I'm not gonna think about it."

"You almost had an enthusiastic acceptance of training," Collette said in a faux-cheery voice. Larent snorted. "Good thing, too. Arian has an idea for a weapon you might like."

Larent made another face as he shrugged. "As long as he doesn't write home, I will try any weapon he puts in my hands." He gave her a gentle squeeze. "Now, how can I help you feel better?"

"I have been trying to come up with an answer for months," Collette admitted. "What do you think will happen next? I was arrested. Lost the throne. Abandoned by my brother. Nearly died. Got yelled at by Whyldon.…"

"Oh, easy answer. You'll get married," Larent replied as though the response was obvious, but his chest suddenly felt constricted, making his normal breathing difficult. He believed

Collette's confessions of love, but loving him didn't mean she wanted to marry to him or anyone else. Still, when she looked at him with those large brown eyes he loved so much, his compressed lungs slowly inflated with a fluttering he associated with her.

"I will, huh?" she asked.

"Yes. Most definitely."

She drew him in for a gentle kiss. "I feel like you should have appeared on my balcony much, much sooner."

"Me too, Freckles," he whispered. "Me too." He initiated the second kiss, careful to stay just as gentle as the first. He wanted more, but he'd meant his promise to let her set the pace.

When the kiss ended, he remained close, happy to be near her and to let her know she was loved more than anything and anyone else in his life. "Are you cold?" he asked.

"I'm outside in the winter without a coat," she reminded him with a grin.

"I can go get it," he offered. He stood and faced her. "And if Whyldon is still inside, I promise I will jump from a window to avoid conflict. It wouldn't be the first time."

"Then go get my coat before I freeze to death," she requested, and Larent obeyed.

Chapter Twenty-One

Arian leaned back in the hay, his blond hair fanning out behind him. Anytime it grew past his shoulders, the curls became too unmanageable. If they ended up on a battlefield, long hair would distract and endanger him. He pondered a trim and other mundane things as he looked up into the rafters of the barn. Anything keeping him from contemplating the situation with Whyldon was welcome. He was angry about so much of it, and he hated how much he was to blame.

Moonlight streamed through an open door a few feet to his left, illuminating strips across the loft. The beams above him curved in intricate patterns. Hay bales sat along the right edge of the loft. Grain and feed storage waited on the left. From below, he could hear the soft meowing of kittens, though he didn't see them.

A noise from behind caught his attention. Arian sat up and reached for the parchment and quill next to him. He gazed over to where Nawalya slept, ready to write down anything she mumbled as she tossed and turned, lost in the dream branches of the tree. Her slumber was much more peaceful than he'd expected, thank the Spirits.

He turned his head to the ladder connecting the loft to the bottom floor of the barn. He raised the hand holding the quill in greeting when Thomas appeared, his cornsilk hair tied back. That was a shame. Thomas had put himself in the line of danger by being with the group, but Arian was comforted by his presence.

"Hey," Thomas said in a hushed voice. When he made it to the platform, he walked over to Arian, boots softly thumping against the floor. "How is she?" he asked as he settled beside Arian.

"Better than expected," Arian replied. "Nothing like when I came to you for arrows."

"Good," Thomas said. He leaned over and placed a kiss on the corner of Arian's mouth. "And how are you?"

Arian might have smiled had the rest of the day gone better. "Upset, guilty, and tired."

"How can I help?"

"I am unsure." Arian put down the parchment and quill. "Correct the mistake I made by not telling Whyldon about Nawalya's visions?"

Thomas leaned against the wall. "From my perspective, letting them work it out seems the most obvious way to address the anger."

"What if they do not work it out?"

"It's possible they won't," Thomas said, looking down at Arian. He reached over and ran his fingers through Arian's hair. "But we aren't going to be able to do anything about their relationship."

"Maybe things would be better, different, if I had done the right thing." Arian sighed, ashamed of his choices. He shifted so he was looking at Thomas. "I justified not taking the visions as seriously as I should have, of wanting them to be untrue. I

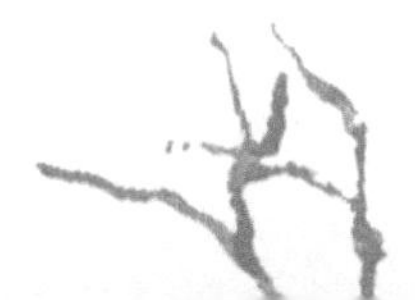

know better. Nawalya saw the destruction of our village, of our people." The last words came out as barely a whisper.

"Did you think it likely the vision about Collette and Larent would come true?" Thomas asked.

"I did not want it to be true, so I pretended the rule of three was a fact instead of a guide we've used in the past," Arian explained. "But I knew the vision might come to fruition."

Thomas was quiet for a moment, and Arian wondered if he'd shared too much or made himself more unlovable and unworthy.

"Can I suggest looking at this from another perspective?" Thomas asked.

"Of course."

"Nawalya saw Collette die, but she did not. Does her survival not suggest the vision was, in part, unreliable?"

Arian pondered this for a moment. "She saw Larent attack Collette and blood, a lot of blood. She interpreted it as Larent killing Collette. So, on one hand, yes. On the other, no."

"Okay," Thomas replied. "But she didn't see Collette dying."

Arian gave a soft laugh, more a huff of breath than anything. He tentatively rested his head on Thomas's shoulder, forcing himself to relax. "How do you manage to stay so positive? You may be worse than Larent but much more tolerable."

"I see no use in remaining negative about things we cannot change," Thomas answered honestly. He took Arian's hand, studying the contrast. His pale fingers were stained with ink, and Arian's tanned and meticulously cleaned.

"I have never been good at avoiding the negative," Arian breathed out. "That's a lie. I used to be very good at embracing the positive aspects of life. I used to be a great many things."

"I think you still are, but I know you struggle."

"Everything feels like a struggle most days," Arian admitted. "Except being with you."

"You will always have me," Thomas promised him. He lifted their conjoined hands and pressed a gentle kiss against Arian's fingers.

Letting out a harsh breath, Arian gathered his courage. He pulled Thomas to him, pressing his lips against the other man's, kissing him fiercer than he had ever dared.

Thomas did not hesitate in kissing him back. Cupping Arian's face, the fletcher moved closer.

Arian shuddered at the touch, his body wanting to flinch away and press closer to satiate the heat pooling in his stomach. Arian wanted things with Thomas he hadn't wanted in years, and it would be so easy to fall into sharing himself so intimately with the other man.

The decision was taken from him when Nawalya started thrashing. He pulled away from Thomas and took up the parchment and quill. As she muttered the word "arrow" five times, Arian jotted it down. She finally settled, and Arian made a humming noise as he set the items aside.

"Sorry," he told Thomas.

"Why?" Thomas asked him.

His cheeks were still a little flushed from their kissing. Arian knew he wanted to see more of it and shrugged awkwardly. "For the interruption?"

"We're here to watch over Nawalya," Thomas reminded him. "We have all the time in the world to explore."

Arian bowed his head in agreement before looking down at the parchment. "She's said 'arrow' twenty-eight times since she fell asleep," he told Thomas, needing a distraction from the other man's lips.

"I wonder what the mention of arrows could mean," Thomas said. He sat back against the hay, his arms crossed in thought. "Do you think she'll need more?"

"I don't know," Arian admitted, feeling defeated.

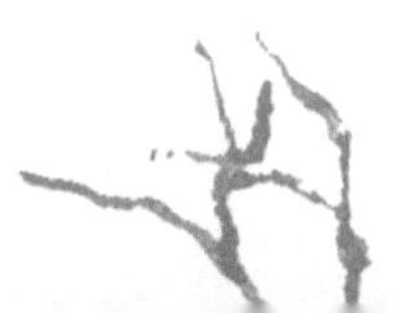

"Then let's relax for now, and we can try to decipher it later."

Arian nodded, glancing back at Nawalya who had trapped herself in her blankets. He considered redoing them but decided she was more than likely warm. "I brought blankets if you wish to sleep," Arian said to Thomas.

"I'll keep them in mind when I'm ready to sleep," Thomas promised. "We both know you won't sleep. Why don't you try to relax?"

Arian nodded, leaned back, and rested his head against Thomas once more. He wouldn't sleep, and nothing felt right, but at least he had this budding relationship.

Chapter Twenty-Two

A light chirping sounded in the distance, catching Rion's attention as he stoked the crackling fire. He saw nothing in the surrounding trees. Night had fallen, and the bird or insect or other creature calling for food or mates was inconsequential to the furrier. Above the roaring fire, fowl roasted on a makeshift spit, the juices dripping and sizzling as they fell into the flames. His stomach rumbled, and Rion helped himself to his store of venison jerky as he waited for dinner to cook.

Across the fire sat Tolan. The other man looked better after he'd had several meals and nights of sleep, but he was quiet and mopey, leaving Rion questioning what Joss had ever seen in him. Oh, he was attractive enough. Rion wasn't blind to tanned muscles and dark wavy hair. Tolan had a charm about him. He just seemed…very sorry.

Rion held up the pack of jerky, then tossed it to Tolan. "You're quiet."

"How would you know if I'm normally quiet or not?" Tolan shot back as he grabbed the bag of jerky.

"We've been traveling together for some days," Rion replied, scoffing at the undue hostility. Rion supposed, in

Tolan's position, he would also be overly sensitive. He tore a piece of jerky with his teeth, chewed, and swallowed before speaking again. "You know, I am not responsible for your problems and concerns."

Tolan possessed the decency to look down in shame. "I know. I'm sorry for snapping at you."

Rion shrugged in response. It mattered very little if Tolan took out his self-pity on him. Rion was a grown man with ample patience. "I know you fucked things up by abandoning your group," he said, getting up to check on the food. "But you've got to get your shit together. Joss isn't going to tolerate this."

Tolan raised an eyebrow. "If she's alive, I'd be surprised if she lets me in the door. She's not the only one I have to worry about."

"She's the one who matters, ultimately," Rion pointed out. He judged the food to be ready and grabbed a nearby cloth so he could remove the makeshift spit from the fire. "I understand a little of what you're going through," he shared.

"How so?" Tolan asked, his tone laced with skepticism. He rose from his seat, gesturing to the food in a silent offer to help.

Rion accepted the help, and the two went through the process of removing the roasted meat from the spit. "Honestly, had Joss not been the queen, I'd have married her. I have no problem admitting as much. The choice not to was never because I didn't feel worthy."

Tolan looked at Rion in surprise. "I had no idea," he admitted, then let out a deep breath. "But I do feel unworthy."

"Why?" Rion asked. With the food extricated and cooling, he took a seat on the stone he'd occupied, a portion of the bird in hand. "She couldn't give a shit about ranks and titles. People are people with her. Always have been."

"If I had rank and title, I would have had soldiers to help her," Tolan argued. "I'd have had sway on a council who did everything they could to work against her. I could have offered her more than my skills in an arena and kitchen." Tolan went back to his seat, carrying his portion of the meal. "The people we were traveling with seemed infinitely more valuable. They had skills, knowledge, and abilities I lack." A hand raised to touch the pendant around his neck, secured on a valuable silver chain. "Whyldon was right about me. I was a liability to her; something to be used against her."

Rion snorted. "Whyldon is very protective of Joss, and with good reason." He didn't say never in all of his life did Rion think the rightful queen would face the hardship of being dethroned and sent into exile.

"I'd be protective of my daughter, too. Queen or not," Tolan said simply.

"It's amazing how many people somehow know her little 'secret,'" Rion laughed. He tore a chunk of roasted fowl with his fingers and took a bite. "You and I view things differently," he said after swallowing. "But part of being with Joss is accepting her role as the queen and having to watch her make decisions against her best interest. Decisions robbing her of happiness. It's having to accept she would be subjected to bullshit she didn't deserve, and knowing there was nothing you could do to make it better. Nothing other than standing by supportively, anyway. I couldn't handle standing idly by while the woman I loved was treated so poorly."

Tolan took a small bite of the bird. "I struggled when I realized what I'd watch her go through. I want to help her, especially now when she's going to have to fight to take her kingdom back." Tolan glared off into the distance. "I'm not good at stepping back."

"Nor am I," Rion agreed. "Which is why I did not marry her." He still regretted breaking her heart, and sometimes, he questioned his wisdom in making such a decision. They ate in more companionable silence than Rion had expected, and he amended his image of Tolan. "I take it your relationship was kept hushed up?"

Tolan nodded. "As much as possible in a castle full of people consistently watching Collette." He laughed and shook his head. "She pushed me out a window more than once in an attempt to hide me from prying eyes."

"Sounds like her, especially if you were insistent on hiding your relationship." Rion took another bite of food, somehow managing to prevent the drippings from soaking his beard. "I wonder how you got her to agree to keep you a secret."

"I don't know, but I think it had to do with her desire to have something for herself," Tolan replied.

"Possibly," Rion said. "But if you wanted to hide it, I'm sure she went along with you."

"She didn't need the added issues of having people degrade her because of me, especially when the fletcher was doing a good enough job."

"She wrote to me about him," Rion said, thinking through some of the letters Collette sent. "She thought he was funny."

"No one else did," Tolan replied.

"And why was her humor anyone else's business?" Rion asked. He'd had his fill of food, and he wiped his hand on the cloth he'd used to protect his hands from the heat. "I'm not saying I'd have tolerated it, but it was her right to choose how to handle it. Just like it was her right to declare a relationship with you if she wanted." Rion tossed the rag back toward his pack. "The lot of you ought to be ashamed of yourselves for trying to deny her autonomy over the little she should have been able to control."

Tolan hung his head again. "You're right, but we were never trying to deny her anything," he said, speaking through the issue slowly. "I know I have been trying to protect her."

"She's not terribly willing to speak up when she needs help," Rion said with a chuckle. It wasn't funny, but it was true. "She's good at keeping things to herself. Not showing emotion."

Tolan scowled. "She never wanted to talk about what happened. She spent a good part of our time on the road joking with Larent or changing the subject." He met Rion's gaze. "She put the Nereid emissary's life above her own when it was clear she was about to be arrested. She let them come for her while I got him out of the city."

Rion watched Tolan clench his hands into impotent fists and didn't blame him. He would have been frustrated in Tolan's position. "Why did she risk her life, do you think?"

"She said it was the best move for the kingdom, which is questionable given who is in charge now." Tolan forced himself to relax his hands. "When I asked her about it, she just… She didn't want to engage at all."

Rion moved from the stone to the ground and stretched his legs out in front of him. "I'm not surprised by anything you just said. Of course, she'd want to get the emissary out. It was the kindest thing to do, making sure the Nereid was safe."

"She didn't need to put herself in danger to help him," Tolan retorted.

"And her decision haunts you?"

Tolan closed his eyes. "Yes. I am still upset whenever I think about it."

Again, Rion found himself sympathizing for Tolan. He'd have been furious in Tolan's position. "She got out, though."

"But she is unhappy. There are things weighing her down she refuses to talk about, except for limited discussions with

Larent." Tolan's bitterness with Larent was evident in the way he spat out the name.

"I think I'd ask myself why Larent is safe for her."

"I wish I knew," Tolan said, running his hands through his hair. "Maybe because he behaves as though nothing matters? Maybe because he makes her laugh and isn't pushing her about the kingdom? I don't know."

Rion nodded. "So maybe the actual problem is, she *is* dealing with things, but just not with you."

Tolan picked up a rock and tossed it back and forth between his hands. "Yes and no. I don't think she's talking out her issues with him so much as trying to escape them, and Larent is more than happy to let her."

"Perhaps she wasn't ready to talk? What she went through... most people wouldn't have come out alive."

"Maybe," Tolan said, though he sounded unconvinced.

"I wasn't there, obviously," Rion said. "But honestly, I think you expected a lot from someone likely operating purely in survival mode."

Tolan groaned and buried his head in his hand. "I kind of hate you, you know."

"I figured. You want someone to buy your bullshit. It wasn't."

"I know my leaving wasn't right. I know I should have done better when it comes to Larent. I know I should have taken her with me when I left for Fythias. I know!" Tolan shouted the last word, throwing the stone across the campsite. "And I know she won't ever forgive me."

"Assuming we find her alive," Rion said quietly.

Tolan deflated with the reminder. "I think you enjoy giving me hope and ripping it away."

"I'm being honest," Rion said. "I would prefer we find Joss alive and well, but I know there was a lot of blood in the clearing. Too much blood."

Tolan let out a breath. "Am I a bad person for hoping the majority belongs to Larent?"

"No. If we are dealing with a scenario where the death is preferred, we might as well hope Joss was not the one who bled out."

"I still feel guilty saying it," Tolan confessed.

"We'll find out what happened," Rion said, offering him some comfort. "And we will go from there. For now, it's late, and I wish to sleep."

Tolan nodded, feeling a yawn coming on. "Sleep well, asshole."

Rion snorted but said nothing. His head cushioned by his pack, he closed his eyes and drifted off to sleep.

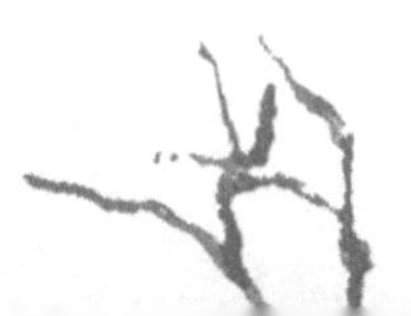

Chapter Twenty-Three

Diana rarely had an evening off, and when she did, she'd found herself drawn into work of some sort thanks to their new royal family. Although Rhoslyn never had a kind word to say regarding Diana's food, she was awfully insistent about Diana maintaining primary responsibility for every morsel of food crossing royal lips.

As weeks had passed since Diana last laid eyes on her husband, she'd made sure to stay out of sight of anyone tangentially connected to Rhoslyn once she was aware her afternoon and evening were free. She'd had to duck behind things and flee from the room on one occasion, efforts which seemed childish to her.

The effort had been worth it, even as she crossed the bridge into the city. She'd been stopped and interrogated by a guard, and Diana had dutifully held up a basket and declared a desire to shop. She was free, and she was allowed to do as she liked with her earnings on her own time, so the guard had no options other than letting her pass.

The walk through the city was quiet and uneventful. Diana didn't appear to catch the attention of those she passed but avoided notice while she made her way to the caves. When she reached her destination, getting inside was a matter of habit. She recognized the location would never feel warm and inviting. Perpetual dampness in the dark felt depressing on the best of days. Still, she stepped forward, guided by torchlight. She nodded in greeting to the guards, then stepped into the open cavern.

Diane immediately spotted her husband in the distance, seated across from Howle. The two created a makeshift table out of crates, and a smattering of cards spread across the table. Neither man looked up, though the shift in Howle's posture suggested he knew she was there.

Diana smiled warmly at the sight of her husband, and her hands went to her hips. "This is a fine thing. I came all the way down here to see you, and you're more interested in cards."

"By the Mother!" Crem exclaimed, placing a hand over his heart and abruptly standing from his seat.

Diana laughed. She could see how worn down he looked, but his exhaustion could not contain the genuine happy surprise at seeing her. He closed the distance between them, gathered her into his arms, and kissed her deeply.

"Hello wife," he said, his voice filled with affection. He looked over to Howle who was chuckling as he straightened the deck of cards.

"Don't glare at me," the older man said. "I knew she was there. I was just seein' how long it to you ta notice."

"He's not the most observant, is he?" Diana asked as she pulled Crem closer against her.

"In fairness to him, he hasn't slept in about twenty-four hours," Howle replied. "I keep offerin' ta wear him out, but he says not without ya present." Howle wiggled his eyebrows.

"He's not joking," Crem confirmed, rolling his eyes.

"If ever the two of you decide to live out your fantasy, don't tell me. I can't handle so much ugly in the mental picture my mind suddenly conjures."

Howle threw back his head and roared with laughter, his long silver and black locks rocking back and forth. Standing, he joined Crem and Diana long enough to clap them on the shoulders. "I'm gonn' head out. No one should be stoppin' by tonight. Enjoy yar time together."

Crem gave the older man a smile. "Thank you, Howle. Be safe." When they were alone, Crem looked down at Diana. "I thought you wouldn't have time to get away till next week?"

"I made time," Diana replied simply. "Besides, I have news."

Concern flashed in Crem's eyes. They walked back to the table where poor excuses of chairs waited, and he glanced up and down, taking in her form.

"It's nothing to worry over," Diana said. "Or rather, I do not believe there is cause to worry."

"Why?"

"Zephraim came to the kitchen to talk," she explained as she took a seat at the table. He did the same after pulling a second chair close.

"And?" Crem asked wearily, with a look equal parts concerned and murderous.

"He is not doing well," Diane explained. "He seems to regret his actions towards Queen Collette, and he trusts none of the people around him."

Crem sagged in his seat, looking all the more worn out. "I know I should ask you to use this, to see if he comes back to the kitchen and to build a rapport with him, but I will not. If anything, this makes me want to ask you to stay away from Zephraim." Crem shook his head. "From the reports Barris gives, it seems as though something happened to shake his faith in Rhoslyn and Riken. Zephraim is sending Riken away and has openly commented on his flirtation with the queen. You may be in even more danger if you become someone Zephraim confides in, Diana." Crem reached out and took her hands in his. "You shouldn't stay in the palace."

"I've been in danger every second I've stayed," Diana reminded him. "And it's good to have someone who can report on his mood."

"Or, you could leave. We could leave. Barris and Howle could run whatever this mess is, and if we still feel the need to get involved, I'm hearing there is a man helping to run the resistance on the other side of the mountains near Galel."

"You're not going to leave and you know it. That means I won't."

Crem gave a sad, almost defeated nod. "I should put you above this. I should take you and go."

Diana offered him an equally sad smile as she nodded. "But you won't." Remaining in Quenall wasn't in question, and she knew if she left the city in order to soothe his worries, she'd be asking to never see him again.

"Would you love me less if I did say 'Fuck it,' and we left?" Crem asked her.

Her heart broke at the question, and she shook her head. "Never. Nothing could alter how I feel about you. I know such a choice would change how you feel about yourself, though."

Crem sighed. "There are so many innocent people who would die if we go back to how Sargarus ruled."

Diana nodded. "Which means we carry on, and we use what we have and know to our greatest advantage."

Looking up to the vaulted cave ceiling, Crem's expression grew resigned. "You should befriend Zephraim. Show him the support he craves. But watch him closely. Make sure you stay close with Barris and his Mers." He looked over to Diana again.

"If anything looks or feels wrong, you leave. Come to me, and we will go."

"I promise," Diana replied softly. She stood from her chair and crawled into Crem's lap. "I would never do anything intentionally dangerous. I would never want to hurt you."

Crem sighed and pressed his lips against her temple. "I know," he said. "I just have this terrible feeling."

"I'd be surprised if you didn't."

"You should have been questioned after I was accused of what happened to Elrick," Crem said. "I keep waiting for it to happen. Or worse."

"I might very well be. With Riken leaving the city, who knows what Zephraim or Rhoslyn might do." She put her arms around Crem's neck, drawing him in for a kiss.

Crem rose, carrying Diana with him. He walked the two further into a cavern, and into a cove hidden by columns of stalagmites reaching for the ceiling. There was a concealed bed, old and small, but clean looking. Crem gently placed her in the middle of the blankets. He climbed into bed, using his arms to hover over her as he leaned in to kiss her. Diana pulled him down, intent on enjoying her evening with her husband.

Chapter Twenty-Four

Riken went over his mental checklist once again as his foot touched down on the landing to Zephraim's office. Before seeing Rhoslyn last night, he'd visited with his most trusted men and given them their orders. Rhoslyn was in charge, and Zephraim was to be heeded, respected, but ultimately ignored.

"King Zephraim's efforts are noble, but foolish," Riken had shared. "Queen Rhoslyn has the best interest of the kingdom and our people at heart. Follow her words as though they are spoken by the Mother herself." Riken's conviction convinced his followers, and he knew they would follow Rhoslyn with near reverence.

He's also spoken privately with Xavier, head of his personal guard and his right hand. Xavier was tall and lean with a boyish face and gold, wavy hair. He was often underestimated, which worked in his favor. Riken trusted Xavier would aid Rhoslyn with every request.

As he stood, waiting to meet with Zephraim, Riken felt as though he was leaving Rhoslyn with every possible tool for success. He ran his hands down his dark green jacket, hoping to remove any traces of dust, then he knocked.

Zephraim granted him access without making him wait, although Riken half-expected a petty, melancholy response, leaving him frozen outside the door. As he watched the king, he wondered if he'd receive any reprimand or snarky remark. Again, he was left surprised.

"I take it you've made your arrangements to travel to Galel?" Zephraim asked. He was positioned at the window looking out to the courtyard below.

"I will be ready to leave as soon as you give the word, my king," Riken said with a low bow. He would play the part as required despite Zephraim not deserving the distinction.

Zephraim nodded but did not look at Riken. "You never did provide the full account of why Collette banned you from the palace."

The king's voice was neutral, almost polite, and Riken was suspicious. He hadn't anticipated the question, mostly because Zephraim had been aware of the general disagreements between himself and Collette even if he hadn't been privy to the details. Riken cleared his throat before answering.

"I was brash in handling a disagreement with Collette over her sudden refusal to allow the Merscale trade without a suitable alternative in place. We kept the disagreement outside the council chambers, but the arguments were often heated. The disagreements came to a head when I informed her I would use my power to stand against her if she did not have a better, faster alternative to the issues our economy would face without the Merscale trade. Collette used this as an excuse to force me out of the palace."

Reflecting back on the tumultuous time, Riken sometimes wondered if he should have strangled Collette to death when they were alone.

"Do you see how being so openly hostile towards the reigning monarch has failed to serve you in the past?" Zephraim asked.

Chapter Twenty-four

"I am being banished due to my anger at the death of Lord Crobán and subsequent request for better action to be taken against those who stand against you?" Riken asked, his voice calm, his face a polite mask, as if they were discussing the weather.

"You're not being banished," Zephraim countered, turning to look at Riken. He was not angry or sad. He was apathetic, an emotion more dangerous than rage. "You're being sent on a mission sorely in need of oversight. But I cannot deny you have tested the boundary with me a time or two, and in front of the council, no less."

Riken bowed his head. "I only wish to ensure your rule is more successful than your father's," he said, sounding appropriately contrite. "If I have been overzealous, I am sorry. I am firm in my belief of your ability to lead this kingdom to great heights." Riken looked up at Zephraim from lowered lashes, fire in his eyes. He believed the kingdom could rise once again if only Zephraim would listen to Rhoslyn.

"My father died, half insane and hated by the world," Zephraim said. He glanced at his desk as if planning to sit, though when he crossed the office, he bypassed it and went to the cabinet where a set of crystal glasses and a decanter waited. He removed the cork and poured dark liquid into each. "His reputation haunted Collette, and it continues to haunt me."

"But before his madness, Sargarus did inspiring things. He expanded our borders, strengthened our economy." Riken patted his chest emphatically as he spoke. "Azmarin became an ally under your father, and worship for the Mother was higher than ever before. Humans stood at the top, where the Mother placed us," Riken said, impassioned, though he did force himself to calm. "My father told me stories of his time on the field of battle with yours. King Sargarus did terrible things, but in most things, he was correct."

Riken knew he was rambling, but this was his passion. Keeping Coralia great and humans on top. Only his love and adoration for Rhoslyn topped the love of country his father had taught him.

"He did amazingly cruel things, and to deny it is to be foolish beyond reason," Zephraim said, shaking his head. He held one of the glasses out to Riken. "I would like for us to be better. To do better. If you don't believe yourself capable of honoring the Mother, of showing the grace and compassion she had in all dealings, our success is doomed."

Riken took the glass, taking a small sip as he considered Zephraim's words. It sounded too much like something Collette would have said, but there was room for interpretation. "How would you show the same compassion the Mother would show?" he asked, interested.

"I think benevolent supremacy is one answer," Zephraim said, taking a sip from his glass. "If we believe the Mother placed humans at the top of the social hierarchy, then we have responsibilities to those beneath us. I believe my father failed by being too cruel, and Collette by being too soft."

"You're not wrong," Riken conceded. "From what my father said, somewhere in the middle of his reign, King Sargarus crossed a line and never came back. Then Collette comes along, and I wish I knew where her ideals came from. Her guard captain, perhaps?" Riken's question was rhetorical because he knew there was no way either of them could speak for her actions. "May I ask what benevolent supremacy would look like?"

"I think I would like to see something similar to what I want from Pontus Bay. We assert our dominance without cruelty." Zephraim took another drink. "We have the right to trade in Merscales, but not through abduction and mutilation."

Zephraim's plan had appeal, though how it could be implemented on a large scale remained unclear. Riken would have to think on it. "Barris does have a good system in place, and his product is better than any others created. I have often wondered how he was able to convince the Mers to work with him the way they do." He gave a chuckle then downed the rest of his glass. "If I wasn't so sure of his loyalty, I would advise you to be careful of him, my King."

Riken placed his empty glass down. "I do wish your sister had been willing to act as you. Your idea enables us to keep our economy strong while we seek change." Zephraim's views were still too soft, but they provided more options for going forward. He would need to inform Rhoslyn.

"Indeed," Zephraim agreed. "For now, you have a long trip to make."

"What am I hoping to accomplish on this trip? What goals would you like carried out?" Riken asked, knowing he would soon be dismissed.

"A general report of the daily business of the trade. Take note on the people in the area. What do they want now that Collette is gone?"

Riken nodded. He could follow orders. Well, he could assign others to follow orders while he took care of other things in the area. "It would be my honor to do this for you."

Zephraim sighed. "Then I will look forward to your reports and your eventual return."

Riken bowed deeply. "As do I, my king."

My Heart,

I will be leaving in a few short hours on orders from our king. While I leave physically, I will remain here with you in all the important. It breaks me not to see you before I leave. To not embrace you once more or feel your lips against mine. Of all my greatest desires and concerns, you are at the center and will forever remain so.

Because I cannot see you one last time, I leave you this letter, my heart, and my right-hand man, Xavier, who will do your bidding as I would. Command him and he will obey without question. He is loyal and all I can leave you for now.

I love you more than life itself, and I will think of you every moment we are apart.

Your always,
Riken

Chapter Twenty-Five

Arian stared out the kitchen window, reflecting on the prior day's events. Nawalya had risen early, exhausted from her restless sleep, but armed with a renewed determination to visit Larent's grandparents for a few days. The distance was close to a four-hour walk, and she could handle herself against possible attacks, so Arian didn't see a need to argue.

As she'd packed her belongings for the short journey, Arian reviewed her patchy revelations. There wasn't much to discuss. She'd uttered 'arrow' repeatedly without context, and even awake and alert, Nawalya offered no insight. "Perhaps a catalyst for change?" she'd suggested with uncertainty as she rose to her feet. Arian was left unsure.

After promising to soon return, and to keep details sparse, Nawalya bid the others, except Whyldon, a temporary farewell, and headed east. If Arian was correct, Nora and Alexander Leassitor would know the full story before the day was out.

Whyldon had taken a walk into the nearby village, perhaps out of a need for space or because Sara thought giving him a task would dull his justified acrimony. Arian wondered if the guard captain felt remorse for the way he'd spoken to Collette, a matter which still angered the elf. Collette, of everyone, least deserved his anger.

Sighing, Arian returned to his breakfast of eggs, bacon, and a strange, but delicious gravy and biscuits. Sara claimed the dish a local favorite, but the remnants of A'lierdeen were a couple days journey from Barcomb Mill, and Arian had never tried it. He looked over to Collette, who was more frequently attending meals at the table. "I notice you are feeling better," he said as he stabbed a piece of biscuit with his fork.

"For longer portions of the day," Collette confirmed. "I still feel like I could sleep about six months."

Arian nodded. Under normal circumstances, she should have been a lot further along in her recovery. Larent's health seemed marginally better, but he'd not been affected by the blood magic and physical wounds Collette suffered. He would give it more thought. "It's a good thing Larent agreed to training." He jabbed a thumb at the man in question entering the room. "After all, he needs help."

Arian looked to Thomas, who sat at the end of the table, eating with one hand and using the other to run a finger along the text of a piece of parchment. Arian almost felt inclined to smile. "I would also like to see your skills as well, Thomas. If you are up to it?"

"I think you'll be more dismayed with my presence than you already are," Thomas replied with a cheeky grin. "But sure."

Arian felt his mood lift slightly at Thomas's cheek. "Well, if your swordsmanship is dismal, then I will have you hide arrowheads on your person. You have good aim with those," Arian said. Skill could always be improved, but some people, like Thomas, possessed a near-supernatural ability to think on their feet.

"Why do I feel like I'm missing something here?" Larent asked Collette as he took a seat. He'd made himself a sizable plate of food, another sign of improved health, though he picked up a slice of bacon and held it out to Collette who quietly ate it.

"Because you are," Collette replied. "Arian might actually smile if we're lucky."

Arian wiped any signs of pleasure from his face just to spite the two. He finished the last of his food and glanced at what Thomas and Collette had left. Seeing Collette's plate was empty, though she hadn't taken much to begin with, he held out a hand in request. "I will handle our dishes, and we will head outside."

Collette remained in her seat. "You'll have fun in the snow."

"We both will," Arian informed her.

Collette let out a short laugh but otherwise did not respond.

Arian rolled his eyes. "Would Her Majesty be of a mind to join me for training?"

"Her Majesty just wants to be asked," Collette replied. "Not told. But yes. I would be of mind."

Arian couldn't help the small puff of laughter despite rolling his eyes once more. "Then let us go. The sooner we start, the sooner we can get out of the blasted snow."

She allowed him to help her up before turning her attention to Larent. "Hurry up. The training is primarily for you. I don't plan on freezing for long."

Larent slowed his eating in a sign of obstinance. "You know, I bet Chuckles thinks you're not as strong as you really are." He paused to take a large bite of food, chewing the bite with an uncharacteristic thoroughness. "You should shut him up. We might get another day of rest."

Arian scoffed. "You need training, Larent. I will not explain why Collette would fail at removing me from the house."

"Whatever you say, Chuckles," Larent said.

"It might be fun to watch her try," Thomas said. He'd finished his meal and taken over cleaning the plates.

Arian rolled his eyes but would soon find himself in the middle of a demonstration. "Would you care to try?" he asked Collette. He moved to the opened space in the kitchen, letting his body relax as he readied his stance. He glared at Larent as he watched the other man open the door leading from the kitchen to the back garden.

Collette laughed at the antics, but she rolled her shoulders. "You were warned," she said. She approached Arian, slower and more at ease than expected, and her arms lifted in a fluid movement. When Arian came within reach, she shoved him, hard.

Arian stumbled and fell back into the snow beyond the open door. He hoisted himself back to his feet and walked back into the house. "Again," he instructed as he planted his feet.

"I didn't think you'd like humiliation so much, Arian," Collette replied. Again, she approached him, her movements swift and fluid. She had technique and form, and the base strength she used when knocking him down could not be ignored.

This time, Arian practically flew out the door and skidded across the icy ground. He ignored the wet snow beneath him as he pondered Collette. "You are not human," he said.

"I knocked you on your ass, and now I'm not human?" Collette asked him from the doorway.

"No," Arian said as he stood, brushing the snow off himself. When he judged himself as clean as possible, he walked back into the house. "Larent, if you would."

Larent nodded and took a position near Collette. He repeated the same movement Collette had made. When he shoved Arian with his not-so-inconsiderable strength, the elf moved, but not like he had from Collette's efforts.

"See?" he told Collette. "You are stronger than Larent."

Chapter Twenty-five

"I don't think it's the strength," Thomas said from his position near the counter. "The response to blood magic… I think it suggests more about you than your display of strength."

Arian nodded. "Your healing magic is like nothing I've ever heard. Sara feels the same way. Now this? Larent said you were strong before, but put it together, and somewhere in your genealogy is a non-human."

"Except, I've never seen an elf, or Mer, or any other with the gifts she has," Sara said as she joined the group. She wore a jacket and hat, suggesting she'd been out, seeing to some task.

"Neither can be eliminated. There are several species of elf and Mer, not to mention fairies and dwarves. They can mate with humans as well," Arian pointed out. "Her powers could come from one of those races."

"Nana says once there were dragons and other mythical creatures who could take human form," Larent offered up. "Not sure if she's telling the truth, but they supposedly granted their offspring with untold powers. Those stories have to come from somewhere."

"There are many possibilities," Sara replied. "Perhaps Arian should dry off. Then we need to discuss what we know, suspect, and what to consider going forward."

Arian excused himself to go to his room to change. When he returned to the kitchen less than ten minutes later dressed in warm and dry clothes, he found Thomas warming a tea kettle, and Sara, Larent, and Collette seated at the table.

Larent had made himself a second plate, and he was sharing every few bites with Collette, who responded without protest or acknowledgement.

Arian grabbed mugs for everyone, distributed them, and took a seat at the table. "I guess I'll start," he determined. "Are there any non-humans in your bloodline, Sara?"

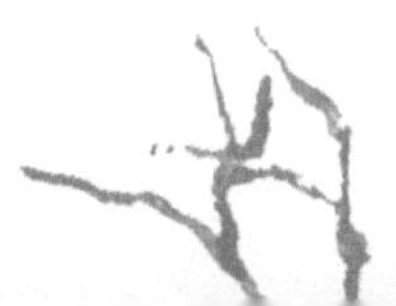

She shook her head. "I don't believe so. Our father kept a meticulous record of the family, but anything is possible."

"Then it comes from your mother's lineage," Arian surmised.

"Does that seem likely?" Thomas asked. He brought the tea kettle over and filled each mug. "With the way Sargarus viewed all magical things and non-humans, I doubt he'd have married Queen Adora if she were from another bloodline."

"The person or people could have been several generations back," Larent suggested. "My family line doesn't have shifters every generation. Most, in fact, are non-magical. I was the only shifter out of six kids."

"So something similar could have happened with Adora, and Sargarus would never have known," Arian concluded. He picked up his mug of tea and sipped. The liquid was darker and sweeter than he anticipated, but it was good.

"Coralian people weren't looking to hide magical affinity in their families until the last generation or so. Magic was permissible, and the promotion of humans above others wasn't an issue," Collette argued. "My mother's family line would have been a consideration, and if she had non-human heritage, someone would have known."

Arian had to concede if the non-human blood came from Adora, it would be much further back. "Fair. We have no way of asking him what he does know."

"And ultimately, it doesn't matter," Sara interrupted. "The ability to suppress blood magic should not have been possible with what we know you inherited from John and this family. Our healing is inherent magic. Blood magic is usually learned. Rather, I've never heard of anyone being able to do it inherently."

"Then we have to consider where the strength potentially comes from," Thomas added. He took a seat beside Arian.

Collette looked at Larent. "The strength of Zephraim's spell felt inherent rather than learned, did it not?"

"Lady, yes," Larent breathed. He handed Collette more bacon and looked up in thought. "A mage tried to control me years ago. They carried around this huge book they constantly referenced." He looked across the table to Arian, his expression contorted into a forced smile. "Remember that one?"

"Yes," Arian growled as he recalled the long-ago mission.

"So you've been targeted for possession before?" Sara asked.

Larent made a face. "Yes and no. Shifters are rumored as easy to control with the right spells. When it was revealed I was a shifter, people have tried to take advantage of my wolf. Never blood magic before, but bad attempts at possession have happened. The mage who targeted me had learned magic, and he was powerful. He just didn't anticipate me ripping his throat out. Perhaps learned magic isn't as potent."

"Not true," Sara said. "You've responded incredibly well to Arian's healing magic, and it is most decidedly learned."

"You should see what happens when he decides to be stubborn," Arian muttered, glaring at the shift. "But learned magic forced upon us is different from the learned magic we accepted."

"How are you so skilled at magic and so ignorant of it?" Sara asked Arian with genuine curiosity. "That is not how learned magic works."

Arian felt heat travel up his neck to his cheeks, and he looked down. "I do not have formal training," he replied. "I was raised to be my people's knowledge keeper, though the elders believe knowledge of magic should be reserved until one was mature enough to handle the responsibility." Arian still questioned what qualified as being responsible enough to learn to harness one's skill, but he did not voice his disagreement.

Larent chose to chime in. "When Arian and Nawalya met my grandparents, Pops taught him everything he knew about

magic, but he thought it was instinctual. The base knowledge… he didn't have it himself to pass on. They were also able to provide Nawalya with insight about her visions, and—"

Arian cut the shifter off. "Our people were unable to explain what Nawalya dealt with regarding her visions, and they were reluctant to seek outside help for fear of casting attention on her. So, between the help provided by Larent's grandparents, and whatever we've been able to find in books, we've built some knowledge and skill, but we know we are lacking."

Sara nodded. She picked up her tea and drank. "Then I would suggest you, Nawalya, and Collette regularly work with me to fill in the knowledge and skill gaps. The knowledge will serve you well, and it might do Nawalya good. She shouldn't be so vulnerable to her visions, and real instruction will help her. I just wish there were more magic users around to share knowledge."

Thomas cleared his throat and placed his tea mug on the table. "Um, there are," he said. He didn't wait for a response. Instead, he brushed his hands together several times. Then he held one out, flat palm facing the ceiling. A bright orange flame emerged, hovering just above the ink-stained skin.

Arian stared at the flame, amazed. He sighed and shook his head. "Anyone else have any secrets they wish to share?" he asked, though he couldn't help but send Thomas a slight smile which faltered when Larent spoke.

"Collette and I are getting married."

Arian's head whipped from Collette to Larent and back to Collette. "You could do so much better."

"You did bring him along," Collette replied. "So you can't object too much." Turning to Thomas, she spoke. "You seem fairly confident with your fire."

"I am," Thomas agreed. He closed his fist, extinguishing the flame. When he opened his hand again, no sign remained. "My father insisted we learn, even with the ban."

"He was smart," Sara said. She looked to Collette. "And how did you learn?"

"Trial and error," Collette responded. "I skinned my knee once when I was outside playing. I wished for it to go away, and when I placed my hand on top, it did."

"And you wonder why we question your skills against blood magic," Arian muttered to himself. "I'm glad both of you managed to find something in way of training. I agree with Sara about needing more."

"Then we will have more," Collette replied.

"Practical training should wait for you until you are healed," Sara told Collette. "The blood magic effects have lingered with you much longer than Larent."

"I agree," Arian said with a nod. "Perhaps Nawalya will return with some of Nora and Alexander's books. They might have further suggestions on treating blood magic symptoms."

"We'll know when she returns," Sara said. "For now, if everyone feels up to it, you should resume the agreed-upon training. I will ask John what he knows of Adora's lineage when he returns."

Arian stood. "Let's go test your strength and toss Larent around in the process."

Chapter Twenty-Six

Darling Thomas,

I should be visiting the blacksmith, and yet, as I sit here in the tree, I have discovered I have a perfect view into the kitchen.

I see you where you stand, chopping vegetables for Sara. I find myself distracted by the sun glinting off your hair, the way your lips curve upward as you laugh at Larent's antics. The way your long fingers hold the knife, firmly but confidently.

I confess I am distracted in a way I have never been before. My heart beats faster in my chest, and I smile as I watch you. I do not know if what I feel is love. But I find myself wanting to experience more of it, with you.

Yours always,
Arian

Letter left for Thomas in their shared bedroom.

A week passed before Whyldon felt calm enough to approach Collette, though guilt stirred in the older guard captain. His anger with Nawalya, and by extension, Arian and Larent, had not waned, but he knew yelling at Collette had been unacceptable. She was his queen, and more importantly, his daughter, and he could not excuse himself for ever treating her less than.

He also suspected, though no one said, the others were waiting on him to make amends. The subtle looks and increased attentiveness to Collette suggested great offense on her behalf. He understood the impulse, even if he could not reconcile it with the decision to keep her possible death by Larent's hands a secret.

Later in the afternoon, Whyldon found the queen seated outside, bundled in her thick leather coat, seated on an old tree stump, and watching Larent train in the distance. The shifter had a natural strength and fluidity to his movements, but the lack of dedicated combat practice rendered him slower and prone to attack. Whyldon contemplated offering advice, but for now, decided against it. He focused on Collette. Her obvious fondness for Larent made it clear avoiding discussion with the man who almost killed her as best for now.

Whyldon knew he would struggle with rationality. So, he pressed his lips together to still his tongue and approached Collette. "How are you doing?"

She looked up, eyes wide in surprise at his willingness to speak. "Pretty good," she replied. "Not as tired as I have been."

"Good," Whyldon confirmed, feeling at a loss with her. He so rarely felt uncomfortable with Collette, but he knew he was at fault. He had crossed a line. "Sara told me about the conversation all of you had the other day."

Collette delayed answering to pull her hair up as a surge of icy wind necessitated it. Whyldon had tied his back earlier in the morning for the same reason, though his hair was shorter and less burdensome. "Yeah, I'm not sure what to make of a lot of it."

"I think I'd feel the same," Whyldon said. He frowned as he watched Larent, knowing the attempts with the longblade Larent held would be more successful with better footing. "Sara asked what I knew about Adora, but I wasn't of much help. She once told me she was chosen, in part, because of her 'pure' bloodline. We could reach out to her family, but I don't know we'd get more information."

Collette crossed her arms across her middle. Whyldon could not tell if she was angry, thoughtful, or cold. "I don't know how we'd ask in a safe way, or if we'd get any sort of response. Didn't my grandparents support Sargarus?"

"They did," Whyldon confirmed. "At least, I know they did until Adora died. Still, I think there's value in trying to find answers. It doesn't matter to anyone here what you might be, but having the information could be beneficial to you." Whyldon turned fully away from watching Larent and looked down at Collette. "I wanted to apologize for yelling at you earlier in the week. You were not at fault for anything surrounding Nawalya's vision."

"I know," Collette said. "And I know you're sorry. I'm not holding a grudge over it."

"You'd have a right to." He paused, considering the wisdom in asking a question he wasn't sure would be well-received. "I just wonder… Why are you not angry with them? They put you in a great amount of danger, and you're only alive by sheer luck." He tried his best to keep his voice neutral, to shield his anger from the discussion, because he knew doing otherwise would be detrimental to the discussion. Usually, the effort was not so difficult.

"I am angry with them," Collette instantly replied, giving Whyldon an almost chastising scoff. "I haven't stopped being angry. They did a shitty thing." She uncrossed her arms, hands going to grip the stump on either side of her thighs. "What does stomping around and grumbling to myself accomplish?"

"I'm not suggesting you stomp around," Whyldon said. "But you should voice your displeasure, at the very least. No matter how you feel about the three of them, they should be made aware."

She shrugged. "We're all aware," Collette replied. "Arian was the one checking my wounds. Nawalya had the vision. Larent's claws tore into my flesh. I don't think there's anything I could say or do to make them more contrite."

Whyldon could see her point. The three, as guilty and responsible as they were, did have to carry the burden of knowing what their silence had cost. Perhaps the knowledge was punishment enough, even though Whyldon didn't view it as his responsibility to punish them. "You're right," he agreed.

"I am, but I don't expect for you to follow my lead on how to handle your feelings. You have a right to be angry, and if your anger means distancing yourself from the three of them, I do understand. Just know I intend to stick with them. If you plan on seeing our mission through with me, you will be around them." Collette went back to watching Larent. "He needs more work," she said after a few minutes of silence.

"He does," Whyldon agreed. "But he's improved, which means he has potential to improve more."

"His footing is his weakness, but I think he'll get better." She looked up at Whyldon again with a sly smile. "You could help him."

Whyldon huffed a laugh and crossed his arms. "If you deem it necessary, I will." Even with how he felt about Larent, if the shifter planned on fighting for Collette, he needed to be proficient in his ability. "Arian mentioned something about a weapon?"

Collette nodded. "No idea what it is, but we should know when he returns. Perhaps we can figure out targeted training from there?"

"I think we'll best know how to help once we know what Arian has in mind," Whyldon agreed. His attention was drawn to Larent when the sounds of training ceased.

The shifter gazed towards the trees, then raised a hand in greeting as Nawalya appeared, looking tired and dirty, but better in a way, calmer. She raised a hand in greeting to Larent, a soft small smile crossing her lips as she approached him and allowed the shifter to pull her into a hug.

Larent held her tightly for a moment. His lips moved quickly, more than likely filling her in and letting her know Arian was in the village. With a nod, she pulled away before swinging her pack around and pulling out a package. Larent paled drastically.

Turning her head, Nawalya nodded to Collette and Whyldon before striding into the house.

Larent remained in his prior spot, eyes studying the package he'd been given before finally looking over the attached letter. He took a moment to scan the contents. Then, he fell back into the snow. "This is for you," he shouted to Collette and held up the package. "Nana sends her love to you and death threats my way."

"He was your choice?" Whyldon posed, having forced himself to ignore the quick greeting Nawalya had given them. He didn't like the distance, but he had no way of resolving the issue for now.

"He was," Collette agreed and rose to join Larent.

Chapter Twenty-six

Grandson,

Your Nan and I are happy to hear you're well. We are also sad to hear about the death of the queen. Nora and I understand what it's like to fail on a mission, and we know you'll take it personally. If you need advice or a shoulder, please write to us.

Nana says write to us anyways, but we know you still have a lot to do. We offered our help, but Nawalya suggested it's best we stay away while your group figures out the best path forward.

Know we love you and are here for you if you need anything. We've sent Arian books on healing and blood magic. Nawalya told us you picked up a magic user during your travels. I doubt the books will help, but one never knows. In the attached package is armor for your magic user, to help protect her from wolf claws, just in case.

Be safe and know you are loved.
Pops

You better bring her home so we can meet her once you complete your mission, young man.

Love Nana

Arian,

I hear you are as well as possible, and you have a young man in your life. You will bring him by when you can, or I will come find you when your current job is finished.

I hope the books help.

Love Nora

Chapter Twenty-Seven

Leaning against a large oak tree, Arian quietly observed as Sara instructed Collette through several possible techniques to access and use her magic. The two women sat on the ground, legs crossed and talking. He'd been invited to join, though he remained a distance from them so he did not interrupt or distract. Keenly interested in the lesson, Arian found himself giving mental reminders to blink and breathe. He'd witnessed several explanations of magic before, but no one managed to articulate it in the logical way Sara could.

"Your magic is complicated," Sara told the queen, reaching forward to take Collette's hands with her own. "You have the family magic, which I suspect works much like my own, but I do not know how intertwined your magic is with whatever else is floating around in there protecting you."

"You know as much as I do," Collette replied. "Arian is the one who suspected there was something more."

"And he was right," Sara confirmed, glancing towards Arian with a smile. She looked back to Collette. "My guess is your blood is from a naturally strong race. One who is not only physically strong but less susceptible to human magic."

"A variety of possibilities remain," Arian said, though he hadn't meant to include himself in the conversation.

Sara nodded, not looking the least bit concerned by his interruption. "You're right, but without more information, it would be difficult to guess."

She relinquished one of Collette's hands long enough to wave the elf over. Arian held back a wince at the open invitation, but he couldn't deny his interest. He closed the distance between himself and the two women and took a seat next to Collette.

Sara gave him a welcoming smile. "You helped to heal her after she was injured. Surely you have some thoughts?"

Arian shook his head. "All I can tell you is Collette is not part elf, nor is she shifter. I have no knowledge of Nereid, dwarf, fairy, or the other races blood can do."

"Show me what you can do," Sara instructed Collette.

Arian observed, though he spotted no outward sign of the magic.

"Shifter is unlikely in general," the older woman said. "You can't shift, right?" she directed to Collette.

"I cannot," Collette responded, her hands dropping to her lap. "And even so, shifters are rare."

"Right," Sara agreed. "Arian thinks not elf, but I'm curious about how the option was eliminated."

"It is a guess based on my village," Arian replied. "A few of the families looked more human than elvish. The bloodline is more diluted. Even so, the children were faster and stronger than human counterparts like Collette." He paused and touched the top of his ear. "But she lacks the most obvious sign, and every person I have ever met with both human and elvin blood has elvin ears."

"Hmm. I am not so certain the ears could be universally true, but I am willing to accept it for now," Sara replied.

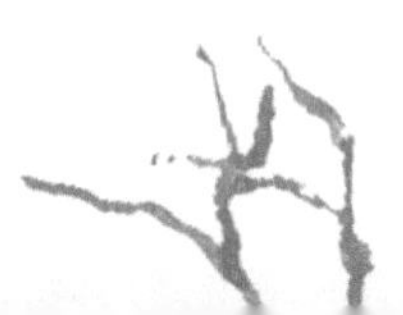

Arian inclined his head. "It is what I was taught growing up, and observed, but it is possible the theory could be wrong. We do not know what elves across the sea are like."

"A good thing to research when time allows," Sara said. She took a breath and refocused on Collette. "Innate magic is a part of you. It should work in the same way breathing or your heart beating works. It should be something you can call upon without strain. I worry because of how long it took you to recover after arriving. Does using your magic usually drain you, or did the blood magic cause your problems after the attack?"

"Usually, it doesn't tire me to use my powers," Collette replied, though she quickly added an amendment. "I have not used it for anything major before. Usually small injuries like cuts."

"Is it possible healing larger injuries might drain her powers?" Arian asked Sara.

"Maybe," Sara replied. "From what I've witnessed, some people have better overall control and practice, and they tend to have more stamina. Theoretically, Collette could achieve the same."

Arian gave Collette an evil little smile. "She would need an injury, a small one, to heal consistently to help her practice, correct?"

"And who are you volunteering to hurt?" Collette asked, brow raised.

Arian's eyes slid to the left, where a certain shirtless shifter attended to chores. "Larent is prone to accidents. Small ones."

"And you think Larent is going to agree to be intentionally injured?" Sara asked skeptically.

Arian shook his head. "If we told him it was to help Collette, I think he would ask how badly he needed to hurt himself." Arian held up his hand at the look Collette shot him. "It was a joke. However, it would be best if we all took turns."

"Then figure that out for yourselves," Sara instructed. "But practice is truly the path forward as Collette already knows how to harness her gifts. Other than practice... we'd need to know more about her history."

"Should she start practicing now?" Arian asked.

"I would recommend it," Sara replied. "What the lot of you are planning will eventually lead to battle. If Collette intends on using her gifts, she should be prepared."

Arian didn't even think about it. Pulling a knife from his belt, he sliced open the back of his hand, hissing slightly at the sting. Bright red blood openly flowed from his wound, and he wordlessly held his hand out for Collette to heal. He didn't realize her upset until she spoke.

"Cut yourself open again, and I'll make it worse," the queen threatened as she took his hand with less-than-gentle movements. Placing fingers along the line of the cut, Arian felt his skin warm as it fused back together, leaving no trace of injury.

"Would you like a warning first?" he asked her.

"I would like for you to not injure yourself at all," Collette replied, dropping his hand.

"I'm going to cut myself again," Arian replied, seeing no reason to avoid another round of practice.

"I'm going to tell Thomas," she replied.

He looked up, surprised by the threat. "I think he will understand. You need practice, and I should assist as I know how to cause the least amount of damage."

"Remember your words when Thomas is mad at you," Collette grumbled, but she motioned for Arian to continue.

"I will accept his anger," Arian insisted. Again, he slid the blade across the back of his hand, and he winced as he realized he'd gone deeper than before. His mistake was not missed.

"You went deeper," Collette complained, snatching his hand with even less gentleness than before. She repeated her

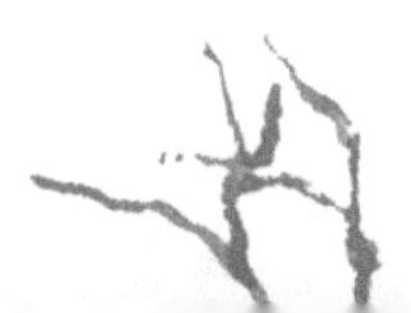

earlier actions, and the warmth of her touch penetrated deeper into his skin.

When she withdrew her fingers, Sara handed over handkerchiefs to both. "You should clean your hands and choose another body part if you insist on practicing."

"Thank you," Arian said, taking the handkerchief and rubbing the blood from his hand. Looking at the unblemished skin, Arian had a thought. "The skin grows back as if new. Would the same happen on scarred skin as well?"

"It is more difficult, but it can be done," Sara replied as she looked at her niece. "The body knits itself together as best as it can without intervention, often resulting in scars. Magic works beyond the body's limitations, and a skilled magic user can avoid the creation of scars. Your scars resulted from not having the strength to continue healing after you were attacked."

Arian pressed his lips together in thought. He had several scars he wanted to keep, but many others he did not want. He also knew Nawalya hated the scars on her back. It was vanity to wonder if Collette could truly rid them of such things, but if she could do it for them, what about others?

Rolling up his sleeve, he showed Collette a thick but inconsequential scar across his upper arm. "Do you mind if I cut here?"

"We might as well try if you're willing," Collette decided.

Arian nodded his consent and was much more careful in the cut. Collette's upset by the depth of his last cut confused him. Thankfully, the newest wound bled less copiously than the cuts on his hand. Collette observed it for a few seconds before lifting a hand again. She pressed her fingers along the cut, and Arian's skin grew warm. He found another question forming on his lips. "When you heal, does the skin of the person you are healing warm up or is it unique to Collette?"

Sara shook her head. "Usually, the only real physical sensation I experience is a tingling in the fingers."

"Collette's healing feels like the sun warming my skin on a spring day," Arian replied.

"I noticed the warmth myself," Sara replied. She nodded to Arian. "How is your scar?"

Arian looked down at his arm as Collette removed her hand, studying the new skin. He gave her an impressed look. "It is gone"

"You remember when you thought you'd be playing escort and protection duty on our little adventure?" Collette asked, amused.

"I am still playing escort, and if taunting the person who tried to kill you means anything at all, then I am still on protection duty as well." Arian's hands moved to the hem of his long-sleeved red tunic but stopped. He wanted to see if she could heal deeper scars, but he was unsure if he wanted to show them to Collette and Sara. When changing, he had always gone into the woods or his own room.

"Would you like to go somewhere less exposed?" Sara asked.

"Please," Arian said, his cheeks reddening.

The three stood from their positions on the ground, and Sara motioned them inside. "Your bedroom," she instructed Arian.

Arian tried to keep how tense his shoulders had become to himself. He wasn't ashamed of his scars, but he had seen others react badly to them.

When they arrived at his bedroom, Sara shut the door behind the group to grant privacy. Taking a deep breath, Arian turned so he was facing the wall as he removed his shirt. He braced himself for a possible bad reaction to not only the amount of patchwork scars across his back but the ugliness of them as well. He tried to remain still as steps crossed the room, stopping behind him.

"Is it okay to touch you?" Collette asked.

Arian swallowed. "Yes." He ignored the slight rasp in his voice and shut his eyes as he felt fingers trace the lines of his scars. She did not pull away or make any sign of fear or disgust.

"Which one do you want to try?" she asked.

Arian ignored the way his skin crawled at the touch. "There is a long jagged one below my left shoulder blade. It goes straight down, almost to my hip."

"She should be able to tackle it," Sara spoke up. "Obviously, you cannot cut yourself here. Would you like one of us to, or should we ask one of the others?"

"Collette can do it, and if she's not comfortable, Larent or Thomas."

"I'll do it," Collette replied, though her voice indicated she was reluctant.

He listened as she unsheathed a blade. "You do not have to. You could get someone else," Arian told her calmly, kindly, and meant it.

"I know," she replied. "But I'm going to, so stay still."

Arian held as still as possible, even going so far as to stop breathing for a moment.

"Follow the length of the scar tissue as carefully as possible," Sara instructed Collette.

The blade pressed against his skin without cutting, a silent warning. Arian let out a deep breath and relaxed his body as he mentally braced for the pain. It came, though it was bearable as she cut into the thicker skin of his long scar. She slowly scored his back, knowing if any of the others walked in, they'd be confused at best.

Finally, Collette withdrew the blade, handing it off to Sara. She then pressed both hands against his back, and the warmth he'd grown accustomed to appeared. Arian sucked in a sharp, stuttering breath. Other than Nawalya, and recently Thomas, no one had spent so much time touching him, and he had to fight to keep from pulling away. He knew for his own sake he would need a moment when Collette was finished. He thought she might as well. When she pulled her hands away, Arian fought from slumping in relief.

"You did well," Sara said. "Both of you."

"Is it fully healed?" he asked.

Sara replied, "Your skin is a little red and obscured from blood, but the scar is gone."

Arian nodded and stepped away from the women to collect himself. "You have an amazing gift. I am more than willing to help you to grow it, but I need a moment before we continue, if you do not mind."

Collette shook her head. "I should probably take a break. I've healed you four times already, and I don't feel comfortable doing more so close together."

Arian motioned for Collette to have a seat on the bed. She looked well enough, but he didn't want to push her too far. "If you need to rest, or some water, let me know."

"No, I'm fine. I just don't like the idea of cutting you open when there is no guarantee I can continue being effective."

Arian nodded and moved to kneel next to Collette. "Next time, we will ask Larent to cut into me so you don't have to."

The door to the bedroom opened, revealing Thomas. "What have I missed?" he asked, eyes going to the shirtless Arian kneeling in front of Collette to Sara and the knife she held.

Arian gave Thomas a small, slightly tired smile and stood. "I've been assisting Collette practice her powers. We have discovered she can heal scars."

"The knife has an explanation," Thomas said, and he shook his head. "You could think of no other way to practice?"

Arian gave Thomas a confused look, glancing at Collette for a moment before saying, "Her powers lay in healing. Would she not need something to heal?"

"Could you not have waited for one of the many natural injuries resulting from farm labor?" Thomas asked.

"With everything coming up, Collette needs as much practice as possible and it is not guaranteed one of us will hurt ourselves." Arian's confusion deepened. "If we had waited, it's possible we might not have learned that she can heal scars thought to be permanent."

"Was her ability to heal scars a needed bit of knowledge?" Thomas asked.

"No, but it is good to know what she can and cannot do." Again, Arian glanced at Collette in confusion. She had warned him Thomas might be upset, but he didn't understand why. Thomas had magic. Had he not experimented with what he could do?

"Right..." Thomas said, and he turned his attention to Collette. "Try and find another way to practice that doesn't involve Arian repeatedly carving into himself," he requested. Without addressing his reason for coming to the room, Thomas saw himself out.

Arian watched Thomas go, then turned to Collette. "I thought Thomas would understand. What did I do wrong?"

"He loves you and does not want you suffering unnecessarily," Collette replied while Sara retrieved a rag and dunked it into the water pitcher sitting on the desk. She ran the damp cloth along the healed cut on Arian's back so he was free of blood.

Arian was appreciative, though he was more focused on Thomas. "Should I go talk to him?" he asked as he pulled his shirt back on.

"Give him time to sit with what we did," Collette suggested. "Discussion when heated won't help, and he's usually reasonable once he's had time to consider a position."

Arian nodded, agreeing with her wisdom. "Do you want to go again?"

"Let's resume this afternoon after lunch," Collette suggested. "You'll have time to talk with Thomas, and I can intercede theatrics from others who will inevitably find out."

Arian pressed his lips together, remembering he had errands to run. "I have to go into town. The weapon I ordered for Larent was due to finish this week." He looked to Sara who had been quiet while Thomas was there, watching Arian, judging him. "Would you like me to pick anything up while I am there?"

"You might want to grab flowers for Thomas while you're out," Sara replied.

"I could, but I was hoping to take Thomas with me," Arian conceded. They could pick up Larent's new weapon, stop by the local tavern for dinner, then head back to the cottage. He knew he was blushing again.

Collette smiled at the confession. "You have a very sweet idea, Arian. You should go invite him and have a good time."

"Do you want me to send Larent here?" Arian asked Collette, refusing to meet her eyes as his blush darkened. Sweet wasn't something anyone had used when referring to him in a long time.

"I'm sure he's already hunting for me," Collette said, standing. "Have a lovely time with Thomas. I will want stories next time we meet."

"I promise nothing," Arian said, barely concealing a smile. He quickly removed himself from Collette and Sara's presence. Taking the stairs two at a time, he almost ran face first into Larent. Unsurprising, the shifter was looking for Collette.

"She's upstairs," Arian said with a smirk. "In my bedroom, recovering."

"Nice try," Larent said, patting him on the back as he passed Arian. "If she didn't see you as a brother, I might have been worried for a second."

"She does not see me as a brother," Arian threw back.

"Whatever, Chuckles. Fletcher is in the barn upset at whatever you were actually doing."

"Thank you," Arian called back. He paused by the door to grab his coat from the rack before going outside, grateful for the shoveled path.

He let himself inside the barn without waiting for admittance and found Thomas pacing back and forth. He truly was upset.

"I see you're done," Thomas remarked before Arian spoke.

"Collette needed a break, and I needed to go into town," Arian replied, feeling uncertain about extending an invitation with Thomas so clearly unhappy with him.

"What purpose do you have in town?"

"I need to pick up a commissioned weapon for Larent." Arian breathed in deeply, steeling himself in case Thomas rejected him. "Would you like to come with me?"

So certain was Arian of the rejection, it took a beat for Thomas's "Sure" to register in his mind. Arian didn't sag with relief, but it was close. "Thank you," he said. "Do you need anything from the house?"

"There is nothing I will need I don't already have with me," Thomas replied.

Arian nodded. "Then let us be off." He awkwardly held out his arm to Thomas and smiled when the other man took it.

Chapter Twenty-Eight

Thomas stood back, watching Arian work through the trans-action with the blacksmith. He wasn't sure what he'd expected with the weapon, and though he could not see all of it from his vantage point near the front of the stone shop, there was no denying the threat.

The blacksmith, an older woman with ebony hair, held up the device for Arian to examine. Three curved blades bloomed from the front of the device, a harness meant to attach to an arm and hand.

"Your work is spectacular," Arian said as he studied the handmade claws. The elf undid one of the bags attached to his belt and handed it over to the blacksmith. "Your requested price, plus more for timeliness and quality."

The woman, who Thomas thought went by Ada, accepted the money pouch. "Be careful with these. The claws are sharp, and your friend could hurt himself and anyone he comes across without proper caution," she said in her deep voice.

"I will advise him before he begins training," Arian replied. He bowed, collected the weapon, and returned to Thomas.

"Do you think Larent will like them?" Thomas asked as they left the shop. The weapons were impressive, but it was difficult to guess how others would feel about anything new.

"I hope," Arian said uncertainly. "They are more similar to what he is used to. What he's meant to be."

Thomas nodded. Despite the lateness of the afternoon, the streets bustled with people. Nothing like Quenall, of course, where one could hardly walk through the marketplace, but Thomas possessed no complaints. He was happy to let Arian navigate them through the crowd. "He never says it, but he hates the restriction of not shifting."

Arian nodded, a slight frown forming. "He has locked away an intrinsic part of himself. In keeping himself safe for Collette, he's removed a sense of self and keener abilities."

"I wish we could help him, but I don't know how we possibly could. Zephraim would have to break the blood magic bond, or Larent would have to die, and I can't see either thing happening."

"You are right. Neither of those is a good option, and Collette has been through enough without any of us entertaining the idea of killing Larent."

"If anything would make her quit now, it would be losing Larent," Thomas agreed, though he wondered if there were others neither knew about.

Arian didn't address his point. "Are you hungry?" he asked instead.

"I could eat," said Thomas.

"The tavern is supposed to be very good," Arian said. "We could go there before returning."

"Let's try it," Thomas agreed.

With a goal in mind, Arian's guidance through the town became deliberate. Thomas was fine with that. Arian was always more at ease with a purpose, and Thomas would never begrudge Arian finding those moments.

Arian glanced over at Thomas when they passed the largest of the crowds. "I am sorry about earlier," he said.

"I know," Thomas replied after a prolonged silence only disturbed by the rhythmic steps on the dirt-covered path. "And I understand the thinking. She does need practice."

"And I would rather her practice now, building up her endurance when things remain peaceful. Neither she nor Sara knows what other kind of magic she has, and I do not think the blood magic was solely responsible for how drained she was after the attack. A small amount of pain seems worth it if it saves a life later." Arian briefly looked at Thomas before turning away. "Learning she could also help remove scars… I confess to being selfish."

Thomas nodded, understanding Arian's desires. Although the other man had yet to share even a fraction of what he'd experienced in his long years, Thomas knew Arian would always be haunted. "I can imagine being able to rid yourself of physical scars would appeal."

Arian mulled Thomas's words over as they arrived at the tavern. Reaching out, he opened the door and motioned Thomas inside. The room wasn't crowded, though enough people sat around, drinking and talking, Thomas doubted they'd receive much attention. They found an empty table in the back corner, small enough for just the two.

"Collette removed a long scar from my back today. One I received in a rather embarrassing situation," Arian shared.

"And what sort of situation embarrassed you?" Thomas asked as he took a seat.

"During a particularly terrible mission, I found myself supported by a rope secured by Larent over a steep drop. As I was lowered, someone I had not realized was watching drove a

knife into my back. Larent pulled me back up, but the person with the blade kept a long strip of skin for his efforts."

Thomas let out a surprised gasp. "You're lucky he didn't hit anything vital, luckier you didn't bleed out."

"I almost did," Arian said, shaking his head. "That experience is why I keep several bottles of blood-replenishing potions in my kit at all times." Again, he gave a small smile. "Imagine me having to walk Larent through the potion process while Nawalya stitched me up."

"Larent making potions seems like something our queen should make illegal," Thomas said, though he turned his attention to the barman who came to ask what they'd like. With drinks and an order of the evening specialty made, the two men found themselves alone again.

"When something is important, Larent comes through. Had I not been bleeding out, I would have worried more about the potion's quality, but he did well in the circumstances."

"Perhaps we should think about having someone else learn to make potions," Thomas said, pausing as great tankards of ale were placed on the table. The dark liquid looked wonderful, and he picked up the sizable mug and took a sip, finding it smoother than he thought it would be.

"I was thinking of asking Collette if she would like to learn. She could then teach Larent. He'd take instruction well from her." Arian paused to take a drink. "Are you interested in learning?"

"I'm always interested in learning," Thomas replied before taking another sip. He smiled at Arian as he put the tankard back down. "You enjoy spending time with Collette."

"Collette is an interesting person," Arian replied. Again, they paused as food was brought to the table, succulent portions of duck accompanying a bed of vegetables.

Thomas's mouth watered in anticipation. "Interesting in a good or bad way?" he asked as he picked up his fork.

Arian began eating as well. "In a good way. She has a sharp mind, and she's handled everything she's gone through better than most would."

"And?" Thomas asked.

"And what?" Arian said with a smirk. "Do you think I should wax poetic as Larent does?"

Thomas shook his head as he chewed a bite of duck. "No, but you are closer to her than you admit."

"I do like Collette, but telling her would ruin her fun, I believe, and would also make her think I want hugs." Arian blanched at the thought.

"I understand your point, but may I make a suggestion?"

"Of course."

"As resilient as she is, she's one of the most fragile people I've met. She needs family, and she's very attached to you. I think she might appreciate a little more confirmation from you."

Arian looked down at the roast duck and vegetables on his plate. "I can try," he finally said.

"Only if you feel the same way."

"I do, or I think I do," Arian said, meeting Thomas's gaze. The trust and vulnerability he saw there warmed his chest. Thomas knew how difficult openness was for Arian. "It's just been me, Nawalya, and Larent for a long time. I forget what it's like to have more."

"What about when this is all over?" Thomas asked, reaching out to put a hand on Arian's. "I don't think Larent will be willing to go off on adventures anymore."

Arian's lips turned up into a small smile. "I have offered to stay on with Collette as her assassin. I am hoping she might let me spy as well."

"I'd think you'd have more to do as a spy. She doesn't strike me as needing an assassin very often."

"One can hope, but anything is possible," Arian said.

"True, and we have such a long way to go and so much we need to accomplish."

"I do hope she intends to head for the Nereid come spring," Arian added. "It's a place I've never been."

Having eaten his fill for now, Thomas wiped his fingers and sat back with his tankard. "It's the safest place to go, and I think she'll get support."

"I hope so. Otherwise, we will have to travel to Fyithas, which will take several weeks in good weather. I do not wish to consider what will happen if we have to cross the ocean to the kingdoms on the other side of the sea."

"Fythias comes with about as much guarantee as Azmarin, and my understanding is your time there was a waste."

Arian's face turned dark as he recounted the events in Azmarin. "It was, and not just because the king decided he owned Collette and tried to assassinate Larent. However, Fythias has always stood against the Merscale trade. They were against Sargarus and his rule. To keep this continent from falling once more, they may lend Collette aid."

"Then we should make sure to cover potential plans to go there with Collette."

"Yes, we must discuss this with Collette." Arian's gaze grew distant for a moment before he shook off his thoughts. Thomas wondered what thought had possessed Arian, but he didn't get the chance to inquire. "What are your plans when all this is over?" Arian asked.

"I'm not sure," Thomas replied. He took another drink as he mulled over options. "I could return to my trade, but I would not like to do anything resulting in distance between us."

"I would like it if you were close by as well. Have you considered becoming an advisor to Collette?"

Thomas had considered the role but didn't know if Collette would extend an invitation. He had spent a lot of his free time in Quenall criticizing her choices, but she was wise enough to understand his critique had been because he believed her willing and capable of doing better. "I would accept should she ask."

Arian smiled again, small and genuine. "I'm happy to hear it."

The two finished and paid for their meal, then left the tavern. Thomas was in no great hurry to return to the house, and he had enjoyed having alone time with Arian. Little opportunity for privacy existed given the task their group had taken on.

"We do not have to go back yet if you would like to look around town. There are a few shops," Arian offered, seeming in no hurry to return either.

"Let's see where the evening takes us?" Thomas suggested.

"I would like that," Arian replied.

The two aimlessly wandered around the small town, chatting and taking in the sights. Barcomb Mill and the surrounding area was lovely and peaceful, and Thomas could understand wanting to spend a life somewhere like the village.

As they walked, Arian reached out and took Thomas's hand in his, unable to make eye contact. Using his other hand, he pointed out the glass blower shop, telling Thomas how he had once wanted to learn when he was younger. They passed the shop, talking or remarking on different things they observed. The longer they walked, the more the stoic elf started to fidget, as if nervous about something.

"You okay?" Thomas asked.

Arian opened and closed his mouth once, twice, then looked around them. "Yes," he said decisively. He pivoted his body, using his weight and grip on Thomas's hand to spin them into the small space between the two houses. He pressed Thomas

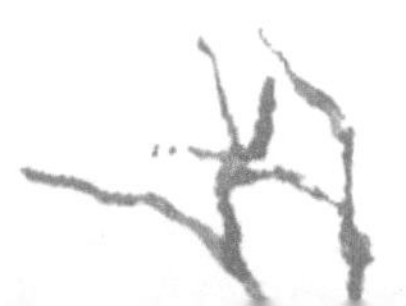

against the wall, bare inches between their bodies as Arian boxed Thomas in.

"Hello," Arian said softly, his breath ghosting over Thomas's lips.

"Hi," Thomas breathed out, the closeness intoxicating him with absolute desire.

Arian stared into Thomas's eyes for a moment before finally asking, "May I kiss you?"

Thomas nodded, unable to say how badly he wanted Arian to kiss him. Arian pressed his body from hip to shoulder against him, brushing his lips against Thomas's once, twice, and a third time before deepening the kiss. Thomas's arms went around Arian, pulling him closer, his mind lost in the taste and feel of the elf.

Arian gave a full-body shudder, but instead of pulling away, he slipped his leg between Thomas's, and his tongue teased Thomas's. The kiss only broke when Thomas's lungs became insistent, and he looked up at Arian feeling dazed by his need for the other man.

Arian let out a harsh breath and rested his forehead against Thomas's. His voice was deep and rough. "I would like to spend the night with you."

"I would very much like that," Thomas replied.

"I can't promise much, touch is hard for me. But I want this, with you."

"We'll work through it," Thomas promised. "Whatever 'it' happens to be."

Arian nodded and pulled away from Thomas. He held out his hand, which Thomas took, and the two men began their journey back to the tavern where they planned on renting a room.

Chapter Twenty-Nine

My Lord Riken,

I write in hopes your plans have easily fallen into place. The work you do to restore the traditional and correct way of things remains our most critical goal. I am just thankful there are so many willing to follow you, to support you in your efforts. As one of your most dedicated followers, I would like to assure you I have followed the letter and spirit of your instructions.

One of your last orders to me was the dispatch of a particular pest. It is my utmost desire to see the task done, but your lady has instructed me to delay my actions a bit longer. You have only been gone for two weeks, and our queen concerns herself with protecting your legacy and legal standing. She is as clever as she is beautiful and serving her has been an honor and pleasure thus far. I shall endeavor to follow through with your orders at the time she deems most suitable.

I hope the time comes soon. Lady Elrick has begun a sly campaign of slander against our queen. Whenever Her Majesty is within ear shot and surrounded by people, Lady Elrick speaks of you in a manner unbecoming a woman of her status. She also seems determined to lay more seeds about your relationship to the queen. She points out the time you spend alone with her, the quiet, intimate looks and whispers. I cannot wait for the day I can remove her from Quenall.

Your humble servant,
Xavier

Wildrun was turning green. Another month or more would need to pass before spring was firmly setting in, but Riken noted the early sprigs of greenery on the trees. He saw and heard more birds, and many of the smaller animals who'd remained hidden during colder months scurried across the manor grounds. Spring would bring new life to Wildrun, and with it, new children from the villagers, hunting with his friends, and all manner of appealing sport.

Riken observed the grounds surrounding his estate from the third-story window of his private office. The windows were draped in lush forest green fabric. Behind him sat an ancient cherry desk, intricately carved by a master craftsman. Looking at it, no one had ever been able to guess its true age. Riken's father had been meticulous in its upkeep. Every few years, it was sanded, buffed, and re-varnished. Even now, it gleamed in the sunlight pouring through the window.

Every other item in the spacious office received the same meticulous care. Nothing was worn, dusty, or neglected, and Riken took pride in the perfect little world his family had created in the confines of the home.

Below, a small squadron of men, his guard commander Cadan amongst them, readied for another journey. Riken watched as they moved supplies to their wagons and did last-minute inspections of their weapons. They'd rested over the past couple of weeks, and Riken knew the men were ready for action.

Riken and the squadron had left Quenall just over a month ago, and as he settled into his desk chair, he felt quite content. Well, with one exception. He missed Rhoslyn terribly. Her beauty, wit, and ruthlessness held his heart. He also hated the very thought of her alone with Zephraim and his flights of fancy and sour moods. He knew Rhoslyn could handle herself against Zephraim, so he didn't worry.

Being back in Wilrun, practically banned from Gadleigh palace, did have its perks. He would be able to further his plans without palace oversight, and thus, strengthen the kingdom. He'd also be able to verify claims of Collette's death. He intended to track down every single person giving the bitch aid and punish them.

King Brath's letter had confirmed Whyldon had been with the group, though Riken was hardly surprised by the guard captain's presence. He'd followed Collette around like a puppy for years, and Riken saw no reason to believe the habit would change along with the circumstances. Larent and Tolan were mere ghosts beyond their short time in the palace. Riken held some interest with them because Tolan was the former queen's rumored lover, but Larent Leassitor was somehow her husband. Riken also knew Larent had been one of many of Zephraim's former, drunken lovers, if Rhoslyn's old letters were to be believed.

An elf named Arian, who'd once been a member of the guard for a handful of months, was also traveling with her. Riken discovered the elf was a survivor of the A'lierdeen massacre, and the knowledge led him to believe they'd seek additional aid from other elves. He'd find and question every single elf he met if necessary. Those who refused to cooperate would greatly suffer.

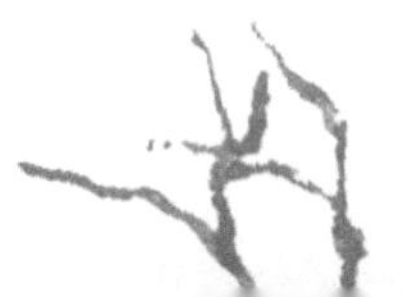

As a precaution, he would be sending a different group to Barcomb Mill. He doubted the traitor would be sitting there, waiting to be found if she were alive, but Whyldon's family was from the area. His sister would, undoubtedly, have useful information. He intended to bring her back to Quenall for questioning.

Striking out against those who sided with Collette was not all he planned to do. He wanted to expand the agreed-upon labor camps. When Zephraim learned of them, Riken knew the king would be angered, but Riken truly didn't care. His time in Galel told him rebels were popping up all over the country. They needed to be dealt with. It was what his father and King Sargarus would have done. If the labor camps did not quell their rebellion, all dissenters would be executed. Rhoslyn had already approved of Riken's plan, and he would see it done.

A knock on the door drew Riken from his thoughts, and he quickly called out for the person to enter. He smiled warmly as a small-framed and tanned young boy with a head of dark curly hair entered his office.

"Lord Riken, the stable master sent me to inform you your horse is ready to leave."

Riken's smile grew. "Thank you, Gwane." The boy beamed at being addressed by name. "I'll head down shortly. You should head to the kitchens and let the cook know I said you could have a tart. You've earned it. I'll let your master know I gave you a break."

The boy's eyes lit up, and he was out the door before Riken could say anything else. He did love children.

Gathering his things, Riken readied to leave, reminding himself once again to send a few more men into Lord Elrick's estate. It would need stability. After all, there was no heir, and soon, there would be no lady.

"Lord Barris said to extend his appreciation," Gisela said to Diana as she carried a near-empty tray into the kitchen. She smiled brightly, placing the tray on the counter near the sink, and slowly went through the process of removing dishes, emptying them, and putting them in the sink for a wash. "I believe he favors you, Diana."

Diana laughed, glancing over at the younger kitchen worker with a fond smile. She was dicing vegetables for stew which would be served to palace staff for their evening meal. It was thick and savory, and though not nearly so grand as what the royal family and their friends would eat, Diana thought it just as delicious. "Lord Barris is very kind, and he praises me anytime I cook something with seafood."

She used her forearm to push hair from her face, more pleased with the subtle contact she kept with Crem's ally. He often found ways to make his presence and awareness known, and it gave her peace when she went long stretches without contact from her husband.

"Lord Barris is always kind," Gisela said brightly. She put the tray away for later use and began washing the noble's dishes. "Everyone he interacts with him thinks the world of him. I wish all the nobles could be more like him."

"You are not the first to think so," a third male voice said.

Both women turned to the kitchen door, and there stood the king. Both women bowed, though Gisela's cheeks burned red with humiliation.

"Your majesty," Diana said in greeting. "It is lovely to see you again. Is there something I can do for you?"

Zephraim shook his head. "I needed to stretch my legs," the king explained.

His expression seemed a bit more cheerful than the last time he'd visited the kitchens, though she acknowledged Zephraim had never possessed much of a cheerful disposition. Diana nodded and smiled. "I can understand. You have been sequestered in meetings most of the day, my king." Diana knew of Zephraim's activities because she had had to prepare meals to be sent up several times. "Shall I get you some wine or something else while you take time for yourself? I have your favorite dessert ready, if you crave indulgence."

Zephraim pursed his lips in consideration and gave her a genuine smile. "An indulgence would be nice."

"I will get it," Diana responded instantly. "Gisela, please go check on Lady Elrick. I know she wanted something to eat before she went into town."

The young girl nodded, bowed to Zephraim once again, and exited the rooms.

Diana began putting together the promised snack for Zephraim. First, she grabbed wine from the dark cupboard. Usually, it went into her cooking, but she could spare it. "Was it Madame Hyacinth who used to make the pudding for you?" she asked conversationally. Wine was poured into the cup, dark and thick, and Diana presented it to Zephraim.

Zephraim grinned at the name. "She used to say she made the fig and date pudding just for me. I remember how deliciously spiced it was. Almost hot. I was sad when she retired and left for Branlin."

Hyacinth had been an old woman when Diana first arrived at the palace. She'd been precise and demanding in the quality of the food prepared in her kitchen, but she'd been kind, warm, and willing to teach.

"We miss her terribly," Diana said. She located her fig and date pudding baked in the early morning and cut an enormous slice for Zephraim. After plating it, she presented the dish and a fork to the king. "We all joke from time to time of her intentionally witholding baking secrets from us."

Zephraim laughed as he picked up his pudding.

"Does it please you, my king?" Diana asked, putting on a hopeful smile. She smoothed the bottom half of her apron, hoping the action came across as an anxious fidget. Once he took the first bite, Diana knew she'd cemented the good mood he would have with her.

When Zephraim swallowed, he took a drink of his wine before answering. "Indeed, it does. You have a real gift, Diana."

"Thank you, your Majesty. I take pride in my work, as do the other members of the kitchen staff, and it is always an honor to feed you." She topped off Zephraim's wine, though he'd barely consumed any of it.

"Good food and drink are appreciated after a long day," Zephraim said, and when Diana's brows raised in what she hoped appeared to be genuine concern, he waved a hand dismissively. "Nothing terrible, I assure you," he said. "Just a very long day with many different items to tend to."

"I see," Diana replied. "I know Lord Riken had been providing you with assistance. Are you seeking someone to fill the role while he is gone?"

Zephraim shrugged, mouth full of pudding. "Perhaps," he responded when he could. "Finding appropriate help is proving challenging."

"I can only imagine," Diana said with a sympathetic nod. "But I know you will find someone." She just wondered what the challenge in replacing Riken might be. She would pass the news off to Barris once an opportunity presented itself. Perhaps he would have insight.

"You have more faith than I," Zephraim replied.

Gisela rejoined them, looking remarkably less cheerful than she had when leaving. "Excuse me, Your Majesty. The queen has requested your presence."

Diana would swear on her life Zephraim rolled his eyes. Still, the king hastily finished the last bites of his pudding and placed the plate on the counter. "Duty calls," he announced, and without another word, he left the kitchen.

Aphros,

Cousin, I wish I had better news to share with you. In the time Ceto and I have been here, we have been unable to find any trace of Queen Collette. As we have traveled south from the gulf, we have investigated several potential locations. I suspect we have encountered individuals who have been in contact with her, but those in Galel have proven secretive with their news. Ceto believes their silence is offered in favor of Queen Collette's protection. My optimism in locating her remains low, but Ceto's positivity keeps us moving forward.

We currently reside in a small inn a couple of days journey from Veitel. Ceto and I have debated the wisdom of getting closer. The southern area of Galel has historically been dangerous for non-humans. At least, it has for the past century. Ceto suggested moving east towards the coast and returning to more northern territories in Galel. However, those plans, as set as we felt them to be, must change.

We have observed movement of materials, wood, and stone into southern Galel. Several of the other travelers we've met at various inns over the past week have spoken of labor camps opening across Wildrun and A'lierdeen. We've heard more tales of non-humans being rounded up by soldiers not wearing the Coralian crest. Humans are rising against the atrocities.

Chapter Twenty-nine

As you know, Ceto and I feel compelled to investigate these rumors. If we confirm them true, you know we must lend aid. We will strive to send news as we can. I hope things are well on your side, and I have better news to report soon.

Jayden

Chapter Thirty

A lunch of sandwiches, fruit, and vegetables sat before the group. The warmer weather required less hardy meals during the day, and the residents of Whyldon's home leisurely ate and talked. Larent took the opportunity to take in the moods of his family.

Thomas and Arian sat together at the table, talking quietly about the group's possible next steps. They'd arrived back from their trip into town less than half an hour ago, and they currently sat so closely together, Larent suspected Arian would either pull back in sudden realization or pull Thomas into his lap. The sexual tension between the two seemed to have lessened, letting everyone know something had happened. Larent would normally poke fun at Arian, but he found he was genuinely pleased for them and decided not to dampen the mood. He hoped Arian avoided self-sabotaging.

Whyldon and Sara stood at the counter, and occasional snippets of their conversation told Larent they were reviewing household finances. Whyldon's slight smile indicated a positive conversation. His general mood had improved over the last few weeks, although Larent knew he was still angry about the concealment of Nawalya's visions. He'd been helping Larent with training, and Larent could measure his improvement.

Still, things were awkward between the captain and Nawalya. Every so often, Larent caught brief glances between the two. He had decided not to get involved, but Larent knew Nawalya had come to a decision of some sort, and as much as he wanted to ask, Larent was afraid of the answer.

Absent-mindedly, Larent held out a piece of toast with jam for Collette, not putting it down until she took it. She gave him a playful glare but easily complied. He knew she was feeling much better, and as a result, she'd been eating more, but Larent found he liked finding small ways to show his love and devotion. Sharing food was an easy demonstration of his care, and his belief had led him to usually carry a small bag of dried fruit or nuts when they left the house. Glancing out the window, the bright sunshine and sparse spots of snow reminded Larent of the mild weather. He decided he wanted to enjoy it. He stood and held out a hand to Collette. "Want to head out for a bit?"

"Sure," the queen agreed. She put her napkin on the table, then took Larent's hand as she stood.

Instead of leading Collette outside right away, he led her upstairs to what had become their bedroom.

"How do you feel about spending the night, not here?" he asked, his grin mischievous.

"I think we probably don't mention it on our way out," Collette replied, her expression playful and bright.

"Well then," Larent said cheerfully. "My pack is ready to go. We can grab blankets, toss them out the window, and they'll never know.

"Then get on it," Collette directed. "Arian gets suspicious when you drag out your funny little plots."

"Yeah, but tormenting Arian is the fun part." Larent stripped two layers of quilts from the bed and folded them as tightly as

he could before showing them into his pack. "You need anything else? It's too warm for the snow."

"We can grab my coat on the way out. I've been in colder weather with less."

Larent nodded and finished gathering a few more needed supplies before tossing the pack out the window. "I'd say we should follow after it, but I'm less likely to get stabbed tomorrow if they see us leaving."

"They'll also know something's up if you try to sneak out the window. Especially after we went upstairs for your proposed outing."

"It would still be fun," Larent joked. They headed back downstairs, past the kitchen, and out into the garden. There, Larent retrieved his pack.

"Where to?" Collette asked, letting Larent lead the way.

"There's a clearing I found the other day, about half an hour's walk. The trees were large enough and closely spaced to protect against the wind and snow while giving a good view of the night sky." He led them toward the clearing. "Feeling up for the walk? I can find something closer."

"Listen to you worrying like Arian," Collette joked.

She was in good spirits, something Larent loved to see. She deserved to be happy, to find joy where she could. And naturally, Larent wanted nothing more than to play along. He gave a full-body shiver. "By the Lady, I would never take away Arian's favorite pastime of worrying over you. Next time smack me."

"I'd rather tease you."

"Whatever makes you happiest, Freckles," Larent said, honestly meaning it. Larent would give and do anything to see her smile. He didn't always voice it, but he made sure Collette never doubted him.

The two walked for some time, fingers laced together, enjoying the comfortable silence. Every so often, he'd point out something silly or interesting, and he wondered how much more there would be to see come spring. They arrived at the small clearing soon enough. The snow was gone, thank the Lady, but the ground was frozen. They had the skills and supplies to make their time together pleasant.

Larent removed the pack from his shoulder and unpacked the blankets. He spread them out on the ground, layering them for comfort. If they didn't prove warm enough, he could always start a fire. "We lucked out. Just frozen ground to contend with," he said happily.

"So no digging of holes while we're out here," Collette observed. "You'll have to find other ways of entertaining me."

"I'm sure I'll figure something out," Larent quipped with a rakish grin.

"Oh, no doubt," Collette replied. Once the blankets were situated, she took a seat in the middle, stretching her legs out in front of her.

Larent settled next to her, draping his arm around Collette's shoulders and pulling her a little closer. "I'll start a fire in a little bit," he promised. "We still have decent daylight."

"A few hours at least," Collette agreed, resting her head against his shoulder.

Larent adjusted long enough to pull one of the blankets around him. They'd been in a clearing before, months ago now, but he couldn't compare the horrific memory with the present. The weather was nicer. They were together, and he planned on marrying her at some point. He also knew he could never embrace his wolf should trouble arise.

"Tell me something," he invited.

"Hmm," Collette replied at first. "I'm pretty sure Arian is getting used to having Thomas's hands on him."

Larent cackled, unable to help himself. "Still not sure he's ready for certain types of touching yet, but you're right."

"I think it's sweet. He deserves happiness and something to look forward to. There's not a lot of time to leisurely enjoy things once spring properly comes."

"True," Larent agreed. "Arian will love recruiting and strategizing once we start gathering an army. Nawalya, too." He pressed his lips against her temple. "There won't be any real time alone for just the two of us, and Lady knows I will miss it more than I can say. Selfishly, I am going to take every opportunity to steal you away. I hope Thomas will do the same for Chuckles."

"I think he will," Collette decided, her voice soft and contemplative. "Though I think Thomas will be busy with the political components of regaining the throne."

Thomas's role in the upcoming struggles was obvious to Larent. Thomas was a great speaker and held an intellect most could not conceive. Despite the name-calling the fletcher had been guilty of in the past, Larent had grown to like and respect Thomas since he'd joined their group.

"Have you decided if you're revealing yourself, or will you lurk in the shadows while Thomas speaks on your behalf?" Larent didn't know what he thought the better option would be, though the household saw many debates on the topic.

"I agree with Nawalya. I have to show myself," Collette said, and Larent detected a hint of uncertainty. "Given the injuries and the weather, I can justify hiding while confined and healing. People will understand the caution. I'm healed now, and spring is coming, so I have to be willing to do the hard thing."

"I think your followers and supporters will understand your decisions," Larent agreed as he gently carded his fingers through her hair. "Many will likely be elated. They'll have a renewed sense of hope for things to get better."

"I hope you're right. We'll know, either way, in another month or so." Collette still sounded uncertain, and though

Chapter Thirty

Larent knew she had to decide for herself, he found himself wishing, once again, for the ability to protect her from everything.

Looking down at her, Larent used his free hand to cup her face. "You're clever, strong, and more of a fighter than most people in your position would be. I will be beside you no matter what you choose to do, even if your choice is running away with me and living out the rest of our lives having grand adventures."

She nearly scoffed in response. "How many times has Arian or Nawalya implied they would go on a literal suicide mission in Quenall and take as many people with them as possible if I decided to do anything other than regain the throne? Even without knowing their possible intentions, I feel responsible for my people, but I can't deny how nice being here and just living has been."

"Just being here with you has been one of the most gratifying times in my life," Larent easily admitted. He let his hand drop to his side, but he continued holding Collette close. "And if you want a quiet life on a farm, I will talk to them. We can come up with another solution for the betterment of Coralia if you want something other than being queen. You deserve to be able to make choices for your happiness, and you deserve to do it without the weight of their impulsive decisions on your shoulders. You aren't obligated to live your life in the service of others."

His words didn't inspire a smile or a laugh, but something contemplative appeared in her expression. "You know, sometimes I think Arian and Nawalya view the world in very simple, almost shallow terms. Like, if they just kill enough terrible people, only the well-intentioned, altruistic people will be left." She let out a sigh and shook her head. "It makes me think of Zeph. He was a good person, once."

Larent leaned back on the blanket, and he reached up to pull her down so she was resting her head against his shoulder. "He was a good person despite the constant sulking and complaints?"

"Yes," Collette confirmed. "I understood some of his apathy. He always felt as though the world denied him love and appreciation. Rhoslyn Almeida used his weaknesses to sway him."

Larent could see it, although the open discussion of Zephraim brought another question to mind. "Does it bother you, knowing some of the things I did with Zephraim for information?"

Collette was quiet for a few minutes before she answered. "I don't think so. You had your reasons, and it's not like I'm judging you for anything in your past. And he's not actually my brother."

"Still, you were raised as siblings," Larent pointed out.

"We were," Collette agreed, though she added context Larent had not considered before. "But not in the way most siblings are raised. Zephraim's mother didn't particularly like me or my mother, even when my mother was long dead. I was the heir to the throne, so she was civil."

"Really? With the way Zephraim used to talk, I assumed you two grew up together. He may have bitched a lot, but I always thought he was fond of you. It's why the whole mess with him turning on you caught us off guard."

"He was fond of me," Collette confirmed. "He still viciously mocked me when I was arrested."

Anger flooded into Larent, and he promised himself he would punish Zephraim for the harm he'd caused Collette. "I'm sorry, Freckles. You deserve so much more than you've been given."

"I'm happy with you," Collette pointed out.

"I'm happy with you as well." Larent breathed in her scent and let the quiet settle around them for a few minutes. "Tell me something else."

"You should tell me something."

He signed, but he knew what he wanted to say. "I'm worried about Nawalya," he admitted. "And I'm afraid to talk to her about it."

"Why?"

"I'm unsure of her mental state since the confrontation with Whyldon. He was justifiably angry and hurt by concealing her vision, but I feel like she's come to the wrong decision about how to proceed with him. She just seems so tired and defeated, and I don't like it." Larent knew better than to attempt resolving the situation, but he wished to do something.

"I think you need to accept we have no way of knowing what is right and wrong for Nawalya, or Whyldon, or the possibility of their reconciliation. I understand his anger even if I don't like how he's expressed it," Collette said, providing reason.

"He yells at you again, and things will not end well, no matter what we did or didn't do," Larent said, a promise he would try to keep. "You're right, though. I can't resolve the issues between Whyldon and Nawalya, but I worry. I also worry Arian is going to sabotage everything with Thomas. And there's nothing I can do about it."

Collette nodded in agreement. "No, there isn't, especially with how much time you spend managing them and their emotions." She offered him a warm smile. "I know you use a lot of humor because of their trauma. You can offer support and advice, but they are going to do what they do."

"Don't we all?' Larent asked. "You're right, and I will be there all the same."

"I know you will, and you've identified another reason why I love you."

"Why?" he asked.

"You just said why," she replied, looking up at him with a playful grin.

"Because I try and take care of two suicidal elves who have more trauma than sense sometimes?" He chuckled and nipped at her nose.

She laughed, her contentment shining in her expression. "How about, because you do not hesitate to care for those you love?"

"I like the way you phrase it better, Freckles," Larent replied. They fell into a comfortable silence. Larent hoped for many, many more years of moments like these with her. "Tell me something."

She looked up at him again. "You should kiss me."

"My pleasure, Freckles," he replied in a whisper, and after small adjustments in their positions, he pressed his lips to Collette's, kissing her slowly. He pulled her closer, enjoying her warmth, her softness. He hummed with pleasure as her arms went around him and her lips coaxed him into a deeper kiss.

He nudged her back against the blankets, not insistent, but as inviting and suggestive as Collette's delectable mouth was proving. Her long, carob hair haloed around her, illuminating her beauty all the more. He followed her down, careful to avoid resting his weight on her while he chased her lips. As they kissed, he ran a hand along her side, the warmth of her skin radiating even through the fabric of her clothes.

His lips moved from her mouth, and Larent brushed his lips down her jawbone and to her neck, delighting in the soft gasps of pleasure escaping Collette. He nipped at the dip between her neck and shoulder, then soothed the spot with more kisses. "Tell me something," he requested in a near pur.

"You shouldn't stop," she replied as her fingers traced up the back of his neck and into his hair.

Larent nipped at her neck again. "What would you do if I stopped, Freckles?"

"Find somewhere to bury you and tell the others you ran off," she said with a breathy laugh.

"Sounds like a good story." A hand moved to rest just beneath her breasts. "I need you to tell me exactly what I'm not supposed to stop doing."

"And why do you need me to be so explicit?" Collette asked.

"Because I need to know you want to be with me as much as I want to be with you," he replied, feeling a little breathless himself. "I need to know what you want and don't want."

She gave him a soft smile, then leaned up to kiss him. "I will," she said when the kiss broke. "Because trust me, I want you even more."

Larent crushed his mouth to hers and finally brought his hands up to her cup her breast through her shirt. He let his thumb trace over the soft material, tempting the little sensitive bud just beneath to harden. He repeated the efforts when Collette softly moaned against his mouth. Encouraged by her response, he continued the gentle brush of his thumb as he kneaded her breast.

She moaned again, soft and intoxicating for Larent. He'd never wanted anyone the way he wanted her, but then, he'd never loved anyone the way he loved her. He knew she felt the same if the way she responded and clung to him was of any indication. He kissed the corner of her mouth, down her jaw, and back to the space on her neck. He nibbled and sucked at the sensitive skin, his body craving more of her as she pressed up against him in response.

When he lifted his head to admire his work, he knew she would have a noticeable mark just above her collarbone. Larent was tempted to leave more nmarks. Experimentally, he opened the first button of her shirt, pushing aside the fabric to reveal more of her skin. Pale and dotted with freckles, he yearned to lavish Collette with attention.

He continued kissing along her collarbone and down as he slowly undid the buttons of her shirt. His lips finally made it to the dip between her breasts, though he kept things slow and gentle.

"You're such a fucking tease," she said and laughed.

"You thought I wouldn't be?" he playfully asked.

He pushed the fabric back, fully revealing her soft, large breasts and her stomach. He took in the various scars, an older one across her shoulder and four newer marks on her side and stomach. Pink and shiny, they demanded attention, and he traced his fingers along the marks. Methodically, Larent kissed each of the scars, starting with her shoulder before moving to her stomach. He would never fully forgive himself for the ones he'd left, and the small act of acknowledging what he'd done felt necessary.

Afterward, he didn't feel quite as playful, so he traced his kisses back up her body and took a rosy nipple into his mouth. She gasped, and her body jerked from the surprise of it before relaxing back against the blanket.

As his tongue circled the hard nub, he relished the sounds of pleasure escaping her lips with urgent frequency. Somehow, Larent restrained himself from giving in to her right away. Instead, he ran his hands down her sides again, one resting on her hip while the other unbuttoned her pants. He then traced his fingers along her stomach once more, then sat up so he could remove her boots. Larent wanted to see all of her, even if he was in no rush. Taking his time with Collette and learning her intimately required patience and meticulous observation.

Boots removed and put to the side, Larent turned back to her. "Lift your hips for me," he requested, and he pulled her trousers down her long legs. When she was completely naked and he could take all of her in, Larent swore he could not breathe for long seconds. Even when he could, he did not hesitate to lower himself down to kiss her deeply. Without one word, he tried to convey the depth of his love for her, his willingness to follow her regardless of the path.

"I love you," he whispered before kissing down her chest and stomach again. He braced a hand on her hip while the other traced teasing patterns along her thighs and around her center.

"Love you," Collette managed through a groan. Prompted by her need, he made feather-light touches across her core, and though Collette groaned again, it was in delicious frustration. "Larent," she said. "You're getting really close to the line."

"What line?" he asked, still inching closer without giving her the craved stimulation.

"You know." He did and watching her body squirm and flush with need drove him to tease her more.

"Do I?" he mused before kissing along her hip bone. "Maybe you should remind me."

"It's going to be a damned shame when you don't return to the house, Larent."

"Oh, it will," he agreed, smiling deviously to himself. "'Cause you'll miss this." Now situated between her legs and close enough to her core, Larent finally gave her what she wanted, licking and sucking at her hot center. He kept his gaze upward, wanting to see every single reaction.

"Fuck," she proclaimed roughly, her eyes closing in sheer pleasure. A hand tangled into his hair, and the gentle pull only encouraged him forward. He spent several long minutes, using every skill and technique he knew to please her. "Larent," she nearly pleaded as he slowed the pace, knowing it drove her wild.

"I've got you," he promised before returning to his target. He began teasing with his fingers as well as his mouth, and when

she gripped at the blankets beneath her, he knew it wouldn't be long, and the thought had him aching with desire.

Just as he knew she was teetering on the edge, he moved to kiss her thigh, and he ceased teasing her with his fingers.

"Fuck," she growled, her growing frustration evident in her tone.

Larent lightly chuckled to himself, brushing his fingers along her inguinal groove. "Yes?" he asked her. He considered pausing to see if she would answer him, but Larent felt as though stopping might be going too far. Besides, he found himself obsessed with the taste of Collette, and he happily lowered his head between her thighs so he could focus all of his attention on her sensitive bud. Teasing put aside, he did everything he'd learned worked best, and even when her muscles spasms and limbs shook, he continued.

Larent loved the way she gasped as he pumped his fingers in and out of her hot core to add to the sensations.

"I swear by every possible deity, Larent..." she managed before groaning.

He glanced up at her, devious glee in his eyes, and sucked on her clitoris. She soon came again, more quickly, but no less intense. He kept a hand on her hip, one Collette grasped as she came and continued holding as Larent's oral assault did not cease. As much the pulsing from below reminded him of his need with every passing second, the sort of pleasure he received from pleasuring her went far beyond anything he'd shared with another person.

"Larent, you have to stop," Collette breathed out, half laughing. "I need a break."

He immediately slowed his fingers. "One more. You can give one more, yeah?" he asked. "If not, I can stop."

Her breathing slowed, though she shook her head. "Fuck, I need...something."

"Do you need this?" Larent asked, making slight changes in the positioning of his fingers so he could massage the sensitive nub with the pad of his thumb. Larent moved back up her body to kiss Collette, letting her taste herself on his lips and tongue. She kissed him back, her movements desperate and clinging as her hips moved in tandem with his hand.

"I've still got you," he whispered against her lips. She held him tighter as she came a third time, just as intense, but rendering her loose-limbed and exhausted. Still, she clung to him long after the sensations passed.

Larent removed his fingers, bringing them up to his mouth to lick before settling beside her, a hand resting on her stomach. "How are you feeling?"

"You treasonous motherfucker," she said with genuine, happy affection.

Larent threw back his head and cackled. "So, I should start again?"

"Fuck no," Collette said with a laugh. "Off limits."

Larent chuckled and sat up just enough to pull a blanket around Collette before settling again. He kissed her and draped an arm around her. He smiled when she closed the distance between them. "I love you, Freckles."

"Love you, too."

He kissed her again, feeling content to stay wrapped up with her for as long as she wanted. "Get some rest. I'll start a fire once it gets too cold. We have all night."

"Okay," Collette easily agreed. "I'm going to want more of you later, though."

"I was thinking the same about you," he replied as he drew her closer. He smiled contentedly to himself as she drifted off to sleep.

Chapter Thirty-One

Morning came far too early, and Collette was tempted to remain bundled up next to Larent on their pile of blankets. There had been no overnight snow, and the fire still burned nearby, though it was slowly dying. She opened her eyes and noted the sunrise, thinking it best to pack up and head back to the house.

Except, Collette didn't want to rise. Exhaustion from the previous night's multiple rounds of sex left her with little desire but to stay where she was. Had she not suspected Arian to show up at any minute and chastise them for leaving without letting anyone know where they'd gone, she might have given in to her whims. Thank the spirits she and Larent had the sense to get dressed.

"We have to go back, soon," she mumbled to Larent. She knew he was barely awake, but she felt him move from behind her.

"It's comfortable here," he said through a wide yawn.

She didn't get up right away. "The fire is burning out."

"But it's not out yet."

Chapter Thirty-one

Collette huffed a laugh, pulling away so she could sit up. She stretched, feeling relaxed in a way she hadn't for months. "Do you want me to leave you out here?"

Larent made a noise akin to a whine and sat up. Collette had learned he was not a morning person in their months of knowing one another, but his current reaction was funny. He automatically reached for her and pulled her into a gentle kiss, one she happily returned.

"Did I help make getting up a little easier?" she asked in a whisper.

"I suppose, even though I resent having to be up," he faux-complained.

"Then let's go back to the house," she suggested. "The bed is warmer, and it's early enough we can get some rest."

"True," Larent agreed. He yawned, stretched, then lumbered to his feet with a lack of grace. After stretching again, he offered his hand to Collette, and when she took it, he pulled her to her feet. She responded by kissing him, arms going around him when he responded so positively.

When the kiss came to a natural conclusion, the two agreed to clean up the site. The blankets were folded and stored, the fire extinguished, and signs of their brief occupancy were erased as much as possible. She half suspected Arian would venture out to make sure they'd done the job well enough.

Once they began the trip back to the house, Collette laced her fingers with Larent's. "I'm surprised either of us can walk," she observed cheerfully.

"There is something to say about the healing power of good sex," Larent casually suggested.

"Shut up," she said, shaking her head.

"There is no proof I'm wrong," Larent insisted. He lifted their joined hands and placed a quick kiss on her knuckles.

"Other than me knowing you're wrong?" she asked. She stepped over a puddle of half-frozen sludge.

He looked down at her, grinning lazily. "And how, exactly, do you know I'm wrong?"

"Because I know the expressions you make when you make up bullshit," she retorted.

Larent let out a gasp and pressed his free hand to his chest in mock horror. "How dare you accuse me of making things up. You'd be too sore to walk if I was lying."

"Who says I'm not sore?" she asked cheekily. "You put in a valiant effort."

"Don't I always?"

"I have no idea. I only have last night to go on," Collette reminded him.

"Don't worry," Larent insisted. "We have plenty of time for more."

They walked for a time before the house came into view. Collette couldn't help but note how different the black and white cottage looked without the excess of snow. It was warmer, friendlier, and she wished she could see it in the summer or autumn when the lush plant life would bring on new experiences. She wouldn't get her wish, she knew. She had responsibilities.

As they moved closer, Collette noticed a tall, broad figure near the door. She stopped walking, not recognizing the person at first. She sensed Larent stopping alongside her, his gaze moving from the person in the distance to take in her furrowed brow.

"Wonder who he is," Larent said.

"Same…" Collette replied, the words having passed her lips before realization dawned. Her eyes widened in delight and a grin spread across her face. Letting go of Larent's hand, she started sprinting towards the house.

"Rion!" she exclaimed as she came within arm's reach, and the tall man lifted her in a great bear hug. She hadn't seen the man in more than a year, but their physical connection and exuberant greeting made it feel as though no time had passed at all.

Rion put her back on her feet and stepped back as he looked her over. "You look like shit, Joss," he said, his tone amused, but the playfulness didn't quite reach his eyes.

"Didn't you hear? I've been chucked out of the palace. Trauma leaves its marks."

"I did hear something about an overthrow, yeah," he replied.

Larent reached them and looked amused and curious if the twitching at the corner of his lips suggested anything. "Damn, Freckles. You have great taste. You'd have to climb him like a tree."

Collette laughed. "I have," she confirmed.

Larent wiggled his eyebrows. "Sounds hot. Maybe one day, you can show me." Larent nodded at Rion. "I'm Larent. You're the famous Rion I've heard so much about."

Rion gave a nod and tilted his head, taking in Larent. "I've heard about you, too. I got a distinctly different impression."

Collette narrowed her brow in confusion. "Who have you been talking to about Larent?"

Larent cocked his head to the side in a sign of confusion. "Not a lot of people outside those here actually know me." He scratched at his stubble then opened his mouth to speak again, only to be cut off as a commotion from the other side of the house caught the group's attention.

Hurried footsteps and Nawlaya calling out had Larent turning to look back. Collette shrieked in horror as Tolan's fist connected with Larent's face from the left. Larent went to his knees, and Tolan followed, raining down violent punches with persistent speed. Somehow, Larent was able to defend himself, and a few long seconds later, Tolan began attacking back.

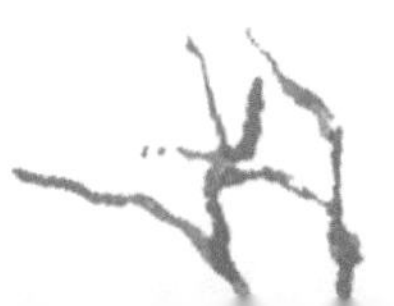

"What the fuck are you doing, Tolan?" Collette yelled, though she doubted she was heard, or paid attention to, given the fury in which he fought. Larent's reaction time and the way he brought his arms up to block the worst of Tolan's blows demonstrated his better skill in hand-to-hand combat, but there was no doubt Tolan was going to beat him to a bloody pulp without intervention.

Rion's arm went around her before she could intervene. "Someone has to stop them!" she insisted.

Arian stepped forward, but instead of stopping the fight, he called out Larent's name and tossed a dagger within arm's reach of the fighting men.

Larent slammed a fist hard into Tolan's side, buying him enough time to grab the dagger. A dark flash of anger registered on the shifter's face, and Collette was convinced Larent intended to use deadly force against Tolan. She didn't want anyone harmed, not when she knew how she would always feel for Tolan.

Larent didn't follow through with her suspicions. Instead, he slashed out at Tolan, the blade catching Tolan from the right hip to the left nipple. The cut wasn't deep, but blood flowed from the wound as the man darted back from Larent and into Arian and Nawalya's awaiting arms. They secured the half-elf tightly. He struggled against them, and Nawalya's patience reached an end. Retrieving a dagger from her side, she slammed the hilt into Tolan's temple in a swift move. The effort didn't knock Tolan out, but it did daze him enough to make holding him easier.

With the fight effectively ended, Collette was able to free herself from Rion's grasp. Quickly going to Larent, she knelt to check on him. Several cuts on his face, the puffiness of what promised to be bad bruising, and bloody teeth told her Tolan had come dangerously close to really hurting Larent. She barely registered Sara, Whyldon, and Thomas standing in the doorway, watching the scene with varying levels of interest and concern.

Putting hands on either side of Larent's face, a strategic and affectionate move, she gently brushed a thumb across his cheek. He needed healing. "Are you okay?" she asked.

Larent gave her a pained smile. "I've had worse, but I'll be alright, Freckles."

"Liar," Collette replied. She ignored Tolan. Taking a deep breath, Collette focused on her magic. The tingling warmth rose in her hands and flowed into Larent. The knitting together of cuts and abrasions registered with her, relaxing her worry for Larent.

Distantly, she felt the struggling presence of the wolf working to hold back the blood magic. Thankfully, Zephraim's influence was restrained for now, and when her hands left Larent's face, she did not feel drained as she had before. "What about now?"

Larent closed his eyes. His hands came up to allow him to brush his fingers across her arms. "Better. Are you okay?"

"Of course," she replied.

Larent gave her a skeptical look and caressed Collette's face. "Are you alright?" he asked again.

"I am," she promised. More quietly, she added, "This isn't like last time. Healing usually isn't very rough on me."

"Good," Larent replied. "I'd ask how the violence affected you, but I'm certain you've seen worse." He sighed and moved to stand, wincing a little with the effort. He glared at Tolan who was still dazed.

"Will you retrieve my medical kit?" Arian asked Thomas, and the fletcher disappeared from the door.

Rion walked over and offered Collette a hand up.

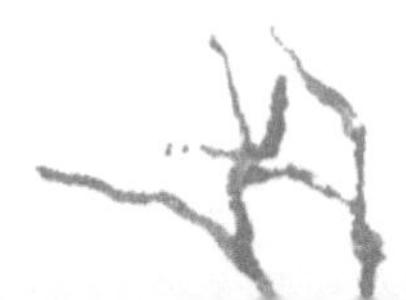

"I guess he's who you meant when you said you'd heard shit about me," Larent said to the taller man, nodding his head in Tolan's direction.

"You would be correct," Rion said.

Collette turned to focus on Tolan who, admittedly, didn't look like he could stand on his own. "What the actual fuck?" she demanded of him in a low, dangerous voice.

Tolan shook his head, then shook it again. He grimaced in pain but met her furious gaze. "You were dead. I was told you were dead, and he did it." Holding up a wrist, Tolan shook his hand so her gold bracelet could be viewed. "We found the clearing."

Collette knew she should have suspected part of the response, but she hadn't. She also hadn't expected to feel so much sympathy for her former lover, and she felt the seething rage drain from her face.

She let out a sigh, and wordlessly approached Tolan to examine him. Her lips pressed together in a thin line as her mind warred over the hurt of his abandonment and her deep desire to protect him and heal him. A particularly nasty bruise was growing darker on his temple, a souvenir of Nawalya's dagger. Without thinking, she reached out and touched her fingers to the warm skin. Tolan flinched back at first, perhaps unsure of who she was or what she was doing. He relaxed after a moment, and the bruise lightened considerably. She repeated the action with the cut across his torso.

Tolan's eyes shone with clarity as the obvious concussion Nawalya had given him vanished. "Thank you," he breathed in relief but then his eyes narrowed.

Collette didn't have to look back as Larent's arms wrapped around her.

"You still okay?" Larent whispered to her.

Chapter Thirty-one

Tolan pulled against Arian and Nawalya's grips. "Get away from her! Don't you fucking touch her!"

"Shut the fuck up," Rion said, glaring at Tolan. "You had your outburst and made sure to drag Joss into the middle of it. Now stop before one of us makes you."

Tolan shrank back immediately and bowed his head. "I'm sorry," Tolan said.

Whyldon stepped from the doorway and out into the yard. His expression was calm, and he held his hands out in small, consoling gestures. He excelled at diffusing most situations, which had been one of the reasons he'd been promoted to guard captain. "Why don't Rion and I take Tolan to talk. Arian and Thomas probably need to check the rest of Larent's injuries." Thomas had just returned from fetching Arian's kit, but he held it while they figured out what to do with Tolan. Whyldon glanced at Collette. "Assuming you are fine with us taking Tolan while everyone cools down."

Collette nodded and took a deep breath through her nose.

"Maybe I should go into the house before you let him go," Larent suggested to Arian and Nawalya. A quick nod from Arian had Larent kissing Collette on her cheek before releasing her. He disappeared through the front entrance of the home.

Once Larent was out of sight, Arian released Tolan, but Nawalya grabbed the former gladiator by the front of his shirt, getting right in his face. "You will not attempt violence against anyone in our party again," she growled, her voice as hard and commanding as Collette ever heard it. "Try anything again, and I will gut you. Collette and Larent have been through enough."

"Nawalya," Arian said softly.

"Shut up, Arian," Nawalya snapped. She pushed Tolan toward Whyldon and went into the house.

Tolan stood dumbstruck before looking at Collette. She read regret and uncertainty in his expression. And perhaps…relief.

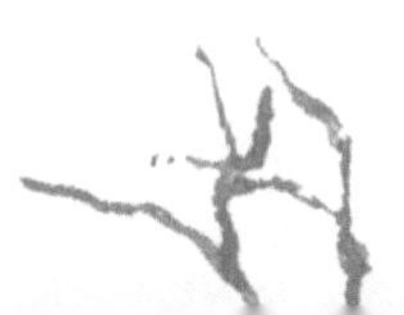

"I'm so happy you're alive," he said. With a small hesitation, he unhooked the bracelet from his wrist and held it out to her.

Something broke in Collette as Tolan held out the bracelet, and she realized the gesture represented the true end of what had existed between them. And she thought being abandoned hurt.

Taking another breath, Collette accepted the bracelet, her jaw set and her mind begging her to remain calm in appearance. She wanted to scream, and she was pretty certain at some point in the near future, she was going to cry. She pocketed the trinket and swallowed. "I'll be back," she told the remaining members of the group. She walked away without waiting for a response, thankful her stinging eyes hadn't betrayed her.

Tolan watched as Collette walked away, and he hung his head and breathed out harshly. He had reacted badly, and he knew it. He hadn't intended to attack Larent, but seeing Collette alive and very happily standing next to Larent with at least one visible love bite… It just set something off in him. Something dark and ugly, and the next thing he knew, he was on top of Larent. His anger, worry, and fear drove him to hurt the man who had caused him so much grief. He closed his eyes and shook his head, ashamed of himself.

"You fucked things up even more than before, didn't you?" Rion observed, though when Tolan looked up, he saw the ginger-haired man staring off in the direction Collette had disappeared.

"He did," Whyldon confirmed. Tolan stood in the front garden with Whyldon and Rion, the others having retreated into the house. "How did you find us, and when did the two of you run into one another?" he asked. He motioned for Rion and

Tolan to follow him, leading down a path away from the house going opposite of where Collette had walked.

Tolan followed without complaint, knowing he was lucky to be allowed there after his obscene display. He spoke first. "I encountered a man who claimed responsibility for killing Collette at a tavern in northern Galel," Tolan explained. "He was showing her bracelet off, so I questioned him. Through interrogation, he admitted to a giant wolf holding primary responsibility for her death."

Tolan had to pause and remind himself Collette was very much alive. The worst had not happened. Rion was able to pick up the story.

"I started hearing rumors of an attack sometime after parting ways with Thomas Fletcher. So I started investigating. Tolan and I both found the campsite where Joss apparently bled out. From there, we used our knowledge and found our way here," Rion said, his boots squelching in the muddy patches of dirty snow littering the ground. He crossed his arms and looked over to Whyldon. "What in the fuck happened after? She looks like she's about half a breath away from falling over, and she should be much more recovered than she is now. I've never seen her so sickly."

"Blood magic happened," Whyldon said bluntly. "She decided she could use her magic against it, while she was bleeding out, and you saw the results. Granted, she's much improved considering she did nearly die."

Tolan sucked in a breath. He knew Larent wouldn't hurt her intentionally, no matter what else had been going on. "Blood magic was used on Larent to attack Collette?" He sighed and tried to pull himself together, shoving his hands into his coat pockets. "Do you know who did it?"

Whyldon nodded grimly. "Zephraim."

The road they walked transitioned from dirt to pebbles, and the crunching noise beneath their feet left Tolan feeling a little on edge. Or perhaps, it was the news of Zephraim. Of everyone who hated Collette, he didn't think Zephraim had it in him. Rhoslyn maybe, but not Zephraim.

"Since when does that twerp have magic?" Rion asked with an outraged scoff. "He can barely brush his hair alone, and I'm supposed to believe he used a blood magic spell?"

"I don't know if he has magic or learned it," Whyldon said, shrugging "I don't even know if the difference matters. However, Collette said she saw him when she was fighting the magic, and it's not as though he wouldn't have the means to carry it out."

Rion uncrossed his arms, but his hands curled into fists by his side. "It makes me want to go to Quenall and have a word with the false king."

"Trust me, I have contemplated it more than once," Whyldon replied darkly.

"I would help," Tolan muttered as he thought over everything. Oh, he really had fucked up.

"Despite what you did, I believe it," Whyldon said. They came to a pause outside a field. Nothing grew just yet, but the ground had been worked. Whyldon turned to meet Tolan's gaze, his expression as neutral as possible even with Tolan's suspicions of harsh judgment. "Where have you been, Tolan?"

Tolan didn't say anything at first, just stood there as he came to grips with one more error in a lifetime of errors. He took a breath, letting the thought go. "I went to get help," he explained. He dug into the pockets of his leather coat, and retrieved a letter, holding it out to Whyldon who took it and began reading.

To Her Rightful Majesty, Queen Collette of Gaillane,

Chapter Thirty-one

My cousin tells me of your troubles and the treason committed against you in the name of continued genocide and economic greed. While Fythias has a long and troubled past with Coralia, I cannot deny your efforts for change, both reported by my cousin as well as correspondence from the Nereids, have suggested a need to reevaluate old positions between my country and yours.

After lengthy discussions with Tolan and much consideration, I invite you to travel to Fythias where you will be my honored guest. Together, we will form a battle plan to take back what is rightfully yours. My resources, including fighters and weapons, will be at your disposal.

Your Obedient servant,
Alaoin Bialaor Eiero
High Ruler of the Fythians

"You've secured an army for Collette…" Whyldon breathed out in complete shock once he'd finished the letter.

"Apparently, I do have family. I just didn't know it," Tolan said.

"Apparently," Whyldon said as he refolded the letter. "Now, I have to ask why you left as you did. Collette would have followed you."

Tolan looked away again. "Because I was angry, hurt, and in a state of self-loathing and stupidity." He pulled the pendant from beneath his shirt, holding it up. The design resembled the seal on the letter, and as Whyldon did not question him, he continued. "I thought it was best if I made the trip on my own in case the necklace meant nothing. I realized my mistake hours later, but I knew I had crossed a line already, so I continued."

Whyldon ran a hand through his hair, as though he wasn't quite sure what to do or say despite his frustration. "Abandoning

Collette when you did was possibly one of the dumbest and most selfish things you could have done," he said, though not unkindly. "And even with the promise of an army," he held up the letter again, "I don't know how receptive she'll be."

"Well, fuck, it's not like she's going to think of herself for once," Rion said, rolling his eyes. "She'll accept the offer, knowing full well what everyone expects from her."

"You've known her disposition for more than a decade," Whyldon replied.

"I don't expect, or want, anything from her. I saw the marks on her neck and the affection for Larent. It's obvious they're together," Tolan said. "If she will take the letter and get an army to help her, that would be something. If I was allowed to travel with you again, it would be a miracle. But I won't ask anything from her. I don't deserve it."

"I think we know at least part of your claim is true," Rion replied with a pitying laugh.

Whldon shot a skeptical look in Rion's direction. "As though you don't?" he asked.

Rion shrugged. "I'm realistic and not making false claims about what I do or don't want."

Tolan laughed bitterly. "Of course, I wish for her to take me back, but I'm not stupid enough to think she would. Especially when she's with Larent."

"And she *is* with him," Whyldon confirmed with a nod. "They both woke up from the events in the clearing, and they decided they were together."

The confirmation told Tolan nothing he didn't already know. Collette and Larent had been building their relationship before he left. Always in subtle, little ways which would not have mattered individually. He pressed his lips together, picturing the whole thing.

Chapter Thirty-one

Whyldon sighed again and looked out into the bare field. "She wouldn't have pursued her feelings for Larent had you not left, and quite honestly, you were contributing to her stress before you left. Larent lets her escape when she needs to."

"I never suggested she would have," Tolan snapped, but he immediately held up his hands. "I'm sorry. I know she'd never betray me, and Larent wouldn't have attempted to facilitate a betrayal. Someone," he said, looking pointedly at Rion, "has helped me realize I've been an ass."

"Someone needed to," Rion replied. He motioned toward the letter Whyldon held. "We probably should talk to her about the promised army."

"I think it's best if the two of you present the option to her. I doubt she wants to see me right now," Tolan suggested. He wasn't about to presume he had her permission to stay. "I can stick around long enough to answer whatever questions she might have."

"Let's let her come back to the house before there is a discussion. I'm sure the others will want to listen in," Whyldon suggested. "We'd been planning on visiting the Nereid when spring came, but the letter could change things."

Tolan motioned for Whyldon to lead the way.

Chapter Thirty-Two

Larent stayed by the door listening to the shit show happening outside. The violent fight with Tolan had been enough, but Larent was genuinely surprised by the way Nawalya snapped at Arian. As he had revealed to Collette, Nawalya had been acting oddly since coming back from his grandparents, and her behavior with Arian further proved it. She came into the house soon after he had, pausing to kiss Larent on the cheek before going upstairs to her bedroom. He knew someone needed to check in with Nawalya, he just wasn't sure he was the right person to question her.

So caught up in his thoughts, he almost missed Collette walking off. Glancing out the window, he watched her go, noting the way she held her shoulders and the way she walked. She was barely keeping it together, and Larent held in the urge to go after her.

Instead, he pulled himself away from the window and went into the kitchen. He fell into one of the chairs by the table and waited for Arian. He would give Collette some time to process all of the shit she'd witnessed. Well, not too much time. He knew how easy it was to spiral, so ten minutes, maybe.

Closing his eyes, Larent started counting to himself, force-fully pushing away thoughts of Tolan's return. He was mostly successful when Arian, Thomas, and Sara came in.

"Basic patch," he told Arian. "I need to go."

Arian took his medical kit from Thomas and began opening it on the kitchen table. "You will sit there until I say you can go," Arian replied.

"Fuck waiting for permission. Freckles just wandered off into the forest alone and hurting," Larent insisted.

The argument left Arian unimpressed, judging by the raised eyebrow. "Has she not gotten mad at the rest of us for not allowing her to roam as needed?"

Larent met Arian's gaze, the corners of his lips downturned. "I'm not going out there to drag her back unwillingly or to make her feel trapped and controlled. If she tells me to go away, I will come back." Larent held out a hand for a potion or something to help him with the pain. Collette had been gone for several minutes, and he was growing anxious.

Arian let out an annoyed huff of breath and went through his kit. The carefully packed bottles and vials clinked together with more force than necessary. Arian held out two items, one a blue bottle Larent recognized as being for pain, and a second jar of a minty-smelling paste for the bruising.

"Make sure you take the liquid first. Then you may go," Arian instructed. He grabbed his kit and went up the stairs.

Thomas watched him. "Sun is barely up, and everyone is already on edge," he observed before following the elf. Larent couldn't help but feel guilty for the emotional labor the fletcher would be undertaking after the early morning events.

Sara stood by the table, hands on her hips. She looked at Larent sympathetically. "Would you prefer I finish healing you?" she asked.

Larent gave Sara a grateful smile. "Could you get the one on my back? Somehow the jackass got a hit." He held out the ointment to her.

Sara took the jaw, removed the lid, and examined the contents. "I don't need ointments and potions to heal you," she replied as she closed it and set it aside. "But you should use it all the same." She prompted Larent to lift his shirt, then pressed cool fingers against the bruised skin and Larent sighed in relief.

"I forgot you healed as well."

"I think so," Sara agreed with amusement. She lifted her fingers from his back and moved position so she was in front of him. "Where else?"

"Can you get my ribs? My face doesn't hurt much anymore."

"I believe my niece took care of your face," Sara pointed out. Again, she had Larent lift his shirt, and she pressed her fingers against his skin.

Larent laughed, finding himself super thankful she'd healed his ribs when he realized how badly laughing would have hurt. "She did, but I'm getting a headache from a combination of stress and my pissed off wolf."

Sara straightened. "I think Arian's pain potion will help with the headache," she pointed out. "The stress, from what I see, will likely get worse."

"I hope the potion works," Larent said, looking down. He didn't know how to resolve the stress. "And I'll be fine. My wolf doesn't like how I got my ass handed to me, or the perceived threat to Collette. He's calming down, though." Standing, Larent stretched his body. "Lady, I feel much better. Thanks."

Sara gave him a warm smile. "No problem. I'm happy to help. You can't exactly go chasing after a certain someone if you're too beat up."

"I would bring myself back from the dead if Collette needed me," he replied, his voice serious. He knew there was literally nothing he would not do for her. He thanked Sara again for her help, and he left the house, jogging in the direction Collette had gone. Thankfully, the ground was wet, and he soon found her footprints.

He followed along to the tree line near the woods, and once he stepped beyond, his tracking task grew a little more difficult. He walked for several minutes, listening and watching carefully for any sound or clue.

Eventually, he found her in a spot several yards into the woods, surrounded by trees and teeming with the sounds of animals waking to start their day. Light streamed through gaps in the tree covering above, and she stood, arms crossed protectively across her chest. Larent froze as he found her. Collette truly was the most beautiful person he'd ever known, inside and out.

"Hi, Freckles," he said gently.

She looked over at him, offering a small smile. She didn't appear to have had the expected breakdown, but her eyes were a little red and glassy, and he felt his heart lurch in his chest. He could think of no reason Collette should ever be sad enough to cry.

"How did you so easily escape Arian?" she asked.

"I told him to piss off," he answered as he approached her, arms outstretched to offer a hug. She walked into his embrace, pressing her forehead against his shoulder as her arms encircled him. He held her close, silently offering every ounce of possible support he could give. "Tell me something," he whispered into her hair.

"I hate almost everything right now," she replied, her voice hollow and sad.

"I don't blame you," he promised. "Tell me what you want to do about it. I will make it happen."

"It's not as though I would actually do what I want," Collette said.

"Tell me anyway."

She was quiet for a few moments, leaving Larent to wonder if she would answer. "I don't want this responsibility."

Larent breathed in deeply and held her closer. He wanted to tell her she could walk away, and he would go with her. He would kill anyone who tried to stop them. He would take her anywhere and live any life she desired.

He knew Collette didn't want to hear any of those promises because she would never let herself walk away. He also knew if he kept pushing, she would eventually force him away, and he couldn't fathom losing her. So, he would support her in a different way. He couldn't take her away from the life she was leading permanently, but he could take her away for a little while.

"Do you trust me?" he asked.

She lifted her head to look at him. "With everything."

He kissed her in response. When he broke, he walked her over to a mostly dry log, indicating for her to take a seat, which she did. "Can you wait for me to come back? Give me ten, maybe twenty minutes, and I'll take you somewhere for a few days. If you'd let me. No questions though," he joked.

"Okay," she agreed simply.

He expected her to refuse the offer, and his expression brightened. "Okay," Larent agreed. I will be right back." He leaned down and kissed her. "I love you, Collette," he said, caressing her cheek. He began the short trip back to the house. Sara was in the kitchen cooking when he entered, though he went for the stairs rather than greet her.

Inside the room he shared with Collette, he made quick work of packing a few of their things in their travel packs. He'd worked less than two minutes when he heard someone at the door. He was relieved to see Nawalya rather than Arian.

"Are you two coming back, or is she done?" she asked.

Larent stopped packing, and he turned to Nawalya. "How long have you known?" he asked, feeling his temper rise.

"About her not wanting to be queen or being on the verge of breaking?" Nawalya replied, looking down. "For a while, either way."

Larent couldn't help but slam his pack down on the dresser with more force than necessary. "From what I've overheard and she's told me, you and Arian have been discussing possible plans to go back to Quenall to handle things if she doesn't want to. You know what those plans do? They put even more pressure on her shoulders, because two elves running full tilt at the castle to kill off all the nobility in sight is a suicide mission. It's juvenile and makes her feel like she can't have one thing for herself." Larent realized he was shouting and quickly held up his hands. "I'm sorry. Shit, I didn't mean to…" He trailed off at the warm smile on Nawalya's lips.

"You should yell at me, and you should be mad at Arian because you're right. Not once have we truly considered Collette and what she wants. I don't think anyone here has, except you. It's time to make things right." Nawalya approached Larent and pulled him into a hug. "I'll deal with Arian. Just focus on getting her out of here." She turned to leave the room, only to encounter Arian in the doorway, arms crossed as he glared.

"Deal with me how?"

Larent swallowed, knowing the needed conversation had the potential to turn into a confrontation. "Collette and I are leaving."

"Leaving? Why?"

"I'm taking her home," Larent replied simply.

"You can't just up and leave because Tolan has appeared, Larent. There is too much to do."

Arian spoke calmly as though he were talking to a child, and Larent wanted to hit him. He might have if Nawalya hadn't stepped up, a finger pressing against Arian's chest.

"Stop treating Larent like he doesn't know what he's doing." Arian took a step back from the quiet anger radiating from Nawalya. "He's taking Collette away because she has reached her limits, and if you would stop and think, you would realize she needs time. Time to not be here. Time to come to terms with what has happened and what she wants. Time without all the stress we've put on her shoulders." Nawalya pushed Arian out of the doorway and strode off. "Let them go."

Larent eyed Arian wearily as he continued to pack, noting the confusion and pain in the elf's expression.

"I know she has been struggling, but perhaps I have missed how much," Arian said.

"Yeah, she's been getting progressively worse, and Tolan showing up didn't help. If she thought you wouldn't go off on a suicide mission, there's a good chance we'd have left already. If she ever told me she wanted to leave, I promise you I would take her and never looked back."

Arian sighed, crossing his arms. "Alright. Just your grandparents' house?"

Larent nodded and resumed attention on the bags. He thought he had everything they would need for a few days, so he gathered them and tossed them over one shoulder. He turned to Arian, ready to leave. "Talk to Nawalya while we're gone. She needs it right now."

Arian made an affirmative noise and stepped back, allowing Larent to pass him. "Be safe," Arian said.

"Always. You too, okay?" Larent headed down the stairs and back outside without another word to any of the occupants in the house. He had more important matters to tend to.

Chapter Thirty-Three

Zephraim's eyes shot open. As he lay in bed, surrounded by darkness, he was convinced he could not breathe. Her face. He'd seen her face in his dream. Pale, thin, and worried, but the face was unmistakably Collette's. Zephraim couldn't recall ever seeing his sister looking so gaunt and exhausted, and he could not concoct any reason his mind would conjure her face, looking so destroyed, while he slept.

He sat up, rubbing at his tired, gray eyes in an effort to self-soothe. Zephraim supposed he shouldn't have been surprised to dream of his sister. She was gone, and he was, undeniably, guilty for his role in her death. He was also terribly sorry and regretful, which were entirely different feelings than he'd expected to have when he'd cast the terrible blood magic spell.

But it hadn't felt like a dream. Even now, Zephraim would swear he'd felt her hands on his face, and his cheeks warming and tingling from her touch. Perhaps he was just imagining things. Still, the lingering unease made him doubtful.

Zephraim thought about going back to sleep, and as he opened the curtains surrounding his bed, he saw the faintest glimmer of daylight filling the room. The fire in the fireplace had extinguished, and the room was much colder with his bed coverings tossed aside. Rubbing his hands together for warmth, Zephraim decided he would find no rest. He rose from his bed, finding the fur-lined slippers he preferred nearby. He slipped his feet into them, then added the layer of his lush burgundy dressing gown.

He felt chilled but warmer, and he decided he would take advantage of the early morning to roam about the castle undisturbed. Leaving his quarters, Zephraim took the stairs to the lower floor of the palace.

Only a handful of servants were up at such an early hour. As Zephraim walked, he passed a man extinguishing lanterns along the corridors. Zephraim nodded to him in passing without stopping.

As he continued, step by step, Zephraim's mind continually went back to his dream of Collette. Was seeing her haunting face the price of blood magic? To be cursed by the specter of his sister for the rest of his life? He deserved it, to be sure. Killing Collette, betraying her as he had, earned him a tortuous existence. He knew, even if he would never say it, he'd fucked everything up, and he had no idea how to fix it.

Without meaning to, he found himself at the doors leading to the palace kitchen. He stood there, listening to the small sounds from inside, half debating on turning around. He doubted Diana Hawke wanted to engage with him. After all, he had the power to pardon Cremisius Hawke for his crimes, and he chose not to. He couldn't see allowing the former commander to return to the palace, let alone duty. Being guilty of murder limited Zephraim's options. He sighed, knowing he was going to bother the poor cook, and he pushed the door open.

Zephraim found Diana by the fire, using a poker to move around wood and ashes, perhaps in an attempt to coax the flames into something brighter and hotter. Her blonde hair hung over

one shoulder, though he noted the loose tie at the base of her neck. Usually, Diana wore it up, and Zephraim was left to conclude she had only been in the kitchen for a few minutes. The wafting scent from the oven suggested maybe an hour at most.

"Hello, Diana," he greeted and stifled a laugh when she jerked away from the fire, dropping the poker on the stone floor.

"Good morning, Your Majesty," she stammered, rising to her feet.

"No need for formalities," Zephraim replied, shaking his head to stop her from bowing. "I know you were not expecting me." The cook looked him over, and he laughed as he realized he was still dressed for bed. Zephraim appreciated having reasons to laugh after his sister inflicted him with mental and emotional assault. "Sorry. I woke far too early and knew I could not get back to sleep."

"It is your palace, Your Majesty. I should think you could wear just about anything within," Diana replied, giving him a genuine smile. She knelt to retrieve the fire poke, placed it in the correct position by the fireplace, and dusted her hands against her clean apron.

"I believe you are right," Zephraim agreed. He looked around the kitchen and saw very little had been accomplished thus far. The hour, and his presence, were to blame. "Would you mind terribly if I made some tea?"

Diana shook her head. "I would be happy to make you some."

Zephraim waved her off. "I can do as much for myself." Without waiting for a response, Zeph began the process of gathering the items he'd need. The kettle was soon filled with water and bubbling on the stove, and he was looking through the options for tea, uncertain of what he would like. A black tea, no doubt, to perk him up.

When he judged the water ready, he used a cloth to remove it from the heat source. "Can I make you a cup?" Looking over his shoulder, he saw her washing off a bowl of fruit, and again, saw the astonishment in her wide eyes at the offers.

"It's not necessary," she said.

"It isn't," Zephraim agreed. "But you are here, and it costs me nothing." Without waiting for a response, he located a second cup and made tea for both. Even as he poured water into the cups, Zephraim wondered why he was being so upbeat, so helpful. He knew his feelings about his dream left him off-kilter, but he questioned his behavior toward Diana. He liked her well enough, and she had never demonstrated anything resembling dislike or annoyance at seeing him, something he couldn't say about many others in his life.

He handed her the drink as he sipped from his own. "This was what I needed," he shared. The warm, earthy tea made him forget the draftiness of the palace, and he drank it in content silence for a few glorious moments. He even smiled as the cook consented to drink from her cup.

"I think a bit of honey might do it some justice," she determined. "Would you like some?"

Zephraim shook his head, feeling the longer red-gold curls gently bouncing on his face. "My mother never allowed honey as I was growing up," he explained, though he never knew why. "I recall, she did like to add dried orange to her tea sometimes. The flavor was unique."

"I recall many from Galel preferring orange in their tea," Diana said. She sipped from her cup once more and set it aside to go back to her washing. "The lords from Myrefall like it with lemon."

"Lemon is more suitable than orange," Zephraim declared with a chuckle. His tea was soon gone, and he decided against another serving. He could call for another soon enough if it was wanted.

Placing the cup near the sink, he watched as Diana moved her washed fruit to the counter. Along the back wall sat a series of knives. She selected a large one, with a thick blade and blunted top. The thing sliced expertly through the dark purple fruit with ease. Diana cut each into halves, pulled out a pit, then halved each piece before moving on to the next.

"Are you sure I can't make you something?" she asked Zephraim.

He gave her a pained smile. "I could not sleep, and I like your company, so I came here. Assuming my presence is okay with you."

"Of course," Diana assured him warmly. "But if one of the workers catches you down here, they're likely to hand you a knife to peel or dice something, Your Majesty."

"I have been warned," Zephraim said with a smile.

The door swung open, and in stepped Barris looking way too awake and cheerful for such an early morning. "Diana," the man declared, practically skipping into the room. "I am in need of tarts. It's life or death." He came up short seeing Zephraim with the cook, but instead of straightening or becoming serious, his smile got wider. "Your Majesty! It is wonderful to see you this morning. Have you eaten yet?"

"He has not," Diana replied.

"I was trying to wake up a bit before dining," Zephraim confessed.

"You look awake enough," Barris insisted. "Please, join me for tarts. Diana always has some set aside for me." He headed over to the oven. "Am I allowed to check today, or is your oven off-limits again?"

"I doubt they are ready yet, but the Mother forbid me from stopping you," Diana said, waving a hand dismissively in his direction.

Grabbing a towel, Barris pulled out two trays of tarts and put them on the cooling rack. Pulling out a plate, he put six aside and left them next to the tray. He grabbed three additional plates and placed two tarts on each before carrying them back to the table. "These are for you," he told Diana, emphasizing one of the plates. "You rose early to cook for me, and the least I can do is offer you one." Barris offered Zephraim a smile and indicated the other plate.

Zephraim took his tea to the table and sat after insisting Diana do as much. "Do you mean to tell me you had our delightful cook rise earlier than she would have to make you tarts?"

Barris looked sheepish and nodded. "It's a bad time of the month for Lynessea. Diana's tarts always make her feel better, so I put in a request last night."

"How very attentive of you," Zephraim said. Rhoslyn never seemed to need similar affection from him. Oh, she would accept them if presented, but the longer they were married, the less genuine her responses seemed.

"She is a good friend and loyal servant. It's the least I could do," Barris explained.

"She sounds like it," Zephraim confirmed. "And you should take her the tarts if she needs them. There should be no delay on my account."

Barris gave Zephraim a warm, understanding smile. "I always try to spend a few minutes with Diana when she grants me a favor. We are fortunate you are here to join us."

Unsaid was the fact that Diana was in the world alone, without her husband to keep her company. Zephraim considered he might need to do something about the Cremisius Hawke situation. "I did not anticipate sharing a meal with anyone this morning. It's quite nice."

"I'm usually down here about this time, if not for tarts, then for tea," Barris replied.

"And you are always welcome to join us as you are able, Your Majesty," Diana invited.

Zephraim nodded in recognition. "I might very well."

"We will enjoy your company." Barris finished off his tart. "I should see myself off. I have a delivery to make, after all. I hope you both have a wonderful day."

"Same to you, Lord Barris," Diana replied. "Please let me know if anything else is needed."

"I'll probably come down for hot water later today, but otherwise I think we're good. Thank you." Barris bowed. "Take care." The lord smiled once more and left the kitchen.

Zephraim wished he had comparable happiness and optimism. "I should leave you to it, Diana. You've been wonderful company."

"I'm so thrilled to hear it," Diana said. She rose from her seat at the table and collected plates and cups. "If you decide you want more than a handful of tarts and tea, please let me know."

"I will," Zephraim said. He stood, brushing his fingers together out of habit. "Have a good day," he added. Like Barris, he left the kitchen.

Chapter Thirty-Four

Xavier bowed when he was granted access to Rhoslyn's quarters. His golden curls swayed with the effort, and though his appearance spoke of boyish charm, his manner attested to something more serious and observant. Riken had chosen well.

At least, he'd chosen a man who could exist within the palace walls and not draw suspicion. Rhoslyn didn't care for Xavier, no matter how capable he'd shown himself to be. His overt confidence and willingness vexed Rhoslyn. She didn't like his familiarity and the lingering closeness. Thankfully, Rhoslyn had not been forced into any specific decisions regarding the man just yet.

The queen sat in the parlor of her allotted quarters, a silver tray of fruit, bread, and other favorites sat on the table before her. Rhoslyn surveyed the man through lowered lashes while sipping daintily from a chalice of chilled juice. Her breakfast had been delivered minutes before by the elf-girl Gisela, and though Rhoslyn's dislike of elves did not extend as far as Riken's, she found Xavier a more tolerable companion.

"Yes?" she asked him after another sip of her juice. She didn't wait for an answer, instead picking up a grape from her tray between thumb and forefinger and popping it into her mouth. The purple fruit's sweetness burst with the first bite, tempting Rhoslyn to select another. "You can't possibly have news so early in the morning."

"But I do, Your Majesty," Xavier replied in a tone flirting the line of insolence. Rhoslyn rolled her eyes and contemplated throwing something heavy at his head. She found him tedious whenever he grew too comfortable, and for some reason, he thought he could not only be comfortable in her presence, but familiar as well. She would have to do something about him if his behavior didn't improve.

"And?" she prompted.

"Your husband was in the kitchen in the early morning hours with the cook," Xavier replied, his expression schooled into calm facticity. Rhoslyn thought he should have the decency to smirk when he clearly wanted to. "And this was not the first time King Zephraim has visited."

Rhoslyn cleaned her fingers on the cloth napkin accompanying her meal, though it was a habit born action rather than a necessity. It remained a stark white when placed beside her breakfast tray. "Who is he visiting in the kitchen, and what is the purpose of those visits?"

"Diana Hawke," Xavier replied and finally approached the table. "I have yet to ascertain exactly why he is visiting her, but from my observations, and the observations of others, they just appear to talk."

Rhoslyn did not speak, but instead picked up another grape. She did not eat it but held it like the other as she thought. Her wrist bent, and the little tidbit of food bobbed up and down a couple of times. "Who else knows?"

"Likely the kitchen workers," Xavier said. "And Lord Barris. He stopped by and dined on pastries with His Majesty and

Diana. I couldn't hear their conversation, but the king seemed more light-hearted than usual."

Rhoslyn put the grape down on the tray. She could imagine what empty-headed Barris and the fucking cook would be filling Zephraim's head with. He was already drifting too far towards Collette's way of thinking, and she'd be damned if they'd go back to those times. She also knew, without having to consider other points, Zephraim would not be swayed from his current path.

"Scare her," Rhoslyn finally replied.

Xavier's responding smile was pure malice. "My pleasure." He tilted his head to the side. "What of Lady Elrick?" The woman had been heard saying she would marry Lord Riken the moment he returned, whether he liked it or not.

"I believe Lord Riken would appreciate efforts to remove her from the possible future he might be subjected to," Rhosyn replied, her voice cold. "We have to wait for the opportune time, though. Lord Riken being on the other side of the country does not mean we act in haste."

"I was instructed to wait until you gave the order, and I shall."

The last word was almost a purr, and Rhoslyn knew she could bide her time until she could no longer deal with him. Rhoslyn decided she was no longer interested in her food. She pushed the tray forward so the maid would know to get it when she came back. "Then do something about her before she publicly smirks in my direction."

"As you wish," Xavier replied with a bow of his head. "Is there anything else I can help you with?" He gave her what was supposed to be a charming smile.

"No," Rhoslyn said. The fingers resting on the chair arm started lightly tapping. "Make sure no one catches you while you carry out your orders."

"Of course." Xavier bowed and turned to exit, but not before giving Rhoslyn a once over.

Rhoslyn scowled as Xavier saw himself out, and she only managed to keep herself seated until the door was firmly shut. She could not recall being openly leered at, and certainly not since she'd been crowned. In a rage, she nearly knocked her breakfast table over, but the potential mess did not bother her. Strolling over to the desk, she took a seat and began a letter.

Riken,

Your man will die before the month is out. Do better next time.

~ R

Lord Riken,

Your fair lady grows more and more unhappy with the social and political state of the castle, and still she tells me to stay my hand until someone suitable can be blamed. I think, were you here to provide guidance and support, she would be more willing to engage in the necessary work. I would never tell you how to act, but a suggestion on your part might sway her into sorely needed decisiveness.

I am saddened to report King Zephraim's increased presence in the kitchen. He favors the head cook. You know, the curvy blonde one who was, or is, married to the treasonness Cremsius Hawke. One might extend the benefit of the doubt where she is concerned. Even so, she should not be so free as to befriend someone so superior to her, and certainly not the ruler of our kingdom. I will deal with Mistress Hawke all the same.

The friendship has not escaped the attentions of Lady Elrick, although she has not used the connection again our queen. Instead, she's uttered shockingly bold statements toward and about the queen. Only this afternoon did I hear her speak of Her Majesty's inability to retain the affections of those she most cherishes. Last week, she dared to theorize about the presumed parentage of any theoretical children born by the queen. The latest insult spoke of a royal baby sporting your dark hair and eyes, unlike those of King Zephraim. I was almost certain your lady would strangle her then and there. I wish you had been here to see it. Certainly, Lady Elrick's time grows lean.

Your lady has started taking meals with some of the lords, ensuring things go to plan. She is quite brilliant, our queen.

Your servant,
Xavier

Xavier slunk from the queen's chambers down toward the kitchen, trying to keep his mind on the things he needed to do instead of the woman whose presence he had just left. Never in his life had Xavier been jealous of Riken. He'd never had a reason to be. Riken's father had saved him from the streets at a young age and raised him alongside his lord. Xavier had always been treated well, rarely denied anything, and often embraced as family. All Xavier had to do in return was provide loyalty and obedience in carrying out orders. Riken had always been generous to followers and harsh to those he felt betrayed him. His generosity and black and white expectations won him loyalty. Xavier's wealth and position in the world demonstrated as much.

But now, looking at the creamy skin, the cinnamon locks of hair, and the long legs he had caught a glimpse of, all Xavier could do was picture the sounds Rhoslyn would make as he plunged into her over and over again. He wanted to bite her creamy skin, marking her as his own. As he walked to the kitchen, he wondered what it would take for him to have Rhoslyn for just a night and what measures he would take to ensure such things. It was a betrayal of his lord, but Rhoslyn made him crazy.

When he was on the landing, he strolled to the kitchens. He stopped long enough at the door to recenter himself. Only then did he crack open the door to peer inside. He grinned viciously as he saw the cook alone.

Xavier watched Diana wiped down the counter surface with a clean hand towel, catching bits of dough or flour in her free hand. When the space was clean, she brushed the contents of her hand into the nearby trash. Xavier pushed the door further open and entered with a swagger. "Hello there, pretty."

Diana looked at Xavier, and she nodded in recognition of his presence. "Hello," she replied. "Is there something you need?"

A smirk grew on Xavier's face as he stalked closer to the cook, slowly boxing her in. He looked her up and down, his eyes lingering on the swell of her breasts. "I was hoping you might have some of those delicious tarts you served the king this morning."

Diana looked at him, the corners of her mouth turned down, unimpressed. "Those were specially ordered by Lord Barris. I'm afraid there is nothing here for you."

Xavier pressed himself closer to Diana, making sure escape would be difficult. She was a pretty woman, though in a much different way than Rhoslyn, so Xavier didn't feel particularly bad about the closeness. "Oh, I would disagree. After all, the king has been spending so much time down here lately, I figure he has to be sampling other delicacies. Maybe I want a sample as well." He ran a hand up her side as he spoke, and he was unsurprised when she pushed him hard.

"You should leave," Diana insisted, though her voice was firm rather than afraid.

Xavier would make sure she experienced fear. "You're feisty," he observed. "I enjoy feisty. I wonder how similarly the king feels." He pushed up against her, a hand sliding to the knife he wore at his hip. "Or how the queen would feel about it."

"You're disgusting," Diana sneered.

Xavier responded by bringing his knife up to just below her throat. "And you, the wife of a traitor, are spending too much time with the king." The glimmer of the blade near her pale throat had him contemplating how far he should take his threats. It would be a real shame to mar such beautiful skin. Her lack of fear made him feel less merciful.

"You should take your concerns to His Majesty, as he has say over how his time is spent," Diana practically growled.

He lifted the knife, pressing it firmer against her chest, but not enough to draw blood. "The queen would rather I take up concerns with you." He was cut off by the door to the kitchen being thrown open. Xavier practically jumped away from Diana, his knife hidden once more on his person.

"Hello, Diana. I could use the hot water bottle we talked about earlier, if you don't mind," Lord Barris said, his voice jovial but his face hard as he strode in and stood next to the cook. His eyes scanned her quickly, and Xavier knew he'd been overheard. Possibly seen.

Diana breathed out and moved away from Xavier. "Of course," she agreed. She retrieved the item in question for Barris. "Were you still planning on going into town, Lord Barris?"

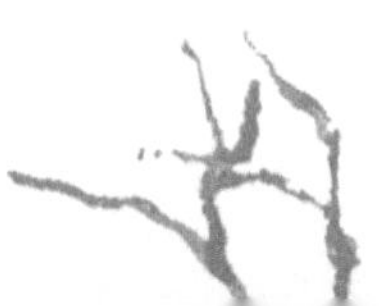

"I was thinking I may have to go out to visit the herbalist for medication. I know you mentioned needing to go to the market today. Would you like an escort?"

"I would be so grateful," Diana replied, keeping her eyes on Xavier.

Xavier kept his eyes on Barris. The Golden Lord watched him just as intently, looming dangerously. Barris was a head taller and much broader, but his own smaller stature didn't stop Xavier from glaring at him as he headed for the kitchen door.

"Then I shall escort you," Lord Barris said.

Xavier left the kitchen. He would have to try for the cook later.

Chapter Thirty-Five

The day proved warmer than any prior. Barris might have enjoyed it had he not been escorting Diana to the caves where her husband resided. People were out, exchanging goods for gold, and carrying on with their day. In so many ways, it seemed as though the city residents hadn't noticed the regime change. He knew better. Non-humans were fleeing the city in droves, hoping to avoid roundups, and it was difficult to gauge what things were like in other parts of Coralia.

Looking over as they walked, he noted the cook was shaken by the encounter in the kitchen. She was doing her best to hide it behind a neutral expression. Barris sighed, thankful he'd been notified by one of his Nereid companions to go to the kitchen. He knew what would have happened if no one had intervened. He decided to push the thoughts from his mind. Forward-thinking was necessary, and he hoped the others would agree.

"I should have asked earlier," he said as they left behind the busy main streets. "Are you okay?"

"I am fine," Diana assured him.

"Are you sure?" he asked, noting her furrowed brow.

She nodded. "Ultimately, nothing happened. I worry about others who remain in the palace. His threats won't end with me." They stepped from the street onto the sandy lane leading to the caves.

"We'll keep an eye out for further problems," Barris promised. He couldn't be present for every conflict or altercation, but he could have readily available witnesses. He would have to figure out how to structure support without drawing attention to his efforts. Fortunately, he would have a little time to think things through.

As they made their way towards the cave entrance, Barris felt compelled to speak. "I'm going to tell Crem about what happened. He needs to know."

"Why would you think I wouldn't want you to?" Diana asked.

Barris shrugged. "I confess my thoughts linger on Lynessea. She hates when I tell her brothers anything, especially when she's been in a spot of trouble. I assumed you might feel the same."

"I don't believe in keeping things from my husband," Diana replied. "I do fear he will want to go after Xavier."

"I'll enlist Howle to make sure he is prevented," Barris assured her as they reached the cave entrance. He motioned for Diana to move forward, and she did without argument. As usual, the journey down the narrow passageways was slow due to lack of light. They encountered no guards, a matter Barris found surprising, but now was not the time to question the reason.

As they moved deeper into the tunnels, the voices of Crem and Howle could be heard. They argued, loudly, and the words echoed off the cavern walls, muffling the message.

"—Rumors of Queen Collette's death arrived in Quenall, most of those willing to fight have either given up or fled," Crem could be heard saying.

"Then we need ta inspire them lad. Ya need ta inspire them. People are bein' shipped off. Rumors are risin' of sanctioned camps openin'. Even if she's dead, we don't have the luxury of doin' nothin'," Howle replied.

"I know, I know," Crem replied tiredly.

Barris might have been amused by the argument had the topic not been so serious. He and Diana quietly stepped into the open cavern, and the two men came into view. Seated at the usual table, the two former guards shared a meal as they discussed options. Barris began to speak, but Diana cut him off.

"You two at it again?" Diana asked as she approached the table. Her tone was filled with the warm teasing she usually reserved for Crem. "Don't you tire of bickering? People might get the wrong idea of who is married to whom."

Howle laughed, hitting the top of the table with the palm of his large hand. "Oh, he's married to ya, lass, but sometimes a man has needs, ya know."

Crem appeared less amused by Diana's appearance. He rose from his seat and went to gather his wife in his arms. "You were not due a visit," he said, his face contorted with worry. He looked from his wife's face and over to Barris. Barris nodded. "Has something happened?"

"Rhoslyn does not like Zephraim's visits to the kitchen, so she sent Riken's lapdog to threaten me," Diana explained.

Crem's growl had Howle rising from his seat.

"Threaten how?" Crem demanded of his wife.

"He cornered me in the kitchen and was threatening me with a knife," Diana further explained.

"Anything else?" Crem asked through clenched teeth.

Diana pursed her lips and raised a brow. "What do you think a man working for Lord Riken threatens to do when he corners a woman with a knife?"

"Just needed to hear you confirm it," Crem said. He released the hold he had on his wife and turned to face Barris and Howle. "I'll be back," he declared, though when he stepped forward, he found himself blocked by Barris.

"Move," Crem demanded.

"You know I can't, Crem," Barris replied evenly.

"Be reasonable," Diana intervened. "You are asking to die if you go to the palace, Crem," Diana reasoned, moving to stand beside Barris. "And what good would you be to me or anyone else if you were dead?"

Crem didn't fight when Howle grabbed him by an arm and forced the former guard commander back to the table. "She's right. I won't go after him," Crem assured the group, and he took a seat without argument. He sighed and ran a hand over his face. "We need a plan in place to watch the bastard."

"I agree," Barris said, deciding to take a seat as well. "I'm going to have my people organize a watch. With Xavier's position under Riken, we'll have to be careful."

"Thank you," Crem said, nodding tiredly. He turned back to Diana. "You cannot go back to the palace. Please tell me you're not going back."

Diana gave her husband a reassuring smile. "I promised you when something dangerous happened, I would leave," she reminded him.

Crem nodded and held out his arms for her.

Diana walked to her husband and practically crawled into his lap. "None of this is your fault. We knew something would happen eventually. We are just lucky it wasn't carried out to his intended conclusion."

"He'd be dead now if it had," Crem promised her.

Barris understood the venom in the other man's voice. It was how he felt when Lord Elrick tried to assault Lynessea. "I'm going to head back and let the king know what's happened.

Chapter Thirty-five

Is there anything else you think I need to tell him?" Barris asked Diana.

"Whatever you do, make sure you do not implicate Rhoslyn in what you say," Diana replied. "He is starting to doubt her, but I fear he will be more resistant if she is outright blamed for anything. I think he can be redeemed enough to make a difference, but we cannot push."

Barris nodded. Her advice made sense, and she had spent more time around Zephraim than the rest of them. He bowed to the group and headed out.

Barris hurried back to the castle, careful not to be stopped by any of the kingdom's– no, Riken's guards. It served no one to labor under the impression any of the guards gave their loyalty to Zephraim. Barris had killed several of them over the last few weeks, though always in response to catching them in harmful acts. He felt no regret for his actions. His beliefs wouldn't allow for it, nor would his morals. Humans so often felt completely intolerant and hateful, and he could not truly consider himself amongst them anymore.

So lost in thought it felt like no time at all before he stood before the king's office door. Taking a deep breath, Barris didn't bother plastering on his usual smile. Instead, he decided to allow Zephraim to see the depths of how much what had almost happened to Diana affected him. With a deep breath, he raised a hand and knocked.

He let himself in after Zephraim granted him entry, and Barris found the king looking out of his window onto the grounds. He shut the door behind him and approached the king. Unlike many, Barris didn't entirely blame Zephraim for what was happening. Although the king allowed himself to be blinded by a pretty face and lies, he was, in many ways, just as much a victim as Queen Collette.

"Yes?" Zephraim asked, glancing over his shoulder.

"Hello, Your Majesty," Barris said with a slight bow.

"Hello Barris," Zephraim greeted. He abandoned the window and made his way to his desk where he fell into his chair. "What brings you by?"

Barris looked down, his normally smiling lips turned down in a frown. "I fear I bring bad news, my king. I removed Diana from the castle for her own safety less than an hour ago."

Confusion formed in Zephraim's expression. "What happened to cause such a drastic measure?"

"I'm sure you're aware I have tried to place her under my protection since her husband betrayed you. I was worried someone might try to harm her, either on behalf of Lord Elrick's memory or some other nefarious reason." Barris made no apologies regarding his efforts. No matter what the kingdom accused Cremisius Hawke of, Diana had been innocent. Barris knew he had to be careful. If Zephraim chose skepticism, he'd be arguing nothing more than Diana's word against Xavier's. "Today I walked in on what appeared to be Xavier Eisenhart attempting to assault her."

"Assault?" Zephraim said and had the good sense to look outraged by the news. "Is she okay?"

"She is shaken, but she says she's alright," Barris said sadly.

"And what of Xavier? Has anything been done about him?"

Barris shook his head. "I only came in at the end, my king. I was more concerned about making sure Diana was alright instead of holding him." Barris was ashamed of not doing more, but Xavier was one of Riken's men. He honestly wasn't sure what could be done.

"You outrank Xavier," Zephraim reminded Barris. "Your word will hold more weight. I will look into this," he promised with genuine anger.

"Thank you. I know the offer will be valued." Barris was earnest in his response. "If you wish to see her, to make sure she's doing well for yourself, I can arrange it," Barris offered. He knew it was a risk, but Zephraim needed other people in his life who weren't Riken, Rhoslyn, or the other nobles, most of whom were only out for their own pockets. He would offer his own friendship, but with everything, he thought it too dis-ingenuous to do so.

"I will take you up on the offer," Zephraim said. He rose to his feet, looking intent. "I am going to handle the situation with Xavier but follow up with me on this issue."

"Of course." Barris turned to leave but stopped at the door. "Zephraim, thank you."

Zephraim gave him a small, brief smile. "Not everyone agrees with the things I think and do, but we might agree assaulting an innocent woman is above us all."

Barris inclined his head in agreement and made a swift exit.

Chapter Thirty-Six

Nawalya hovered just outside the kitchen door, listening to the others talk. Discussions drifted from when Sara's seasonal farm hands would return to the chores reserved for after breakfast. No one brought up Collette, though she supposed no one really knew what to say or think since she and Larent fled the cottage.

The elf knew she was partially responsible for the uncomfortable silence surrounding Collette. She'd returned from the Leasstitor home short-tempered and withdrawn. Her time with Nora and Alexander had been good, cleansing. Without Arian there to intervene, Nora and Alexander had laid down very hard truths, truths they had been trying to say for years but were always prevented from sharing. Those truths needed to be discussed with Arian, but Nawalya hadn't been sure what to say, or how to properly convey what she'd realized.

Entering the kitchen, her head held up, she took in the scene before her. Whyldon sat next to Thomas, who sat next to Arian at the table. Sara and Rion were cleaning dishes, and Tolan was preparing vegetables. The scene was peaceful and cordial, and it allowed Nawalya to feel more secure in her next actions.

Nawalya swallowed a few times, going over what she wanted to say in her head one more time before finally speaking. "Arian, Thomas, would you please come with me outside? I wish to speak with you about something."

Without hesitating, Arian rose, took his plate to Sara, and with a quick thank you exited the room. The move prompted the same from Thomas.

Nawalya smiled at Sara. "I promise to return them to help with chores."

"The chores will be here when you are done," Sara replied reasonably. "Don't feel rushed."

Nawalya nodded and turned to face Whyldon where he sat, feeling nervous. She owed him so much more than she was capable of giving. "I am sorry, Whyldon, for not telling you about my vision. I acted selfishly, multiple times, by not telling you and Collette. Again, I'm so very sorry." The words felt rushed, but sincerity laced her words.

Whyldon appeared to not know what to say in response. In truth, other than practiced civility, the two had not spoken much in the last several weeks. Still, Whyldon slowly nodded a couple of times. "Thank you."

Nawalya almost sighed in relief, but she managed to nod while giving him a small smile. She had not expected him to beg her back, and she happily accepted his acknowledgment. She left the house, feeling the tension in her shoulders ease a bit. She knew apologizing to Whyldon had been the easiest part of the day. The next discussion would prove infinitely harder.

The air was much chillier than it had been in the last week. A glance towards the gray sky told her they could expect fresh snow. Looking ahead, she spotted Thomas and Arian in the distance, so she trudged ahead, appreciative of their chosen distance from the house.

Nawalya stopped in front of one of the fallen logs she'd seen Collette and Larent use a few times and thought about sitting down for a minute, to have the conversation face-to-face with Arian. She decided to pace instead, feeling too anxious to remain in one place.

"We need to talk, Arian," she began but immediately shook her head. "No. I need to talk, and you need to listen. Thomas, I need you to moderate, to make sure we don't fight or get off topic."

Arian crossed his arms but nodded. She could tell he wanted to know what was going on but was hesitant to have this conversation. Her attitude as of late had been quite different since her return.

Nawalya paced back and forth as she considered how to express her thoughts without hurting Arian. She decided to start by posing a question.

"When Whyldon was yelling at Collette and me about my vision, you stepped forward to stop him. What was your reasoning?" Nawalya asked softly.

Arian narrowed his eyes, a sign of his uncertainty, as if looking for a trap in her question. "Whyldon had no right to yell at Collette. She had nothing to do with our choice to hide your vision."

Nawalya nodded. "So you were only going to try and redirect his anger from Collette?"

"And from you," Arian admitted.

"Why from me? You were the one who said the consequences of our decision to conceal my visions was on Larent and my shoulders. I deserved his anger." She closed her eyes and took a breath. "Were you going to lie and say it was your idea to hide the truth?"

Arian narrowed his eyes, a sign of uncertainty. "I was going to redirect his anger at me."

Chapter Thirty-six

"Why?" Nawalya asked again.

"Because you have never handled personal conflict very well. Your mental well-being could have been affected by what happened. I wanted to lessen your burden."

Nawalya pondered Arian's answer, and while she had an idea of how to address some of Arian's reasoning, she turned to Thomas instead. "What do you think of his answer?"

"You want my honest opinion?" Thomas asked. His words came across as hesitant, but his eyes conveyed an understanding of the truth.

"Yes, please," Nawalya replied.

Thomas sighed and nodded. "I think the two of you, and Larent on occasion, enable each other to embrace the things hindering your growth and wellbeing, and often to your detriment. Arian trying to take the blame for a decision the three of you made is a prominent example of the behavior."

Nawalya made a lazy motion to Thomas. "You see, Arian?" she asked, and when he looked at her in confusion, she continued. "You treat me like a child. There are a million examples of you enabling me to hide behind you so I can avoid the consequences of my own choices. I won't even touch on how we treat Larent." She had to direct her gaze away from Arian as she spoke, knowing he was hurt by her words, no matter how true they were. "I love you like a brother, Arian, and there have absolutely been times when I have needed your intervention. Thomas is right, though. So were Nora and Alexander. We don't deal with our trauma, and we don't try to improve our conditions. It's time to heal."

Arian blinked hard and sagged like a stringless marionette. "You agree with her?" he asked Thomas.

Thomas rose and walked over to Arian. "Staying buried in your trauma has been easier for you in many ways," Thomas replied thoughtfully. "And you're both uncertain on how safe

it would be to heal. But, I know you have needed it for a long time."

"Healing is terrifying," Nawalya said in a quiet, honest voice. "Arian feels the same way."

"Where would we start to deal with what we've been through?" Arian asked.

Thomas shrugged. "Sara has said, more than once, she thinks she can help Nawalya learn better control over her abilities. Refining skills over her visions would be a start."

"I plan on asking for her help as soon as we are done here," Nawalya replied before looking back at Arian. "This will be hard for both of us. From now on, when I make questionable decisions, I will deal with the consequences. I'm not saying I won't ask for your advice or help, but I need to be an adult. This whole situation with Whyldon has proven that."

"How?" Arian demanded, and Nawalya could see anger in his eyes, not at herself or Thomas, but at himself and the idea of change. "How does that warrant such a change?"

A part of Nawalya wanted to back down, to give in and not fight with Arian, to not cause him any more pain or confusion. If she did, she knew nothing would change. Nothing would get better, so instead she straightened her back and got right in his face.

"Out of everyone here, we should have understood what the loss of Collette, his daughter, would have done to Whyldon. We should have told him, and instead, I made up excuses, not out of love, but like a child trying to hold on to her favorite toy. For spirits' sake, Arian, I have had that man's voice in my head for over a century, and yet I was able to treat him so poorly. I was so easily able to lie to him. You know what that tells me?" she demanded. "I wasn't afraid to lose him because I love him. I was afraid to lose the idea of him. If I had truly loved him, then he would have come first. But no, I put myself, and my own wants, first, and I've been enabled every step of the way. Collette almost died, Arian. She almost died, and I'm responsible."

Arian closed the distance between them, and though Nawalya's eyes remained locked on her oldest friend, the others trickling out of the house did not escape her attention.

"Collette's attack is not your fault," Arian insisted. "And of course you love–"

Without thinking, Nawalya reached out and grabbed Arian by the edges of his gray coat, shaking him hard. "No. You aren't in my head. You don't get to tell me how I feel!" she yelled.

She took a breath, forcing herself to calm. Thomas had stepped closer, and he looked ready to defend Arian.

"Whyldon is real," she began again. "He's honest and true, and I'm not. I'm an assassin and a thief. I enjoy being those things, and not once has he ever judged me for it. In return, I lied to him and kept parts of myself from him. That is not love. It can't be. I need to heal so I can determine if I am a good partner for him, much in the same way you need to heal for Thomas. I am not a child. I am not your responsibility. I am your friend."

"Let him go, Nawalya," Thomas said firmly, placing a hand on her shoulder. "We can make points without assaulting each other."

Nawalya released Arian immediately. "Sorry," she said, ducking her head in slight shame. She didn't want to focus on Arian's shocked, hurt expression.

Thomas let his hand drop from Nawalya's arm, and he took Arian's hand. "Let's go for a walk so everyone can calm down. You and Nawalya can pick this conversation up later, okay?"

Arian nodded quietly, and Nawalya knew he was thinking over everything. "I'll be here when you're ready," she said.

Nawalya watched them walk off, feeling horrible guilt over the end of their conversation, but relieved for the hard truth to be spoken. The two emotions balled up in her chest, similar to a panic attack but never quite tipping over. She took a breath and started back towards the cottage. Tolan was outside collecting water, and Whyldon was in the distance, ax in hand. She presumed he was splitting wood if the ax he carried was any indication.

Tolan stopped working as she approached, a look of severe confusion on his face. She realized he was behind on most of the changes in their lives. "Are you okay?" he gently asked.

Nawalya couldn't help but laugh. "No, not at all. I will be, eventually." She rested a hand on his shoulder. "You are a complete idiot, and I am angry with you, but I am glad you're back."

Tolan blushed. "I'm glad someone feels that way," he muttered to himself before motioning to Whyldon. "What's going on there?"

Nawalya shook her head. "Later, I have things to do now, but later." She offered him a brief smile before going inside. She found Sara at the counter, kneading dough. "Excuse me, Sara?"

Sara turned to look at Nawalya. "Yes?"

Nawalya licked her lips, suddenly feeling nervous again. "Is your offer to teach me to control my visions still open?"

"Of course," Sara warmly replied. She picked up the dough, balled it up and dropped it on the flat surface of the counter. "I think you've suffered far too long."

Nawalya gave Sara a small shy smile. "Thank you."

"You're welcome. Controlling magical gifts isn't terribly difficult once you have some practice. I wish someone would have granted you the time and patience before now."

"My people were too scared. I was too scared," Nawalya admitted. "Fortunately, I still have time to learn."

"You do," Sara agreed. "It's never too late."

Chapter Thirty-Seven

Yawning, Larent slowly blinked awake. He wasn't sure what time it was thanks to the heavy curtains over the window, but based on the light peeking through, he knew it must be late morning. Rolling over, he looked at Collette, still asleep, her hair spilling around her face and contrasting with the cream bed linens. Larent found her breathtakingly beautiful, an observation he increasingly made any time he looked at her.

He didn't want to wake her, not when she looked so relaxed and peaceful, but she would need to eat soon. He also had no doubt Nana would have a large breakfast spread prepared in the kitchen. Larent reached out and pushed a lock of Collette's carob hair from her face. He earned a soft groan of protest for his effort. He chuckled at her response and leaned over to kiss her cheek. "I know my bed is amazing, but it's time to wake up."

"Why do you like treason so much?" Collette sleepily grumbled. When she opened her eyes, she shifted around so she could snuggle with Larent.

He wrapped an arm around her, pulling her closer. "Because every time you accuse someone of treason, you wrinkle your nose in the cutest way."

"I do not," she argued. "I'm a very scary, intimidating woman. Nothing cute at all."

"Oh yes," Larent agreed, chuckling. "Very scary and intimidating."

"Asshole," Collette replied affectionately.

"True," he agreed with a laugh. "But we should get up. Nana said she would make breakfast, and with you here, she will make something special." He knew Nana already loved Collette based on the reception from their arrival, so he had no doubt of the meal awaiting them in the kitchen.

"Then get up and stop distracting me," Collette said.

"Oh, am I distracting?" Larent asked, running a hand along her side. She was the distracting one, and he couldn't understand how she couldn't possibly know as much. "How distracting?"

"I haven't gotten up, have I?" she asked.

Larent was tempted to stay put. To enjoy one another however they desired, but he knew his Nana would want them fed. So, he reluctantly suggested the responsible thing. "Come on, then. Let's go eat." He kissed her once more before releasing her. They both got out of bed and went through the process of dressing, washing their faces, and cleaning their teeth.

As they left the room, Larent smiled to himself, enjoying how much less tense the hours in his childhood home had made Collette. He also loved her being here, around his grandparents. She'd pause in their short walk to the kitchen to look at art hanging from the walls or admire the finishing of a cabinet. Larent appreciated the eclectic collection of tapestries, sketches, and paintings lining the walls of his home, and not everyone always had. Collette's admiration brought him joy.

The kitchen was a whirl of utterly controlled chaos when they arrived. Nora Leassitor stood near the oak counters, her long blonde and silver hair done up in a messy bun which was held up by what looked like ornate knitting needles. Flour, batter, and other remnants from her frenzied cooking sat splattered across her clothes and arms as well as the brick wall behind the counter. Nora took no notice as she hummed, stirred, and plated various components of her elaborate meal, her movements graceful and fluid.

A quick glance told Larent their breakfast would have no particular theme. Some of the items reminded him of the meals he'd enjoyed in Quenall, others came from more distant lands and people, and he wondered if Collette would enjoy them. Struck by the realization he didn't know how much traveling she'd done, Larent filed the thought away for later investigation. Another two dishes sat to the side, and Larent grimaced as he realized these were Nana's experiments. They might be delicious, or they might go to the pigs. He would have to warn Collette.

At the round dining table, also oak but scratched and scuffed from years of use, was Pops. Perched on his nose sat a pair of spectacles Larent's grandfather didn't need but loved for some unknown reason. Dark chocolate eyes merrily scanned pamphlets, though Larent did not inquire about the contents. Behind Pops, a large open window provided a view of the distant woods. The bright sun shone on his umber skin and salt and pepper hair. Chirping birds sang as they flew by, basking in the unseasonably bright, warm weather. Larent thought he would need to make use of the good weather before the day was out.

"I thought the two of you might sleep in," Nana said from near the stove. "I'm not quite finished, but feel free to dig in." She paused in her preparations long enough to kiss Larent and Collette on the cheeks. Larent realized his Nana was a small woman, but standing next to Collette, he realized his grandmother was a good six inches shorter.

"Larent insisted we get up," Collette explained, and she shot him a devious look. "He was either anxious to eat, or he doesn't like sharing his bed."

Larent shot her a scandalous look. "I love sharing a bed with you."

"Uh-huh," she replied with a flirtatious grin. Larent found himself contemplating the wisdom of throwing her over his shoulder and taking her back to his bedroom because of her lips.

"Eat," Nana and Pops said at the same time, prompting Collette to obey. She took the plate Nana offered and began helping herself to food.

Leaning in close, Laren whispered, "Let me try these two first." He pointed to a caramelized vegetable dish and something resembling a rich meat pie.

"Why do you need to try them first?" Nora asked sweetly.

"Leave the boy alone," Alexander said, giving Nora a wry look. "He knows how you like to experiment with food. Our poor girl doesn't."

"Ruin all my fun." Nora snapped the cloth she had on her shoulder at Alexander, popping him gently on arm. "He's right, though. I haven't tried it yet."

Larent grinned to himself as he added food to his plate. Being home was such a wonderful experience, and he wondered why he'd gone so long without visiting. Well. Other than his time keeping Collette from being arrested and executed again. "I missed you two."

He went to the table with Collette, and as had become a habit, he glanced over to her plate, seeing she'd served herself small portions of just about every dish. Nana was good at many things, but cooking would always remain at the top of the list.

A slight tap on his side from Nana's towel as she walked by reminded him to stop watching Collette and eat himself. "What all are you making?" he asked as he picked up his fork.

Chapter Thirty-seven

"I decided to get started on lunch," Nora explained, and Larent wondered where exactly said lunch would go given the quantity of food they were expected to consume for breakfast alone. "Don't give me that look. You're both far too thin."

"I can promise to eat as much as possible," Collette replied after swallowing a bite of something bready, fried, and drizzled with honey. "This is delicious."

Nana beamed. "I'm glad to hear it. We picked it up from a group of elves in Fythias years ago. If you have a favorite dish, let me know."

Collette shook her head. "I'm not picky about the type of food I eat." She nodded in Larent's direction. "I know he can be, though."

Nora pointed her wooden spoon at Larent who shook his head. "No, ma'am. Not me. I am not picky at all and will eat anything you make."

"You better," Nana said firmly.

"You can't overfeed them, Nora," Alexander said without looking up.

"Larent is going to need sustenance given all the training he will do while here," Nora argued.

Larent groaned and dramatically said to Collette, "Save me."

"I would be interested in seeing what your training entails, actually," Collette replied. "Everyone does it differently, after all."

"You are more than welcome to watch or join," Alexander replied in his deep, soothing baritone. He put his pamphlets down and surveyed her over the top of his spectacles. "You are not expected to, though. If you'd rather rest, read, cook, go for walks, or anything else, you are more than welcome." He cast his grandson a look of disapproval. "Unlike our grandson, I've heard you don't need to be refreshed in all forms of fighting."

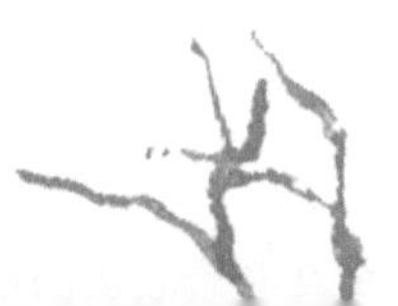

"I have been training since I was five or six," Collette confirmed with a nod. "And I enjoy the process of practicing."

"Then you are welcome to, young lady," Alexander said and smiled when Nora finally sat down to eat.

Several minutes were spent eating and chatting about light topics. Larent delighted in listening to Collette's exchanges with his grandparents. She was funny and observant, qualities he'd long recognized in her. His grandparents responded well, and the shifter found himself wondering how often she might like to return to the home when the opportunity arose.

"Oh," Nora exclaimed as she dabbed at her mouth with a napkin. "We have a large library," she informed Collette who listened in interest. "I have a section for those of us with more refined tastes."

"Smut," Alexander added before taking a large gulp of tea. "She means those books are full of smut."

"Why must you ruin my fun?" Nora asked, gently smacking her husband's arm. "A woman has to have hobbies, and since I was forced to give up my favorite one—"

Alexander cut her off. "No one forced you to give up anything, woman."

Collette met Larent's gaze, amusement shining in her eyes. He leaned forward and whispered, "They are always like this."

"Oh yeah?" she replied leaning a little closer, and damn, he was distracted again.

"Yeah," he replied. "It's worse when Nana has wine."

"Once. You only witnessed it once," Nora insisted.

"And I was scared for my life!" Larent dodged Nora's swiping hand.

With a laugh, Alexander stood, his empty plate in hand. He walked over to the sink to clean his dish. "You were twenty-two, and you saw nothing. You weren't scared for your life."

Larent looked at Collette. "I was."

"I have to ask what it is you didn't see," Collette asked.

"Don't you dare, young man," Nora warned, shaking her index finger in his direction. Larent considered his options, and once a decision was made, he braced himself. "I saw a drunk Nana dancing with veils and slowly removing her clothes for Pops," he said, then immediately jumped out of his chair to avoid Nora's dish towel.

Nora sighed and rolled her eyes before casting a warm smile at Collette. "Would you like more food, dear?"

"Oh, no thank you. I had plenty, and it was all delicious."

Nora responded with a pleased crinkle of her eyes, and she rose from her seat, gathering empty dishes to take back to the sink. "You two go get ready for training. I've got the kitchen, and I'll be at the family altar if anyone needs me later."

Larent went around for a hug and kiss from his Nana and a firm pat from Pop before moving to leave, only to pause when Collette was drug into a hug from Nana as well. Laughing, he held his hand out for Collette and extracted her from the kitchen. "I'm so glad you're here."

"So am I," Collette replied. She glanced back at the kitchen and asked, "Family altar?"

"Where did you think I got my spirituality from?" Larent joked. "There's a shed on the far side of the property. Nana converted it to a family alter forever ago." They found his bedroom and shut the door behind them, creating a sense of privacy even if Larent was fairly certain privacy was almost non-existent.

Larent kissed her. "They seem to like you, and I'm glad you like them."

Her arms went loosely around his waist. "How could I not?" she asked. "You are so much like them."

"Pops is too serious for me to be like him."

"I would argue, you know," she replied.

Larent laughed and kissed her before pulling away to get ready. "Training with Pops won't be easy. Expect bruises. The man trained soldiers well over a couple of centuries." Larent shrugged, then let her go so they could change into appropriate clothing.

"Wouldn't be the first bruise I ever got," Collette replied.

"I know, but neither of us are completely healed. Just be careful," Larent requested. He would never ask her to avoid anything she was genuinely happy to participate in, but he thought the reminder of their current physical reality was a fair thing to broach.

She smiled at him. "I usually do. You know, except the one time when I nearly died."

Larent laughed, knowing he shouldn't. "Yeah, except the one time." They were soon ready, and Larent found himself looking forward to seeing an exchange between Pops and Collette. He thought his grandfather would approve of her capabilities and dedication to practice. He reached for her hand and sighed contentedly when she took it.

After a quick walk down the hall and into the kitchen, Larent felt his excitement to work with Pops growing. He released Collette's hand and leaned over the flour-covered counter to kiss Nana on the cheek, only for his grandmother to catch his hand before he could pull away.

"You know what, dear? I could use a little help. Do you mind staying for a moment?" Nora looked past him to Collette. "Go ahead and join Alexander. He can help you pick out some weapons. Larent will be along in a minute."

Collette didn't object, and she stepped outside, leaving Larent alone with his grandmother.

Larent turned to his Nana with a look of suspicion. She rarely asked or wanted help when it came to her kitchen.

Chapter Thirty-seven

"Don't look at me like that, young man. Take a seat," Nora instructed.

Larent knew he was in trouble but quickly sat down and settled in. Experience taught him obedience was the best response when Nana wanted to chat.

"So, Nawalya mentioned a few things while she was here, and you, young man, need to answer some questions."

Larent swallowed hard. This was going to be one of those Come to The Lady conversations, though he wasn't sure what he'd done to warrant an interrogation. "What type of questions?"

Nora pressed her lips together. "Have you apologized to Collette for chasing away the man she loved? The man I know, not too many years ago, you were also in love with?"

"What? He left of his own accord," Larent said, standing.

"Sit your ass back down," Nora ordered, and Larent took his seat. Nora put both hands on the edge of the counter, looking Larent in the eyes. "He did decide to leave, but you forget, I've met him. I know how insecure he was and still is from the sound things. I also know how much you loved him and how hurt you were. It seems like you've never really let go of your hurt."

She waited for him to acknowledge her theory. Larent nodded to keep the peace.

"You lash out when you're hurt and angry. You use your words to dig at a person until they can't take it anymore. We both know what you did to Tolan the moment your group hit the road."

Larent looked down in shame. Nana was right. He had thrown barb after barb at the half-elf, meaning to hurt him, to make him feel useless, and his insults had contributed to the choices Tolan made.

"I thought so." Nora came around the counter and lifted Larent's chin so he would look at her. "What you did was wrong. I understand he hurt you, but you should have moved on instead of letting it fester. You took actions that caused everyone, including Collette, real pain." She let her hand drop, but Nora crossed her arms over her slight frame and leaned against the counter. "Was your poor treatment of Tolan motivated by your desire for Collette?"

"No!" Larent immediately insisted. "By the Lady, no."

Nora breathed out a sigh of relief. "Good. I didn't think you'd do something so cruel, but I had to check." She smiled reassuringly. "Why did you go after Tolan so harshly?"

Larent was quiet for a while, gathering his thoughts, because he wasn't sure he could explain himself. Tolan's betrayal sometimes felt new, and Larent recognized he was to blame for not doing enough to forgive and move forward. "Because it hurt, when he left me, almost more than anything else ever has. We had such a connection, and he refused to try. He ran the moment I told him I loved him. Yet, there he was with Collette, so easily telling her he loved her."

He closed his eyes as he considered his motivations and feelings, and he knew at some point, he would have to contend with the inadvertent pain his actions had caused Collette. He'd also have to deal with Tolan in a less than shallow way. "Something inside me just wanted to hurt Tolan, and so I did everything I knew to hurt him without attacking him. And it was wrong. It was so, so wrong."

"And he left her, at least in part, because of you," Nora said gently.

"I wasn't trying to break them up. If I had tried…" Larent let out a deep breath. "Well, I would have done it differently. That's for damn sure. I never dreamt he would leave her, Nana. Not over some spiteful jabs. She is worth everything."

Nora uncrossed her arms and placed a hand on Larent's shoulder. "It's obvious she feels the same way about you, even as new as your relationship is. You're going to have to deal with your unresolved feelings regarding Tolan at some point, or you're going to hurt her just as badly."

Larent winced at the thought.

"It seems as though you are left with very few options." Nora held up a finger. "Get over it, ignore him, and let it go." She raised another finger. "Befriend him. He's a good kid, and friendship wouldn't be terrible." She raised a third and final finger. "If the two of you can forgive him, bring him into the thing you're creating together, and fuck the anger and hurt out of everything."

"Nana!" Larent exclaimed.

"Oh stop," Nora said with a light swipe of her hand. "You think your Pops and I haven't brought others into our world? When you live as long as we have, sometimes it helps to have a third, or fourth, or fifth companion. I'm old, not dead," she pointed out as Larent grimaced. "Either way, you need to apologize to Collette and let your anger at Tolan go. We raised you better."

Nana took a deep breath, and Larent knew there was more.

"Now, it took a bit to get it out of her, but we need to talk about Nawalya and Arian."

"There's nothing to talk about," Larent said, confused.

"Oh really? You don't let Arian boss you around, smack you, and throw knives at you? You aren't dismissed because you joke around? You don't tiptoe around Nawalya, treating her like a child and never letting her do anything for herself? Honestly, Larent."

"Hey," Larent defended. "Arian is often right, and most of the time, the hitting and the throwing knives are in jest. And Nawalya has issues."

"Most of the time is not all of the time," Nora replied with a shrug. "Arian has a lot of anger issues, and he's been allowed

to remain stuck in the same place he was in forty years ago when your Pops and I found them. Nawalya isn't much better."

"You know what they've been through," Larent argued weakly.

"I do, but they aren't children anymore, and from what I'm hearing, you allow them to get away with pretty much anything. Their poor treatment stops right now. You are not dumb, and you are not the butt of others' jokes or their errand boy. You are a grown, intelligent man, and we taught you to take care of yourself. Joke around, play the fool if it helps you, but stop being the fool. That woman out there is going to need a lot more from you than the play acting. Step up. For her, for them. Be the man your Pops and I know you are."

Larent looked down and thought over Nora's words. In the end, he had to admit she was right. He had allowed himself to be a fool, in every critical way. He did treat Nawalya as if she were breakable and enabled Arian's rage and anger. Collette would need more from him as they continued. But could he be everything they needed?

"Hey now," Nora said. "I had the same talk with Nawalya, and I'm sure at some point I'll talk to your girl, or your Pops will. This isn't all on you, and if you try and take it all on, it will break you. Your little group needs to lean on each other for help, support, and growth. If you don't, this mission and our kingdom won't make it. You can do this. You're strong enough, smart enough, and all of us love you. Now get out there and get your ass kicked. Sounds like you need it."

Chapter Thirty-Eight

Four days had passed since Larent arrived, bringing with him a woman Alexander never thought would grace their home. Both looked tired and stretched thin, but Collette looked broken in a way Alexander had seen in others whose lives had been filled with hardship. Her overt suffering made it easy to like her, to forget who her father was, and the abject horror he had inflicted on so many. Alexander would never hold someone responsible for the actions of their parents, especially when the person had been a child. Still, the connection lingered in his mind.

Alexander was also keenly aware of the love radiating from Collette whenever his grandson was in her presence. Knowing Nora would pepper them with relationship questions, Alexander intervened, asking her to swear to leave them alone. Larent and Collette would marry or not, and given Collette's position in the world, Alexander felt as though Larent needed the opportunity to decide what he ultimately wanted for himself.

Turning his thoughts back to training, Alexander focused on Collette and Larent who were occupied with hand-to-hand sparring. Larent had improved by leaps and bounds since they arrived. He was able to contend with Collette in a fight rather than being taken down in a few minutes. Alexander had expected to be impressed by Collette from what Nawalya had told him, but he hadn't been ready for it. Whoever was responsibile for her training had ensured she would not only survive a fight but a full-scale war. She was prepared for and anticipated, the worst. Unfortunately, the training also resulted in the near suffocation of the natural softness Alexander detected in her. Despite her tough demeanor, an innate kindness flourished, and Alexander found the existence to be a Lady blessed miracle.

Alexander snapped out of his meditation as Larent lunged for Collette. He got tossed for his troubles. The girl had good aim, and Larent skidded past a tree. He wondered if anyone had spoken to her about her strength. She smelled human enough, but his bear told him there was something more there, buried underneath the scent of wildflowers and spring rain. He would consult Nora, as her cat's senses were a little more refined than his.

"Okay," he called out to Collette. "Time for a break. You're thrashing the poor boy more than normal."

"He's being sloppy," Collette pointed out, her tone showed a teasing fondness for Larent more than anything. "I'd almost think he likes being tossed around."

"Only by you," Larent quipped, studiously avoiding Alexander's glare.

"Do I need to make sure you're too worn out to move for you to take your training seriously?" Alexander asked in a deep, even voice. He wouldn't push his grandson as far as he threatened, but he knew Larent would straighten up.

"No, Pops. Not at all," Larent replied.

"Good. Go check on your Nana," he instructed, earning a suspicious look from Larent. His grandson jogged off towards the house, and Alexander had a few minutes alone with Collette. "Walk with me?"

Her hands dropping to her sides after securing her hair into a loose bun. "Sure."

Alexander's hands went behind his back as they started walking toward the property line. He and Nora lived modestly, but they'd secured a larger lot of land over the years. It allowed them freedom in how they lived. At the far corner of the Leassitor land, a small wooden fence sat, and Alexander met the item, running a calloused hand around the top as they walked.

"You're a good fighter," he shared.

"I am," she acknowledged, following alongside Alexander. "I didn't have much of a choice but to learn, and the skills have been useful."

Alexander's lips turned down in a harsh frown. "Whoever pushed you hard enough to be so skilled should be punched in the mouth. Every child should have a childhood. There's no way you did."

"You're not wrong, and not just because I learned to fight from a young age," she agreed. "But given the life I've led, I can't be resentful."

Alexander came to a sudden stop and turned to face Collette. "Yes, you can. No matter what sort of life you've led, the things forced on you were unfair. You, young lady, are allowed to be resentful, angry, sad, or whatever other feelings you have. Whoever taught you otherwise needs a good thrashing."

Collette didn't respond at first, the only sound issuing from the birds and near by livestock. He glanced at her now and again, noting her thoughtful expressions shifting from shock to denial to something he couldn't quite identify.

"Again, you're not wrong," she said.

Alexander chuckled, though his heart broke for Collette. "I'm happy to hear it. Too many people struggle with managing emotions. They can eat you alive if you ignore them too long."

"I have managed my feelings well enough all these years," Collette replied. "There's a balance there, acknowledging and working through what I feel while protecting myself from others who'd love to cause me harm. It usually works."

"I hope so. From an outsider's view, it looks like you carry a lot on your shoulders without acknowledging the cost." He gave her a soft smile he knew resembled Larent's. "Would you mind if I asked you a personal question?"

"You can ask, but I might not answer."

A deep laugh left Alexander's lips. He could see why Larent was so smitten. "I asked my grandson why he brought you here. He told me about Tolan, but he also mentioned he wanted to give you a reprieve from everything. As you can imagine, he didn't tell us what everything entailed. I was hoping you'd be willing to tell me what he thinks you need to escape from."

She didn't withdraw from him as Alexander partially anticipated. Instead, she let out a sigh. "Being queen."

"And why do you want to run away from it?" Alexander prompted. Larent had not unilaterally decided she needed a break. When she looked off in the distance, Alexander thought the question was likely difficult for the girl.

"Anyone with a lick of sense in their head wouldn't want the responsibility. Having served for three years, I can attest to how difficult and demanding the job is." She crossed her arms, something he noticed she did when she felt vulnerable. "Every effort I made was challenged and used against me. People used their dislike and disagreement to assault me, betray me, and arrest me. And all of those terrible things happened before I ever set foot out of Quenall."

"It sounds like a shit time," Alexander agreed, knowing it was an understatement. "But I have to ask, why do you keep trying?"

"Because someone must. Someone who genuinely wants better for Coralia than what we had under Sargarus." Collette shrugged again. "Someone else could do it, but let's be honest, I'm best positioned. I have a legitimate claim. I have the power to do something others would have to cultivate."

"All valid reasons," Alexander readily acknowledged. "But even so, it is your life. Whatever you choose to do, there should be enjoyment somewhere in the midst of everything else. I would hate to see you suffer more."

They resumed walking, staying close to the fence even if no reason existed.

"I do get joy, you know, because I know what I was doing improved lives," Collette said after a stretch of quiet contemplation. "I hate the political games and the pressure, but I know I'm doing the right thing."

"You are," he assured her with a broad smile. "Larent and Nawalya think you are a good and effective ruler."

"I tried to be."

"That's all any of us can do. Of course, Nora would tell you to take it a step further and murder any who questioned your efforts," Alexander said, shaking his head.

Collette snorted. "As tempting as the idea sounds, I feel like adopting murder as a policy against those with different viewpoints would make me every bit the villain."

"I've said something similar to Nora," Alexander chuckled again, though he looked back in the direction of the house. "Shall we head back? I fear Larent will come looking for you soon."

"Probably," Collette agreed, and the two turned their backs on the fence.

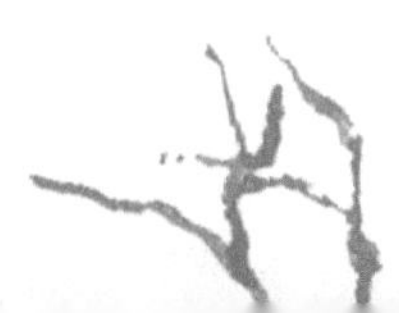

Chapter Thirty-Nine

As Larent strolled into the house, he knew Pops would start a conversation with Collette. He trusted his grandfather with his life, and he knew the older man would do nothing to bring him, or Collette, harm. Still, Pops didn't know Collette. Not really. Larent was willing to admit he was still learning the intricate facets of Collette, a byproduct of persistent observation. He knew she would put Pops in his place, if needed.

Nana immediately put Larent to work kneading dough. He'd spent hours growing up standing at this very counter working dough of some kind over a sprinkling of flour. Today, neither he nor Nana felt the need to talk. Their conversation hit all of the important points, and Larent could enjoy the companionable silence as he counted the minutes Collette was gone.

He heard the distinct sound of hooves on the wooden floor. Looking over, Larent laughed as he took sight of a couple of goats. This wasn't the first time animals managed to find their way inside, and given the outside chill, Larent couldn't blame them.

"Oh, dear Lady, not again." Nora groaned. "You monsters, get out." She snapped her dish towel in their direction, making absolutely no impression on the goats. "Go get your Pops," she instructed as she continued trying to persuade the goats to listen. "They're afraid of my cat, but not his bear."

"Okay, okay," Larent agreed, laughing all the while. He jogged out of the house but came to a stop as he found Collette and Pops heading in their direction. "Goats are in the house again," he called out, earning a sign from Pops.

"Damn it," the older man said, shaking his head. "You two go wander. Rounding up the goats will take a minute." Pops didn't wait for a response. Instead, he walked away from Collette before shifting into a gigantic bear. His skin and clothes seemed to rip away as his spine curled down. Thick, shiny black fur emerged, and Pops moved with a swiftness the bulk of the bear rendered impressive.

Larent had always loved watching the change, and he was inspired to do research into shifter magic if the chance ever arose.

"Isn't he beautiful?" Larent asked Collette as she joined him.

"He is," she replied, her eyes trained on the running bear. "His shifting differs from yours, but I'm not sure I can explain how."

"I think his shift is smoother, maybe," Larent ventured as a guess. "But I've never heard anyone compare them before."

"Given my lack of familiarity with shifters, naturally I'd compare the ability when given the chance," Collette replied.

"Beyond our spirituality, I don't know a whole lot. There aren't a lot of us." He leaned close and playfully whispered, "And you know I can't fully trust Nana to keep from exaggerating about things."

"I have noticed your family's spirituality," Collette replied with a conspiratorial grin. "At least a time or two."

"Just a time or two?" Larent asked, holding out a hand for her to take. He smiled softly, feeling himself relax as their fingers laced together.

As they'd been instructed to wander, Larent led them with no real plan. The sun was out, helping to combat the chilly wind, and animals of all kinds could be spotted along their makeshift trail. They passed a pin where an old pig covered in large black spots happily wallowed in the mud next to a trough. Larent wondered when Nana decided she liked pigs. He'd have to ask, but the thought left his head as Collette waved a trio of fingers at the animal. Lady, he needed to get his near worship under control. He found himself wondering what Pops had said to Collette, but he knew she would divulge the conversation in her own time. So, he posed a familiar question.

"Tell me something."

Collette looked up at him as they walked, and Larent once again found himself in complete awe of her. She was so beautiful and strong, and for some reason, she had chosen him when she might have had anyone she wanted.

"I maintain, you are very much like your Pops," Collette replied.

"Why?" Larent asked with a startled laugh.

"I know you, and I have spent months learning your heart and demeanor. Your Pops made many observations today I've heard you make. It's an easy parallel to draw."

Larent eyed her slyly. "So he told you to run away with me, then?" he asked, mostly teasing.

"It's possible," she quipped back. "Do you want me to run away with you?"

Larent shrugged. "I want whatever you want. If you want to stay here forever, I'm good. If you want to continue fighting for the kingdom, I'm equally as good. I'll be good with another, unnamed option."

Collette stepped around a discarded farm tool, long rusted beyond use, and Larent paused long enough to pick the thing up and toss it further from their path. "What if I was undecided?" she asked as they resumed their stroll. "What would you want, then?"

"To help you figure out what you truly wanted without pushing you either way," he replied. "Admittedly, not pushing would be challenging for me because I know you don't really want to be queen, and even if you wanted the role, it's brought you so much pain. I don't think you'll walk away, though, and I've accepted your decision." He gave her hand a reassuring squeeze. "Besides, what I want doesn't matter nearly as much as what you want."

"What you want absolutely matters to me, Larent."

He brought them to a stop and pulled her against him. "All I want is to be with you, Freckles. It doesn't matter to me if you decided to be a farmer, an explorer, or a queen."

She gazed up at him again, her expression content, if not happy. "I want to be with you, regardless."

"Same," Larent repeated. "No matter what." He kissed her, but soon had them moving again. "Nana brought something up when you and Pops were talking," he shared. "I think I agree with her."

"About what?" Collette asked.

He sighed, feeling his mouth grow thin at the seriousness of his grandmother's words. "I know I've said it before, but I am sorry how I treated Tolan."

Collette's brow went up in confusion. "Why?"

Larent was grateful they were moving, and he could look ahead as he explained his thinking. "I know Tolan chose to screw up, but had I not been so hard on him, so vindictive and nasty, he might have made different choices. I'll always regret the role I played in what he did to you, and I'm sorry."

He dared to look down at her, fearing she might be angry with him, even though he hadn't hidden his behavior from anyone. Instead of seeing anything resembling fury in her expression, she just nodded.

"You were an ass to him at times, but like you said, he chose to leave. I'm not going to waste energy being upset at you about it, especially when your contributions had very little to do with me."

"They absolutely didn't," Larent confirmed. "You were happy with him at one point."

"I know," she replied. "Truthfully, I've been heartbroken since I was arrested. Tolan showing up out of nowhere was just a final straw for me."

"I don't see how you couldn't be. You cared for Zephraim, and you still have a real love for Tolan. I'm surprised you decided to give me even the smallest of chances."

"You make me happy, and I deserve happiness. I'm going to take it when I find it," Collette said with a shrug. "As much as I love the people we are with, they wouldn't have a lot of patience with me if I decided to wallow in how I really feel about everything outside us."

"Which is bullshit when you considered how long they've wallowed in their own trauma. I think only Thomas and Whyldon would have any room to say anything, but they are generally less demanding on you."

They were far enough from the house, they'd probably miss a summons to return. Tired of their aimless path, he redirected them towards the woods. Collette liked the woods, which made the choice obvious for Larent. "What do you want to do once we leave here?"

Collette sighed. "I suppose we need to start thinking about our plans when we leave Barcomb Mill. With the snow melted and the two of us healed, we have little excuse to linger."

He cast his gaze over her again, genuinely surprised by her decisiveness. Larent doubted Pops had bullied her into a decision, but he felt like their conversation must have motivated her into a firmer stance. "It sounds like you've made up your mind."

"I've accepted I'm not going to step down from my responsibility," Collette explained, shaking her head. "If I'm willing to acknowledge my refusal to quit, I need to be less passive about moving forward."

Larent stared at Collette for a few heartbeats, taking in the way the sun glinted off her hair, the firm set of her lips, and the renewed fire burning in her eyes. He knew right then he would follow this woman anywhere. He would step out from behind Arian and Nawalya and forge a new path forward with Collette. Something in him had shifted, finally falling into place. He would stand by her side, never faltering, supporting her in any and all ways he could. He would learn politics for her if he had to and be a consort worthy of the queen before him. He would give his life for Collette, and he would forever place her happiness and safety above his own.

"Then we plan on moving forward," Larent easily accepted. "Are you still willing to go to the Nereids, or do you have another goal in mind?"

"They are the safest bet, and I'm hoping they will be receptive."

"Can we stay a few more days before we head back? Or do you want to leave sooner?" Larent was good either way, but he wouldn't mind a few more days with her and his grandparents. It would also help him get this need to be with her, wrapped around her, under control before they hit the road and they would no longer have time for cuddles and slow love making.

"We can manage another few days."

Larent grinned. "Perfect. Then you can go back and kick everyone's ass."

Collette laughed. "Should we go see if your grandparents managed to handle the goats?"

"Unless you want to do anything else?" Larent said, playfully wiggling his eyebrows as he backed Collette against a tree.

"I could be persuaded."

"And I can be persuasive," Larent said. He boxed her in against the tree, his body pressing against hers as he lowered his head for a kiss.

Chapter Forty

Riken rode slowly into the village, his chestnut stallion's deliberate pace demonstrating just how unhappy mount and master were. To his right rode Cadan, his army commander. Cadan made an imposing figure. He sat tall on his horse, and his broad shoulders, dark hair, olive skin, and deep gray eyes marked him as skilled and dangerous. Cadan scanned the area in silence, taking in every detail of the village. Riken knew Cadan was a loyal man, and with the letters he'd received from Quenall regarding Xavier's behavior, Riken needed reassurance of loyalty.

Behind them rode three soldiers hand-picked for the mission. The rest of Cadan's men waited in the forest, all aware of their orders. The day promised violence, and their willing compliance ensured success.

The elven village was exactly how Riken had pictured it. Wooden huts were spaces in circular patterns near the north side of the settlement. Some were new or well-maintained, while others sat splintered and faded under the sun, a fire hazard waiting to happen.

The buildings, Riken assumed, had their own rudimentary plumbing a striking difference from the more advanced accommodations found in the cities and larger human estates. Dogs and other domesticated animals lazily wandered about, pausing to chew on grass or rub against the exterior of a dwelling. Such was the way of the elves, to live simply and close to nature. Riken didn't understand making such choices. Convenience, cleanliness, and the advantages he found with human-designed and ruled areas made more sense. Nature-loving elves lived barbarically, and the village proved it.

As they rode on, Riken spotted who he assumed were town elders standing near an intricate stone fountain, waiting for them. Elvish women pulled grubby little children into their huts, perhaps detecting the threat he posed.

A memory of a past conversation slunk to the forefront of his mind. An elderly elf, the only elf his father had trusted, once told Riken to never trust elves. They lied to protect their own, and they always lied to humans. It was advice he lived by when dealing with these creatures. He wondered what lies would be shared.

Arriving in the town center, Riken and his men quickly dismounted, and two of the men grabbed the horses by their reins. Cadan and the third man, a young soldier with red hair, stepped forward and bowed ever so slightly to the elders who returned their gesture with head nods. A sign of disrespect if ever there was one, but Riken kept his face pleasant while Cadan and the other man did the same.

"We were not expecting you, Lord Riken," said the eldest elf. His long gray hair cascaded down to the middle of his back, presenting a semblance of vitality. The elder was helped forward by a woman who bore some resemblance.

"Strange. I sent a messenger over a week ago. I wonder what might have happened to him," Riken pondered out loud. He knew his man had been here and gone off to meet the soldiers on their way to Barcomb Mill.

The old man's face remained calm but several of the others shifted their weight and their eyes, telling Riken all he needed to know about how the day would go.

"Let us go to the community building, and we can see what you want," the old man said.

So he'd chosen to stick with deception on top of the disrespect, evidenced as the old elf turned his back on Riken. The community building sat just beyond the village center, large enough to hold a few hundred, but no more impressive than the smaller dwellings. Riken might have been insulted by the suggestion to go there had it not been the finest building to offer. His team followed inside, and Riken had to fight against rolling his eyes at the sight. A fire burned in the middle of a large room. Around it lay a covering of lush rugs, blankets, and cushions. The walls held paintings, tapestries, and other culturally significant decorations. Tables sat against the walls, some for food preparation, some for crafts, and others for who knew what, all of which Riken dismissed.

On one side of the fire sat a series of raised seats. The elders sat down, then motioned to the pillows on the ground. The position would place Riken and his men lower than the elders. Riken nodded to Cadan and the soldier to sit while he loudly planted his feet. He knew the elders should speak first. It would be considered the height of disrespect to start the conversation, but he considered the social faux pas fair since he didn't know who he was speaking to.

"Elders, I have come here on behalf of your king and queen to request your help in gathering information on the people who have been helping the convict Collette Gaillane."

"Why would you assume we know anything of the criminal queen?" one of the younger female elders asked. Gray threaded through her blonde hair, and her ancient body bent forward much like her companions.

"Because two of them are elves," Riken answered. "A male named Arian Tal'Dela and a female called Nawalya. From my research, the male is a survivor of A'lierdeen. Yours is the closest village still standing. A well-known truth about elves is their insistence on sticking together. One would assume the lone survivors would come here at some point." Riken watched all the elders carefully, but it was the female helper who gave them away, her eyes widening slightly at the names of the elves.

"We know of none by those names, nor has the queen been here," the head elder spoke up. "It is true elves stand together, and we did send aid to A'lierdeen. When our people arrived, however, there were no signs of survivors and none showed up here."

Riken pressed his lips together. "I was afraid you'd make a claim of ignorance." A tap to his right hip had Cadan and the soldiers on their feet, weapons drawn. All the elders except the head rose to their feet and backed away, fear in their eyes. Riken's gaze remained fixed on the head elder.

"We have done nothing to warrant your hate and violence," the old man said calmly, his gaze obstinate and confident.

"Oh, but you have. You have lied to me. The woman recognized the names of the elves," Riken pointed out.

"They are common enough names, especially Nawalya. It means loss in our language, and only those who have suffered greatly would call themselves such."

"Be that as it may, she recognized both names, not just Nawalya."

The old elf smirked as he rose to his feet. "It is not treason when there is a false king on the throne. You were right. We received your message, and we prepared for your arrival." The elder clapped his hands and waited as if something was to happen. When nothing did, he clapped again, the smile fading from his face.

"Were you expecting someone? Guards perhaps?" Riken asked before clapping his own hands, the effort mocking. A second passed before the door to the center opened, letting a symphony of screams and terror enter along with two of Riken's soldiers. He glared at the elder. "I also came prepared."

The soldiers and Cadan advanced on the elders, subduing them before the three soldiers drug them from the center, leaving only Riken, Cadan, the elder, and his helper in the room. Cadan roughly grabbed the elder and brought him to Riken before the old man's legs were kicked out from under him. He collapsed with a cry of pain to the floor. The woman tried to rush to his side, but Cadan grabbed her.

Unsheathing his sword, Riken held it against the side of the elder's throat. "Tell me what you know, or he dies."

Tears poured down her face, but there was no mistaking the anger in the woman's eyes. "Two people using those names were here twenty years ago. They helped us fight off raiders who were stealing our animals and burning our crops. We do not know if they were from A'lierdeen. We just know they came to our aid."

"Were any others with them?" Riken asked curiously.

"A man named Larent, human. He helped them fight off the raiders."

Riken couldn't contain the satisfied smile spreading across his lips. Her information gave him so much more to research and confirmation of a long-term relationship. "And they haven't been back in recent months?" He pushed his sword closer to the old man's throat, drawing a small amount of blood.

The woman screamed in rage. "No! By the Spirit, I swear it. We haven't seen them since they killed the raiders."

"Finally, some honesty," Riken said sweetly. "I thank you for it." As the word left his mouth, he drove his sword into the old man's back and through his chest. The elvish woman screamed and thrashed anew as Riken cleaned his sword on the dead elder's body.

"Put her with the others," Riken ordered Cadan. The commander pulled her from the tent, paying no mind to her screams of rage and pain.

Looking down at the body, Riken sighed in pity before looking around at the community building. He wondered if any of the artifacts were worth monetary value before deciding it didn't matter. He walked from the building into organized chaos. The soldiers he had stationed in the woods had done their jobs beautifully, having stormed the village, subdued guards, and rounded up everyone.

The screaming woman was handed off to another soldier. Candan stood by a young man with a shock of orange hair and a round face. He was visibly distressed by the events. Riken would have to ask how the boy was recruited for the mission.

"Is there a problem soldier?" He let the words linger as he and Cadan watched the young man.

"It's Farner, sir," Cadan informed Riken.

"My Lord, what about the children?" Farner asked.

Riken couldn't recall looking and sounding so young, and he knew he'd never held the sort of sympathy he read in Farner's expression. Looking back at the group of elves who were slowly but proficiently being forced into the center of their village, Riken honestly felt bad for them. These savages refused to submit to the rightful rule of their leaders. They spit in the face of the Mother and lashed out violently. Despite the terror he had to inflict, Riken made a decision he didn't expected.

Turning to Cadan, he issued new orders. "Have your men gather the children and any carers who are in no shape to fight. You," he added, pointing to Farner. "Go help." The young soldier left without hesitation, and Riken grabbed Cadan's arm before he could join. "Keep an eye on him. If he's too soft on the elves, deal with him."

"Of course, my Lord. Farner's family has been loyal for generations."

"All it takes is a second of doubt, of pity, for one to lose their way. We need loyalty and commitment amongst my troops."

Cadan nodded and went to help the others. Riken watched dispassionately as children were torn from their parents. Cadan walked the line, picking out the few adults he deemed safe to care for the children. The remaining elves were backed together into a tight circle, many unable to resist due to injury or restraint. The screaming and crying got louder as dry brush and wood scraps were placed around and next to them. The elves were covered in oil.

Moving closer to the circle, Riken held up his hand, all activity in the village stopping as cries echoed out. "Your elders refused to help me, to help your royals. All I wanted was answers. Answers as to who was helping the convicted queen, and your elders lied to me. As such, I find all of you guilty of treason. Enjoy your last moments."

Riken stepped away, and his men stepped forward, torches in hand. They set fire to the village and its people.

Chapter Forty-One

Thick, pungent smoke lingered in the air, though the active, swirling gray plumes of a powerful fire had long faded into feeble wisps of translucent vapor. The stench of charged flesh came in waves, escalating in intensity with each passing breeze. Here and there, scorched tree branches hung low over the remnants. Skeletal fingers searched for the now-lost society.

The ashen sky blocked out all traces of hopeful sunshine, casting the remains of wooden structures into frightening shadows of what had been. A field of what once might have been wheat sat abandoned save for the plows and tools.

The soft earth beneath Ceto's boots shifted as she explored the rows of burnt-out huts scattered at one end of the village. Every so often, she passed the charred remains of an animal, though the acrid smell forced her to cover her nose and mouth with a scarf. She prepared for something more horrendous.

Every step she took echoed throughout the empty streets, and her golden eyes constantly shifted, looking for potential danger while trying to avoid trodding on the dead. The attack appeared sudden. The wooden huts gave way to what Ceto assumed were the social and business areas. Kilns and ovens, recreation spots, and other areas to carry out daily work survived the fire in better condition than the huts. A court, where Ceto assumed sports or games were played, looked nearly untouched.

Various trinkets lay scattered along the roads, some recognizable while others sat in piles of ash. A washer carrying their linens towards the creek left behind an old basket, half burned, the singed clothing within looked mostly unharmed. A baking sheet, dented and tossed into a random doorway, had likely held bread and other decadent treats not so long ago.

In the village center sat a blackened stone fountain. The haunting silence served as a reminder of the once bubbling water, of the laughter of children. Around the fountain lay the remains of dozens of bodies, and Ceto paused in her steps, eyes widened in her desperate sadness.

"This was brutal," Ceto said, her voice a whisper.

"This was intentional, planned, and executed with efficiency," Jayden replied gravely, coming up beside her. He'd been the one to spot the smoke when they'd been packing up their camp. His lips pressed together, and his eyes narrowed as he took in the scene.

"Why do you think they were targeted?" Ceto asked.

"Because they were elves?" Jayden suggested in a harsh voice before shaking his head. "I somehow doubt there was a real reason. They probably pissed off a noble or someone who could afford hired hands." He shook his head again. "They'll tie the massacre back to Queen Collette, you know."

Ceto nodded, her anger bubbling just below the surface. "They will," she agreed. "And the false king will justify more brutality."

Carefully, she walked a half circle around the bodies, tallying the number of the dead. "There are too many of them to bury."

"I know, but we can't just leave them here," Jayden replied. He remained in place while she walked, so she looked over, alarmed when he gasped.

"Ceto, I don't see any children," he said in a voice laced with horror.

Somehow, Ceto had overlooked the lack of children, and her golden eyes frantically searched the mass of bodies. He was right, and she felt a new sense of terror creeping up her spine. "You think whoever's responsible took them?"

"Yes," he breathed out. "We must let Aphros know they've started abducting children. The last time Coralia waged war against non-humans, the children were targeted first."

"We'll write to him as soon as we figure out what to do here," Ceto assured him.

Jayden's mind was quickly made up. "We need to bury the dead. Then, we will track the responsible monsters."

"Of course," Ceto said without hesitation. She took a breath, calming herself. "How do you propose dealing with the burials?"

"The only way we can. Find tools, dig a trench, and move them."

"Let's get started, then. We have a long day ahead of us," Ceto suggested.

Aphros,

Ceto and I came across a destroyed elvin village. Everyone was murdered, the village burned, and the raiders took the children. We are certain the responsible party is troops from Quenall. Ceto and I have changed course, and we will be tracking the perpetrators.

Chapter Forty-one

Please, use our information to call as many people to our kingdom as possible. We can't lose any more children.

Jayden

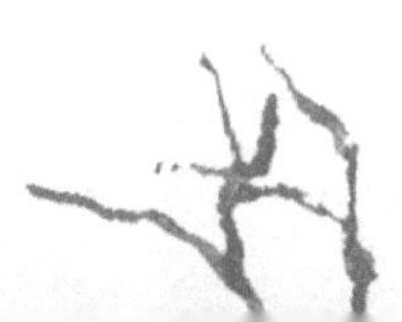

Chapter Forty-Two

Tolan looked down at the sleeping woman in his bed, her carob colored hair spilling across her face and pillow. He barely resisted the urge to reach out and brush the silken strands from her cheek. He knew Collette hadn't slept well these last few months, so instead of waking her, he studied her delicate features, soaking in her beauty. The rare peaceful moments they shared always brought him joy, even as he wrestled with his ever-growing affection for her.

He had come to realize he had never felt this strongly about anyone. His feelings for Collette terrified him. He wasn't worthy of her, in any way, yet he loved her, and he was almost positive she returned the feeling. The way she lit up when he entered a room, the way she reached for him when no one else was around, the way his name fell from her lips… How could it be anything else?

With his internal acknowledgment of his affections, Tolan pondered leaving Quenall before either of them fell harder than they already had. It would hurt less in the long run when she eventually found someone more worthy than a bastard kitchen worker with arena experience. Yet, he didn't leave the bed. He

292

couldn't. Instead, he finally gave into the urge to brush her hair away from her check, his fingers gliding over the smooth skin, wincing as Collette stirred.

She made a soft noise of protest, as though leaving sleep might offend her more than any other notion. Still, when her eyes fluttered open, dark orbs half hidden by sleep-heavy lashes, she gave him a soft smile.

"Hey," she said.

"Hi," Tolan said softly. "Go back to sleep. It's still early."

"Okay," she replied just as softly, closing her eyes as she snuggled up closer to him. She did not drift back to sleep, but instead allowed them both to exist in content silence for a stretch of time.

Tolan held Collette close and considered all the ways he was not, nor ever would be enough. He decided to push those thoughts away. He was in love, and he had no desire to fight it. Kissing the top of her head, he resolved to embrace what they'd grown to be for one another. She was worth staying for, no matter how bad an idea it was.

As light streamed into the room, he pondered ignoring his duties, but Collette interrupted his thoughts.

"Aren't you supposed to be in the kitchens by now?" she asked.

"I don't want to go," Tolan admitted with a soft, self-deprecating laugh.

"Then don't," she said, opening her eyes and looking up at him. "You could tell Diana I held you up."

"That's a sound plan, but what of your advisors and Whyldon?"

"What of them?" Collette asked. "I'm their queen. They can wait while I enjoy your warmth."

"Very true." Tolan pulled her closer, avoiding mention of the nobles who ran her ragged, pulling Collette in different

directions in an attempt to undermine the changes she wished to make.

"You should still be more afraid of Diana," Collette teased, more awake now. "Even my position might not be enough to save you from her wrath."

"Everyone should fear Mistress Hawke," Tolan agreed, his voice affectionate and playful. Collette could alway redirect his negative thoughts. "She is a formidable woman, but unless you wish me to go, I am happy where I am."

"I cannot recall when I have ever wished you to go," she replied, her fingers running along his bare chest in light touches.

"Oh, I think there has been a time or two," Tolan said with a laugh. "Or else you might not have pushed me from the window."

"You enjoy being pushed from windows," Collette insisted.

"What makes you assume that?"

"You keep letting me do it."

"What if I just enjoy your hands on me? Even if it's to push me out said window?" Tolan asked playfully.

"You can never doubt I look for reasons to touch you," Collette replied.

"I love you," he said without thought, freezing up as he realized what he said. No matter what he knew about their mutual feelings, he'd never voiced it.

She looked up at him again, though she remained as she was, half on top of him, a leg draped across his, while her head rested on his shoulder. "I love you, too."

Tolan gave Collette a soft smile, once more pushing away his doubts as he kissed her. He could do this, with her, for her. He could do this.

Tolan stood in the small amount of shade offered by the north side of the house. He'd spent the morning chopping wood, and the cool morning air did nothing to prevent him from turning into a sweaty mess. Pulling his shirt off, he wiped sweat from his forehead. He tossed the item over his shoulder and made the short walk to the decorative table Sara stocked with a water pitcher and cups. He poured himself a glass. Thirst quenched, he leaned against the cottage and experienced a full-body shiver as his bare skin touched the cold siding of the house.

Tolan considered going inside to wash up and grab a new shirt, but a small popping noise followed by a disgruntled shout drew his gaze. Several feet from the house, Arian stood over a portable potions table, the contents of his once carefully packed medicine kit meticulously laid out. The elf, and every vial and bottle, were covered in a sticky, purple substance glowing brightly.

"It has never blown up before," Arian complained bitterly to Sara.

Thomas stood near, laughing outright while Nawalya sat cross-legged on a log a little further away. She studiously complied with the exercises Sara assigned for better control of her visions.

Arian snarled at the purple mess and grabbed for the potions book Sara provided. He carefully turned the pages, eyes scanning the contents. Eventually, he reached for a fresh container to mix a new elixir, then slowly added each until he had a swirling, translucent liquid. Arian glanced at the book again, muttered something over the potion Tolan couldn't hear, and upended the contents onto himself and the table. Everything glowed for a second. Then, magically, the purple sludge disappeared, leaving everything clean.

Tolan shook his head and looked away as Sara stepped forward to ask Arian a question. Sara and Thomas had been working with Arain and Nawalya for a few days to improve their natural and learned magical skills, leaving Whyldon,

Rion, and himself to pick up the bulk of the chores. With spring approaching, Sara needed to make sure she was ready for planting.

Nawalya slowly came out of her meditation, giving a small shriek that roused Tolan from his thoughts. He squashed his first instinct to ask if she needed help, knowing it would be rebuked. Standing, the female elf turned toward the forest, a bright smile spreading across her face.

Tolan redirected his gaze, spotting the reason for Nawalya's happiness. Collette and Larent had emerged from the forest, hands intertwined, laughter on their lips, all contributions to the beautiful pairing they made. A pang of jealousy formed in Tolan's chest, and he had to push it down, lest he make another stupid move.

He pulled his shirt back on, knowing retreat into the house would look worse than standing there shirtless. Still, he did not move to greet Collette and Larent as Sara and Thomas did. He remained by the house, drinking in the sight of Collette.

"You're looking so much better," Sara said, leaning in to hug Collette with a familiarity he assumed was fostered in the time he'd been gone.

"Do I?" the queen asked curiously.

"Yes," Larent confirmed before Sara could reply. "You're always beautiful, but you're radiant today."

Tolan frowned to himself, not because Larent was wrong, but because he was jealous. He wished he could be beside her, holding her hand, kissing her, complimenting her. He'd ruined their closeness with his decisions.

"You're biased as fuck," Collette replied with fondness, and Tolan's eyes went up to Larent. Admittedly, the shifter's usual attractiveness bordered on radiance as well.

"Of course he is," Sara said with a gentle laugh. "And he should be."

"And biased or not, I'm not wrong," Larent added with a grin. He leaned in and kissed Collette but pulled away when Sara cleared her throat.

"I know you cannot help yourselves but indulge in one another, but perhaps you'd like something to eat? I can let Arian and Nawalya take a break," Sara said.

"Take a break from what?" Larent asked.

Thomas, who took up residence next to Sara pointed toward the potion table. "Arian has been working on his healing magic." Then he gestured to Nawalya. "She's been working on meditation techniques to manage her visions."

"Really? Well, shit. I'm proud of you guys," Larent said, earning rude gestures from both elves. He chuckled and redirected his attention back to Sara. "I'm good on food. Nana made sure we ate before we left, and she packed us up with extra for the journey." He looked to Collette, checking in dutifully. "Are you hungry?"

The queen shook her head. "No. I've never eaten so much in my life. I'm actually pretty certain Nora didn't sleep the whole time we were there."

"She took cat naps," Larent replied.

Tolan couldn't help but chuckle at the lame joke, and he even smiled to himself as Collette smacked Larent's arm.

"Shut the fuck up," she said in a playful voice, and Larent responded by pretending to sew his mouth shut.

Tolan's grin disappeared as his gut clenched. He decided to go inside and wash up. The privacy would allow him to pull himself together.

"Tolan, wait up!"

Glancing back, Tolan watched as Larent whispered something to Collette, who looked apprehensive and skeptical. Still, she nodded before giving Larent a soft kiss. Then Larent

jogged over to catch up with Tolan, who gave the shifter a skeptical look.

"I promise, by The Lady, no violence. Well, unless you start it." Larent's smile was slightly more vicious than Tolan liked, but he knew if he turned the wolf down it would make him look like an ass and hurt his chances of being allowed to stay.

"Yeah, fine," Tolan replied, and reluctantly, he motioned for Larent to follow him into the house. They would be out of earshot and sight, but not so far away should the two men start fighting again. "What?" he asked when the door was closed. He winced, noting the harshness in his voice.

"I deserved that," Larent said, surprising Tolan. "I took Collette to see my grandparents, and Nana gave me a verbal ass-kicking about a few things."

Tolan's brows narrowed in confusion. Whatever Larent was doing, it wasn't the gloating warning to stay away from Collette he'd expected. "And?" Tolan prompted.

"And Nana was right, of course. She always is." Larent looked down and away. "I never really let myself get over you and your decision to leave me, and as a result, I said and did some pretty horrible things. I wanted to say I'm sorry."

Tolan's jaw dropped in surprise. He knew he looked like a wide-eyed, gaping fish.

"My behavior doesn't excuse what you did to me and Collette. You'll have to apologize to her at some point because you owe her as much." Larent shrugged. "I doubt we'll ever be friends, given our history, but I wanted to say I am sorry all the same."

Tolan managed to close his mouth, but he was blinking really hard, his brow scrunched as he tried to let what Larent said sink in.

Larent laughed as he patted Tolan on the back. "Also I forgive you for trying to kill me. I'm sure you had your reasons, but I don't want to hear them right now."

His peace said, Larent took off, leaving Tolan floundering, completely unsure of what to do.

"I take it you're feeling better after your trip?" Whyldon asked while Collette went through her pack, determining what to unpack.

She was seated cross-legged on the bed, completing the task with a leisure she rarely utilized. Meanwhile, Whyldon had taken a seat in the desk chair, cluing her in on his intention to talk. She didn't mind. She knew she needed to check in, to reassure him of her good health and mental state. "I am," she agreed, tossing a shirt to the side. It needed washing, and a bit of sewing to repair a hole near the bottom. "Getting away from everything helped me refocus."

"So you didn't flee because you wanted to avoid Tolan?" Whyldon asked.

When Collette looked up, she spotted the mischievous twinkle in his eye. She glared at him in return. "Like Tolan Dethenal can run me off. I was already at the end of my very long, frayed rope. I'd have needed the time away, regardless." She found a leather pouch for storing jerky and other sustainable food items when traveling. Finding it empty, she put the pouch aside so she'd remember to fill it.

"We've noticed," Whyldon acknowledged. He leaned back in the chair, the front two legs leaving the floor, his legs long enough to help with the balance. "I should apologize for not recognizing it earlier and intervening."

"How would you have intervened, exactly?" she asked, her lips turned up in amusement. "Did you plan to stop Zephraim, or do something later in the timeline of my life falling apart?"

"You know, I'm unsure, but had I been more cognizant of what you have been dealing with internally, I'd have been more proactive," Whyldon replied. "Either way, we need a path forward."

"We have a path forward," Collette said. "Figure out how to either get support or raise an army. I suspect the Nereid might be willing to help, but we could be surprised."

"They owe you for what you did for their emissary," Whyldon agreed. He scratched his chin and continued. "You may not want to hear this, given your history with Tolan, but he brought another option back with him."

Collette didn't look up from her sorting, though she paused long enough to make a gesture to continue.

"The high king of Fythias has offered his army. Tolan arranged it, if it is something you want."

She looked up, seeing no hint of jest in Whyldon's face. If he was right, if Tolan had secured her an army and backing from a strong nation, she could win back Coralia. "How the fuck did he get me an army?"

Whyldon lowered the chair onto all fours. "I don't know all of the details, but he has an official letter confirming the offer. Fythias is a well-respected nation, and their willingness to work with you suggests others would follow."

"Does this mean I have to talk to him?" Collette asked, knowing the answer. His presence in Barcomb Mill meant the others hadn't deemed it necessary to throw Tolan out. She could make him leave, of course, but she knew she wouldn't issue such an order even without the promise of an army.

"At some point, I suspect you might," Whyldon said, though both he and Collette looked over as a gentle knock sounded on the heavy door.

"Yes?" Collette called out. The door opened, revealing Larent.

"Mind if I join?" he asked.

"I suppose," Collette said, her consternation over Tolan temporarily forgotten.

A grin grew on Larent's face, and in a few steps, he was on the bed with Collette, arms around her waist, and chin on her shoulder. "Pretend I'm not here."

"You need to be here for what Whyldon shared," Collette replied. "Apparently Tolan found an army for me, and Whyldon says I have to talk to him."

"Oh, shit. How?"

Whyldon pulled a letter from his pocket and handed it to Collette. "He has connections to the royal family in Fythias."

Collette opened the unsealed letter, eyes scanning the brief message. The seal and signature looked legitimate, and even after everything Tolan had done, she doubted he would forge a letter to earn their favor. She handed it over to Larent.

"Wow, really?" he said, browsing the parchment. "Is he a royal?"

From the hallway, a voice said, "Yes, actually. I am." Tolan stepped into the doorway, and Larent bowed his head against Collette's shoulder, muttering an apology about not closing the door.

Collette met his presence with a neutral gaze. She knew she should be thankful for what he had accomplished, but she was also brokenhearted, despite her relationship with Larent, and she wasn't ready to be welcoming. "I take it you didn't know as much before you ran off?"

Tolan shook his head. "I suspected I had some sort of connection to an important family," he said, holding up his necklace to show the pendant.

Collette wanted to roll her eyes at the motion, but she restrained herself knowing he had a reason. "You must have used the libraries in Quenall. Your pendant has always looked Fythian to me."

Tolan nodded in response. "The pendant earned an audience with Alaoin, my cousin, and the High King."

"So you are officially a royal, and you've secured an army for me," Collette said. "At what price?"

Tolan gave an awkward shrug. "Giving up any rights to the throne was the only condition. He and his advisors used a lot of political talk I didn't understand, but they argued I theoretically had more right to be king than my cousin did." He sounded distinctly unhappy about the prospect.

"Why did you agree to his stipulation?" Collette asked.

Tolan raised an eyebrow in confusion. "My cousin was trained from birth to rule, and from what I saw, he's done a damn good job. I was an arena fighter. Then I worked in a kitchen. How would I begin to be a good ruler?" He shook his head. "I went there for help, and what he asked of me was more than fair."

"Maybe, but you have more rights to a throne than I have, based on your story," Collette argued. She didn't miss Tolan's eyes darting in Whyldon's direction. "I will accept your reasoning, but know if I catch you moping again like you were before you left, I might kill you where you stand."

"Or she'll have Arian do it," Larent interrupted. "He volunteered to be her personal assassin."

"Perhaps, rather than issuing threats, we should think of productive ways to move forward?" Whyldon suggested. "If we are to go to Fythias, we should forgo plans for the Nereid Kingdom. Travel would be different."

"True," Collette conceded. Other than packing, she could think of only one other reason to delay their stay in Barcomb Mill, and Collette knew she had not taken the opportunity to refine her magic as she should. She could worry about her lack of foresight later. Decision made, she called out, "Arian!"

The elf appeared beside Tolan a few moments later, his quick steps imperceptible. "You called?"

"How long do you need with Sara before we leave?" Collette asked.

"An hour, but I cannot speak for Thomas and Nawalya," Arian replied.

"We should likely wait until morning if that suits," Collette said. She didn't want to rush anyone who was not ready. A small delay would also provide everyone with a nourishing evening meal and a night of rest. She'd speak with Sara about what she could do to work on her magical abilities since she wouldn't have further opportunity to properly train.

"Morning might be best," Arian agreed after pausing to consider.

"Good," Collette replied. "Make sure everyone's food storage is restocked if you can, my brother. I know I'm empty."

Arian stared at Collette for a minute in total silence before an eyebrow went up. "Of course, sister," he said, his voice sardonic on the last word.

Collette grinned at the response. "Thank you."

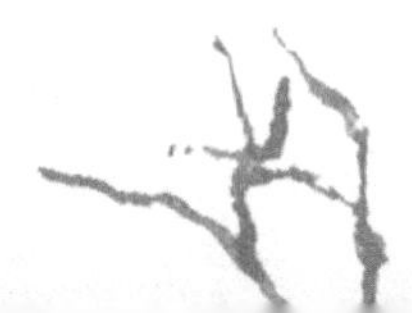

Chapter Forty-Three

Arian headed to the room he shared with Thomas, silently grateful he hadn't unpacked all his things while they resided in Barcomb Mill. Thomas, on the other hand, would need a lot more time to gather his belongings. Entering their shared room, Arian was unsurprised to find Thomas lying on their bed reading. He couldn't help but stand there looking at the blond man.

These last few weeks had been… Well, rough was a nice way of putting it. Arian had been sullen since his conversation with Nawalya. Their fight? Whatever it was, he had not been the best of company. He would need to make it up to Thomas and eventually talk to Nawalya. Just maybe not right now.

Moving to the dresser, Arian started to pack the small amount of items he had out. "Thomas, Collette would like to leave tomorrow," he said softly.

Thomas put his book aside and sat up, his leisurely movements showing no motivation despite the warning. "Where would she like to go?"

"She has decided on Fyithas. Whyldon informed her of Tolan's army."

"And is Tolan allowed to travel with us?" Thomas asked, light eyes twinkling in amusement.

"She did not say he was, but I am assuming so." Arian paused. "Not to say she will not throw him overboard once we are at sea."

"He might deserve it." Thomas finally stood and began a slow circle of the room to collect his things. "Someone might warn him when the time comes all the same."

Arian tilted his head in thought. "I will leave that in your hands."

"Why mine?" Thomas asked as he rolled up a sheet of parchment. "You know him better."

"Because I believe you are the only one who may mind if he is tossed overboard." Arian paused to reconsider. "Rion might care."

"Rion might," Thomas agreed. "But you won't?"

Arian shook his head. "It would be a waste, especially since he may be needed in negotiations. However, if Collette sees a need to throw Tolan overboard, I will be there to lend her a hand."

Thomas snorted in response, his lips turned upward in a smile. Finding his bag, he began packing away his papers with gentle care. "I'm sure you are very happy to assist her."

"In most things," Arian admitted.

Thomas gave the elf a knowing grin, and he focused on his papers for a little longer. Eventually, his things were consolidated into his travel pack. "I think I have a couple of things downstairs…"

"Would you like me to go find those items for you?" Arian asked, leaning against the dresser, his packing finished.

"If you would like," Thomas replied. "I can see your eagerness to be ready to leave the second the sun is up."

"It is less an eagerness to be gone and more a desire to be doing something productive." Arian did not add his need for distraction from his spiraling thoughts.

"Any particular reason?" Thomas asked, approaching him slowly and placing a hand on Arian's cheek.

Arian thought to pull away from Thomas's hand but chose to lean into it instead. "Things have been very hard since we arrived here."

"More or less since leaving Quenall?"

"On a personal level, harder than since we left Quenall."

"Tell me why," Thomas asked quietly.

"It's everything. Whyldon, Nawalya's changes since returning from Nora and Alexander's, Tolan arriving, and Larent and Collette leaving. It has been a lot." Before Collette nearly died, Arian had been more than capable of handling whatever came their way, or he felt like he had. But the emotional implications of their mission had exploded in a way he was unable to cope with, though he thought he hid it well.

"What we are trying to accomplish is an incredibly difficult task, and it's only natural we would suffer along the way," Thomas said, his voice gentle and affectionate. He brushed his thumb along Arian's cheekbone. "How you're feeling makes sense and is reasonable."

"It does not feel reasonable. I have an aching emptiness where nothing I've done seems right." Arian shivered slightly, but he remained close to Thomas, craving his touch even knowing he wasn't quite used to it.

Thomas moved closer, cupping both sides of Arian's face. "You have been so crucial from the moment you helped Collette leave Quenall. You've defended her. You've kept her alive. And other than Larent, you are the person she most relies on."

"And yet…" Arian closed his eyes as Nawalya's words echoed in his head. "I have treated Nawalya as a child, disrespected Larent, and taken away Collette's choices. Choices I had no right to make."

"Nawalya allowed you to treat her as you did," Thomas argued gently. "I would even suggest the way she behaved demanded your indulgences." He carefully wrapped his arms around Arian's waist. "Your dynamic with Larent is mutual, and you both need better boundaries with one another."

Arian leaned forward into Thomas's embrace, controlling his breathing as he rested his head against Thomas's shoulder. "I have always treated her with care, even before everything went wrong. I have always worried about her, but she has allowed me to do so. I also allowed both of us to wallow in our past. I have turned down offers of help, and now I wonder if she turned it down because I did."

Arian knew it was a silly thought as soon as he said it. Nawalya was her own person. He sighed, knowing he needed to address the next point. "Larent has a new fire in his eyes. I believe boundaries will be a discussion we have soon enough. He's bad at impulse control when he has something weighing on his mind."

"Then have a conversation with both of them," Thomas encouraged. "I doubt either want a fight from you, but the dynamic has forever changed, and it was always going to require discussion."

"What if I do not wish for things to change?"

"I don't think you have a choice, Arian," Thomas replied." Larent is not going to abandon Collette to go on missions with you anymore. I also get the sense you don't want to go back to the way things were before you came to Quenall to investigate the new queen."

Arian sighed into Thomas's shoulder. "You are very right."

"I know," Thomas said with a gentle laugh. "And whatever you decide, I plan on following you. This mission is only the beginning of the life I want to live with you."

Arian pulled Thomas tighter against him as the words registered. He forced away the intrusive thoughts telling him he was unworthy. At least for the moment, he would trust Thomas's words. If he kept hiding from his feelings, and from Thomas, eventually Thomas would walk away. Arian did not want that. Pulling away slightly, he gazed at Thomas for a moment before kissing him heatedly. He could use more of these hidden moments in his life.

Thomas responded eagerly, his lips and tongue teasing Arian's senses with overwhelming need. He hardly noticed the few steps their bodies made to get closer to the bed, and Arian didn't object when Thomas nudged the elf back onto the bed. When Arian was settled, Thomas followed, straddling him.

Arian closed his eyes. "Spirits, Thomas," he said, his voice rough. His hands ran along Thomas's sides and down to his hips, and Arian couldn't help but pull him closer. Their lips met again, and Arian groaned as Thomas began a slow and teasing grind against him. His body shivered with pleasure. Arian briefly wondered if he would make a better showing than he did the first time they'd shared. Thomas's tongue chased those thoughts away and soon Arian found himself thrusting up in reaction to the way Thomas moved against him.

"Tell me what you want," Thomas prompted between kisses.

"You. I want you," Arian breathed out.

"Okay," Thomas returned. He leaned back just enough to begin undoing the buttons at the top of Arian's shirt.

Arian shuddered as Thomas's finger brushed his bare skin, and he couldn't stop himself from thrusting up against Thomas. Arian ran his hands up and down Thomas's back one more time before moving them to undo Thomas's shirt. He helped

Thomas out of his shirt, taking in his pale skin. He then allowed Thomas to help him out of his own.

Arian took several steadying breaths as his chest was barred to Thomas once more. The fletcher had yet to flinch away from his scars, but a part of Arian still worried. Thomas looked down at him, running his hands down the elf's chest in reverential desire. He leaned in and kissed Arian.

Arian's breath caught in his throat. Thomas's hands moving on his chest almost overwhelmed him, but Arian knew he was safe. Returning the kiss, Arian allowed his hands to roam the revealed parts of Thomas's body. As they kissed, Thomas adjusted positions, and he gently pushed Arian's shoulder, encouraging him to lay back on the bed. The slow, intentional movements allowed Arian time to process each change and escalation of passion.

"You still okay?" Thomas asked.

"Yes," Arian breathed out as he followed Thomas's instructions. The rest of the words he wanted to say caught in his throat. He felt dizzy as Thomas kissed him again, then began trailing kisses along his jaw and down his throat. Arian let his eyes fall shut, not bothering to contain the moan. One hand bunched in the sheets under him. He felt Thomas's eyes on him, as the kisses moved lower, and he groaned again as Thomas's tongue swirled around his naval. He was almost distracted from Thomas unfastening the top button of his pants.

"Spirits, Thomas." He buried a hand in Thomas's hair.

"Lift your hips for me," Thomas directed, and Arian complied, trousers and shoes soon discarded, leaving him naked.

Thomas's hands ran up and down Arian's thighs. His pale eyes met Arian's, his expression warm and adoring. "Still okay?"

Arian nodded after allowing himself a moment to adjust to the touch. "Yes," he added in breathy emphasis. The response encouraged Thomas to lower himself, resting his weight on

his forearms. Arian could feel his lover's breath against his straining erection, the man's tongue teasingly running along the underside before finally taking Arian into his mouth.

A noise that seemed somewhere between a moan and scream left Arian. His mind zoned in on nothing by the sensations created by Thomas. A hand twisted into the bedding beneath him and his other hand buried itself in Thomas's cornsilk hair. He groaned softly as Thomas's head began bobbing up and down, a sound of pleasure rumbling in Thomas's throat.

Arian threw his head back as the sensations, and Thomas's name became a litany as the man drew him closer and closer to the edge. When Arian spilled, the hot intensity pushed him into a place of, albeit brief, peace. He held no worry or anxiety, his mind completely focused on the moment he shared with Thomas. When Thomas sat back on his haunches, he dabbed at the corner of his mouth with a finger, grinning down at him.

Arian couldn't help the small chuckle at the satisfied grin on Thomas's lips. Shaking his head, Arian reached out and grabbed Thomas, pulling him down for a kiss. He tasted himself on Thomas's lips, and it made him crave the other man all the more.

"I was going to request you fuck me," Arian shared.

"Trust me," Thomas replied between kisses. "I have every intention."

Arian's breathing turned harsh as he pulled Thomas down for another kiss. Yes, they needed to leave in the morning. Yes, they had to save the kingdom, but maybe, just for tonight, he could be selfish.

Chapter Forty-Four

Morning came, trickling in with an easy calm, assuring Collette she'd picked the perfect time to leave Barcomb Mill. Her heart ached at the thought of abandoning the serenity of the cottage and farm, a place where she'd recovered and connected more deeply with Larent and Arian, and where she'd embraced the familial ties she had to Whyldon and his family. She swore to one day return for something more akin to leisure. She had much she wanted to learn from Sara.

Crawling out of bed, a task often made difficult by Larent, Collette went about the task of preparing herself for the long day ahead. She was searching for her boots when she heard movement from the bed.

Larent lifted himself on his elbows, his eyes blinking in sleepy, slow movements. "Time to get up Freckles?"

"You could probably get a few more minutes if you need them," Collette said fondly.

"Only if you're sure," Larent said, his eyelids already closing.

Collette laughed. "I am."

"Okay," Larent said as he settled back against the bed. His eyes shut as he murmured, "I love you."

Leaving Larent in the bed, Collette headed downstairs, finding herself surprised by the quiet of the house. She had been certain Arian at the very least would be up, but as she walked into the kitchen, the only person she spotted was Thomas.

"Morning," Collette greeted.

"Morning," Thomas replied as he removed a kettle from the stove. "I think we'll be getting a later start than anticipated."

"I take it you and Arian had a late night," she commented.

"We did," Thomas confirmed with a grin. "Still didn't drown out the noise from your room."

"You can take up your concerns of noise with Larent," Collette quipped.

"He would see the question as a challenge. I'm not sure you could handle any more enthusiasm from him in one sitting," Thomas said as he went about steeping tea. He gestured towards his task, silently asking if Collette would like some. She nodded.

Nawalya walked through the kitchen, and upon spotting the two, she sent them both a small glare. The dark shadows under her eyes gave them more than enough information as to why she was unhappy. She made a quick exit without talking to either of them.

Thomas snorted. "We're in trouble."

"I maintain it's Larent's fault. At least on my end."

"You might, but I will take credit for anything I might have caused," Thomas replied. Seemingly satisfied with the tea, he poured a couple of mugs for each of them. "Besides, there is time for the others to catch up on sleep since we're having a slow morning."

"True," Collette said. She accepted the mug from Thomas and sipped from it, a hand idly playing with the ends of her loose hair. She needed to put it up because traveling with it down always turned out to be a royal pain in the ass.

Sara emerged into the kitchen, looking much more alert than Nawalya had. She smiled at both. "I'm surprised the two of you are the only ones up."

"Nawalya stomped through not long ago," Thomas shared. "I believe she didn't sleep well." He sipped his tea with an expression of innocense.

"I can't imagine why," Sara joked. She picked up the kettle and used the remaining hot water to make her own tea. "Did you need help braiding your hair before you set off?"

Collette almost nodded, but she paused as she considered the offer. "Actually, would you mind helping me cut it?"

Both Sara and Thomas looked at her in surprise. She supposed she understood why. Her long carob hair, thick and wavy, remained well cared for despite the weeks on the road and the illness brought on by injury and blood magic. Ridding herself of the burden would mark a physical change more noticeable than the scars often covered by her shirt.

Sara did not question her. "We can take care of your hair once you finish your tea."

"I'm about done, but finish yours," Collette insisted, only for Sara to abandon her tea so she could guide her niece to a chair.

"It won't take long, and I can always brew more tea," Sara insisted. She fetched a pair of scissors once Collette was seated.

After a brief discussion, Collette sat still as the snapping sound of scissors and hair echoed around her ears. She paid little attention to the quick drop of hair around her face and onto the floor beside her. Each falling lock left her feeling lighter, more assured of the path forward, and she found herself wondering why she hadn't cut her hair sooner.

Collette's hair soon fell to just above her shoulders. Instantly feeling lighter, the queen raised a hand, letting her fingers run through the remnants of her tresses. She glanced down, seeing the lengths of hair scattered along the ground.

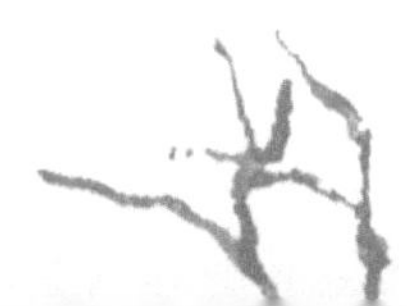

"You'll be harder to identify," Thomas observed, forcing Collette to look up.

"I think so," she agreed.

"You look nice," he added, as though uncertain if she regretted the choice or not.

"Thank you, but vanity is not why I did it," Collette said with a grin.

"Of course not," Sara said, putting a hand on the queen's shoulder and squeezing it.

Collette smiled up at the older woman, one who so resembled her. She would miss Sara, and again she knew she would come back whenever she could. "I should help clean up," Collette said.

Larent stumbled into the kitchen, temporarily preventing Collette from rising. He was obviously still half-asleep as he sat down heavily next to Collette, almost missing the chair. Extending an arm across the table he laid his head down on it and turned sleepy eyes to Collette. "You are so beautiful," he said, following it up with a large yawn.

"Thank you," Collette said, reaching out to run her fingers through his hair. "You can go back to bed. Hardly anyone is up."

"I tried, but you weren't there so…" He closed his eyes, relaxing.

Collette laughed, rising to her feet to help Sara clean her hair from the floor. Thomas, meanwhile, decided to brew more water.

The house slowly grew louder as various members rose and made their way to the kitchen. As Rion took a seat across the table from Larent, Sara dished out a creamy porridge in bowls, passing them to Thomas to hand out. Catching Collette's gaze, Rion raised a curious brow as he took in her changed appearance, but he said nothing about it.

"I thought we'd have left by now," he commented.

"Too sleepy," Larent muttered as he sat up to accept the food from Thomas.

"You ought to be," Rion said after swallowing a mouthful of porridge. "From what I heard, neither you nor Joss got much sleep."

"That one didn't either," Larent said, motioning to Thomas.

"We weren't as loud as you," Thomas shot back with a grin as he joined the table.

"Then you weren't trying hard enough." Larent gave Collette a sleepy grin. "I mean, I was accused of treason at one point last night."

"I'm pretty certain Arian and I can't commit treason against the other," Thomas pointed out. "It's not the best comparison."

Larent laughed. "Okay, true." He looked at Collette. "If they were louder than us, do you consider it treason?"

"If they were disruptive, perhaps," Collette replied.

Larent laughed, though he quieted down as Tolan walked in. The half-elf looked concerned for a minute as if he didn't know if he should be there. Thankfully, Sara intervened by handing over breakfast, and he took the bowl to the table and sat beside Rion.

"So they would have to break shit?" Larent asked, deciding to keep the conversation going.

"Would breaking something have disrupted us?" Collette returned with a grin, carefully keeping her gaze away from Tolan. She would eventually have to deal with him in a more civil manner, but Collette wasn't ready.

Larent's grin grew. "I'm surprised we didn't break the bed."

"I'm thankful you managed to avoid destroying my furniture," Sara said. She smiled as Whyldon entered the kitchen, looking more rested than many of the others. She pushed a bowl toward him. "Eat up, John. You have a day of travel ahead, assuming everyone feels up to leaving."

"Apparently, Thomas and Arian kept everyone up," Collette said with faux innocence, causing Larent to snort.

Most people finished eating by the time Arian stumbled into the kitchen, his pack hanging from his shoulder. He dropped next to Thomas and placed a small, sweet kiss on the other's lips before stealing Larent's cup of tea.

Larent opened his mouth to complain but decided to get a new cup.

"You seem exhausted, Arian," Collette observed, grinning in his direction.

"Not at all," Arian said as if he wasn't about to fall asleep at the table.

"Perhaps we need to delay leaving," Collette observed. Again, she ignored Larent snorting.

Arian shook his head. "No, I will be more awake shortly."

"I'm already awake enough to go," Larent said before looking around. "Did Nawalya eat?"

Thomas shook his head. "She stomped through, shot dirty looks, and left when it was just Collette and myself."

"She should eat before we leave," Arian said with a sigh as he exchanged glances with Larent.

Tolan pointed his spoon at the two. "If she doesn't wish to eat…" He gave Arian and Larent a meaningful look.

Larent raised his hands in surrender. "I wasn't going to try and force her to eat."

Arian gave a tired sigh and nodded at Tolan. "This will take getting used to."

"She's a grown woman," Thomas added. "If she eats, she eats. She knows we plan on leaving."

Arian just leaned against Thomas, his eyes on his bowl.

"When did we want to leave? After we clean up or was there more we needed to do?" Larent asked.

"We're in Galel," Whyldon said in response. He'd finished his food and was now rinsing the bowl and spoon. "If we want to find a safe encampment for the evening, we need to leave within the next hour or so."

Rion nodded. "I don't think there's anything but flat land for miles. We might have to settle for a village since we're presumably going north." He took a final spoonful of porridge and swallowed. "I'll go get my things."

Whyldon said, "We can decide what to do for the evening depending on where we are by early afternoon."

Everyone made gestures of affirmation while Tolan collected some of the empty bowls to take to the sink. "I'll let Nawalya know when we're leaving and that food is available if she's hungry," he shared with the group before heading out. Whyldon dismissed himself to grab his things, with Thomas leaving moments later to do the same.

Arian eyed the door Tolan exited before reaching down to his pack and pulling out a long package. "Larent," he said, noting his friend had knelt to retrieve something from the ground.

"What do you need?" Larent asked.

Arian made a tossing motion, waiting for Larent's nod before throwing the wrapped item.

"Shit, it's heavier than it looks." Setting it down, Larent grinned at Collette. "Freckles, Chuckles got me something."

"Are you going to open it?" Collette asked and caught an amused glance from Sara who had taken up responsibility for post-breakfast cleanup.

"What if it tries to bite me?" Larent asked with a chuckle.

"It is not going to bite you," Arian said.

"Not that you have a problem with biting," Collette pointed out.

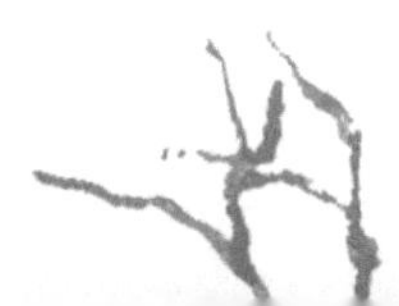

"True," Larent said as he unwrapped the item, only to stare at it in shock as the paper revealed the bladed gloves. "Arian?"

Arian looked away from Larent, refusing to make eye contact. "You are shit with a sword. I assumed a weapon like this would be more comfortable given how often you use your claws in battle." Arian finally met Larent's eyes. "We can practice on the road."

Uncomfortable, Arian moved to the sink to start dishes for Sara.

Collette moved closer so she could examine the weapon. Metal and skeletal in shape, she could see the wisdom in Arian's idea. "These are beautiful," she murmured, putting a hand on Larent's back. "You will excel in using these with a little practice."

"I think so, too," Laren said carefully, picking up one of the weapons. He slid his fingers into the round holes, seemingly crafted for fingers, at the bottom. He closed his hand into a fist and raised his hand in examination. The four long claw-like blades curling towards his palm made for deadly promise. A brief smile appeared on Larent's face, showing his clear comfort with his new weapon compared to the sword.

"How does it feel?" Collette asked.

Larent twisted his wrist, moving the claw in small motions. "Good. A little heavy, but it's a good weight. I think I can use these."

Collette nodded, pleased with Arian's thoughtfulness. It didn't replace the ability to shift, to allow the wolf to take over, but it was closer and better than the sword. She glanced over and noted Arian, who looked so tense his shoulders were almost touching his ears. "Arian, can you help?"

"Of course," the elf said easily, relaxing slightly when no overt displays of thanks were given.

Chapter Forty-four

"Thank you, my brother," Collette replied. "Now we should get ready to leave."

Arian nodded as Larent removed the gloves. "I am going to help Thomas collect our things," he shared before leaving.

"I have no idea how to pack these up," Larent declared. "Wanna help me figure it out?" Larent gave Collette a big grin.

"You probably need to wrap them," Sara said from her position near the sink. "Then you can more safely store them in a bag."

"Thanks, Sara," Larent said happily, before looking back at Collette and wiggling his eyebrows.

"Go do as she says," Collette said, resisting her lover's subtle suggestion.

Larent gave her a small pout in jest. If she went upstairs with Larent, they would have been delayed. He rewrapped the weapons and left the kitchen, presumably to finish packing.

"You are going to have your hands full keeping up with Larent," Sarah observed when it was just the two women. She turned to her niece and approached her, her face aglow with genuine affection. "I have so enjoyed getting to know you."

"I've enjoyed getting to know you, too," Collette returned. "I cannot express how much I regret having to leave."

"Leaving is only temporary," Sara replied. "As are your struggles. The world will right itself, and you will end up where you belong." She took Collette's hands as she had in the days and weeks before, a motion Collette associated with comfort and home. "You will be here again."

"I hope so," Collette replied, and though she'd promised herself as much, she wondered how long she'd have to wait. "Are you going to be okay once we leave?"

"Of course," Sara replied. "You have enough to worry over without adding me to your burden. Focus on regaining the

throne and working with Arian. Both of you are too talented with healing to limit yourselves."

"I will," Collette promised. She could cry over the prospect of leaving Barcomb Mill and Sara. She might still.

"Good." Sara relinquished Collette's hands. "Now be on your way. You have a long day of travel ahead."

Chapter Forty-Five

Ian slowly wiped down the bar counter in front of him, stopping every few minutes to gather an empty mug and place it by the sink. He was in no rush to serve any of the soldiers—what a joke—in his tavern. A young haughty looking soldier standing a few feet down the bar waited impatiently for Ian's acknowledgement. Ian didn't give him the satisfaction of an upward glance.

Instead, he kept an eye on his female employees as they served the men, deftly avoiding groping hands and ignoring the lewd jokes at their expense. Ian felt impotent, watching those workers go through the harassment and torment. If he interfered, the monster leading the soldiers would give him trouble.

Finally turning to the young soldier demanding drinks, he poured and slid a drink in his direction after collecting payment. Charging double for these buffoons soothed a little. Alone again, Ian's eyes darted to the far corner where Lord Riken sat with one of his men. A man called Cadan sat nearby, and the two drank and laughed as though the world were not falling apart. One of Ian's older barmaids stayed close, seemingly ignored by the two, but taking in every word they said. Thus far, she'd signaled nothing of importance back to Ian.

Counter cleaned, Ian spent several minutes refilling pitchers for his workers and individual mugs for customers. Now and then, when a free minute found him, he'd look back to the lord. Riken was attractive. He had a handsome ruggedness and strong jaw most found delicious to behold. Ian was reminded of the Nereid he'd encountered some months back. He shared the same dark hair Lord Riken possessed, but they bore no additional similarities. Riken was attractive in the same way any dangerous creature was. Gorgeous, perfectly shaped, but just as you realized something was amiss, the animal would strike.

Lord Riken looked up from Cadan, eyes scanning until he caught the gaze of one of the barmaids. He motioned towards an empty tankard, and she walked by to fill it. The glare he gave the poor girl reminded Ian of Wildrun. Under its pretty stone and well-dressed people lived an infectious rot of hatred, malice, and elitism hidden under the guise of following the Mother. Ian knew, if Riken had his way, he'd spread the rot to the rest of Coralia.

To the east of the mountains separating Quenall from the rest of the country, the people loved Queen Collette and her support of Nereid rights. They had been wary of her at first, given King Sargarus's preference for destruction and genocide. She'd proven herself kinder, more inclined to justice and fairness, and with each decision, she'd won the love of her people. People like Riken had fought back, spilled blood, and committed treason because they didn't like her decisions. No doubt, had she not escaped, they'd have killed her for protecting more than just the humans.

He hoped the rumors of her subsequent death were just rumors.

Unlike many of his companions, Ian was well-traveled, and he'd made the trip to Quenall for the queen's twenty-fifth birthday. He remembered watching her in her little dais, laughing and joking with a stream of visitors. She'd looked young but comfortable in her position. Seeing her in all her finery did nothing to conceal the young queen and her mates when they'd visited his little tavern some months back. She'd a mouth like a sailor, and the ability to drink like one, too. He hadn't told anyone, of course, not even the extremely attractive Nereid who'd come asking. Ian felt bad about keeping the knowledge to himself, of course, but he wouldn't put his queen in danger.

A pounding at the back door caught his attention, and he quickly waved his sister over to man the bar. Only a few people would use the back entrance, and only if it was urgent. Ian walked calmly until he was out of sight, then hurried to the door. Throwing it open, he motioned the two men in before shutting the door against the cold. Spring might be coming, but it was still colder than the Mother's tit.

Ian motioned for the two men to follow him deeper inside, but they both shook their heads, neither of them moving from their spot.

"We have to get back out there," Morrley said in a gravelly voice. His blond hair stuck to his forehead as he pulled off his cap and wiped his hand across his forehead. "Survivors were found from the elven village Lord Riken burnt down."

"What?" Ian asked in shock. "No one could have survived." He glanced over his shoulder as though Riken stood right behind him, listening. "Be careful. We have no actual proof he was responsible, and he's in the tavern right now. You don't want to make accusations he'd retaliate against."

All three men looked back toward the dining area before Morrley spoke again. "Two hunting parties weren't at the

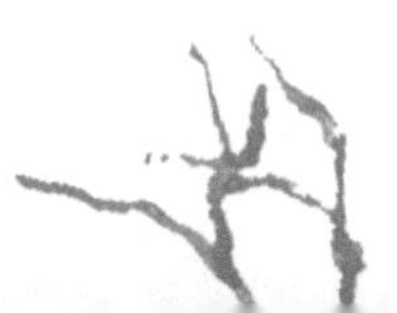

village at the time of the attack. They saw wagons with their people in them and followed them to one of the new labor camps. They say the soldiers wore Lord Riken's crest."

Ian swore violently, then looked at the other man, Gaillard, who wouldn't meet his eyes. Ian knew his night was about to get worse. "Tell me," he said softly to the small dark-haired young man.

"We went north to Barcomb Mill to visit Sara Whyldon," Gaillard began. "More of Riken's men were there to arrest her, calling her a traitor to the crown. When she demanded proof, one said it was obvious someone other than her had been staying there. She tried to claim it was hired help, but she was arrested. They are taking her to Quenall for questioning."

The young man sounded close to tears, and Ian reached out, placing a hand on his shoulder. "Did you find anything else?" Ian asked calmly.

"After the soldiers left, we went in and searched the house. The soldiers were right. Other people had been there, and it looks like they left recently."

Ian nodded even as his heart flew. It had to be the queen. Taking a deep breath, Ian centered himself and made a plan. "I know you want to get back to the elves, but I need one of you to get my brother. I need him to take over the tavern for a little while."

"What? Why?" Morrley demanded.

"Because I'm going to go check on those elves. Then I'm going find the queen."

Chapter Forty-Six

Three days on the road, and Rion was having the time of his life. He'd been very familiar with Whyldon and Collette from his years in the guard. He also knew Tolan well enough from traveling together. Observing Thomas, Arian, and Nawalya, whom he didn't know well, had interested him because he was observing new and complicated dynamics.

He grinned down at Collette, who'd help him set up camp while the others hunted or gathered supplies for the evening. He surveyed his former lover, the woman he would have married in another time and place. She was as beautiful as ever. Perhaps more so, but he couldn't ignore the lingering strain in her expression or the contemplative silence when she was not actively engaged. The lack of genuine laughter and playfulness compared to the last prolonged time they'd shared with one another startled Rion. He wished he could resolve her sadness, but she would have to be the one to do it.

She did not want to talk about her state of well-being, so he engaged her in a different way. "So Nawalya lied?" he asked, picking up on a conversation from earlier in the day they hadn't been able to finish.

"By omission," Collette clarified, driving a stake into the ground. She tugged on the rope when she was done and nodded her head as she found the setup acceptable.

"You dying is a pretty big thing to omit, Joss," Rion said, eyebrow raised.

"I'm aware." Collette started on another tent.

"And?" Rion replied.

"And?" Collette asked, shooting him a look. "My feelings on the matter have been made known, and we've moved on."

"No one is scarred." Rion shrugged. "Keeping a secret like possible death deserves a larger response." He shook his head at the stubborn pout on her lips and decided to move on. "How've you really been?" he prompted Collette. "Beyond nearly dying?"

Collette went back to her task. Every now and then, her eyes pointed to the sky in thought. She'd defaulted to the habit when she didn't know the answer to his questions or wanted to avoid answering them, and Rion scratched at his beard, wondering if she knew about the tendency.

"Honestly?" she asked, and when he nodded, she said, "Exhausted. Sad sometimes. Lost, though, admittedly not as much as I have been."

"Very strong feelings, then," Rion remarked. "I mean, fuck Joss. After everything you've been through, I think most people would have given up by now. You probably should, if ruling makes you miserable."

"You are not the only person who thinks so," she replied. "But I know myself, and I've chosen to embrace my position rather than fight against it.

"I understand why you continue. There are more people, both in our immediate group and elsewhere, expecting you to solve all the world's problems. Even the lad I brought with me thinks the fate of Coralia, the Nereid, and probably some random dwarf in a faraway land, rests on your shoulders."

"Doesn't it?" she asked. "I mean, I know there are other people out there who could take responsibility, but I don't think anyone worth the role would willingly accept the burden."

"Who gives a shit?" Rion said. "Almost no one cared what being queen did to you and forced you to suppress. Many of them still don't. They want what you promise without ever thinking about you, and when you are back on the throne, they won't make sure you are well and happy." He motioned to her with a free hand. "You allow them the luxury because you're willing to throw yourself in the line of fire as long as one less person suffers."

Collette snorted, though she paused in her renewed efforts with a different stake. "You make the same complaints you always have."

"And you still ignore them as though I'm not right." He sighed and shook his head before offering her a reassuring smile. "I'll support you, no matter what. Loving you and your bull-headed decisions is a burden I will bear for the rest of my life. Just like the burden of knowing you will do the stupidest shit in the name of saving the faeries, or whoever else happens to need help. I think you'll benefit from having more voices telling you doing something else is okay."

"I've never once tried to save faeries," she gave in a mumbled argument.

He laughed, the sound boisterous and rich. "If you haven't, it's solely because you've not come across one asking for help."

They went back to setting up camp, a feat he and Collette had shared a number of times over the years. It felt nostalgic, and Rion was forced to contend with how much he'd disconnected from her in order to keep the nostalgia and longing at bay. He doubted he would have the luxury of staying away for the foreseeable future.

He looked towards the woods as a murmur of voices and crunching leaves alerted him. "I think our party returns," he mentioned to Collette. He was proven right when Arian stepped out of the trees, soon followed by Nawalya.

"Arian," Nawalya said, a large pile of wood in her arms. She marched around Arian and turned to face him, effectively trapping him in conversation. "I understand your argument. I truly do. When I yelled at you weeks ago, I did not say things correctly, but I still meant what I said. I allowed you to treat me as if I am incapable of taking care of myself, of taking responsibility for my own actions. Your support and care these last decades are so much more appreciated than you will ever know, but it has to stop now." She reached out and put a hand on his shoulder. "The change will be hard on both of us, but if I allow you something as simple as coming to find me to tell me I need to eat, we will fall back into our old patterns."

Arian hung his head. "I understand, but it will not be an easy habit to break."

"I know. Spirits, I know, but maybe we can try and compromise. Instead of saying 'Nawalya, food is ready. You must come and eat,' you just say the food is ready and allow me to choose when I partake."

Arian chuckled. "Are they not the same thing?"

Nawalya lightly smacked the back of his head. "They are not. Now, you stay here. I am going hunting."

"Would you like company, Nawalya?" Collette offered, pulling Rion's attention to her.

Nawalya looked at Collette as she moved to grab her bow and quiver. "Yes, please."

Collette grabbed her own hunting supplies. "Tell Larent where I've gone if he returns before we do," she instructed Rion and joined Nawalya.

Chapter Forty-Seven

Barris stood in the shadows of the courtyard just off the queen's garden, his eyes on the king. Zephraim sat alone on one of the many ornate marble benches, head hung low, suffering from a prolonged state of melancholy. Despite all of the grievances Barris held for the man, he couldn't help but feel sympathy for the abject loneliness Zephraim must have felt.

"Are you even listening to me?" came a soft-voiced question from the woman standing beside him.

"Of course," Barris replied.

"What did I say?" she asked, an indigo eyebrow rising in challenge.

Barris smiled widely and looked down at the love of his life. "You said you have your brothers split between watching Xavier and Rhoslyn. Xavier has laid low since his threats toward Diana and Zephraim's heated response," he replied. "You also said Rhoslyn has been holding meetings with the remaining nobles, but she's making them look like chats over tea. All of which means we can't move against either of them."

"What else?" Lynessea asked sweetly.

"The Rebellion has trickled to almost nothing thanks to the rumors of the queen being dead, and if not for Diana, you would worry Crem might try something rash to drum up support."

"Fine, you were listening," Lynessea conceded. She glanced around before giving him a playful shove.

Barris hated the need to always be careful, aware of whose eyes were on them at any given time. He just thanked the Goddess small signs of affection were often considered more important in the Nereid culture. It meant it was easier to keep his hands to himself.

"Are you watching him again?" Lynessea asked.

"Of course."

"I think he's a lost cause," Lynessea said, crossing her arms.

"The Goddess says most are lost and need a light to guide them home," Barris countered.

"Sometimes I feel allowing you to become one of us was a mistake," Lynessea said with a gentle laugh.

"Only when I use my teaching against you." Barris smiled brightly before looking to Zephraim. "I think he needs a friend, a real friend. Someone who isn't there for what he can do for them."

"You realize you are not that friend. While, yes, you would want to be a real friend to him, as long as he stands to murder our people, you will try to use him."

"I know," Barris breathed out. "He seemed happier when Diana was at the meal we shared. I just feel like I need to try."

"Try but remember when he finds you're basically a Nereid, he's going to be pissed."

"Oh, I know." Barris intertwined their pinkies. "I love you."

"I love you, too. Go get him, sunshine." Lynessea pulled away and walked back into the castle to give her brothers more orders.

Taking a deep breath, Barris stepped from the shadows into the light he loved so dearly and walked towards Zephraim. "Hale and good day, my king."

Zephraim looked up, the shadows beneath his gray eyes evident in the bright sunlight. "Hello, Barris," he returned.

"How fares the day?" Barris asked, lowering his voice to what he hoped was a tolerable level when he saw how tired and stretched thin Zephraim was. Staying on Zephraim's good side remained critical, especially when the king's slow spiral was growing more obvious.

"Well enough, though I admit to sleeping poorly last night," Zephraim shared. "It makes facing the day difficult."

"Yes, it would," Barris said. "Is there anything to be done to help you sleep better?" He motioned to the bench next to Zephraim for permission to sit down next to the forlorn man.

Zephraim gave a quick nod. "I will likely inquire about a sleeping draft before turning in for the evening."

Barris's brow furrowed. "I've heard the sleeping draft can become addictive. I know of a plant with medicinal properties that might help you. The roots are supposed to relax the body and enable natural sleep," Barris offered.

"I'm willing to try if it would make you feel better, Barris."

Barris shook his head. "I wouldn't ask you to do it for me. Simply do it for yourself and only if you're comfortable."

"I need to do something," Zephraim said with a sigh. "I keep seeing her face," he said, running a hand over his eyes.

Barris wondered whose face was haunting Zephraim. His mother? Rhoslyn? Diana? He didn't know. "Whose face?"

"Collette's."

Barris did everything he could not to gape at the unexpected response. Could the king be experiencing doubt or guilt? "Zephraim, none of what has happened has been ideal in any way." He didn't want to say Zephraim wasn't at fault, because

Collette being on the run was Zephraim's fault, and they both knew it. Still, he did want to comfort the other man. He just wasn't sure how. "The news said a bandit killed her."

"Do you honestly think a bandit could take my sister out?" Zephraim asked quietly.

Barris shook his head. "Not at all. Truth be told, I don't believe she's dead. I believe something happened, but Collette is alive."

"I hope she is," Zepheaim replied, keeping his gaze locked on the ground by his feet, shoulders slumped. "I just doubt it."

Barris knew it was bold of him to do so, but he couldn't help but reach out and place a hand on the older man's shoulder. "She's alive and more than likely planning your downfall." He gave Zephraim a bright grin to show he was mostly joking.

"If she is alive, she is absolutely planning to come back and take the kingdom," Zephraim agreed, though his words were far more serious than Barris's.

"She won't come alone," Barris added. "The Nereid will help her."

"Of course," Zephraim agreed. "She'd need the help. It's the only smart move."

"Especially if you keep the alliance with the Azmarins while relying on the army Riken is building." Barris tilted his head, examining the king. "Are you planning to fight her?"

"I'm sure there are those who feel as though I should," Zephraim replied, his words given with such deliberation, Barris was uncertain how Zephraim might feel, let alone act. "But if the opportunity exists, I would be interested in trying to mend what has happened."

Barris gave Zephraim a small, sad smile. "Collette is an amazing woman, you know. I doubt she remembers it, but when we were young, she changed the course of my life with a few

words of advice. I'm sure she would be willing to forgive what has happened, but you need to take the first steps."

"If she is not alive, I cannot mend things," Zephraim pointed out. "Hoping she breathes does not make it so."

"It's more than hope. She's too bright a light to go down quietly. No, she'll be back, though an announcement of a pardon might draw Collette back in." Barris knew he sounded overly hopeful in his words, but Zephraim's statements led him to believe they could intervene and prevent further disaster in Coralia. His hopes were shortly disrupted, however.

"And who are you suggesting his majesty pardon?" Rhoslyn asked as she stepped through the interior corridor and into the garden. She looked as lovely as ever, cinnamon hair intricately styled and perfectly placed. Bright green eyes framed with dark lashes radiated the same beauty the young queen was known for. The set of her mouth and the intensity of her gaze, however, showed suspicious curiosity.

Barris met Rhoslyn's intense gaze, and he gave her the brightest of smiles. "Why, Collette of course." His smile grew even brighter. "After all, the Mother teaches we should forgive those who have passed into her arms. A post-mortem pardon would help with some of the unrest." Turning to look at Zephraim, and knowing Rhoslyn couldn't see it, he winked at the king.

"Am I to understand you think a pardon of any kind should be issued to the woman who killed my brother and tried to commit treason by appealing to our ally?" Rhoslyn demanded of Barris. She turned to Zephraim. "And you're entertaining this?"

Barris didn't wave her off, but it was close. "His Majesty wasn't entertaining the idea, not truly. We were simply discussing some of the ways we could quell the unrest His Majesty has noted in the kingdom without either enslaving or killing anyone." Barris didn't bother addressing the accusation of

Collette killing Rhoslyn's brother. No one really believed her guilty of the crime.

Zephraim inclined his head in agreement, though the motivation to do so remained concealed behind a wall of neutrality. "Truly, my dearest. Never would I entertain pardoning the person responsible for Wrenn's death."

Such interesting phrasing. Barris was all the more curious. He smiled in response and changed the subject.

"How is our queen doing on such a bright day?" he asked, not caring one bit. Barris was willing to give Zephraim a chance, but when it came to Rhoslyn, he would end her life himself if he could get away with it.

Rhoslyn glared at Barris, full lips set in a frown. Without addressing him, she turned from the group and retreated back into the palace, her heels clicking on the ground with a ferocity she never displayed.

Barris knew he would have to be careful going forward. He waited until she was out of sight and earshot before he laughed. "I believe I angered your wife."

"She's certainly not happy with you," Zephraim confirmed. "But she's been less charitable, in general, since Riken left. I'm not supposed to have noticed."

Barris nodded. "I think none of us are supposed to notice." Barris studied Zephraim. "I take my own life in my hands speaking my opinion, but I'm sorry this happened, to you and Collette."

"You're not the only one," Zephraim replied with an honesty he had not expected.

"What are you going to do about it?" Barris asked.

"You ask a question I continue to ponder," Zephraim said.

"I am willing to do whatever I can to assist," Barris promised. He stood from the bench, looking down at Zephraim. He wanted to reassure the older man, but he knew nothing he could

say would help. "I will prepare the plant I offered for you, your Majesty, should you choose to use it."

"Thank you," Zephraim replied. "I'm sure I will."

"I shall leave you with your thoughts." Barris gave the king a bow and dismissed himself. He had much to share with his wife and Cremisius Hawke.

The door to Rhoslyn's private chambers crashed against the stone wall, the sound echoing throughout the corridor, and likely down the stairs. Rhoslyn gave the noise no mind, despite her usually careful attention to a calm demeanor. She was angry, and Barris's open challenge to her authority had gone unchecked. She needed to move carefully, to deal with the attempts to sway her good-for-nothing husband to the wrong side.

She took a breath and shut the door more carefully, pointedly ignoring Xavier who sat at a desk near the office area of her chambers. "Have you gotten around to dealing with Lady Elrick yet?" she snapped.

He raised an eyebrow at her, lowering the papers in his hand onto the desk. "No, but as you and my lord instructed, I have been waiting for the right time and the right cover." He looked down at the papers, then back at Rhoslyn, his eyes raking over her form. "It is now the right time, or it will be in a few days."

"You need to get it done," Rhoslyn replied, glaring at the obvious ogling. She was going to have to deal with him. "I have another mission for you, and I cannot have your attention divided."

"Consider it done," Xavier said simply, a smirk playing on his lips. "What else can I assist you with?"

The phrasing made Rhoslyn's skin crawl.

"You will keep your eyes and tongue civil, or I will remove both," she warned Xavier, though his lack of response suggested he did not believe her. Rhoslyn hated to further bloody her hands, but she wouldn't hesitate the next time he did anything to annoy her. "As for the business needing oversight, I witnessed Lord Barris arguing for Zephraim to pardon Collette. Zephraim did not immediately shut him down. You can imagine I have concerns."

Xavier stood at the mention of Barris, his brows knitted together in thought, his papers forgotten. "I will watch the lord and his filthy Mers, but you should write to my lord. He holds Barris in high esteem. He will be able to recommend a path forward."

"Lord Riken is kept informed of news here," Rhoslyn replied. She walked over to the table holding wine and other libations. She poured a glass without offering any to Xavier. He was already too bold without alcoholic encouragement.

"Then I will deal with Lady Elrick and monitor Lord Barris. Any limits I should be aware of?"

"Do not kill him. Not yet anyway," Rhoslyn decided. "He may not be guilty of anything more than empty-headed altruism. I want to monitor him, and I do not want us to act without hearing from Lord Riken."

Xavier nodded. "How have your meetings with the lords gone? Do you need me to have anyone else watched?"

She shook her head. "The rest of the nobility in the city have fallen in line. For now, I am satisfied."

Xavier smirked and crossed to the door, keeping more than an arm's length away from Rhoslyn. "Let me know if you need any other needs satisfied, my queen." He looked her up and down once more, his gaze stopping on the low cut of her dress before bowing his head and stepping from the room.

Rhoslyn, for her part, downed the wine and took a seat at her desk. She had a letter to write.

Riken,

Once again, I find my trust in your judgment falters with every interaction I face with Xavier. He is arrogant, untrustworthy, and his gaze lingers far too long. You and I will have many discussions upon your return, and you might not appreciate the resolution.

I came upon Barris issuing sympathetic ideas regarding Collette to Zephraim. He needs to be monitored.

Rhoslyn

Chapter Forty-Eight

The forest surrounding the planned camp offered peacefulness that couldn't come with prolonged discussions, and Collette understood Nawalya's choice to retreat. The tittering of animals and nature was often preferable to stubborn resistance, and as much as Collette loved Arian, she knew he would have to make small adjustments to the way he had lived for decades.

The two women walked in comfortable silence, barely a sound issuing with each step, increasing the chances for successful hunting.

"I'm surprised you were able to talk Larent into leaving your side earlier," Nawalya said in a near whisper.

"He volunteered, believe it or not," Collette replied in the same low voice. Although she never begrudged a second spent with her lover, she hadn't missed the increased neediness he'd exhibited since their return from Nora and Alexander's.

"He's trying to make sure he doesn't suffocate you by giving you space," Nawalya guessed.

"Probably," Collette agreed as they walked further into the woods. With spring slowly arriving, the forest was filled with life, though they were content to pass many of the creatures they came across. A doe and her baby made for poor, cruel targets, and the birds too light a meal to justify the work.

"Perhaps we should look for rabbits or quail," Nawalya suggested.

Collette nodded. They'd had many decent feasts on both over the months, so no complaint existed. Quail and rabbit also made for lighter transport and disposal, because Collette could never forget she was in hiding.

Pondering on the potential decision, she nearly missed Nawalya holding out her arm, forcing Collette to come to a stop. Nawalya had not spotted an animal. The wide eyes and set jaw alerted Collette to danger. She reached for her dagger.

"Someone's here," Nawalya whispered and pointed to crop of thick brush. Crouching behind the bushes wasn't the best solution to the problem, but it was the most convenient. Collette held her breath as heavy footsteps reached her ears, and in the distance, she spotted four figures entering the clearing. As they drew closer, she identified three as elves and the fourth a human.

"Are you sure she came this way?" the human asked his companions.

"Yes," replied a lean elf with long, russet hair. He paused and bent down to examine the ground, fingers hovering above the forest floor. "These tracks match the ones from earlier." He rose, fingers hovering in the air, wiggling back and forth as those walking before coming to a stop.

"They stopped there," he said, pointing to the ground about a foot away.

The human let out a sigh of relief. "Queen Collette!" he tried, the word lifting at the end as though in question. "Your Majesty!" he tried again. "If you can hear me, if you are near, please come out. We are in desperate need of your help."

Collette looked over at Nawalya, her brows raised in question over the reliability of these claims. She knew it was foolish to trust them, but if they genuinely needed help, was it not her job to comply?

Nawalya's lips pressed together, eyes focused on the men. She tentatively shook her head as another elf spoke.

"My queen, my name is Indir. We are only a few of the survivors from the village of Urhadell. Lord Riken burnt our village to the ground with most of our people trapped in the village square. He took our children and the adult survivors to a nearby labor camp a little ways from here. Please, I beseech you. Aid us in saving our people."

Nawalya's hand rose to her mouth, sadness and rage flooding her face along with a deep red flush. Although Collette would never know all the details of the trauma her companion and Arian had faced, enough similarities had been described. Collette had to do something. Nodding to Nawalya, Collette rose from her position, facing the men. Nawalya did the same, her bow strung and ready in case they were lying.

"Oh, thank the Spirits," the human male said upon spotting them.

Collette remained where she was, letting Nawalya hold the others off until there was more information. "Lord Riken burned your village?" she asked, the first words she'd exchanged as queen with an outside supporter in months.

"Yes," breathed Indir. "We were out hunting when it happened, but based on a message we received prior, he was there to see if we had housed you." His gaze held no anger or blame, just sadness. "We assume he did not like the answer our elders gave."

Collette's guilt sat in her stomach but rose as she realized just how many people might have died because Riken was looking for her. "Where is the camp?"

"Half an hour east," one of the blond elves said.

The other blond elf stepped towards Collette. "Lord Riken holds hate in his heart for elves. He would have found another reason to hurt us. His search for you was a way to justify his intentions."

Collette looked to Nawalya. "We have to help," she said without question.

"Of course." Nawalya directed her attention to the four men. "Our camp is back in that direction." She gestured vaguely behind them. "Can one of you please find and inform our companions?"

One of the blond elves nodded. "I will go."

"Here," Collette said, removing the gold bracelet from her wrist and handing it to him. "Show them this so they know you're telling the truth. Arian might attack first otherwise."

"Will this be enough?" the elf asked.

"If not, my partner calls me 'Freckles,'" Collette replied. "His pet name for me should suffice."

The elf took his leave, and Collette hoped reason worked in his favor.

The human, emboldened by the action, spoke up. "We should go. Hopefully, your companions can catch up quickly."

Collette and Nawalya agreed, and they began the trek toward the camp.

"My name is Ian, Your Majesty," the human finally introduced. "I am the keeper of an inn you stayed at several months back."

"I remember you," Collette said, thinking back on the night the would-be assassins revealed themselves. "Did you know who I was then?"

Ian nodded. "I would never have revealed your secret. I know those in Quenall have hunted for you, and your life is in danger. If things weren't so dire, I'd not ask you to risk your safety."

"My safety isn't my concern," Collette replied. The area they traveled through grew brighter, and she knew they'd soon leave the shelter of the forest. She recognized fear bubbling up at the thought of abandoning the safety of caution, of laying low, but she had no choice.

The group came to a stop once they reached the edge, and Ian turned to look at Collette. "I thought you should know, two Mers are looking for you. A male named Jayden and a female named… Sitos. No, Citi? Ceto. Ceto was her name."

Collette had no idea who Ceto could be, but Jayden... It had to be the same one. "Jayden was supposed to be back in the Nereid Kingdom. I got arrested so he could escape. Why is he looking for me?"

"Everyone thinks you're dead or has heard news of your death. They didn't believe it and came to find you. Jayden said it was to offer help."

Collette felt... happy? No. She was relieved to know she was needed and wanted. And to learn Tolan had gotten Jayden to safety. "I have been injured and in hiding. People thinking I was dead was the point," she explained.

"A good plan," Ian confirmed. "Jayden and the Nereids are not the only ones looking for you. Perhaps I should be sorry to draw you out of hiding, but your people need you."

"And they are going to have me," Collette confirmed. She gestured toward the edge of the woods. "Tell me what you know."

Ian nodded and jutted his thumb in the direction of the camp. "This is one of many labor camps, my queen. From what we've surmised, they've been filled with dissenters, human and non-human alike. We also know the Merscale trade was reinstated by royal decree."

"What?" Collette demanded, alarmed.

Indir nodded this time. "Pontus Bay is the only approved location, but as you can guess, others seek to be involved. Lord Riken will turn his attention to the trade once the camps are established. For now, Lord Barris runs the only legal operation."

Collette out a breath. The world had fallen into chaos since she'd been on the run. "Anything else?"

Ian grimaced. "Seven nobles have died in Quenall. Cremisius Hawke has been charged with the murder of Lord Elrick and inciting a rebellion. Last we heard, they can't arrest him because they can't find him." He shrugged. "It also seems Lord Riken has more to do with the hostilities coming from the capitol. He's on this side of the mountain for now."

"Then we find Riken and deal with him," Collette determined.

"Agreed," said Ian.

Nawalya moved to stand beside Collette, having spent much of the conversation in whispers with one of the blond elves.

"I would not be surprised to find Lord Riken, or some of his men, near the camp. Not if he is in the area. He's a cruel bastard, and he only values humans."

"Let us hope we do not encounter him," Indir said. "He travels with soldiers, both to carry out orders and for protection."

"Of course he does," Nawalya said. "He'll need help to terrorize Galel."

Indir and Ian exchanged looks. "I'm afraid we have heard news from Barcomb Mill. Riken had Sara Whydon arrested on charges of treason. She is to be taken to the capitol for trial. It happened the day after you left."

Collette briefly stopped breathing. "They have Sara?"

"Yes," Ian confirmed.

"When we finish here, do you think you can send word to Cremisius Hawke?" she asked, knowing Rhoslyn would have Sara killed without an intervention. Crem might be in time to help. It was that or go after Sara herself.

"Of course. I have a few people who can get in and out of Quenall safely, and if needed, I'll go myself," Ian promised.

"Shall we discuss the camp?" Nieven asked, motioning the group forward. They walked to the other side of the treeline, where seven elves came into view. "If you look beyond the trees, you will see the encloser, my queen. Our scouts told us this is a newer camp. There are twenty or thirty guards posted."

"At most, we are outnumbered three to one," Collette summarized. "Any guards we can easily pick off from a distance?"

A black-haired elf stood and beckoned Collette to come stand beside him. "They have not erected the wall yet. Eight people take turns patrolling the grounds in groups of two and four. We may be able to take them out with arrows, but we are low. Every shot would have to meet its mark."

"I have plenty of arrows, and I do not miss," Nawalya, indicating the full quiver on her shoulder.

"We need to take them out as quickly as possible," Collette said as she surveyed the camp. "I don't know how much time it will buy us, but it would reduce the number we'd have in direct combat." Distantly, she spotted what looked to be a makeshift barracks for guards, or so it seemed by the two uniformed men standing nearby. "What's that?"

"It's where the guards sleep when not on shift," another elf informed her.

"That will be our second target," Collette established.

"Any other targets?" Nawalya asked as she readied her first arrow.

Collette shook her head. "No immediate ones I can see. If we cause enough of a disturbance, we'll have a greater chance of subduing the rest while we get the prisoners out." She started counting the number she could see from their position. "Do you think we can get those on perimeter duty out of the way without detection?"

Nawalya looked over the camp, most of which remained obscured by the guard barracks, her eyes moving over the different groups. Nawalya gave a decisive nod and notched an arrow. "Those of you with bows, ready yourself." She glanced over at Collette. "Tell us when."

Slowly, the guards circled into the line of sight, two at first, then four.

"Get ready," Collette said, her voice low and commanding. She could hear Nawalya take a deep breath as she drew back on her bow, growing still as she waited. Four of their party followed suit, leaving nothing but her thudding heart sounding in her ear. As the fifth and sixth soldiers appeared, Collette leaned forward.

"Now," she ordered.

Nawalya released the first arrow, a second flying before the first landed, a third releasing in quick succession. The first arrow struck the guard through the right eye, and he dropped. The second guard didn't have time to register his companion's death before he went down, an arrow through his neck. Five guards went down before the others noticed something was wrong. One ran toward the warning bell, only to fall as an arrow sprouted through his chest. For the moment, no one living knew they were there.

"We've got to move," Collette directed, and they carefully closed the distance between the trees and the open camp. Staying low, and hopefully out of sight, they approached.

Without perimeter guards or a border wall, getting into the camp felt too easy. Collette glanced around cautiously, hand on the hilt of her dagger as they crossed into the campgrounds. Even with the sun up, preparations for the evening provided some safety. For now. Up close, Collette saw no windows in the barracks, and they remained virtually invisible to the remaining guards. Riken and his men had been arrogant in the construction.

"How do you wish to proceed?" Nawalya whispered.

"We need to locate the base of the prisoners," Collette replied. "Once we know where they are, we can determine how to strike."

Moving around the barracks, more of the camp came into view. Poorly constructed entrances to underground mines sat along the eastern and southern parts of the camp. Nearby sat a series of straw huts, low built and small. One was much smaller and shabbier than the others, possibly holding the children. "The prisoners will be in the mines," Nawalya said. "And are those huts for sleeping? Spirits, they would have to crawl to enter."

"A person forced on their belly is less likely to fight than a person on their feet," Ian said.

"We'll deal with as many of the guards as possible before we attempt rescue of the prisoners and children," Collette determined.

"That's risking a fight by moonlight," Ian replied.

"We are risking every life if we try to rescue them now," Collette argued. "It's too quiet. The guards are nowhere to be seen, and we've been in the camp too long without signs of other people."

Nawalya looked around. "We could light the barracks on fire to draw people out." Her expression turned thoughtful. "Or I could head into the camp pretending to be lost."

Collette wasn't sure what the best solution was, but ensuring the safest escape for prisoners and children seemed obvious. "Three of you, scout the camp. See if anyone is around, guards or prisoners alike. If you see a guard, dispose of them. The more we take out now, the fewer we deal with later. Once we're certain we've handled the guards, we'll need to secure

the building holding the children. Once we are certain we've done as much as we can, Nawalya can cause a disturbance, drawing people out of the mines."

The three elves nodded and dispersed, leaving Ian and Nawalya with Collette. "Think we can take the camp before the boys arrive?" Nawalya asked, a gleam in her eyes that spoke of danger and death.

"I'm kind of hoping Arian didn't kill the messenger," Collette replied. "And if they come, there's no telling what will happen if we don't have something going already." She grew silent, thinking carefully as they continued moving. "Where are the rest of the guards?"

"If the camp runs like the old ones under Sargarus, they'll work the mines all day and all night in shifts," Nawalya mused aloud. "Half the guards should be asleep in the barracks while the rest are down in the mines with the prisoners."

"There are no windows to the barracks," Ian pointed out. "We can guess they haven't spotted us because we can't see them."

"Then we check through the door," Collette decided, knowing they were inciting violence with the choice.

Nawalya moved first, slowly scouting the perimeter of the barrack, pausing every few feet to check for stray guards. When they reached the door, she glanced back to make sure Collette and Ian were behind her. Nodding, she turned back to the door and grasped the makeshift handle, easing it open a few inches.

Whispered voices sounded from the interior, no more than three of four distinct rumbles. Nawalya looked at Collette for instructions as she removed her hand from her dagger, instead reaching for the smaller throwing knives hidden on the other side of her belt.

"How many?" Collette asked in the softest of whispers.

Nawalya opened the door a little bit more, her eyes scanning what she could see. "Seven but I cannot see the entire room."

Seven. They could take seven, and judging by the size of the barracks, another half dozen might be in there as well. So twelve or thirteen soldiers. "Our odds?" she asked Nawalya just as quietly, grinning with a willingness to take on the challenge.

"Very, very good," Nawalya said, her smile bloodthirsty.

Collette looked back to Ian who nodded his agreement. "Let's go."

Permission granted, Nawalya kicked the door in, her knives flying in the direction of the voices. The dim light of one lone lantern illuminated part of the barracks, allowing the intruders to see two knives hit their targets. A third knife lodged itself in a burly, balding guard's large bicep. He ran at the group, tripping as his foot caught an unseen object on the ground. He yelped as the knife in his arm plunged deeper from the fall, and Nawalya went after him, finishing the job before he could rise to his feet.

A fourth guard, this one lanky and stinking of filth and alcohol, rose from a bed with a shout. He went for Collette, never pulling a weapon and perhaps hoping his size would suffice. Collette didn't have to use her daggers at first, instead ducking down, causing him to fall over her, landing with a thud. In one swift movement, she went down on a knee, driving her daggers into his back. Ian covered her, driving his sword into the stomach of a man who came running.

Nawalya pulled her knife from the dead guard and threw it at another coming for Ian while Collette kicked the knee out of another man wildly swinging a sword far too big for him. She drove the blade of her daggers into his neck, pulled them out, and went to take on one of the men trying to tackle Nawalya.

The room stilled after the next two kills, the coppery smell of blood permeating the floor.

"Make sure we got everyone here," Collette ordered.

Nawalya went from body to body, slitting each throat, just in case. Ian grabbed the lantern and circled the room, pausing

to nudge one of the fallen with the toe of his boot. "I think we got them all," he reported.

"Good," Collette said, ignoring the blood splatters on her hands and clothes as the lattern swung around, bringing the dark red stains to her attention. "We need a distraction to help clear out the mines and get the children to safety."

"I'll make it happen." Nawalya retrieved her throwing knives, cleaning them off on the bodies before tucking them away on her person. She positioned her dagger where it wasn't easily seen and held out her bow and quiver to Collette. "I will need a moment."

"Whatever you're doing, Ian and I will position ourselves outside the barracks. If you pass Indir and the others, warn them," Collette instructed.

Nawalya nodded and proceeded to smear blood across her face and other body parts. Using her bloody fingers, she shook out her hair, fluffing up parts and twisting others, leaving her disheveled. Nawalya then closed her eyes for a moment, and when she opened them, her face looked more open, helpless, and her eyes glassy. "Do I pass as a damsel in distress?"

"That or a war criminal," Ian said, though nothing in his tone suggested negativity. Collette laughed at the observation.

Nawalya smiled. "I have done this before, Larent's idea. He always swore a woman screaming for help would bring every man running. He was right." She gave a delicate shrug. "Shall we proceed?"

Collette nodded, and the three left the barracks, finding the sun slowly sinking in the sky. In the distance, she watched their elf companions quietly relocate scared, traumatized children from their small dwelling into the nearby forest. "Make it quick, and keep them from looking back at the camp too much," she said to Nawalya. As Nawalya walked away, she passed the group of elves who'd broken away and directed them back to Ian and Collette.

"What is the plan?" Indir asked as he joined them.

"Nawalya is going to cause a distraction," Collette shared. "We anticipate the guards and prisoners will come out of the mines. We'll need to act decisively as they come. Identify the guards, take them out."

"Right," Indir said.

Nawalya, meanwhile, let out a blood-curdling scream as she ran into the center of the camp. "Help! Please! We've been attacked."

No response came at first, and Collette felt her heartbeat grow rapid. What if they knew what happened and refused to come out as a result? What if the prisoners below were now suffering? So many questions ran through her mind, none of them coming with answers.

Just as her worries hit peak anxiety, men emerged. Dressed in dark uniforms and armed with swords, they had almost no time to prepare for Nawalya as she threw herself into the arms of one who hadn't drawn his weapon.

"Help, please help. My friends and I were attacked in the woods." She looked up, playing the helpless and delicate woman. "There was a large group. Just in the woods." She pointed away from the barracks towards where Collette and the others had first checked out the camp.

While the man Nawalya had attached herself to tried to comfort her, the oldest of the soldiers, if his salt and pepper hair was a sign, sighed. "Go get more of the men from the mines. We can't have bandits out here."

A young man, who might very well be a teenage recruit, ran back into the mine entrance calling for assistance. Eight men quickly joined him.

From her position, Collette debated her next move. She needed the guards to have more distance between themselves and the mine entrances. An idea occurred to her, and she looked at the bow she held for Nawalya. Lifting it, she tested the draw, finding she could work with the weapon, although she usually needed something a little longer. Retrieving an arrow, she notched the arrow, aiming at the guard at the back of the new group. She let it fly, hitting the man in the neck.

Nawalya let out a helpless scream of terror as the guard went down. The older guard cursed and shouted for his men to form up.

Beside her, Indir let loose another arrow, hitting another man, bringing about more screams and shots. More guards began trickling out of the mines, prisoners appearing behind them. Collette saw them chained together, some by ankles and others by wrists. She pulled back another arrow, hitting another guard in the eye.

Nawalya backed away from the guards, some of them following behind as others rushed toward the forest in pursuit of the nonexistent bandits. Only when prisoners remained did she attack, her long dagger pulled from her hip in a fluid motion. She dug it into the nearest guard's neck before dragging it down his spine. Without pause, she moved to the next, slitting his throat.

As the guards realized what was happening, they turned their attention to Nawalya. Collette looked at Ian. "Someone needs to figure out how to get the prisoners unchained. The rest of us need to help Nawalya."

Indir and the dark-headed elf ran to tend to the prisoners without hesitation. Ian nodded in the opposite direction, and the remaining members of the group ran to join the fray.

Nawalya was a whirlwind of graceful movement as she ducked and weaved around the guards who came for her. She took her hits as she could, leading them away from the prisoners. As she was joined by the others, Collette swore she saw her sigh in relief, especially when Ian prevented the older guard from injuring her by running him through the chest.

As Collette engaged with a younger man, stout and solid on his feet, she counted the remaining soldiers and dodged a swing from an ax. The strength of the guard didn't make up for his lack of precision, though Collette knew she'd want to avoid the path of the blade. The next time she ducked, she managed to take herself out of his direct line of vision. Grabbing a discarded sword from the ground, she made a quick jab to his side just as Nawalya drove a knife into the back of the man's knee. As he fell, the women moved to the next enemy.

The battle ended with most of the guards dead or too injured to move. The few remaining, younger guards who were at least a half-decade younger than Collette, were rounded up by a few of the elves. They could decide what to do with them later. The prisoners had been moved from the mine entrances toward the center of the camp, Indir working diligently to remove chains.

"Any major injuries?" Collette asked as she, Nawalya, and Ian approached the center.

"A few scratches. Nothing life-threatening." Nawalya looked down at Ian's arm. A long, but shallow slice ran the length of his forearm.

"What about the prisoners?" Collette asked.

"I have not had a chance to look yet, but from a glance, malnourished and dehydrated, but not enough to have severe health problems," Ian replied. "I don't know about the condition of the children."

"We need to check," Collette said as she looked ahead. "Everyone will need to be moved from here as quickly as possible. Someone will eventually come along and discover what's happened. I won't have them subjected to more torment."

She brought their trek to a stop and reached out for Ian's arm. He extended it, confused, even more so when she pressed her fingers to the injury and the wound healed, leaving nothing but slightly reddened skin behind.

"Your Majesty?" Ian asked, blinking.

"We don't have time now," Collette replied, dismissing the question as they began walking again.

As they drew closer, Collette took in the low murmuring of those who were freed. "The queen…" someone spoke, the words almost inaudible amid the number of voices. Elves, humans, and Mer stood out, and as she imagined the possible reasons they would be here, her lips pressed into a thin line.

"It would seem you've been recognized," Nawalya remarked as the murmuring swelled.

"Seems so," Collette said. She'd expected to feel anxiety, to feel judged or unworthy. None of those feelings arose. Instead, the uncertainty of the past months seemed to shift as something more solid settled in.

"The queen has come to rescue us?" the quiet voice of a young Nereid asked.

"Yes," Nawalya announced unexpectedly. "Queen Collette came to help."

Cheers erupted, thankful and loud in ways Collette hadn't heard before. Not when it came to her rule, anyway.

"Was not expecting that…" Collette said, mostly to herself.

Nawalya snorted, as if she wasn't at all surprised by Collette's reaction.

"You should speak," Ian invited, his smile broad and hopeful.

Collette nodded, unsure of what to say. She licked her lips and took a breath. "Please," she implored the gathering, using her hands to motion for quiet. The crowd obeyed, eyes eager and bodies at attention. Collette swallowed, taking a breath. The words finally came to her. "I owe all of you an apology.

For not acting sooner. For not stopping these atrocities against you and others as thoroughly as I should have."

She glanced at Nawalya who gave her a warm, encouraging smile, prompting her to continue.

"Months ago, I was accused of crimes I did not commit, arrested by people who did not have the power to arrest me, and driven from Quenall in the dead of night with a handful of followers who willingly took on the risk of standing by my side. The usurpers planned on killing me to silence me and prevent me from interfering in their plans." She placed a hand on her side, even now feeling the long scars left by giant wolf claws. "They nearly succeeded. Those in power in Quenall will claim it was the right move to bring Coralia into a new era of wealth and success." She paused, breathing again. "I wish I could say Coralia thrived, that it flourished with ingenuity and power. That our people did not go hungry, or worse, fear their leaders. Sadly, there is much to fear." Collette shook her head, her jaw set as she looked out at the faces of her people, tired and ashen. They deserved better.

"They promised you my overthrow would be a symbol of change. Change which would bring about a new era of prosperity and hope, and once again, Coralia would stand as a beacon of light for the world. Their promises have proven empty. The man who calls himself your king has been enslaved by the whims of those laced with cruelty and hatred. In the months since Zephraim claimed the throne, villages have burned, labor camps have formed, and elf, Mer, and human detractors have gone missing, you amongst them. Coralia finds no glory in violence and mutilation, not in the subjugation of its people."

The confirmation of her identity and her words sparked a renewed interest in the crowd, and Collette wanted to reassure them of her intention to fix everything, even the existing problems from before the overthrow. "Coralia deserves more from its leaders, and I promise tonight is just the beginning of what we are going to do. I will not tolerate the cruelty you and countless others have faced. I will regain the throne, and I will set things right. Permanently. I swear upon my name, Collette Venora Josselyn Gallaine, Queen of Coralia, and upon my life."

The words echoed into the dusky evening, promises Collette intended to fill, no matter what it took.

She watched the faces of those who had been rescued, tired and curious, perhaps questioning. Looking at Ian, she opened her mouth to issue a new order, but she paused as the first of the crowd lowered themselves into a bow. Others followed, human, elf, and Nereid alike, until every person, including Nawalya, bowed to Collette, their queen.

A hand went to Collette's heart, thankful beyond words for their support. She could do nothing but return the gesture, and once again, the group broke out into cheers. Collette couldn't help but laugh.

Nawalya did not join them. Her head turned with a snap, and Collette's gaze trailed after hers. "What is it?"

"Someone's coming on horseback. Several someones," Nawaya conveyed.

"Fuck," Collette breathed out. This late in the day, she doubted they'd find friendly company in the newcomers. "We need to distract the riders," she said and motioned to the crowd. "And we need to get them to safety. Now."

"What type of distraction do we need?" Nawalya asked the queen.

"Something to keep those approaching from finding our people free from their captors," Collette replied. Looking at Ian and Indir, she said, "Get them back to the forest and lead them as far away as you possibly can. If anyone is in a condition to help protect the group, there are weapons scattered on the ground. Grab them and be careful."

"Right." Indir turned to the group. "Her Majesty wishes you to follow us into the woods. Grab any sword, knife, or weapon you come across. We must be swift." The rescued prisoners moved in a frenzy, the younger and healthier began gathering supplies while the others were hurried away from the camp center and into the forest.

"Go with them, Ian," Collette commanded over the sounds of organized chaos. "They need someone to get them somewhere safe, and I know you can do it."

"What about you, Your Majesty?" he asked, voice pitched high.

Collette and Nawayla exchanged looks.

"We're going to meet our guests," the queen said.

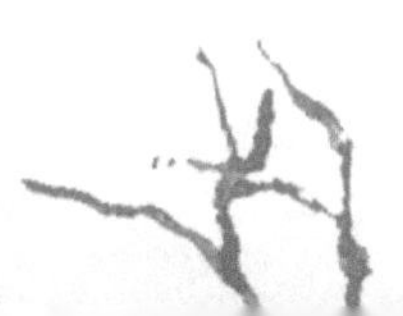

Chapter Forty-Nine

"Okay, we have an agreement. You stop threatening to stab me and start taking my ideas more seriously, and I'll leave your more sordid past shenanigans out of my jokes and such?" Larent asked Arian from where he was sitting next to the blond elf.

"Yes, fine. We have an agreement," Arian said before rising to his feet and pacing along the outer edge of their camp again. From his posture, Larent knew Arian was glaring into the forest as though he could will Nawalya and Collette's return. Larent had hoped their discussion, on boundaries and treating each other better, would have distracted him, but no.

The rest of the camp's anxiety over their departure was less obvious. Tolan and Whyldon spoke softly about plans in Fythias, but every so often, one of their gazes traveled toward the trees. Rion had settled back against a log, absentmindedly whittling a stick. Larent didn't know if he was shaping anything in particular and he didn't monitor the woods, but the set of his shoulder was tense. Thomas sat close to the fire, reading, the most relaxed of the group.

"They'll be back soon, Chuckles," Larent said for what felt like the hundredth time.

"They have been gone an hour, and it's going to get dark soon," Arian replied.

"And? They can handle themselves," Larent replied, trying to sound reasonable. "You know, it's possible they wanted time be ladies instead of surrounded by the lot of us."

"Nawalya mentioned hunting," Rion pointed out, his knife working a long curl of wood from the stick. "Hunting can take more than an hour."

"I am aware," Arian snapped, impatience lacing his words. "Something feels off."

Larent wanted to take his word for it, but at the same time, he couldn't help but think Arian's focus was crossing recently set boundaries. "Are you sure you're not worried because we're not watching over them?" he asked. Larent expected the glare he received in response, but not the way it slid off Arian's face as Thomas gave the elf a warning look.

"It is possible," Arian admitted, only to turn around suddenly. "Someone is coming our way."

"I take it you don't think it's them," Rion said, rising from his seat and tossing the stick aside.

Arian cocked his head to the left and concentrated. "One person. Heavier gate than either Nawalya and Collette's. Coming from your side at a fast clip."

Arian pointed at Rion. Thankfully, it was no consequence to stop the elf who came sprinting into the camp. Rion extended an arm, a movement the elf did not see, as he ran head-first into the furrier and fell on his back, gasping.

Larent was up and moving even as Arian was upon the intruder, straddling him and placing a knife at the elf's throat.

"Where did you come from?" Arian demanded. The strange elf raised a hand, causing Arian to press down with his knife. The glint of gold registered with Larent and Tolan.

"Arian, stop," Tolan insisted. "He's got Collette's bracelet."

"How did you come in possession of anything belonging to Her Majesty?" Whyldon demanded, closing the distance with solid, heavy steps.

"She gave it to me," the elf said in a panicked voice.

Larent knelt and took the bracelet from the elf, putting it into a side pouch on his belt. He wasn't going to let something she so dearly valued get lost in what was promising to be a skirmish.

"Why did she do that?" Arian growled.

"My village was attacked," the elf explained. "Burned down and people killed. The survivors who were not captured came across the queen in the forest. There's a labor camp. She went to help."

Larent blinked as the elf's words settled in his mind and saw Arian pull back. He imagined Arian was flashing back to the distant past, but he shoved it off.

"You mean to say the queen has gone to fight guards at a labor camp?" Tolan asked from behind Arian.

"Yes," the elf said, breathing out in relief. "She said one of you calls her 'Freckles.'"

The pet name he'd given Collette had Larent moving across the camp for his new weapons. He knew Collette would be fine as would Nawalya, but he wanted to be prepared anyway.

Arian jumped to his feet and held a hand out for the elf, hauling him to his feet with no other apology.

"How far away is the camp?" Whyldon asked.

"About a forty-five minute trek from here," the elf shared. "They went with three of my companions. Another seven wait near the camp to join them."

Chapter Forty-nine

Arian froze, his face growing red. "Twelve people? To take a labor camp?"

The rage in Arian's voice caused Larent to cringe and Tolan to take a step back. Larent believed in Collette, but the last time he'd seen a labor camp, it had been protected by seventy-five guards.

Rion gave Whyldon a look rather than address Arian. "Sounds like Joss," he said, shaking his head.

"Unfortunately," Whyldon replied, worry etched around his eyes.

"The camp opened last month. From our count, there are thirty guards and about twice as many prisoners," the elf explained. "The odds aren't ideal, but better than they will be in the coming weeks."

Arian gave a barely noticeable sigh. Quickly, the men gathered their weapons and stashed their items. They could come back to camp afterward. Tolan was tucking away a couple of knives when he stopped, alert to a new surprise. Two people emerged into the clearing. A woman with iridescent glimmers along her neck and arms, accenting vivid red hair, and another man, taller, with dark hair and a reddish glint to his skin.

"Jayden," Whyldon said in astonishment.

"How are you here?" Thomas asked, excited.

If the Nereid ambassador was surprised to see them, he hid it well.

"Captain Whyldon, Tolan, Thomas," Jayden said, sheer fondness in his voice as he recited Thomas's name. Larent didn't miss the soft growl issuing from Arian.

"What are you doing in Galel?" Thomas asked, then he shook his head and amended. "What are you doing in Coralia?"

"Looking for you," Jayden said, then paused. "Well, looking for Queen Collette. We came to offer assistance."

"Collette has departed to take down a labor camp," Thomas replied. "We were going to find and assist her."

Jayden didn't look surprised. "We are more than happy to help," he offered, motioning to Ceto.

"We received word the Merscale trade had been restarted. We know she is against it," Ceto said. "We also heard she died, but our king did not believe the news. He will be thrilled to learn she is alive, fighting slavers."

"Yes, fine. Join us," Arian nearly barked, impatient anger radiating from him. "We need to leave now." He pointed to the stranger elf. "You. Lead the way. Quickly."

Chapter Fifty

Collette heard the approaching sound of hooves, her human ears failing her until it was almost too late. The sky had darkened considerably. Distantly, she made out the forms of four riders, the colors on their uniforms and regalia confirming the presence of the man she somehow knew she would see.

"It's Lord Riken," she shared with Nawalya, thankful they'd put distance between themselves and the camp. Their position, concealed behind several layers of bushes off the road, made it impossible for Riken to spot them.

Nawalya let out a soft growl. "What do you want to do?"

As the riders drew closer, they could hear Riken laugh as if he had no care in the world. "Cadan, you worry too much. I brought two guards like you requested. We didn't need a small army on this trip."

"As you say, my lord," Cadan replied.

Collette glanced back in the direction of the camp, and even though they were too far away to see it, she knew they couldn't possibly be safely in hiding. "I have to delay them."

Nawalya looked hard at Collette. "There are only four."

"I know," Collette replied. "It's not a matter of stopping them. We've got to buy time for those back at the camp." Collette took a deep breath through her nose, a decision made.

"I'm going down there." She looked over to Nawalya. "Do not intervene until you have to."

Nawalya gave Collette an unhappy look but nodded. "When Arian arrives, I'd plan on lying about what you're doing."

"Oh, Arian is never going to forgive me about tonight," Collette replied. A brief check of her weapon, Collette took another deep breath and walked away from the security of the bushes to the worn road where Riken and his men traveled. She came to a stop in front of them, her expression neutral and calm as she waited to be recognized.

Riken spotted her but was slow to stop his mount. Confusion transitioned to recognition, tinged with shock and disgust. "You're alive?"

"I am," Collette confirmed. "You'll have to congratulate Zephraim for his attempt to kill me the next you see him."

Confusion briefly clouded Riken's face, but he pushed past it. "I think I'd rather you tell him instead," Riken said. A grin grew on his lips, his eyes darkening in anger as he slid off his horse. The large man to his left moved to do the same, but Riken held up a hand. "Stay on your damn horse. It's only Collette."

He spit out her name like a curse.

"Sir," the man said firmly.

"Stay there, Cadan. I'm tired of you questioning me." Riken waved the other two off their horses so they could join him.

"It sounds as though you have problems with your followers, Riken," Collette observed, forcing her posture to remain relaxed and unconcerned. Riken's irritation with Cadan proved interesting, and she wondered if the dynamic always existed.

"He worries when there is nothing to worry about. Unlike your experience, I don't worry about being betrayed or replaced." Riken grabbed a rope from his bag and handed it off to one of the helmeted soldiers.

Collette laughed, pressing a hand against her chest. "Do you mean for me to worry, Riken? Surely, you cannot be serious."

"You never knew when to take something seriously, did you? Your fatuity is one of the many reasons you were a failure as a queen." He and the two guards advanced on her, though more cautiously than Riken's taunts would have Collette believe.

"I've never been able to take you seriously, Riken," Collette replied, her tone bored and mocking. "The way you simper over Rhoslyn Almeida is enough to tell me how easily emasculated you are." She offered the man a sympathetic smile. "And how is my new sister-in-law?"

"She is doing quite well and proving herself a much better, wiser queen than you ever were," Riken tried to taunt. Behind him, Cadan had risen higher in his saddle. Riken chose to move forward. "Tell me, Collette. Are you all alone out here? Did your allies realize you're full of nothing but empty words? What about your rumored elf lover? Did he finally tire of you?"

Riken stopped within arms reach and motioned the soldiers to pause.

"Oh, are you interested in trying your luck with an elf?" she asked with a wry grin.

A clear desire to strike Collette rose in Riken' eyes. "Unlike you, I don't degrade myself with filth."

"Struck a nerve, Riken?" she asked, her smile slipping away into something a little less playful.

"No, it serves as a reminder of how much better our kingdom will be once I put your head on a pike." The soldiers grabbed Collette one on each arm in a bruising grip and pulled her closer to Riken. "Secure her to one of the horses. She doesn't have to be comfortable."

Collette simply laughed at him. "Good plan. It might work well for you."

"Why are you always so fucking smug?" Riken spit out, halting the soldiers in their orders.

"Because I find this whole situation hilarious," she replied, ignoring the two men who flanked her.

"Why's that?" Riken demanded, getting in her face.

"Sir!" Cadan said. Riken held up a hand to silence the soldier.

Collette did not flinch. She simply tilted her head back enough to meet his gaze. "Because you're pathetic and weak."

Riken's posture and demeanor changed into something less refined, meaner. "I think I'm going to enjoy showing you your place while I drag you back to Quenall."

"I can't wait to see you try."

Riken's hand twitched before it balled into a fist. "My father was right. Sargarus should have beaten you more often."

"You know what's so sad about your father, Riken?" she asked him.

Riken sneered. "You should watch what you say next."

"Do you really think I'm afraid of you?" she asked.

"You should be."

"I'm not," Collette assured him. "You are nothing but a sad, pathetic man taking Zephraim's scraps and hoping and praying you don't further shame your father while he rots in his grave."

She knew she'd crossed a line before the sentence ended. Riken's face twisted in rage, and he pulled his arm back and punched her.

A muffled groan of pain left her mouth at the impact. Pops of light clouded Collette's vision for several long seconds, and she was certain she remained upright because the soldiers held her. A metallic taste filled her mouth, and without reaching up to touch it, she knew her lip had split. Blood pooled down her chin, hot and thick. She spit out a mouthful and looked up at Riken again, lips twisted in a smile.

Riken swung again, this time aiming for her stomach.

"Sir, she's baiting you," Cadan warned.

Riken paused snarling, but realized Cadan might be right. "Secure her," he ordered the guards, who still held her arms.

Collette laughed again, ignoring the blood running down her chin. "You still think you're hauling me to Quenall?"

"Of course I am," Riken said, ignoring the fact that Cadan was starting to dismount.

"Then you're a fool," Collette said. Without warning, she kicked out, the heel of her boot meeting Riken's kneecap with as much force as she could muster and wrenched her arms from the soldiers. Her shoulder pushed Riken to the ground.

The soldiers lunged after her. One went down with an arrow through his chest, and the other a dagger to his throat, the weapons appearing from different directions. Cadan, in his rush to get to Riken, was lucky the arrow meant for him missed by inches as he threw himself to the ground.

Riken, from his place in the dirt, tried to go for his sword.

"Draw on me, and I will fucking kill you," Collette warned, her teeth bared. She kicked him in the side for good measure.

Riken tried to turn to catch himself but ended up face down in the dirt. "You bitch!" He spat out and tried to kick Collette with his good leg, going for a weapon, any weapon.

"You better hope that's all I am," Collette taunted him, easily dodging his attempts to fight back. "You better pray I am merciful."

"Fuck you," Riken shouted, his right leg in obvious agony as he tried to move away and stand.

Collette laughed, then used the back of her sleeve to mop the blood from her face. "The only reason I don't run you through is because your death would be more motivation for pursuit than your shattered pride…and knee." She looked over to Cadan. "Come collect your boy!"

Cadan moved quickly to Riken's side.

Riken yelled, "Kill her, kill her."

"Touch her, and I'll gut both of you," came a rage-filled voice from behind Collette.

"And we'll help," came another voice from further back. An arrow landed with a thunk close to Riken in warning.

"Run back to Quenall," Collette said, thankful for the backup even with the success of the evening. "Tell them I am coming. Warn them what happens when you go after my people."

Cadan drug Riken to the horses, a cold rage in his eyes as he ignored Riken. It was the matter of moments for him to get Riken, his knee obviously broken if not shattered, on to the horse and ride them out of there.

Collette watched them ride away, though with nothing but the stars and moon to light the evening sky, the ability to watch was limited. She finally turned around to see the others. Arian and Larent she had expected but not Jayden Drake.

"You're supposed to be back in your kingdom," she accused.

"I was in my kingdom. I am here now," Jayden replied, his manner easy going and relaxed than it had been in Quenall.

"I would be pleased to see you had I not just fought a man who is responsible for imprisoning some of your people," Collette said. She looked at the others. Even at night, Arian's palpable anger was apparent. The elf stood feet from Collette, Larent behind him by a few steps, watching Arian warily.

"You… you…" Arian started and stopped several times, his mouth working with no real words coming out.

Collette hesitated in responding, knowing Arian was angry. She understood why. She'd run off with little consideration for the party, putting herself in danger. Rather than wait for Arian to explode, she made the decision to close the distance between them and throw her arms around him in a tight hug.

Arian's whole body tensed up for a moment. Then he relaxed, his arms coming around her in a quick, yet firm and comforting return hug. "I understand, but I am very angry."

"You have a right to be," Collette acknowledged as she released him. She dabbed at her bleeding lip again, the pain of it making itself known as adrenaline wore off. "Can you believe that bastard punched me?"

"I saw it, actually," Arian growled out.

"I wish I could say I was surprised," she replied, holding her fingers near her lips. Her skin grew warm and tingly as her lip knitted back together. Gingerly, she prodded it a couple of times before she was satisfied.

Arian moved to look closer at her face, examining the injuries from the punch. He looked back when Larent tapped his shoulder.

"Be mad later, or better, be mad at that one." Larent pointed to where Nawalya was emerging from the bushes with Thomas. Arian gave Collette a long hard stare before stalking off in their direction.

"Where are the others?" Collette asked, aware Tolan and Whyldon had not appeared.

"They stayed back at the camp to help organize a safe passage for those who were freed," Jayden replied. "My travel companion Ceto is with them."

"Good," she replied. She didn't want to think about what a confrontation with Whyldon might be like. Not when Arian was so heated with her.

"When they are safe, would you care to accompany us back to my kingdom?" Jayden asked. "In speaking with your companions, I hear you have an offer of aid from Fythias. They are our allies, and I think we could convince them to join us once you are safe within our borders."

A genuine smile bloomed on Collette's face. "Yes. That would be perfect."

"Good. I'll head back to find Ceto and let her know the plan." Jayden took his leave, leaving Collette alone with Larent.

"So, I hear you had an adventure?" Larent said with an amused grin.

Collette flashed him a smile as she gingerly pressed different parts of her face, healing the sore and bruised spots. Riken had a nice punch. "It's been a long evening. I'm just sorry you missed it."

"Oh, I bet." Larent watched her, his eyes checking every visible part, but otherwise he held his worry in. "Freckles," he said, noting what must have been obvious regret in her expression. "Sometimes you have to have fun without me. Besides, if this is what you and Nawalya chose to do for lady time, who am I to complain?"

"Lady time?" Collette replied with a laugh. Determined she was as healed as she could be, Collette wiped as much of the remaining blood away from her face.

"You know, time without the men to do whatever you want, like kill slavers."

She laughed at the explanation. "Spirits, I love you."

"I love you too." He held out his arms for Collette, who immediately went into his embrace. "I'm so glad you're okay."

"I know," she replied quietly. "But I had Nawalya with me, and there was no way I wasn't going to make it back to you."

"I know you can take care of yourself," Larent assured her, holding her close. "I didn't let myself worry until I saw that bastard hit you. Then, I was just angry. You did great, Freckles."

"I let him hit me," Collette pointed out. She looked up, concerned. "Are you okay?"

Larent didn't answer right away. "I knew you had a plan, but it's difficult to watch someone hurt you." He let out a wry chuckle. "Also, holding Arian back wasn't fun at all."

She nodded. "I've never seen him so angry."

"Incandescent with rage is how Thomas phrased it," Larent said with a small laugh. He grew quiet, observing her in the dark, then leaned down to kiss her. "You ready to go find the others? I hear we're taking a trip to the Nereid kingdom."

"We are," Collette replied, relieved to know so much of their immediate future was planned and in safe company. She pulled away from him but took his hand. "You ready?"

"I'm following you."

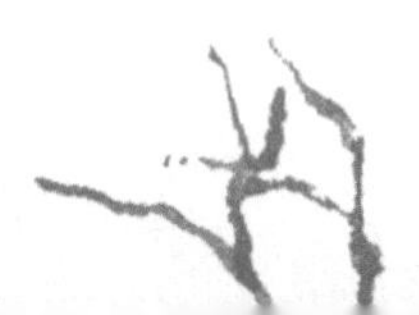

Chapter Fifty-One

Riken,

Our beautiful Queen Rhoslyn has finally given me permission to loose my hand on Lady Elrick. The foul woman has proven to be a thorn in our side long enough. Lady Elrick rejoices in spreading rumors and lies about our benevolent queen and trying to topple her rule. I have a plan in place, one which will resolve our problem without suspicion or blame. I shall have it enacted by the end of the week, if not the end of the day.

In more pleasant news, the fair queen has more use for me after this mission. The esteemed Lord Barris seeks a pardon for the treasonous former queen, postmortem of course. Zephramin did not shut the idea down, which, as you much suspect, concerned our fair queen. She has asked that I keep an eye on Lord Barris once Lady Elrick is dealt with. I cannot wait to see where her blood thirsty plans lead us after this.

Xavier

Barris crouched low on the roof of one of the many warehouses of the merchant district, his eyes never leaving the abandoned-looking carriage. He wanted to go down there. He wanted to stop what he knew was happening in the carriage, but Lynessea had pointed out saving Lady Elrick did them no favors. The woman was a viper who watched Barris the same way she watched Riken. If Riken became unavailable, Lady Elrick would come for him, and the very idea of her hurting his people if she found out his secrets boiled his blood. Lady Elrick emerging in jewelry made from the skin of Lynessea's people soon after Pontus Bay was allowed to establish the Merscale trade meant she could never be trusted.

The carriage door opened and drew Barris from his thoughts. He inched closer as Xavier exited, blood on his shirt and a dagger in his hands. Barris expected him to leave immediately, but instead, Xavier leaned against the carriage, waiting. Barris watched the area, eyes scanning from ground to rooftops where he spotted a figure moving north. For a moment, he worried he would have a fight on his hands. Then realized who it was. Barris pulled down his mask so he would be able to speak freely as Lynessea slid down next to him.

"Two of Riken's lackeys are bringing the pastry chef. You know, the one who works by the main square. From what I could overhear, he was in a dalliance with Lady Elrick and has been loudly upset about her deciding to end things. They've already killed him, but they are going to toss him in the carriage with Lady Elrick and make it look like a crime of passion."

Barris watched as the two guards came into view, a body between them. "If he's been loud about his unhappiness, people may question it, but no one will look into it."

Xavier straightened, motioning the two to move faster. Arriving at the carriage, they shoved the man inside. Then Xavier went to work. Barris couldn't see inside the carriage, but

the shadows from the open door told their own story of Xavier arranging the murder scene to his liking before the three went their way, the guards to the barracks, and Xavier to the castle.

"Come, you can inform Zephraim of what has occurred, and if that monster is with Rhoslyn…" Lynessea trailed off. The two stood, pulling their masks back up. Without the courtesy of discussion, they took off across the rooftops, the town flying by as they jumped.

They reached an unwatched area of the castle wall, security more lax since they thought Collette was dead. The two climbed the walls of the castle, then snuck up to their room, happily unnoticed. Barris quickly changed, kissed Lynessea, and rushed out to Zephraim's office. He knew Lynessea would go to find her brothers. Hopefully, they had notifyed Crem of what had happened tonight. Barris wanted Lynessea by his side, but if anything went wrong, he could not risk her.

Barris rushed to Zephraim's rooms only to almost knock the man over in his haste. "Your Majesty!"

Zephraim's alarm was evident in the narrowed brow and slight frown he wore. "What has happened to bring you to me in such distress?"

Barris took a deep breath. He knew he was taking a chance, but he had to believe Zephraim had truly changed. Their kingdom and their lives depended on it. "I just witnessed Xavier murder Lady Elrick and cover it up by placing the body of a jilted lover with her to make it look like he did it. He has since returned, and I believe is headed to the queen's quarters."

Confusion rose on Zephraim's face. "Why would he…" Zephraim did not wait long enough to answer the question before heading in the direction of Rhoslyn's chambers.

Barris followed. Zephraim deserved to know Xavier reported to Riken, and Riken all but reported to Rhoslyn. When they arrived at Rhoslyn's rooms, Zephraim did not pause to knock, instead, throwing the doors open. He walked inside, pausing as he stepped into the area serving as her office. Barris overheard raised voices from the interior rooms.

"What do you think you are doing?" Rhoslyn could be heard demanding from, presumably, Xavier.

"Taking what I'm owed," Xaver's voice could be heard saying.

As Zephraim hurried to the back, the distinct sounds of struggle could be heard. Zephraim tried the door to the room Rhoslyn was in. A twist of the handle proved it locked. More concerning noises came from the other side, including something heavy slamming against the other side of the door. Had Xavier turned on Rhoslyn?

"Rhoslyn!" Zephraim called out, gaining no response. He looked back to Barris. "We've got to get in there."

Barris looked at the door and hissed. "It's solid, but if we work together, we can take it down." He backed up and motioned for Zephraim to join him. "On the count of three."

Neither men had weapons, a fact they couldn't pause to consider.

"One," Barris began, turning his gaze back to the door. "Two." Barris flexed his fingers, ears straining for more information. "Three."

The two men ran at the door, throwing their weight into it. It remained solid, despite the apparent cracking.

"Again?" Barris asked as he backed up and prepared to run at the door again.

"Yeah," Zephraim agreed.

Barris took a deep breath. "One." He braced himself and prayed to his Goddess silently. "Two." He let the breath out. "Three."

They ran at the door again, and thankfully, the door gave way, breaking at the junction where the handle and lock were placed. The door swung wildly back, clattering against the stone wall.

The two men stumbled into the room, straightening immediately as they came across Xavier, who was pressed up against Rhoslyn, a predatory leer on his face. No matter what Barris thought of Rhoslyn, she did not deserve what Xavier was threatening.

He and Zephraim moved forward, only to pause as a knife appeared in Rhoslyn's hand.

"This is the last time you will ever get too familiar with me," she said, her voice full of venom. She did not wait for the blond man to reply before plunging the knife into his throat. Blood sprayed from the wound, hitting Rhoslyn's hand, face, and neck without her giving it notice.

Barris could only watch in horror as Xavier grabbed his neck and collapsed to his knees, blood pouring despite efforts to stem the flow. He fell over dead before anything could be done, though Barris knew Xavier's life was over the second the knife appeared. He was horrified but also upset that any proof of possible wrongdoings by Rhoslyn were gone. He eyed Zephraim, wondering what the false king would do.

"Rhoslyn," Zephraim began, only for her to glare at him.

"I am so tired of dealing with incompetent men," she said, tossing the knife on the ground beside the dead Xavier.

Barris said nothing, just watching events unfold, hoping he didn't have to put himself between the two.

"What do you mean?" Zephraim asked, horrified by the scene in front of him.

"Just what I said," Rhoslyn replied. "Do you know how often I have watched the men around me make the most absurd choices? My brother liked to bait your sister and start problems with others. You have moped around for months. Riken doesn't know when to keep his mouth shut." She looked down at Xavier's body. "And he couldn't keep his hands to himself."

Barris inched closer to Zephraim. The last thing they needed was a dead king, false or not. Even so, Barris had a terrible feeling that Rhoslyn had plans worse than death.

"What are you saying?" Zephraim asked, hesitantly.

"I'm done allowing you and others to play at leading," Rhoslyn said. "Going forward, you all answer to me."

Barris was flabbergasted. "You can't just declare yourself in charge," he insisted, but further protests died in his throat. The longer Barris considered the circumstances surrounding Rhoslyn, the more he realized how much trouble Coralia was in. Riken controlled a majority of the guards in Quenall. Rhoslyn controlled Riken, and her closed-door meetings with high-ranking nobles meant she likely swayed them. Barris's look of bafflement soon changed to one of dawning horror.

Rhoslyn surveyed both men, her expression cold and impatient. "I've always been in charge," she stated plainly.

Barris couldn't deny her words. Dear Goddess, he let so much slip past him. He considered the knife on the ground for a second and wondered how bad things would go if he lunged for it and handled Rhoslyn now.

"Guards," Rhoslyn called out, drawing their gazes back to her.

"Rhoslyn," Zephraim tried again, his voice full of surprise and hurt.

"Save it," Rhoslyn replied.

Barris pressed his lips and placed his hand on Zephraim's arm. "No need for guards. "We'll go." His smile was less bright and had more teeth than normal.

"Good," Rhoslyn replied. "You can send someone to clean him up," she said, nudging Xavier with the toe of her shoe.

"Rhoslyn," Zephraim tried again, though he did not pull away from Barris. "Can we please—"

"No, Zephraim," Rhoslyn snapped. "Go to your rooms, leave me in peace."

Barris pulled Zephraim from the room, motioning to a few guards to help the queen. He waited until he was sure they were away from listening ears and watching eyes.

"It's okay," he murmured. "We'll handle this."

Crem,

Rhoslyn murdered Xavier for assault and has declared herself ruler. I witnessed the crime, as did Zephraim. We cannot move against her. The attempted assault justified her actions, and she holds power over Lord Riken and his force. We have no way of striking against her—yet.

I don't know when I'll be able to get away or next meet with you. I need to be here for Zephraim and to find out Rhoslyn's next steps. Our work, now more than ever, must continue.

Barris

Book Club Questions

1. Why do you think it took Collette discovering the labor camp to step back into the role as queen?

2. Did Whyldon overreact or underreact to the revelation of Nawalya's vision? What, if anything, would you change about his response?

3. Did Tolan have justification for leaving Collette? Should Collette forgive him now that he has returned?

4. Was Collette too kind in allowing Riken to live? Why do you think she allowed him to return to Quenall?

5. Why do you think Ian lied to Jayden about seeing Collette and her travel party? Would you have made the same choice?

6. Should Whyldon have focused more on Collette's mental and emotional well-being, or was he right to primarily concentrate on making her battle ready?

7. Why do you think Arian was so willing to treat Nawalya like a child for so many years? Why did Nawalya tolerate his treatment?

8. What does Collette's decision to move on with Larent suggest about her relationship with Tolan?

9. Larent frequently uses the phrase, "Tell me something," when talking to Collette. Why do you think he does this?

10. What theme of the book did you most relate to? Why?

Author Bios

Kate Jenkins enjoys writing fantasy, sci-fi, and romance as much as she enjoys reading them. She lives in a small town in Idaho with her autistic teen who is her whole world, her parents, and between them, four dogs and six cats. When not hanging with her son, she loves gaming, especially first-person shooters and asymmetrical horror games she can play with friends. She's a K-pop enthusiast and harbors a secret love of K-dramas and Anime, much to her mother's displeasure as she's slowly being sucked into them with her. Her favorites tropes are currently enemies-to-lovers, there was only one bed, coffee shops, time travel fixes it, and soul mates/soul identifying marks. She is hopeful one day she can talk her co-author into writing these with her.

Morgan Moreau is a lover and writer of all kinds of fiction, including fantasy, history, crime and mystery, and modern-day stories. She is an enthusiastic lover of *The Little Mermaid*, as is evident in her vivid red hair, mermaid tattoos, and growing Ariel collection. Morgan also loves all things pirates, especially those who "wear fine things well." She lives in Alabama with her dog, Scarlett, and dreams of getting more. Her current passions include higher education, animal rights, and watching the 1995 *Pride & Prejudice* at least once a month. In addition to her current literary loves, Morgan is a fan of vampires, pirates, and superheroes, and she hopes to incorporate this into future works.

A sneak peak from the upcoming sequel, *Legends of Coralia: The Marked Queen*.

The wooden platform gleamed in the morning light. Like the surrounding buildings, the harbor was decorated in bright, pastel colors of blue, white, and coral, a beautiful depiction of Nereid life for all to see.

Aphros smiled to himself, listening to the comforting splash of waves and feeling the breeze on his face. His ashen curls swayed in the wind, almost dry since arriving on land an hour before to greet his guests. His scales glittered under the bright sun, proudly and brilliantly proclaiming him a Nereid king. He inhaled, taking in the salty fragrance with an appreciation he could hardly describe.

In the distance, the expected ship rocked in its moorings as the passengers descended. Aprhos stood far enough back he could not yet make out faces, though he thought it fairly obvious the woman with shoulder-length chocolatey hair flanked by a group of men must be Queen Collette.

Though slight of frame, her taller stature and strong shoulders and arms told him she would be a formidable foe should things turn violent, and Aphros knew, at some point, attacks would come to the kingdom.

"They made good time," Aprhos observed without looking at Ceto.

"The weather and sea have been cooperative," Ceto replied from beside him, beaming with excitement. "The Goddess Galene wanted them here."

"She did," Aphros agreed, smiling to himself. "And your excitement is palpable. You have been out here long before I." Ceto was dry and well-groomed, characteristics one could not always associate with the woman. She preferred her time below the surface, and when she appeared on land, it was last minute, and usually dripping. Her earlier return to the island, after spending time on the now docked ship, left Ceto with

strong opinions regarding Collette. "I believe you are much more taken with the queen than even Jayden."

"A person who takes on the world to seek justice deserves recognition, do they not?"

"They do," Aphros replied with a nod.

Ceto turned to look at him fully. "I believe she has earned the great honor of being marked."

More books from 4 Horsemen Publications

LGBT Romance

AJ Buchannan
Orchestrated Love

Eskay Kabba
Hidden Love
Not So Hidden
Signs of Affection
Deeply Devoted to Him
Honest Love
A Plane and Simple Connection

Lucas LaMont
Roman's Reckoning: Type 6
Mikaél's Moment: Type 6

Stephan's Resurgence: Type 5
Anastasia's Arrival: Type 6

Stormie Skyes
Check Yes, No, or Maybe

V.C. Willis
The Prince's Priest
The Priest's Assassin
The Assassin's Saint
The Champion's Lord

Fantasy

D. Lambert
To Walk into the Sands
Rydan
Celebrant
Northlander
Esparan
King
Traitor
His Last Name

Danielle Orsino
Locked Out of Heaven
Thine Eyes of Mercy
From the Ashes

Kingdom Come
Fire, Ice, Acid, & Heart
A Fae is Done

J.M. Paquette
Klauden's Ring
Solyn's Body
The Inbetween
Hannah's Heart

Lou Kemp
The Violins Played Before Junstan
Music Shall Untune the Sky